PRISM

VOL. 1

TO MY MOM & DAD,
FOR SHAPING WHO I AM.

TO MY BROTHER & SISTER,
FOR KEEPING ME GROUNDED.

TO MY FRIENDS, WHO ALWAYS
BELIEVED IN MY POTENTIAL.

TO EVERYONE WHO SHORED UP
MY BROKEN PARTS AND REMINDED
ME OF THE MANY POSSIBLE FUTURES
WHEN ALL WAS ECLIPSED.

THIS IS FOR YOU.

SLOANE LEONG
Creator

ARIANA MAHER
Letterer

DARIUS OU
Logo Designer

HALEY THURSTON
Creative Consultant

NEOTENOMIE
Original Soundtrack

SHANNA MATUSZAK
Production Design

IMAGE COMICS, INC.

Robert Kirkman: Chief Operating Officer
Erik Larsen: Chief Financial Officer
Todd McFarlane: President
Marc Silvestri: Chief Executive Officer
Jim Valentino: Vice President
Eric Stephenson: Publisher / Chief Creative Officer
Corey Hart: Director of Sales
Jeff Boison: Director of Publishing Planning & Book Trade Sales
Chris Ross: Director of Digital Sales
Jeff Stang: Director of Specialty Sales
Kat Salazar: Director of PR & Marketing
Drew Gill: Art Director
Heather Doornink: Production Director
Nicole Lapalme: Controller

IMAGECOMICS.COM

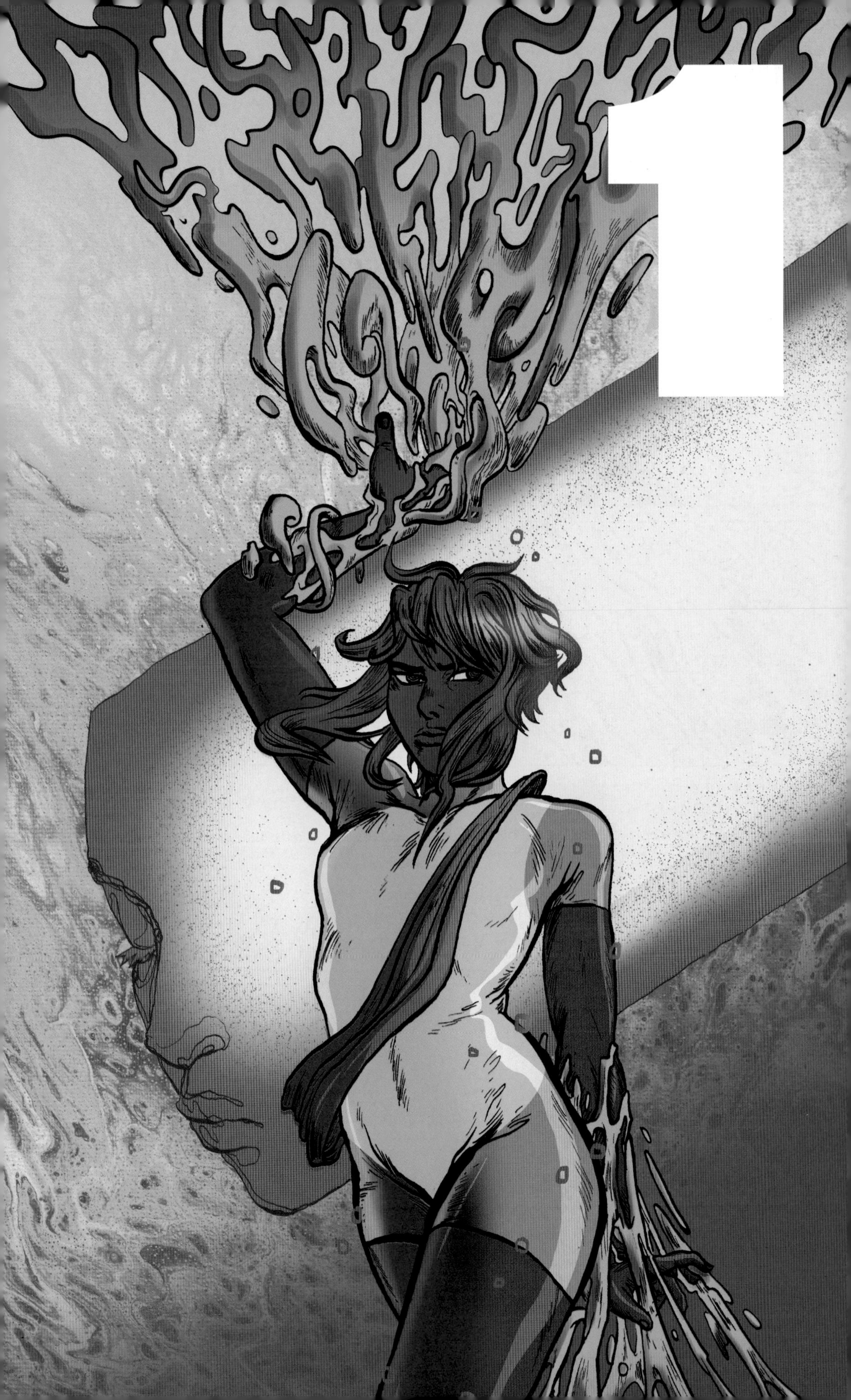
1

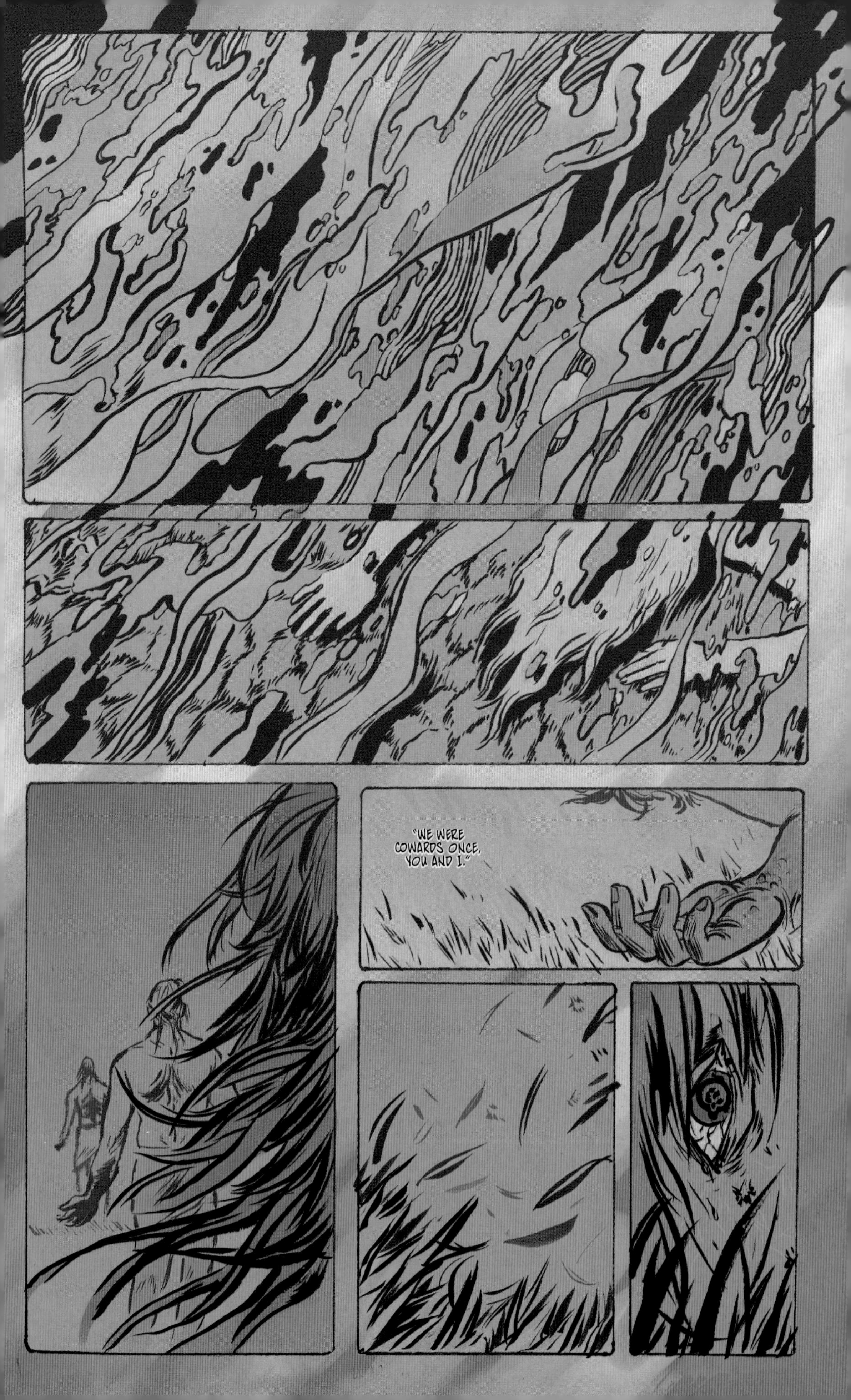
"WE WERE COWARDS ONCE, YOU AND I."

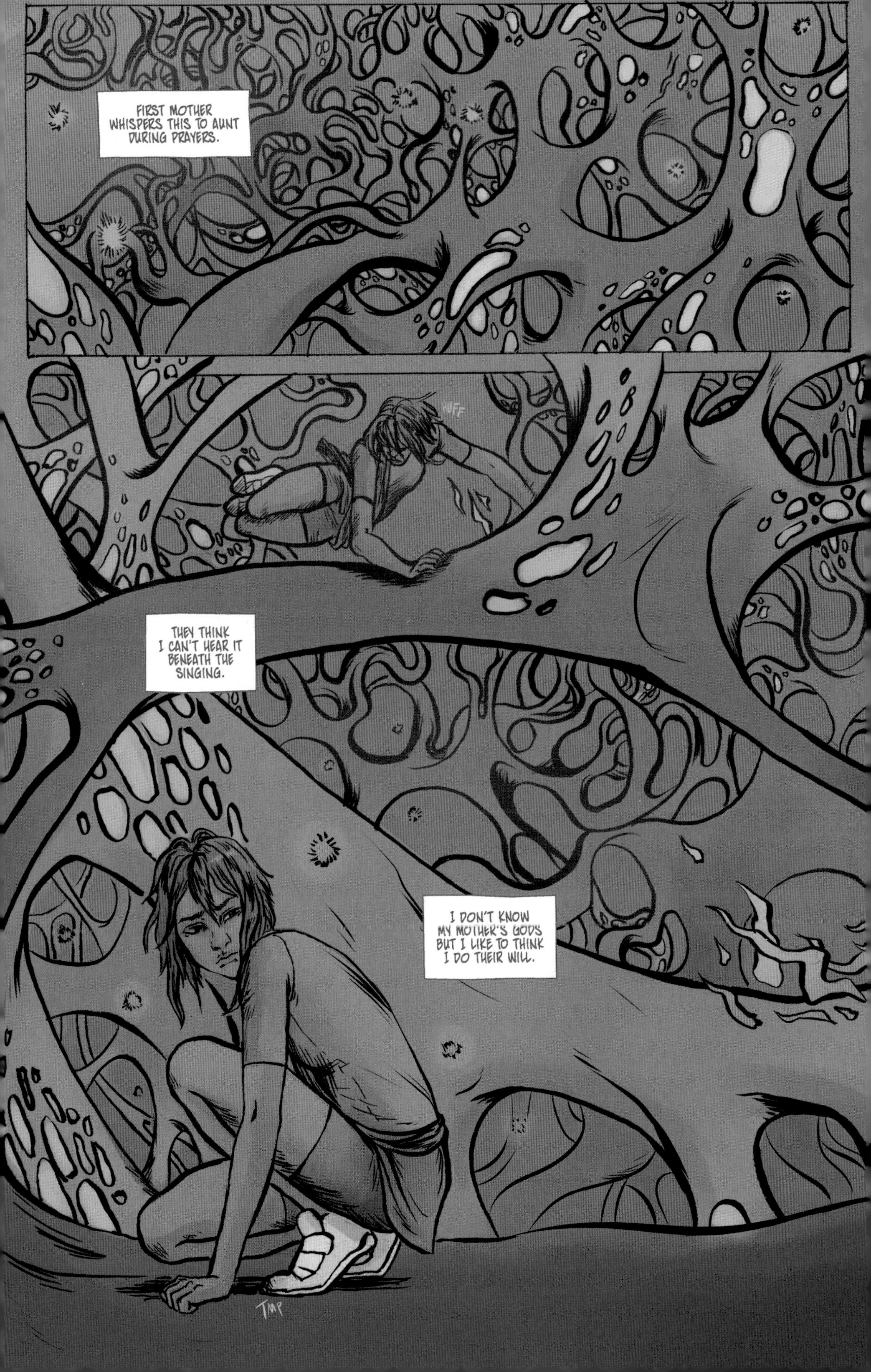
FIRST MOTHER WHISPERS THIS TO AUNT DURING PRAYERS.
HUFF
THEY THINK I CAN'T HEAR IT BENEATH THE SINGING.
I DON'T KNOW MY MOTHER'S GODS BUT I LIKE TO THINK I DO THEIR WILL.
TMP

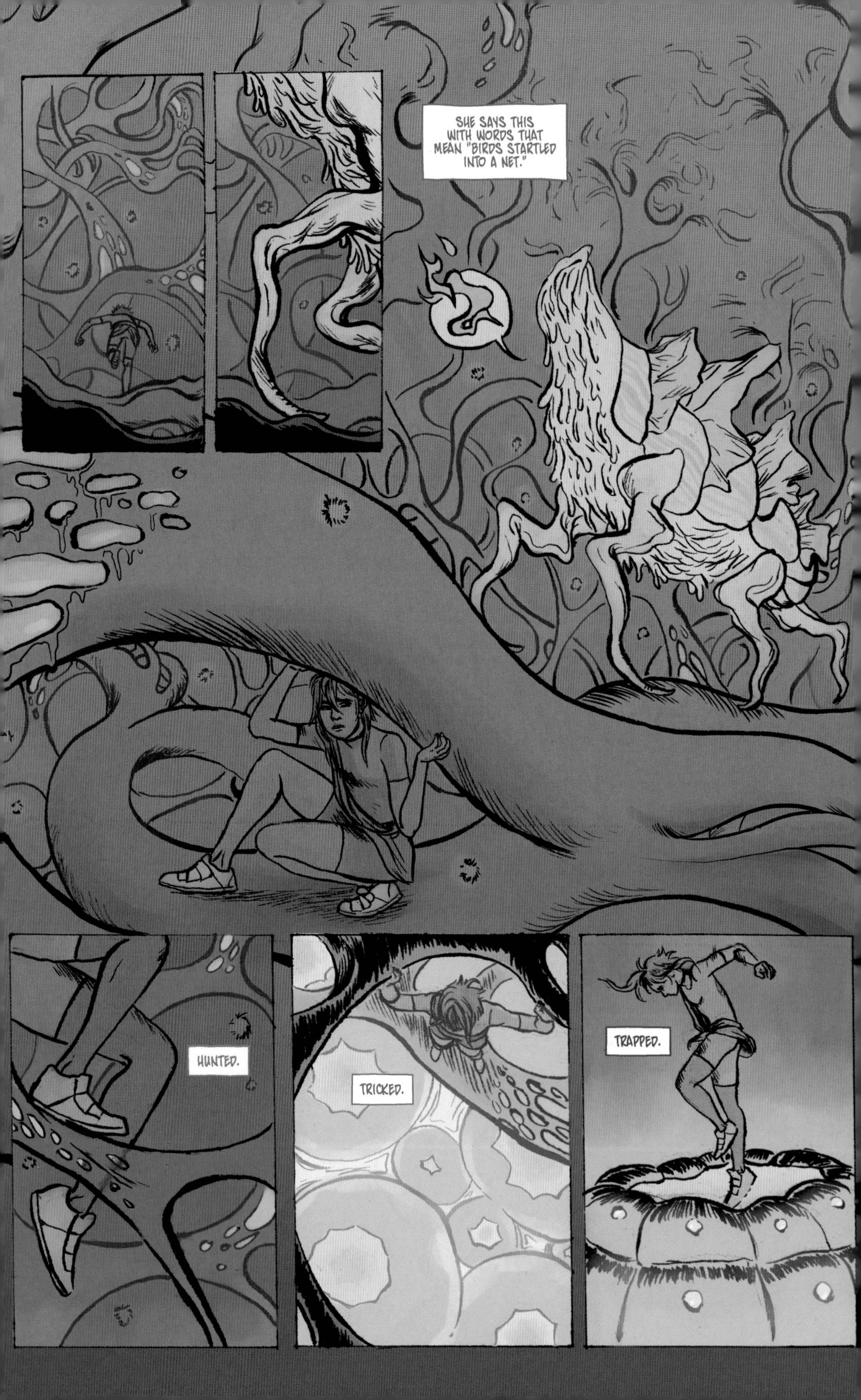
SHE SAYS THIS WITH WORDS THAT MEAN "BIRDS STARTLED INTO A NET."
HUNTED.
TRICKED.
TRAPPED.

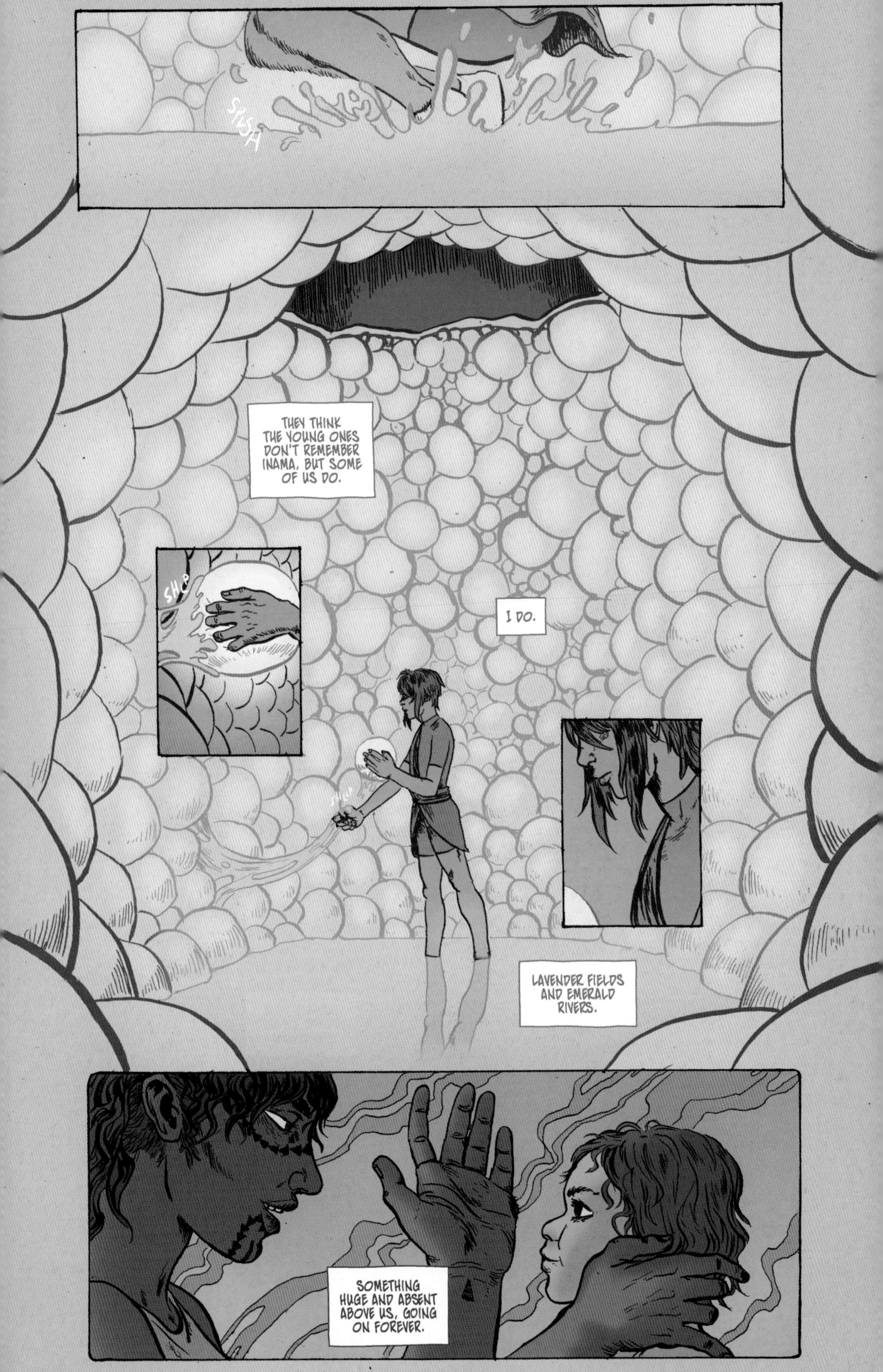
SWSH
THEY THINK THE YOUNG ONES DON'T REMEMBER INAMA, BUT SOME OF US DO.
SHLP
I DO.
SHLP
LAVENDER FIELDS AND EMERALD RIVERS.
SOMETHING HUGE AND ABSENT ABOVE US, GOING ON FOREVER.

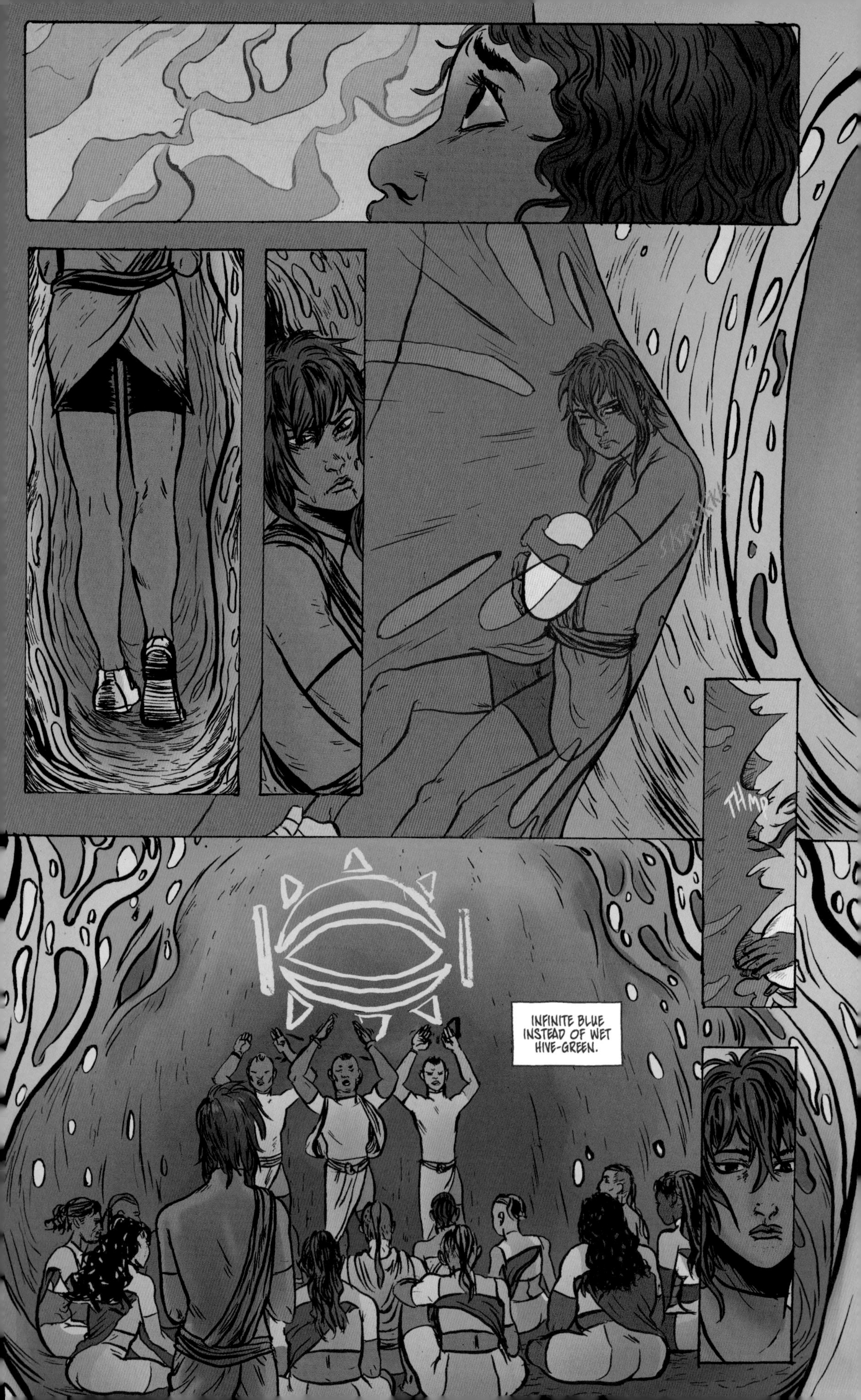
THMP
INFINITE BLUE INSTEAD OF WET HIVE-GREEN.

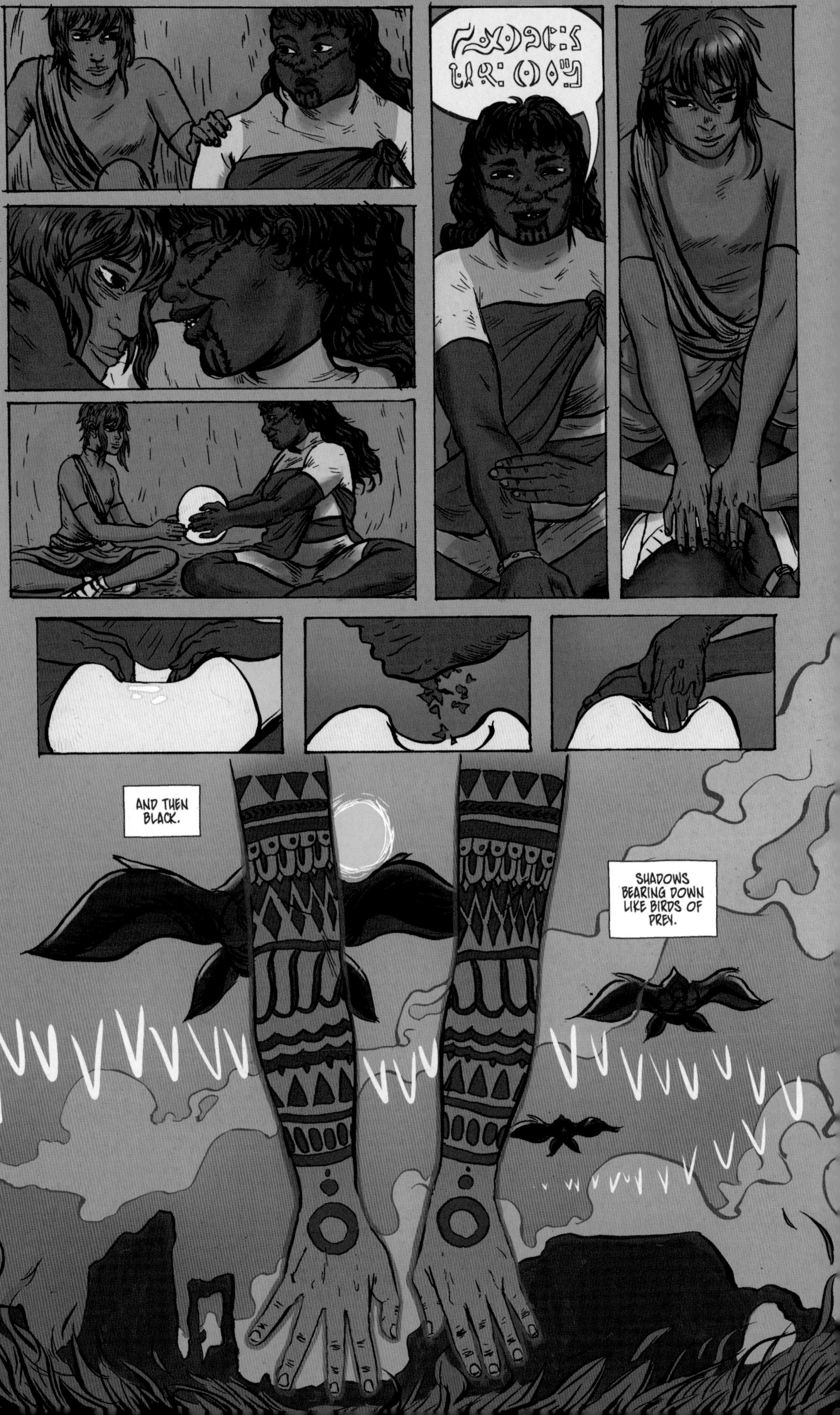
AND THEN BLACK.
SHADOWS BEARING DOWN LIKE BIRDS OF PREY.

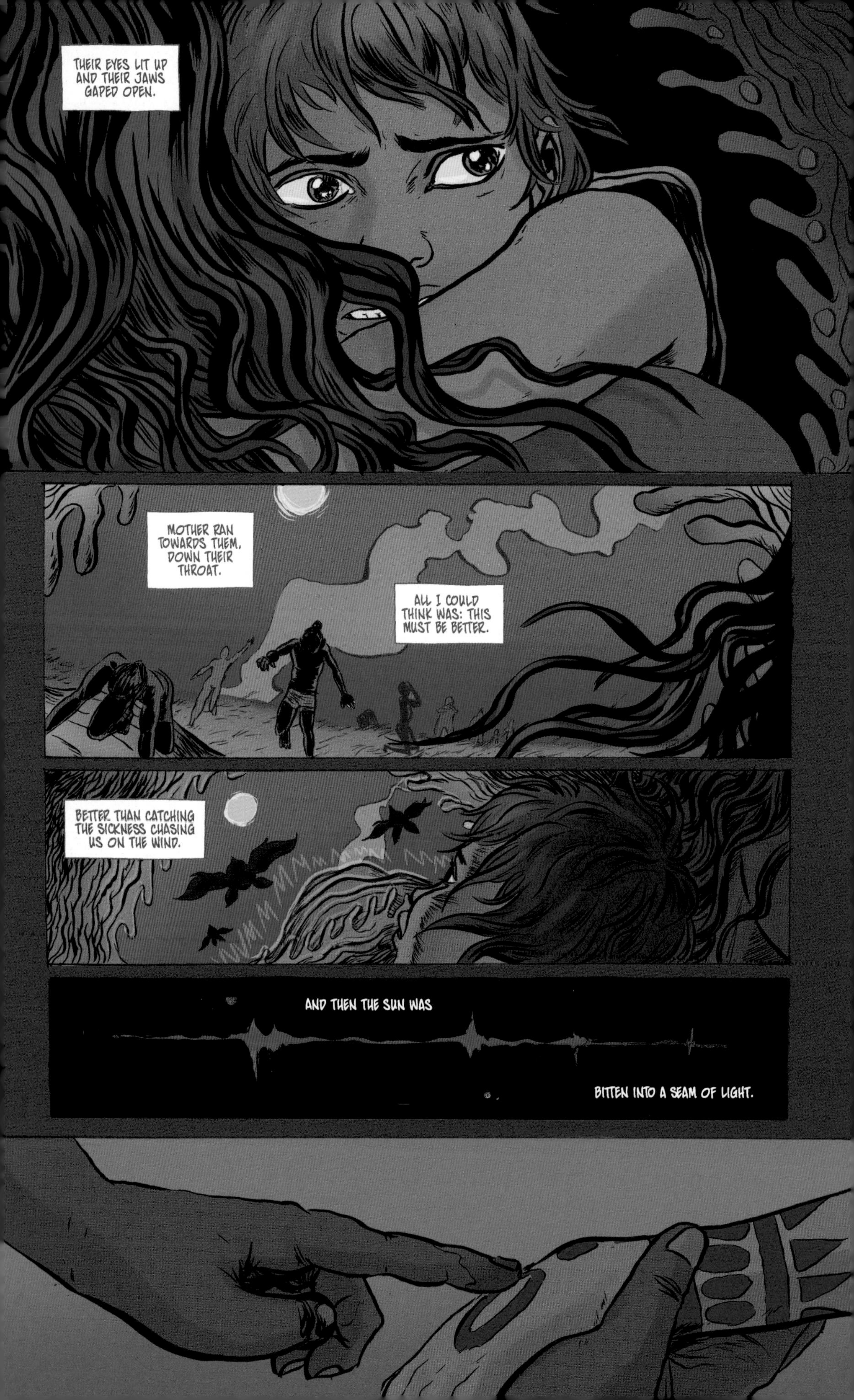
THEIR EYES LIT UP AND THEIR JAWS GAPED OPEN.
MOTHER RAN TOWARDS THEM, DOWN THEIR THROAT.
ALL I COULD THINK WAS: THIS MUST BE BETTER.
BETTER THAN CATCHING THE SICKNESS CHASING US ON THE WIND.
AND THEN THE SUN WAS
BITTEN INTO A SEAM OF LIGHT.

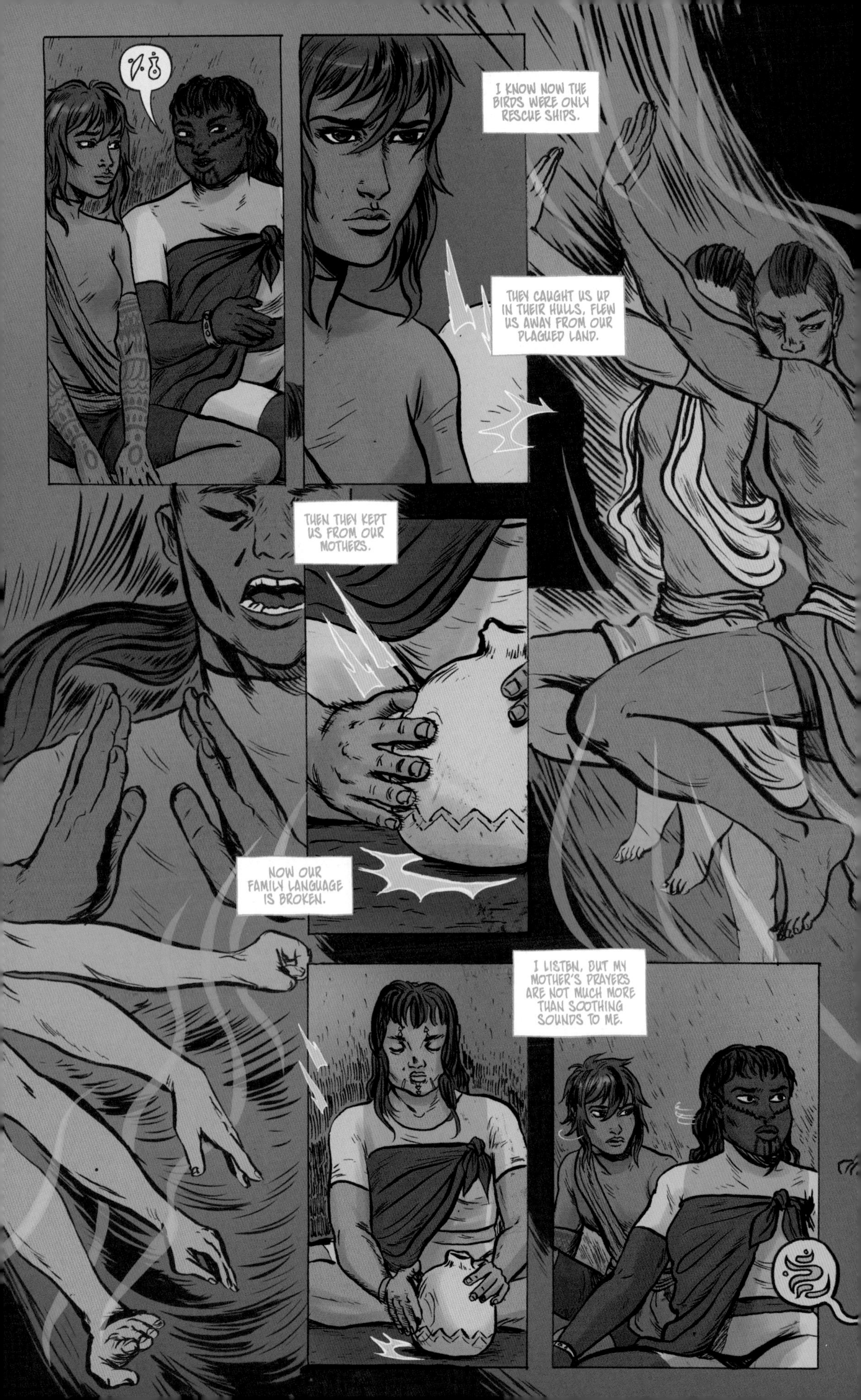
I KNOW NOW THE BIRDS WERE ONLY RESCUE SHIPS.
THEY CAUGHT US UP IN THEIR HULLS, FLEW US AWAY FROM OUR PLAGUED LAND.
THEN THEY KEPT US FROM OUR MOTHERS.
NOW OUR FAMILY LANGUAGE IS BROKEN.
I LISTEN, BUT MY MOTHER'S PRAYERS ARE NOT MUCH MORE THAN SOOTHING SOUNDS TO ME.

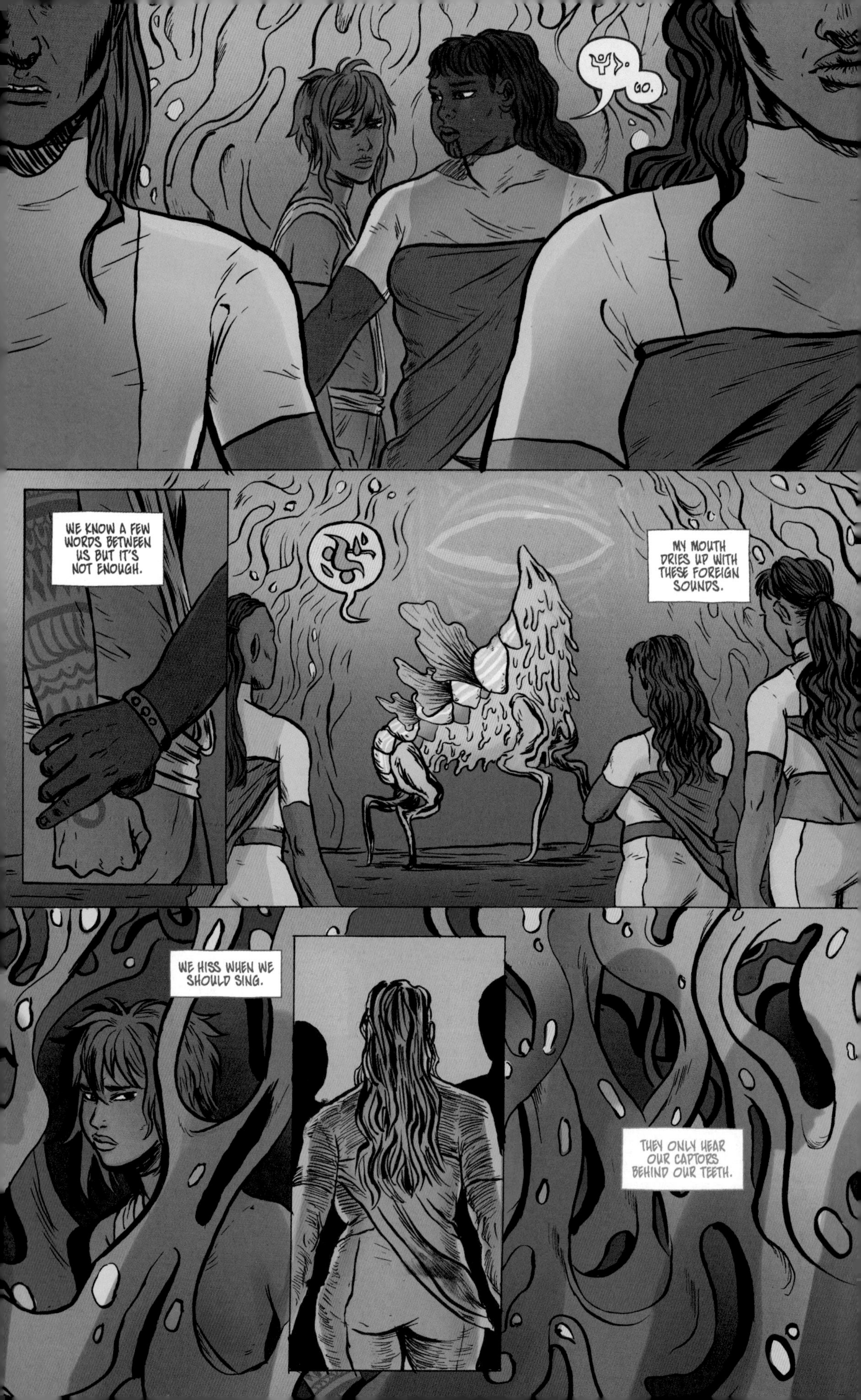
GO.
WE KNOW A FEW WORDS BETWEEN US BUT IT'S NOT ENOUGH.
MY MOUTH DRIES UP WITH THESE FOREIGN SOUNDS.
WE HISS WHEN WE SHOULD SING.
THEY ONLY HEAR OUR CAPTORS BEHIND OUR TEETH.

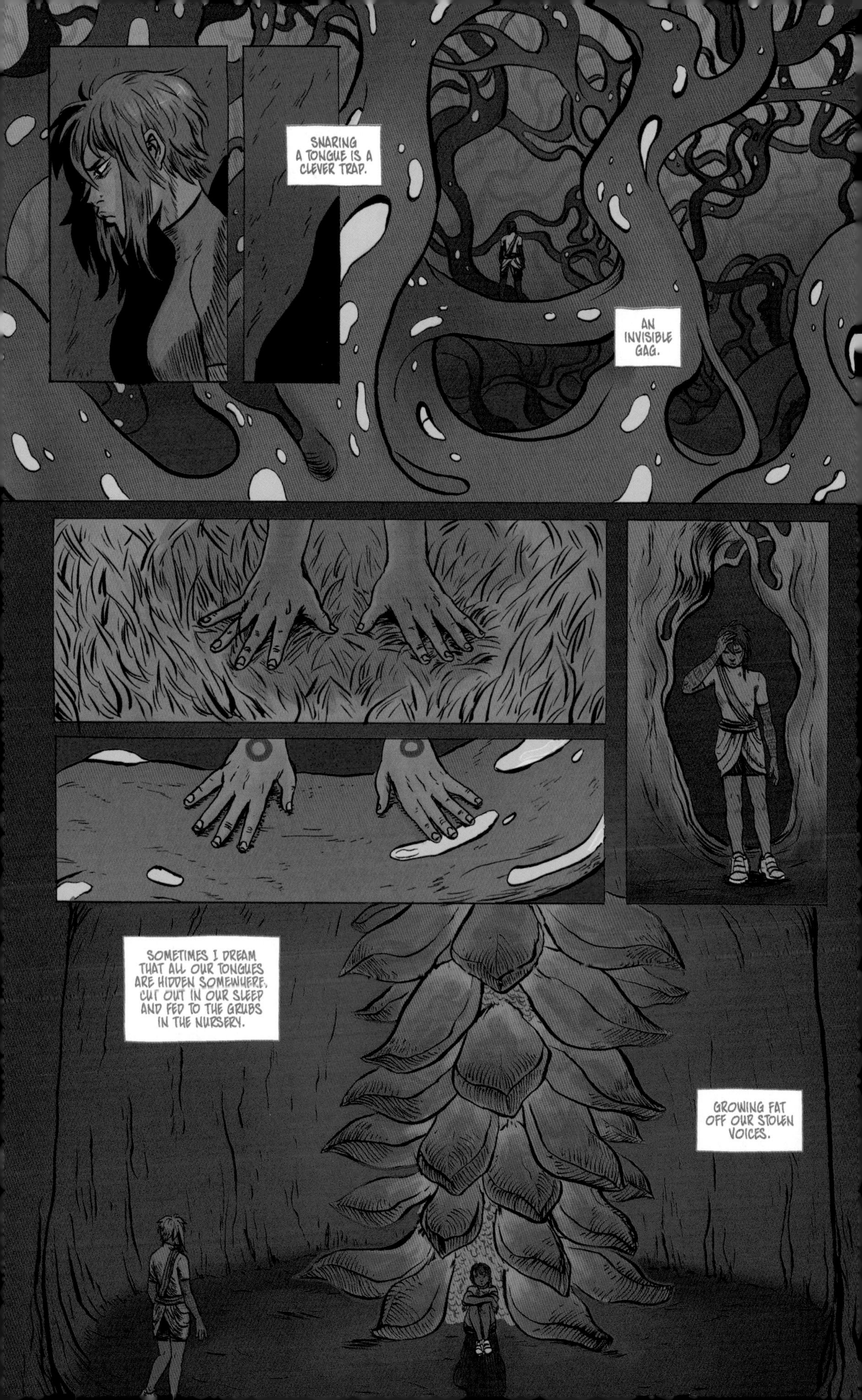
SNARING A TONGUE IS A CLEVER TRAP.
AN INVISIBLE GAG.
SOMETIMES I DREAM THAT ALL OUR TONGUES ARE HIDDEN SOMEWHERE, CUT OUT IN OUR SLEEP AND FED TO THE GRUBS IN THE NURSERY.
GROWING FAT OFF OUR STOLEN VOICES.

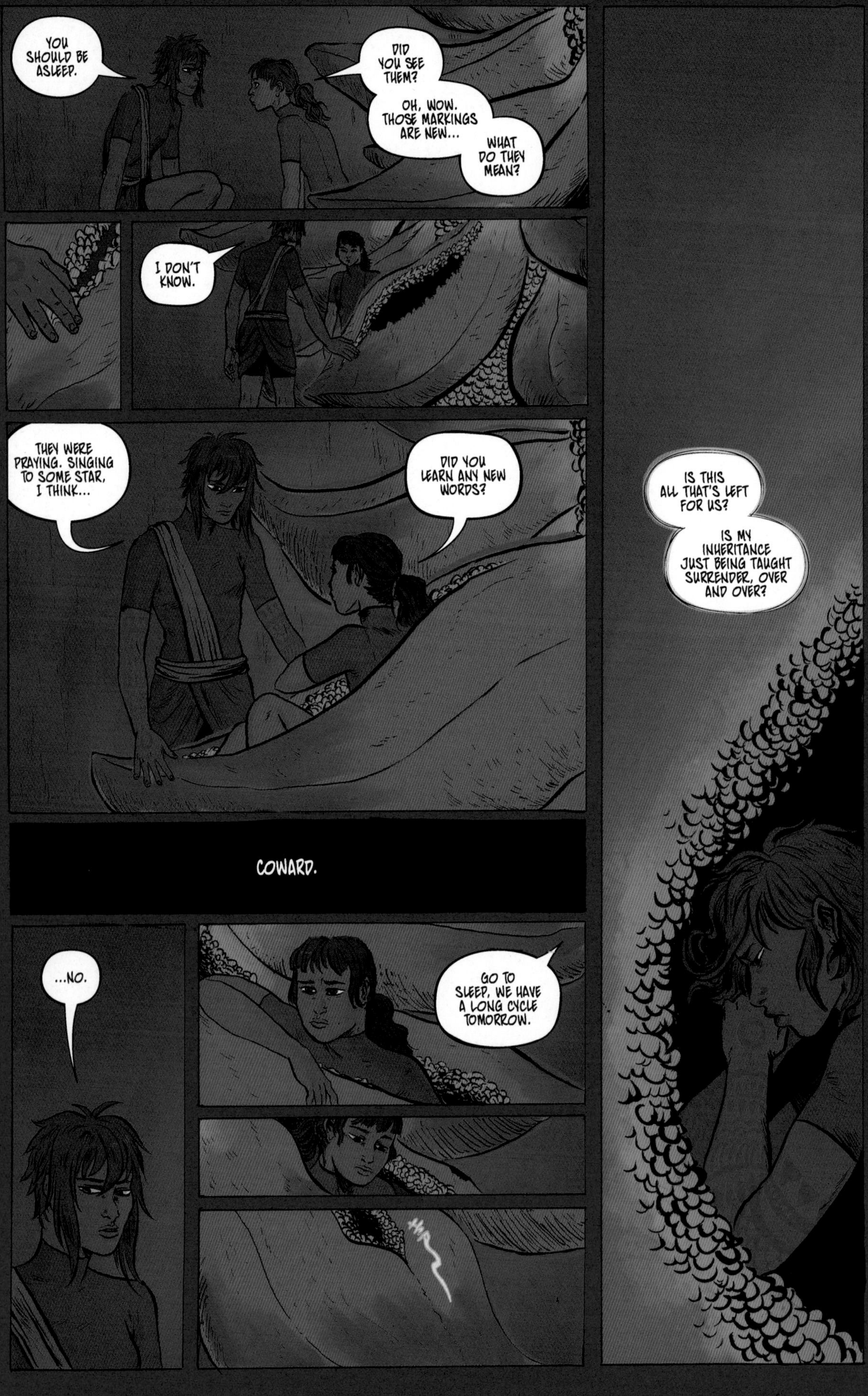
YOU SHOULD BE ASLEEP.
DID YOU SEE THEM?
OH, WOW. THOSE MARKINGS ARE NEW...
WHAT DO THEY MEAN?
I DON'T KNOW.
THEY WERE PRAYING. SINGING TO SOME STAR, I THINK...
DID YOU LEARN ANY NEW WORDS?
COWARD.
...NO.
GO TO SLEEP, WE HAVE A LONG CYCLE TOMORROW.
IS THIS ALL THAT'S LEFT FOR US?
IS MY INHERITANCE JUST BEING TAUGHT SURRENDER, OVER AND OVER?

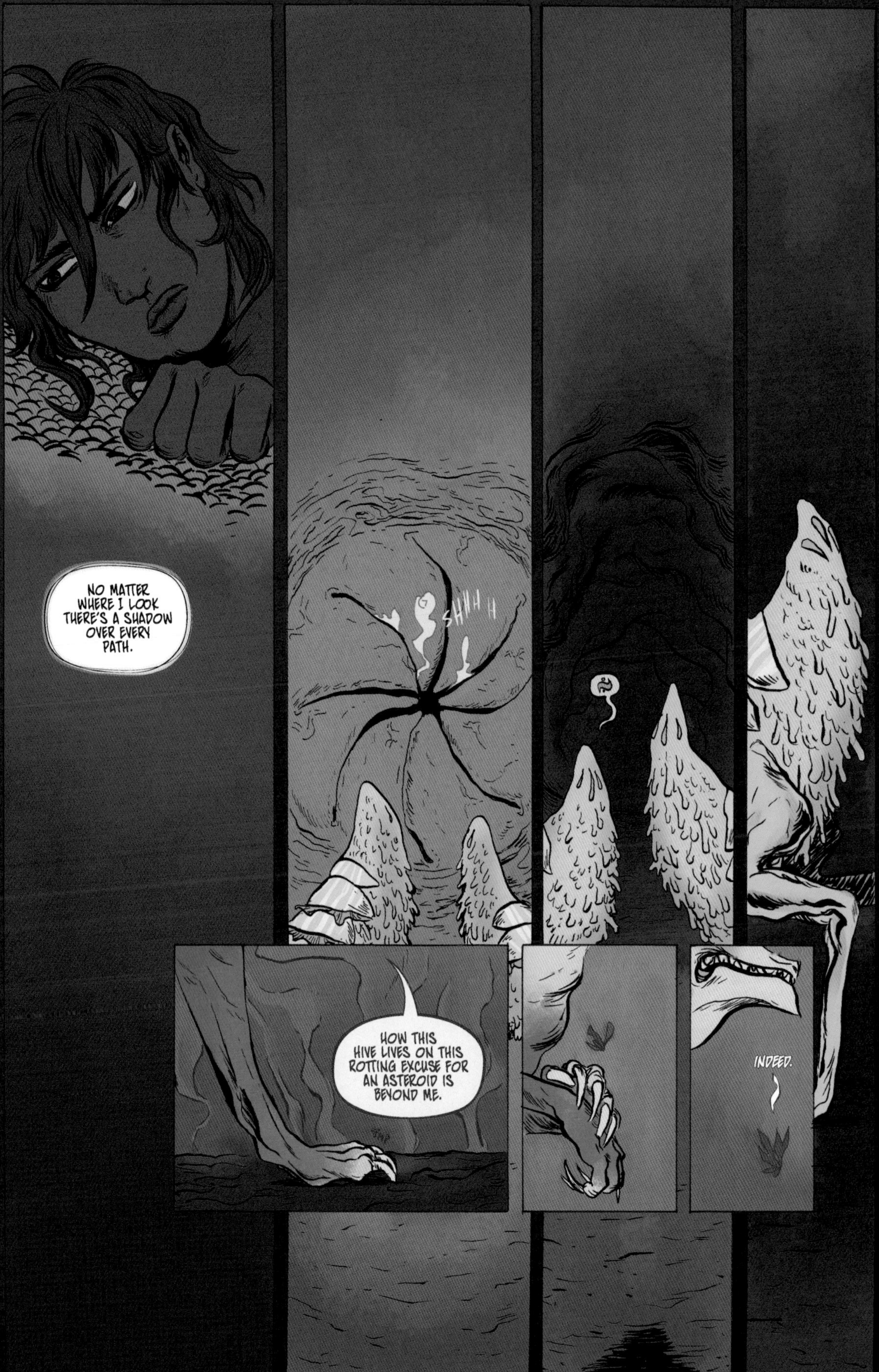
NO MATTER WHERE I LOOK THERE'S A SHADOW OVER EVERY PATH.
SHHHH
HOW THIS HIVE LIVES ON THIS ROTTING EXCUSE FOR AN ASTEROID IS BEYOND ME.
INDEED.

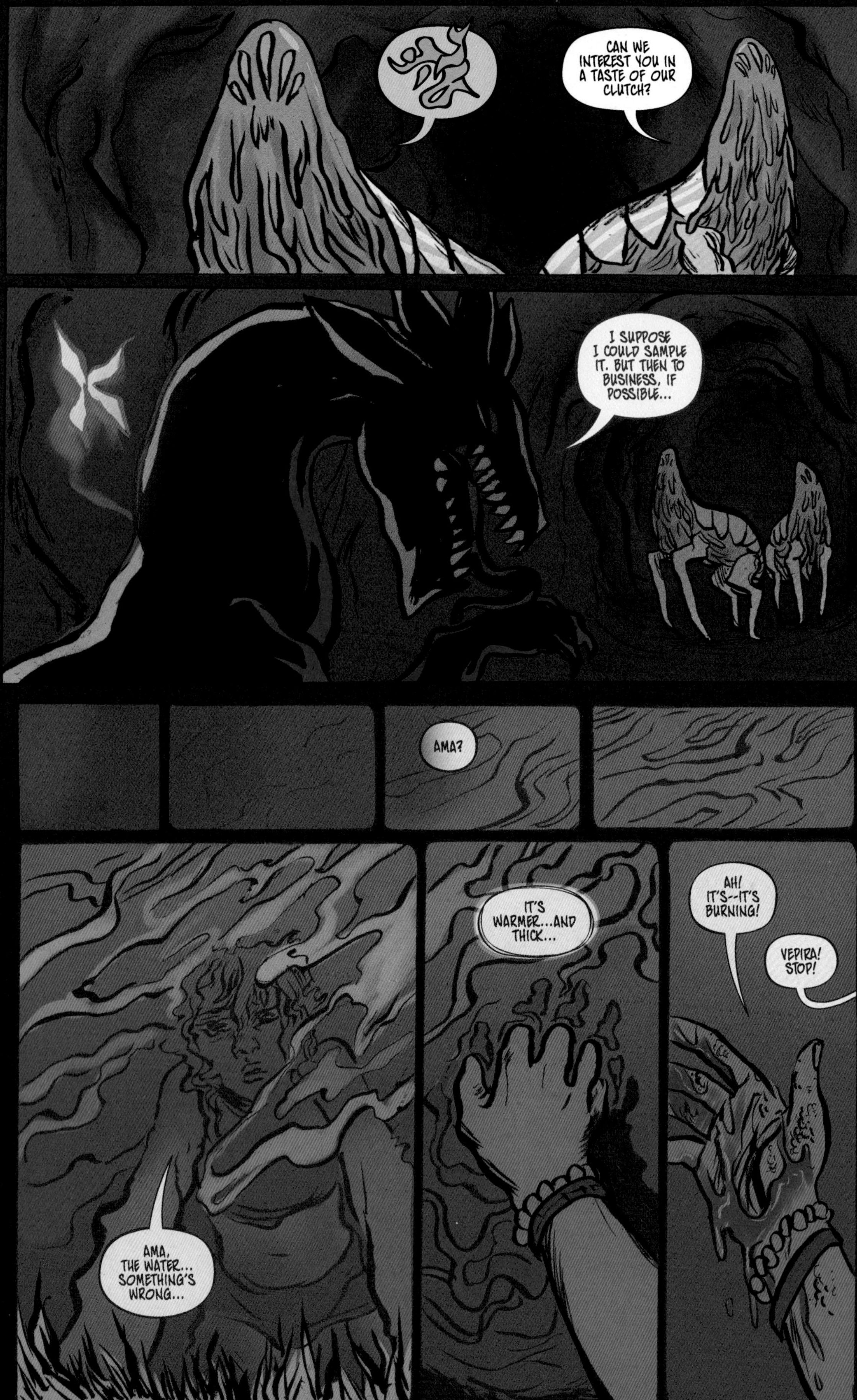

CAN WE INTEREST YOU IN A TASTE OF OUR CLUTCH?
I SUPPOSE I COULD SAMPLE IT. BUT THEN TO BUSINESS, IF POSSIBLE...
AMA?
AMA, THE WATER... SOMETHING'S WRONG...
IT'S WARMER...AND THICK...
AH! IT'S--IT'S BURNING!
VEPIRA! STOP!

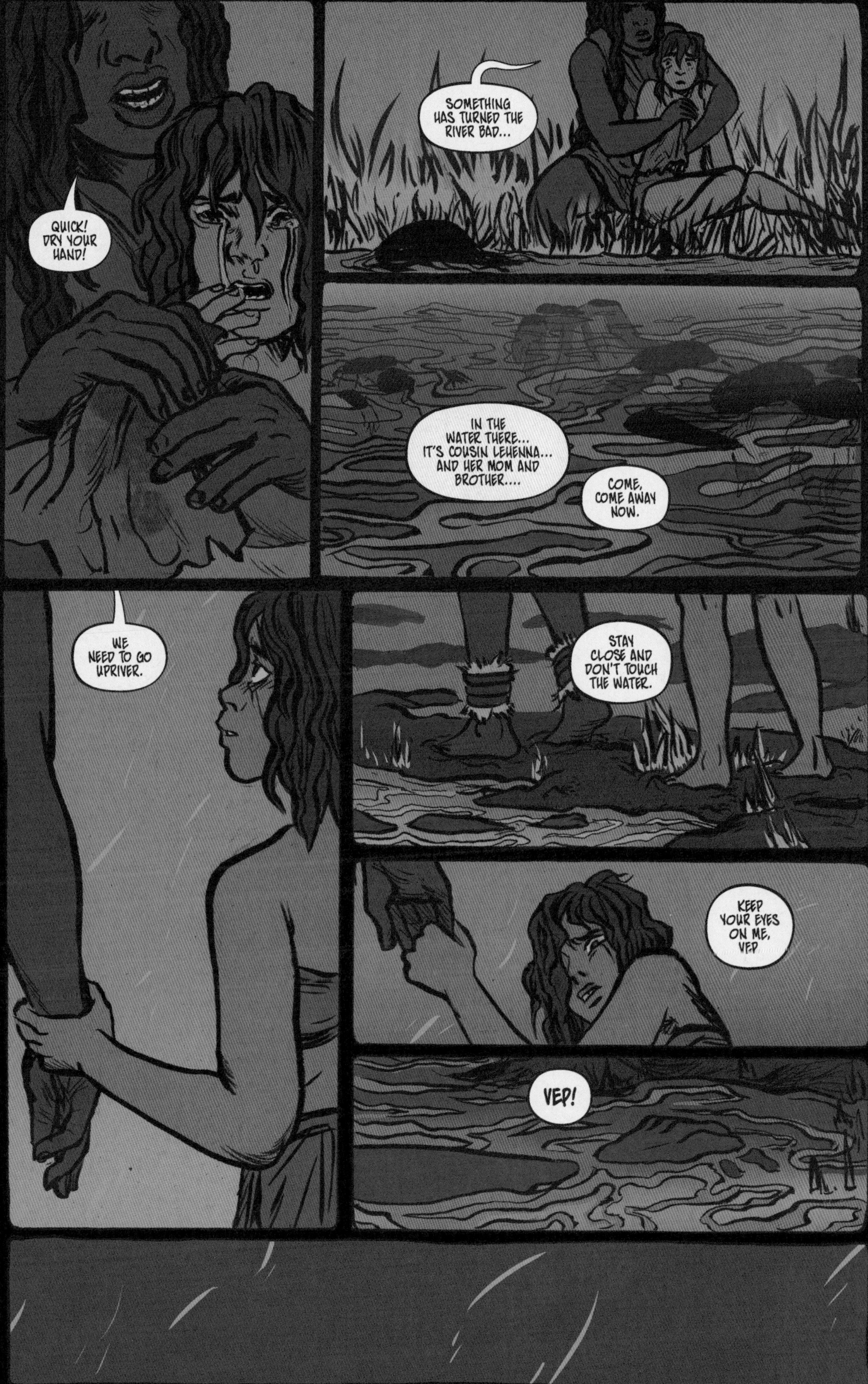
QUICK! DRY YOUR HAND!
SOMETHING HAS TURNED THE RIVER BAD...
IN THE WATER THERE... IT'S COUSIN LEHENNA... AND HER MOM AND BROTHER....
COME, COME AWAY NOW.
WE NEED TO GO UPRIVER.
STAY CLOSE AND DON'T TOUCH THE WATER.
KEEP YOUR EYES ON ME, VEP
VEP!

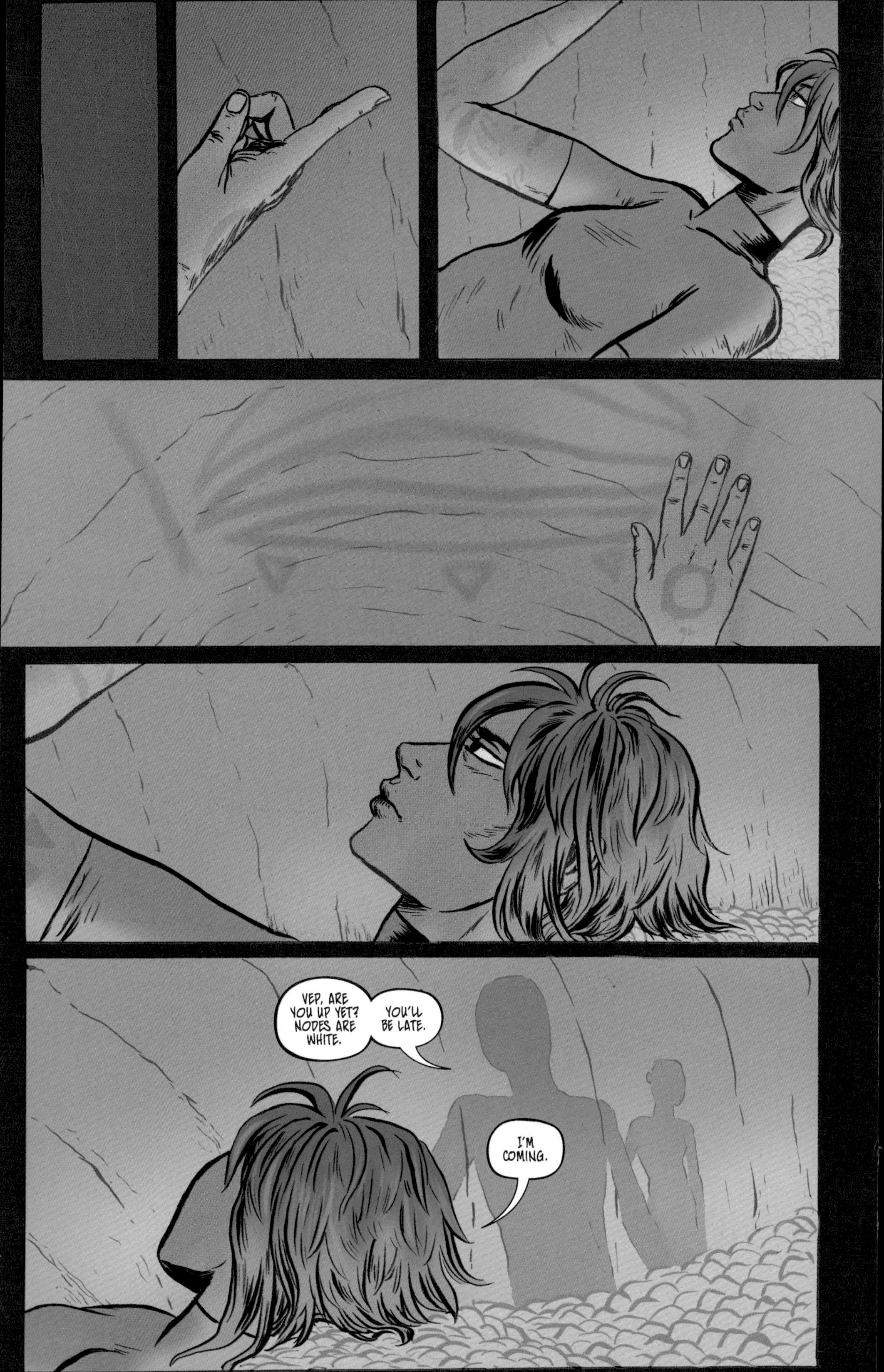

VEP, ARE YOU UP YET? NODES ARE WHITE.
YOU'LL BE LATE.
I'M COMING.

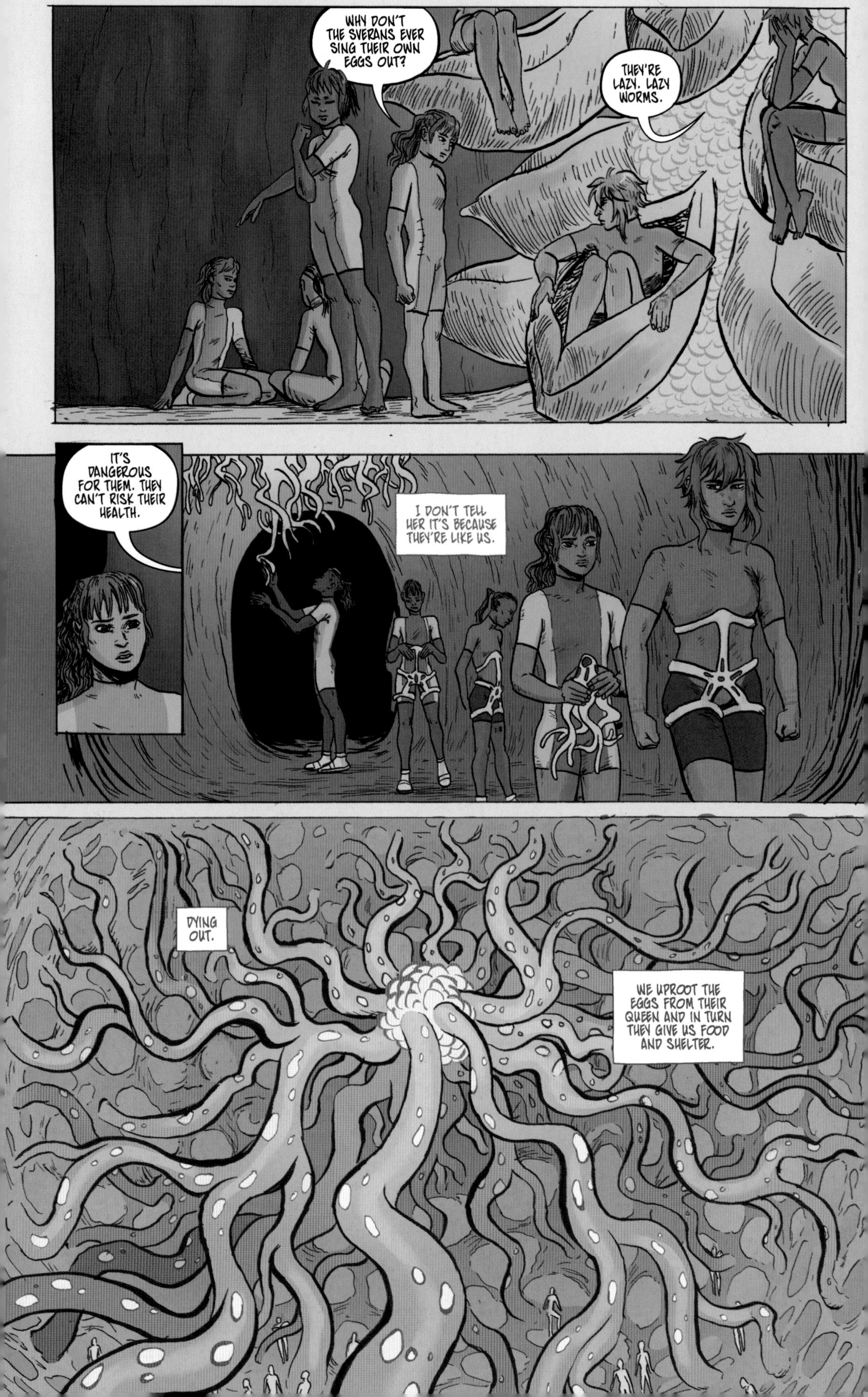
WHY DON'T THE SVERANS EVER SING THEIR OWN EGGS OUT?
THEY'RE LAZY. LAZY WORMS.
IT'S DANGEROUS FOR THEM. THEY CAN'T RISK THEIR HEALTH.
I DON'T TELL HER IT'S BECAUSE THEY'RE LIKE US.
DYING OUT.
WE UPROOT THE EGGS FROM THEIR QUEEN AND IN TURN THEY GIVE US FOOD AND SHELTER.

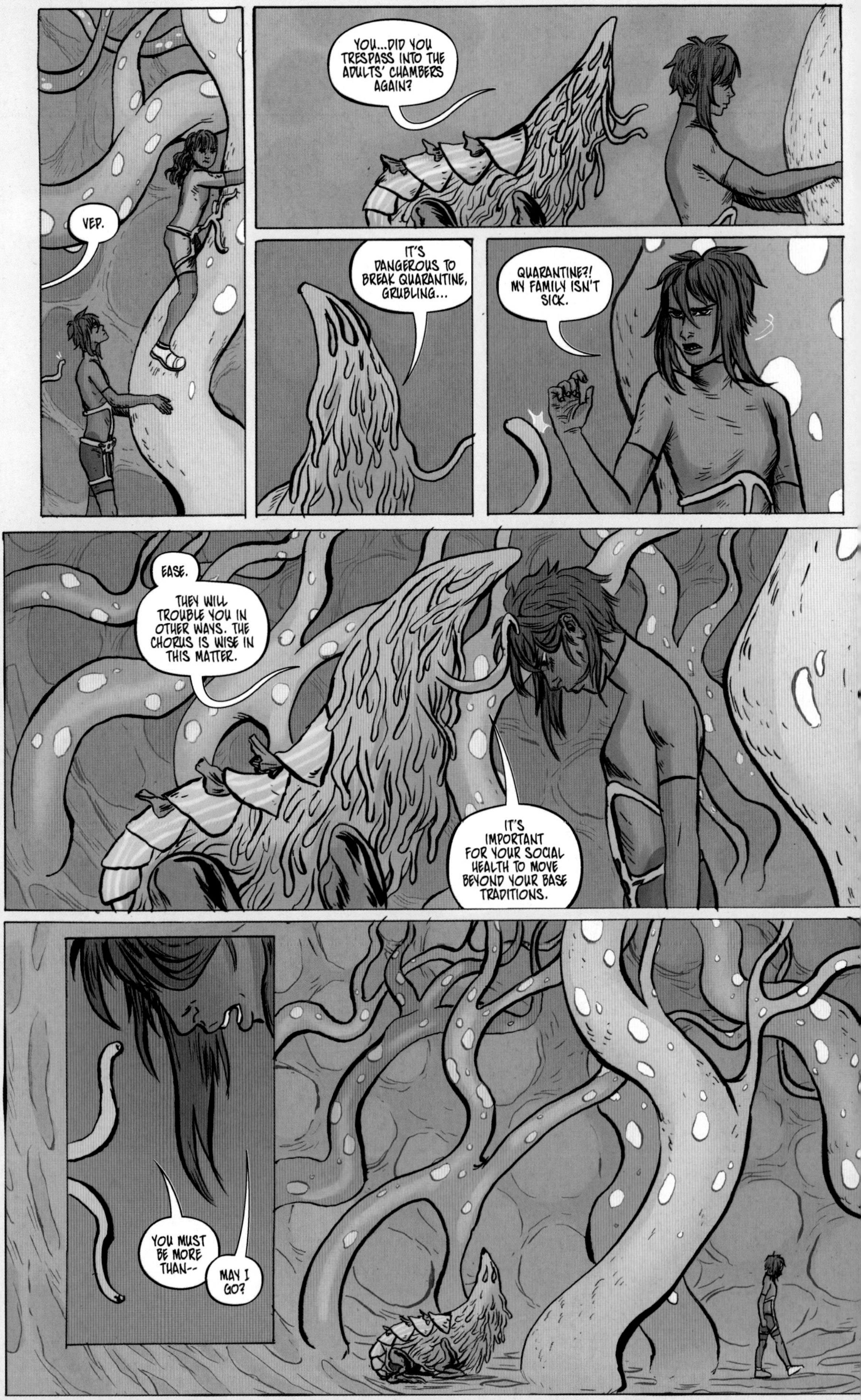
YEP.
YOU...DID YOU TRESPASS INTO THE ADULTS' CHAMBERS AGAIN?
IT'S DANGEROUS TO BREAK QUARANTINE, GRUBLING...
QUARANTINE?! MY FAMILY ISN'T SICK.
EASE.
THEY WILL TROUBLE YOU IN OTHER WAYS. THE CHORUS IS WISE IN THIS MATTER.
IT'S IMPORTANT FOR YOUR SOCIAL HEALTH TO MOVE BEYOND YOUR BASE TRADITIONS.
YOU MUST BE MORE THAN--
MAY I GO?

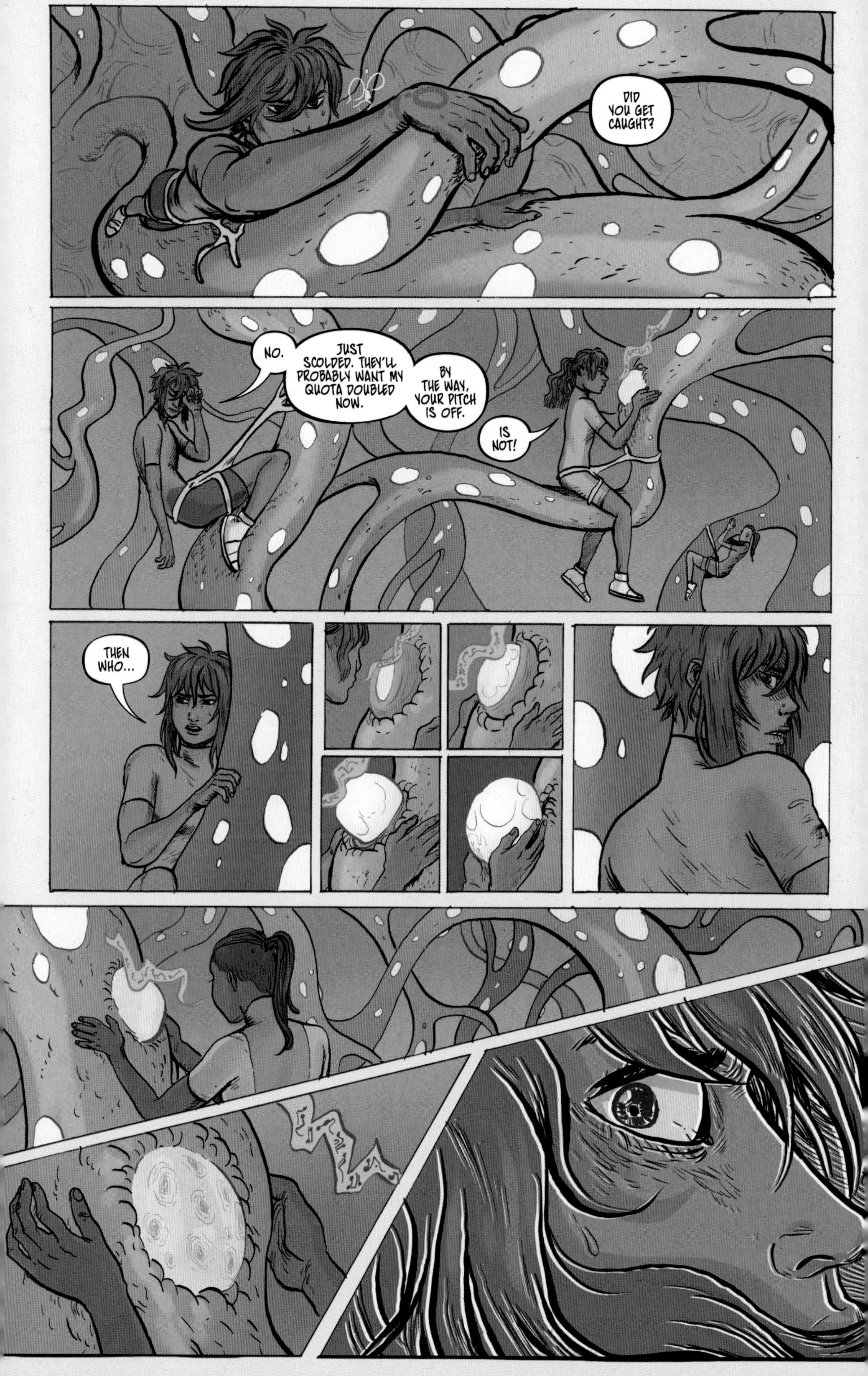
DID YOU GET CAUGHT?
NO.
JUST SCOLDED. THEY'LL PROBABLY WANT MY QUOTA DOUBLED NOW.
BY THE WAY, YOUR PITCH IS OFF.
IS NOT!
THEN WHO...

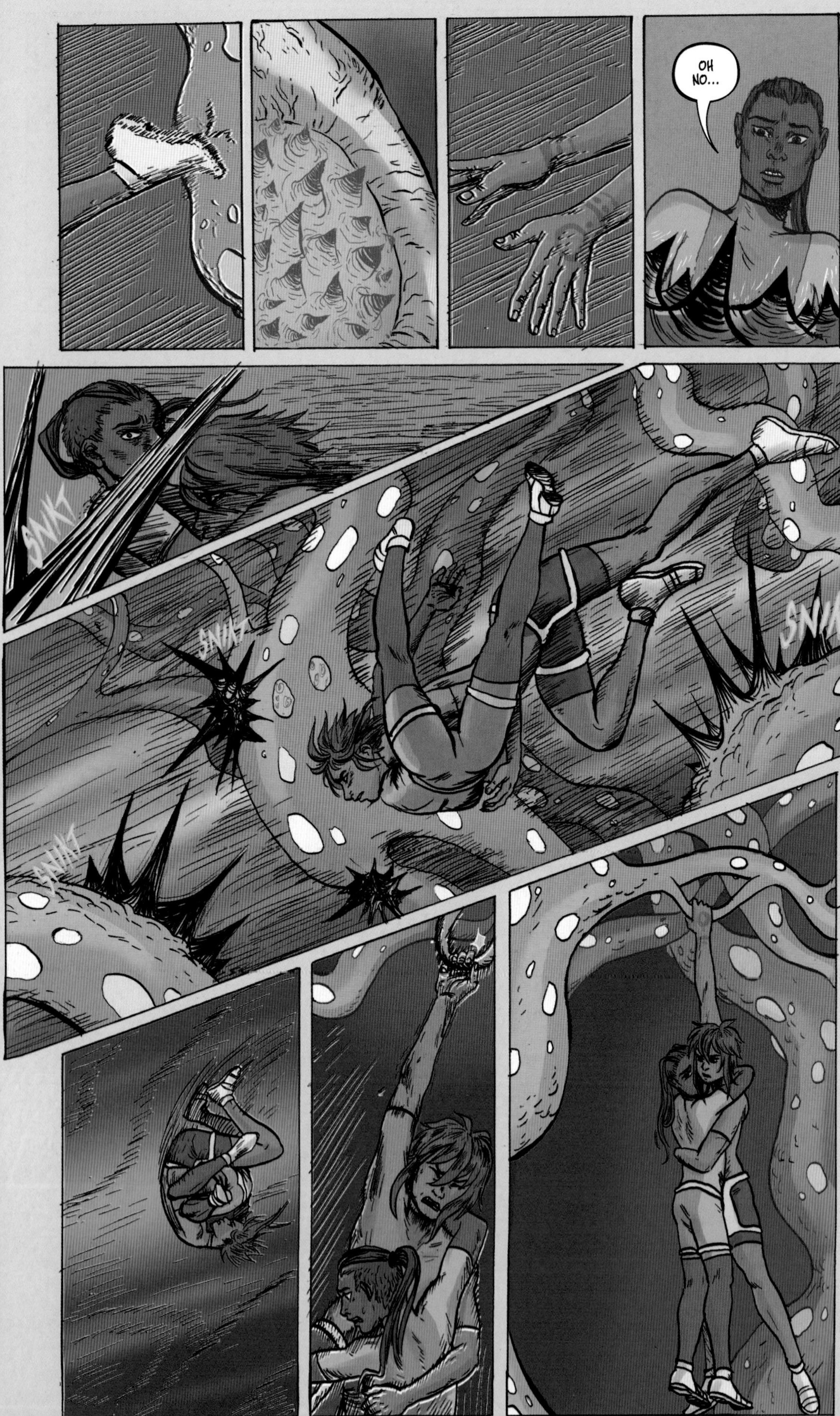
OH NO...
SNIKT
SNIKT
SNIKT
SNIKT

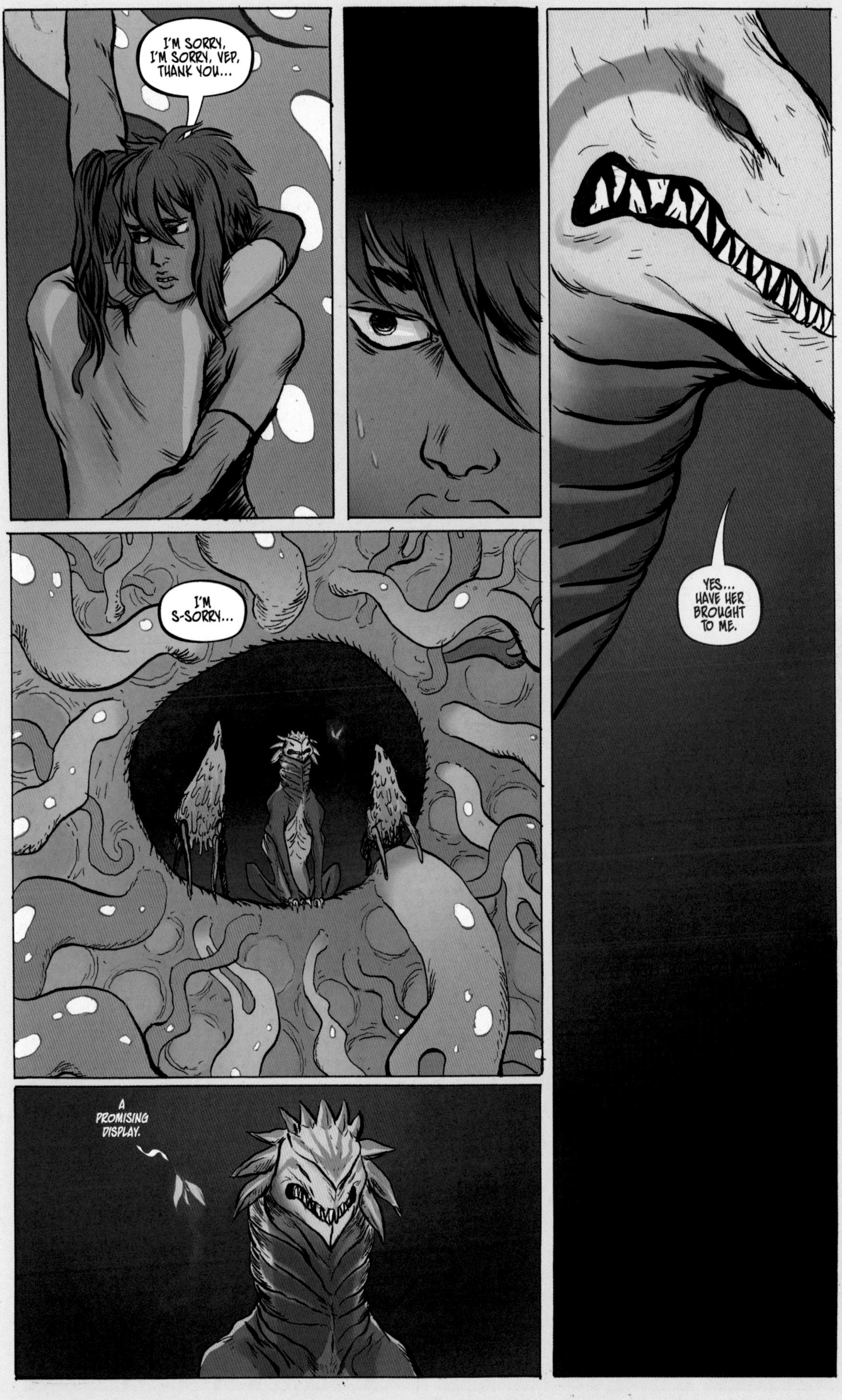
I'M SORRY, I'M SORRY, VEP, THANK YOU...
YES... HAVE HER BROUGHT TO ME.
I'M S-SORRY...
A PROMISING DISPLAY.

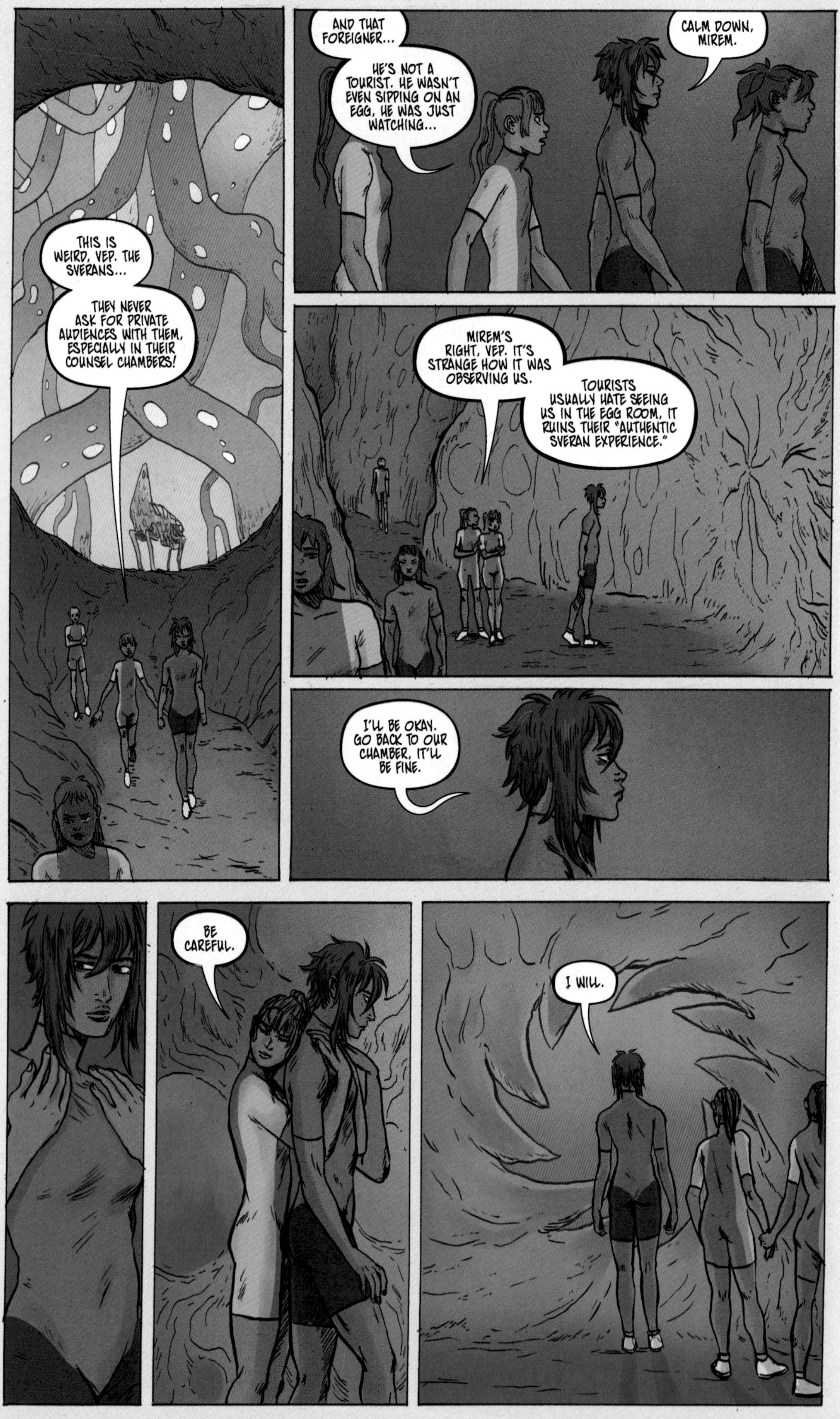
THIS IS WEIRD, VEP. THE SVERANS...
THEY NEVER ASK FOR PRIVATE AUDIENCES WITH THEM, ESPECIALLY IN THEIR COUNSEL CHAMBERS!
AND THAT FOREIGNER...
HE'S NOT A TOURIST. HE WASN'T EVEN SIPPING ON AN EGG, HE WAS JUST WATCHING...
CALM DOWN, MIREM.
MIREM'S RIGHT, VEP. IT'S STRANGE HOW IT WAS OBSERVING US.
TOURISTS USUALLY HATE SEEING US IN THE EGG ROOM, IT RUINS THEIR "AUTHENTIC SVERAN EXPERIENCE."
I'LL BE OKAY. GO BACK TO OUR CHAMBER, IT'LL BE FINE.
BE CAREFUL.
I WILL.

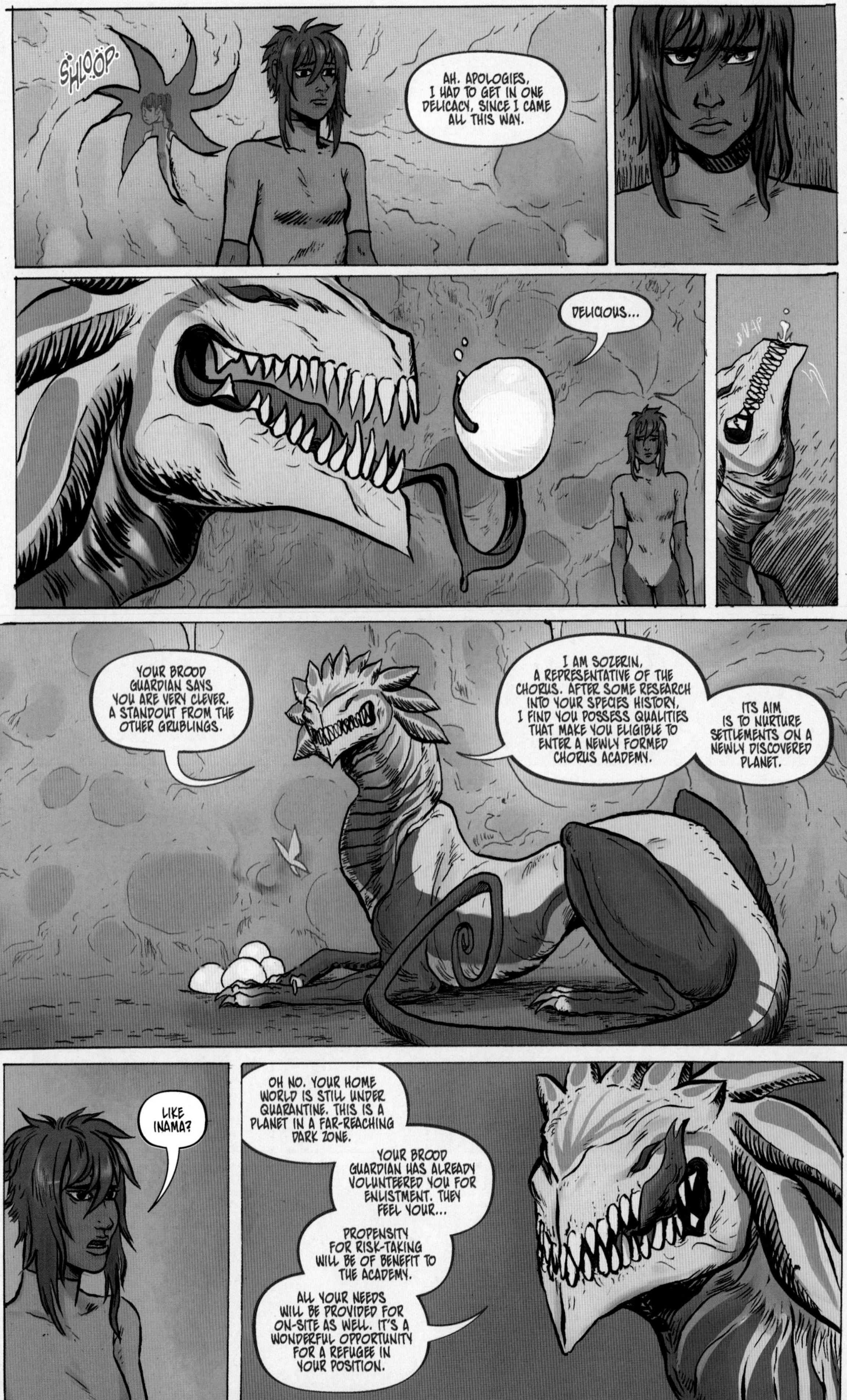
SHLOOP.
AH. APOLOGIES, I HAD TO GET IN ONE DELICACY, SINCE I CAME ALL THIS WAY.
DELICIOUS...
YOUR BROOD GUARDIAN SAYS YOU ARE VERY CLEVER. A STANDOUT FROM THE OTHER GRUBLINGS.
I AM SOZERIN, A REPRESENTATIVE OF THE CHORUS. AFTER SOME RESEARCH INTO YOUR SPECIES HISTORY, I FIND YOU POSSESS QUALITIES THAT MAKE YOU ELIGIBLE TO ENTER A NEWLY FORMED CHORUS ACADEMY.
ITS AIM IS TO NURTURE SETTLEMENTS ON A NEWLY DISCOVERED PLANET.
LIKE INAMA?
OH NO. YOUR HOME WORLD IS STILL UNDER QUARANTINE. THIS IS A PLANET IN A FAR-REACHING DARK ZONE.
YOUR BROOD GUARDIAN HAS ALREADY VOLUNTEERED YOU FOR ENLISTMENT. THEY FEEL YOUR...
PROPENSITY FOR RISK-TAKING WILL BE OF BENEFIT TO THE ACADEMY.
ALL YOUR NEEDS WILL BE PROVIDED FOR ON-SITE AS WELL. IT'S A WONDERFUL OPPORTUNITY FOR A REFUGEE IN YOUR POSITION.

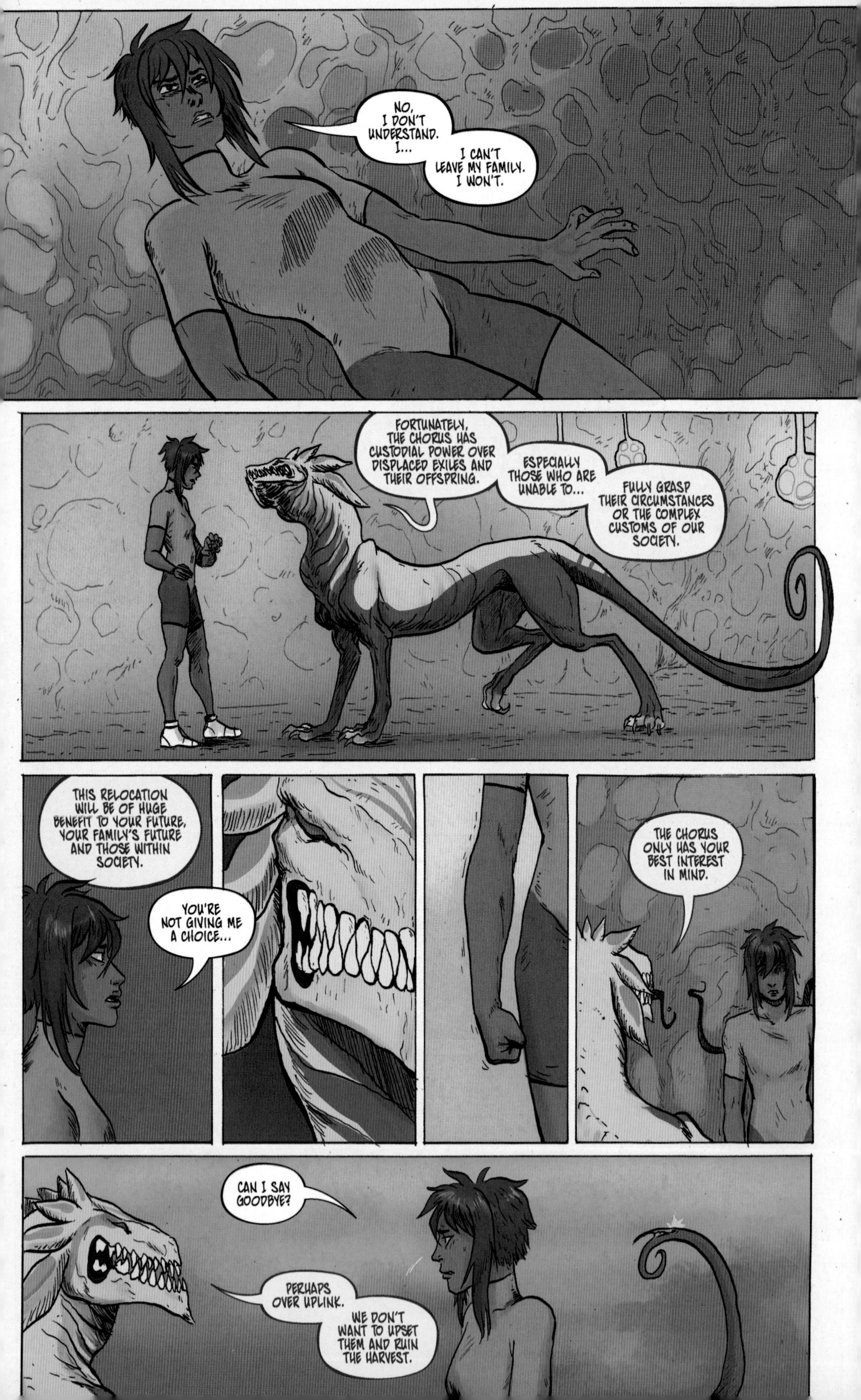
NO, I DON'T UNDERSTAND. I...
I CAN'T LEAVE MY FAMILY. I WON'T.
FORTUNATELY, THE CHORUS HAS CUSTODIAL POWER OVER DISPLACED EXILES AND THEIR OFFSPRING.
ESPECIALLY THOSE WHO ARE UNABLE TO...
FULLY GRASP THEIR CIRCUMSTANCES OR THE COMPLEX CUSTOMS OF OUR SOCIETY.
THIS RELOCATION WILL BE OF HUGE BENEFIT TO YOUR FUTURE, YOUR FAMILY'S FUTURE AND THOSE WITHIN SOCIETY.
YOU'RE NOT GIVING ME A CHOICE...
THE CHORUS ONLY HAS YOUR BEST INTEREST IN MIND.
CAN I SAY GOODBYE?
PERHAPS OVER UPLINK.
WE DON'T WANT TO UPSET THEM AND RUIN THE HARVEST.

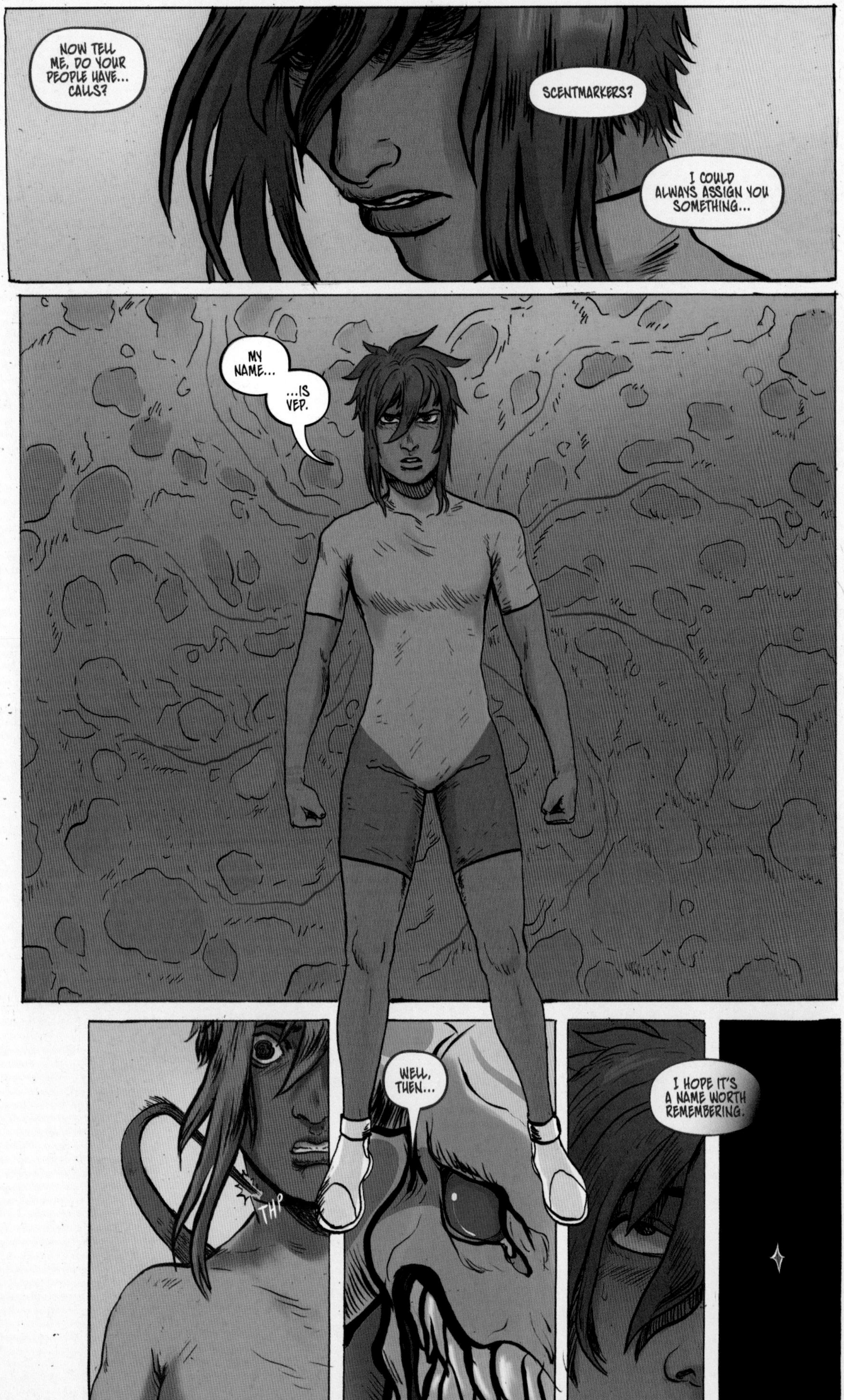
NOW TELL ME, DO YOUR PEOPLE HAVE... CALLS?
SCENTMARKERS?
I COULD ALWAYS ASSIGN YOU SOMETHING...
MY NAME...
...IS VEP.
THP
WELL, THEN...
I HOPE IT'S A NAME WORTH REMEMBERING.

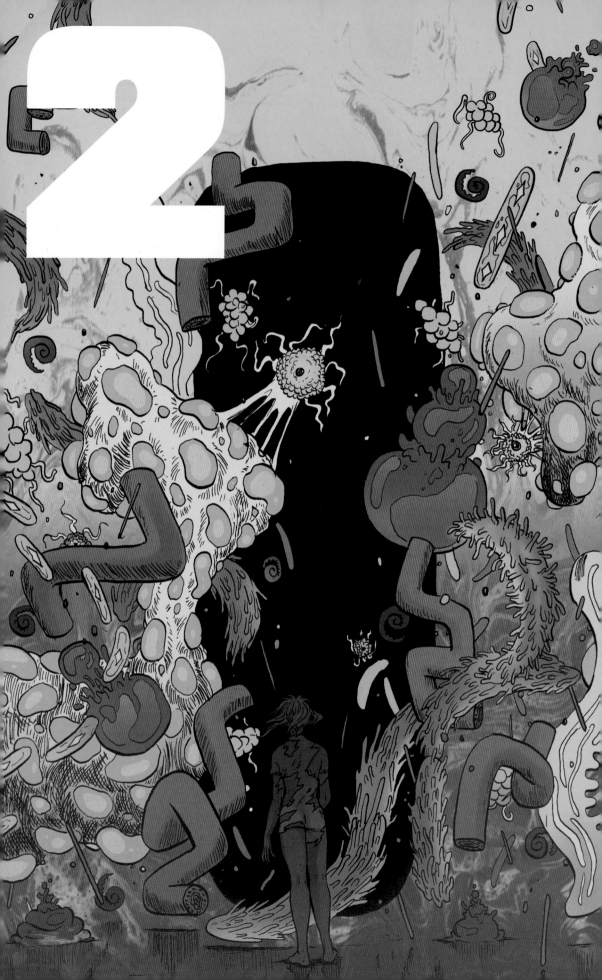

WHEN THE BLACK SURF PRESSES ASHORE

AND THE RAINS WET US THROUGH

THE SHELL STILL HOLDS US ALL

UNDER THE EYES OF THE STARS

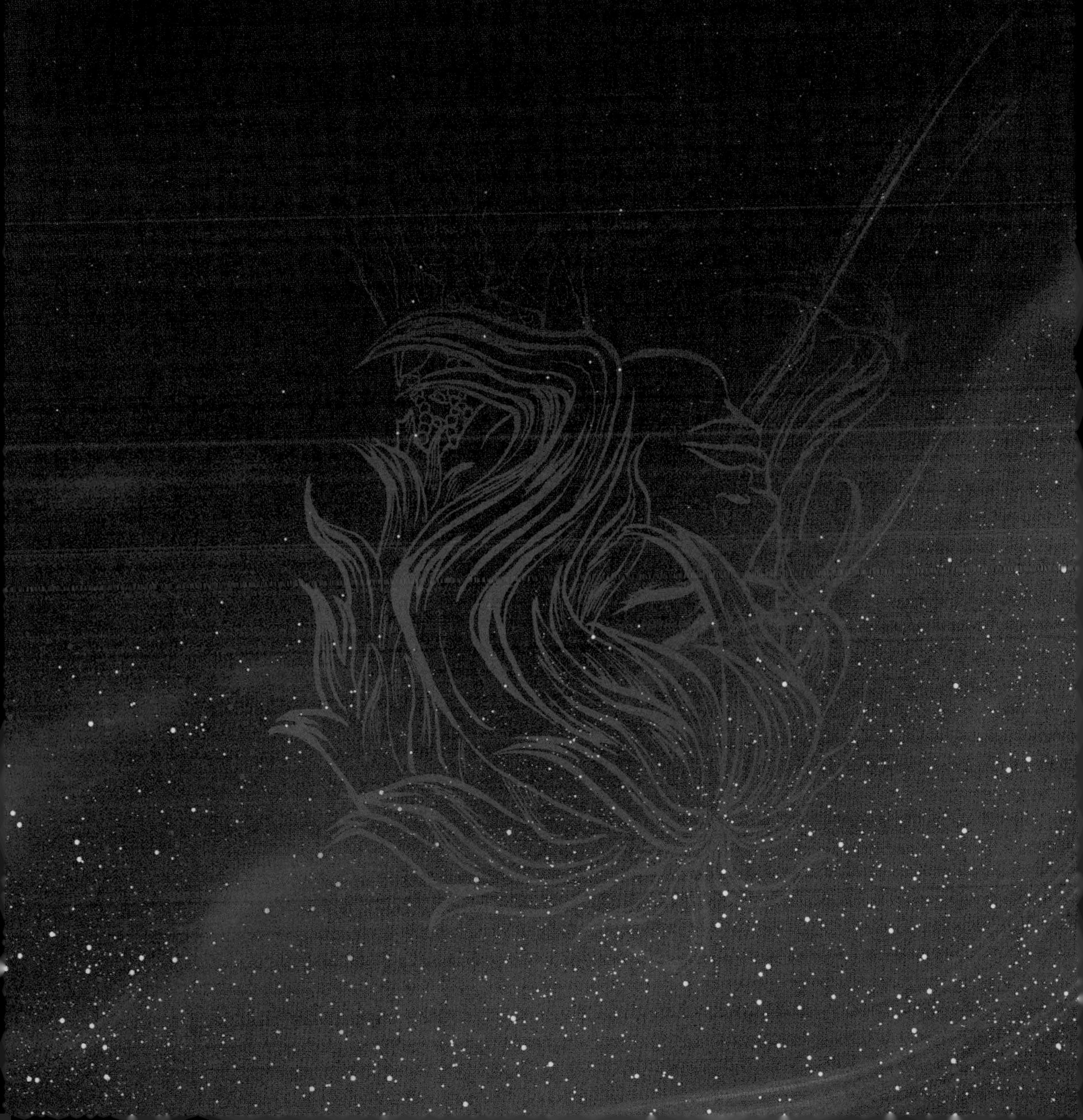

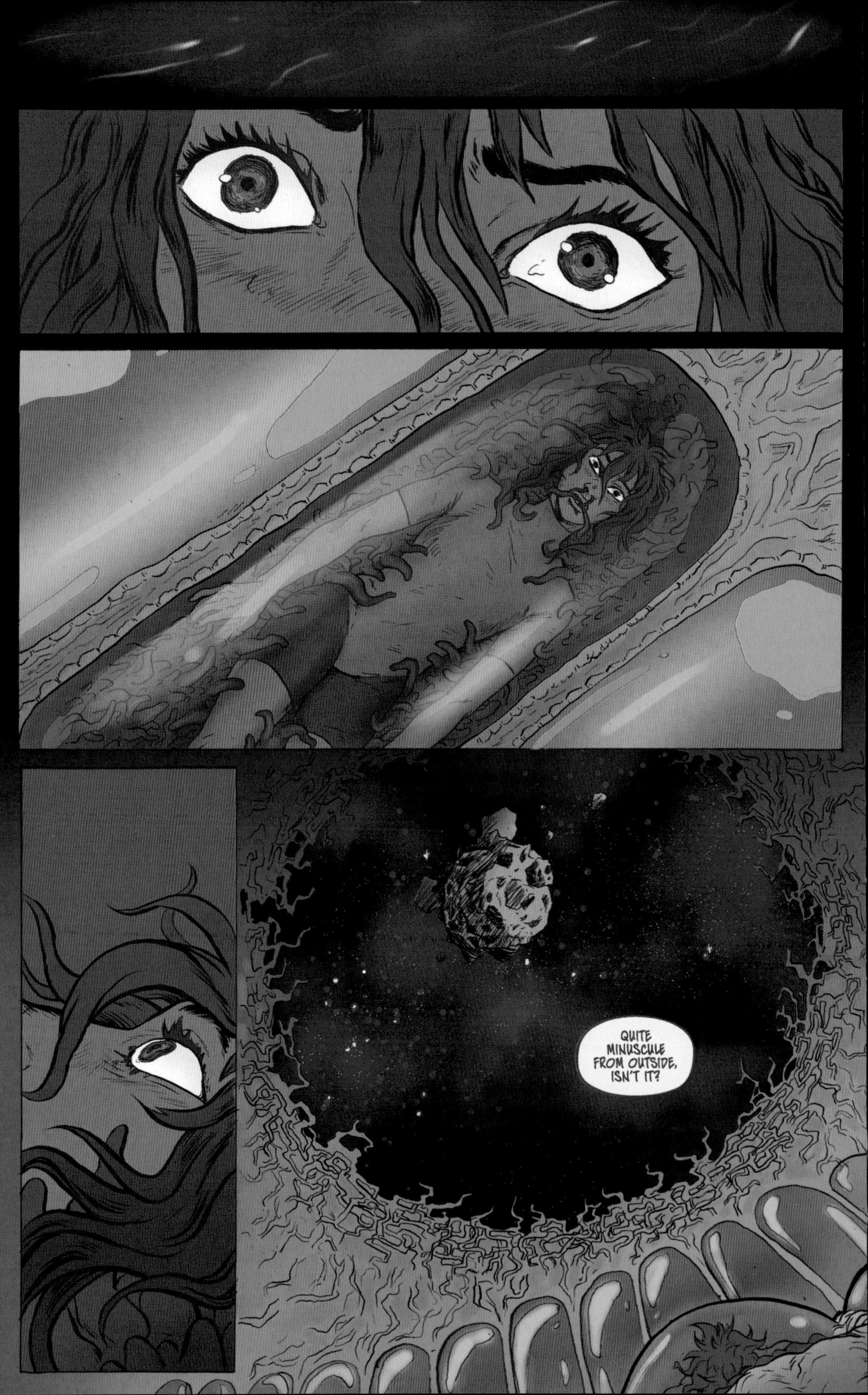
QUITE MINUSCULE FROM OUTSIDE, ISN'T IT?

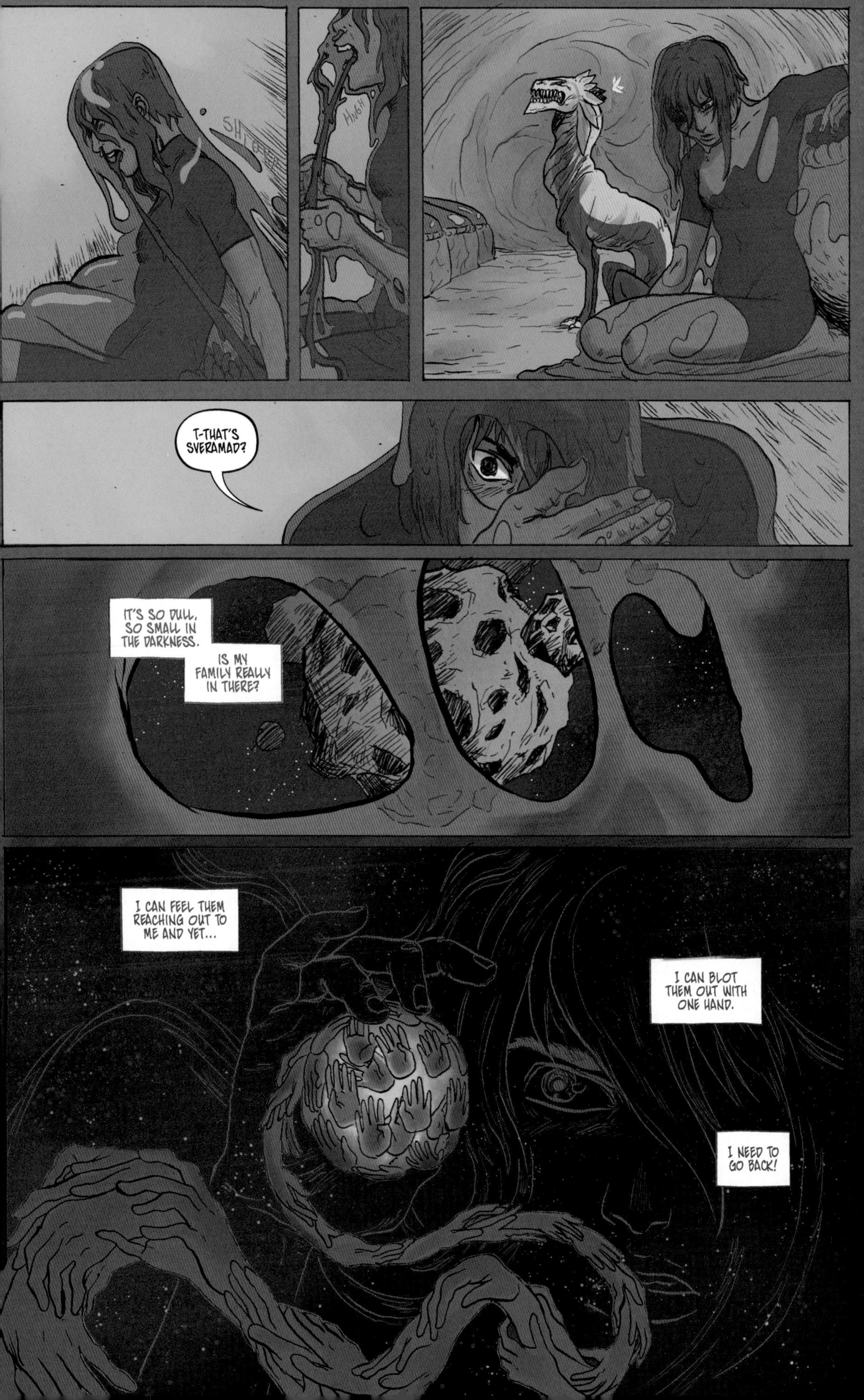
T-THAT'S SVERAMAD?
IT'S SO DULL, SO SMALL IN THE DARKNESS.
IS MY FAMILY REALLY IN THERE?
I CAN FEEL THEM REACHING OUT TO ME AND YET...
I CAN BLOT THEM OUT WITH ONE HAND.
I NEED TO GO BACK!

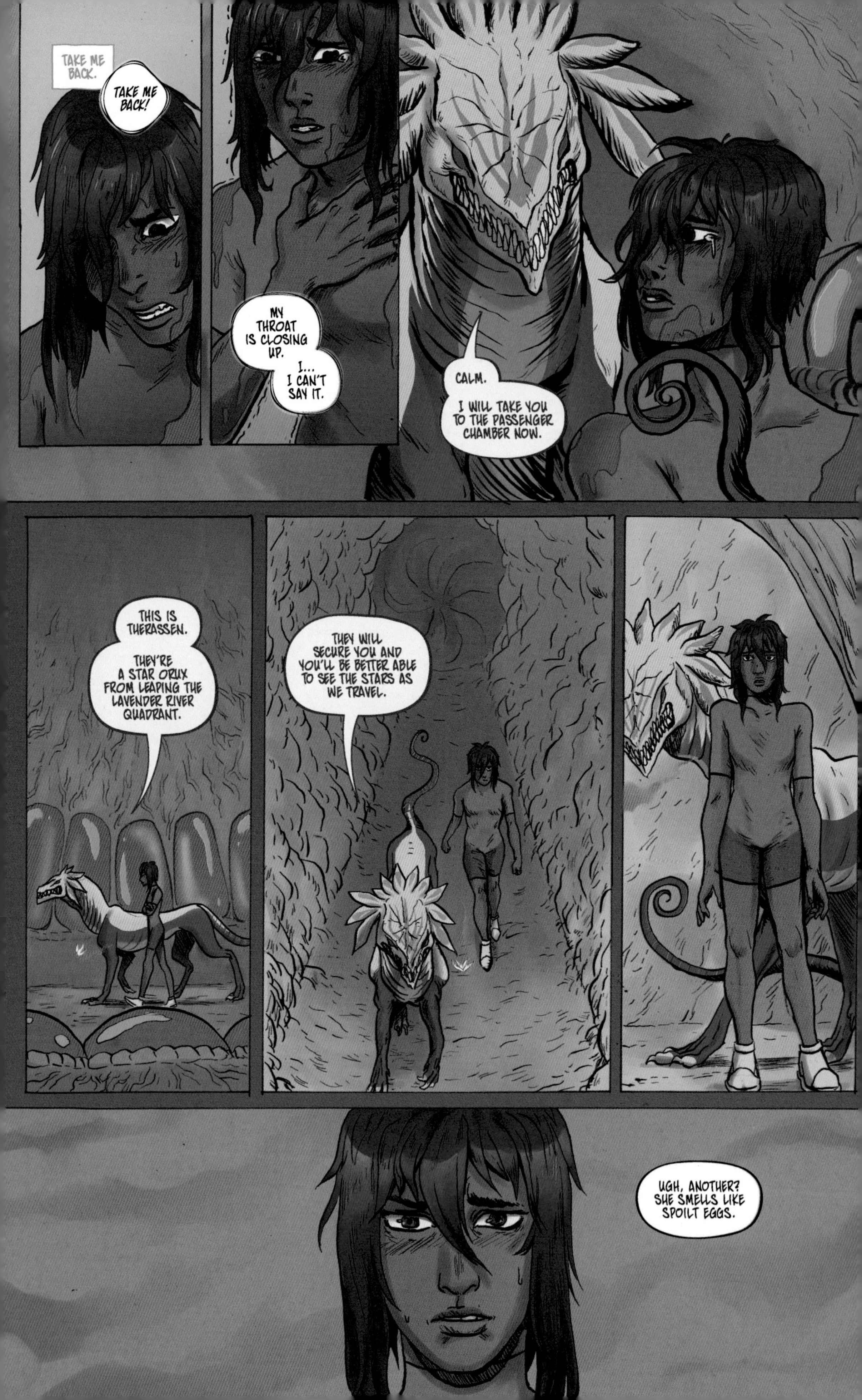
TAKE ME BACK.
TAKE ME BACK!
MY THROAT IS CLOSING UP.
I... I CAN'T SAY IT.
CALM.
I WILL TAKE YOU TO THE PASSENGER CHAMBER NOW.
THIS IS THERASSEN.
THEY'RE A STAR ORUX FROM LEAPING THE LAVENDER RIVER QUADRANT.
THEY WILL SECURE YOU AND YOU'LL BE BETTER ABLE TO SEE THE STARS AS WE TRAVEL.
UGH, ANOTHER? SHE SMELLS LIKE SPOILT EGGS.

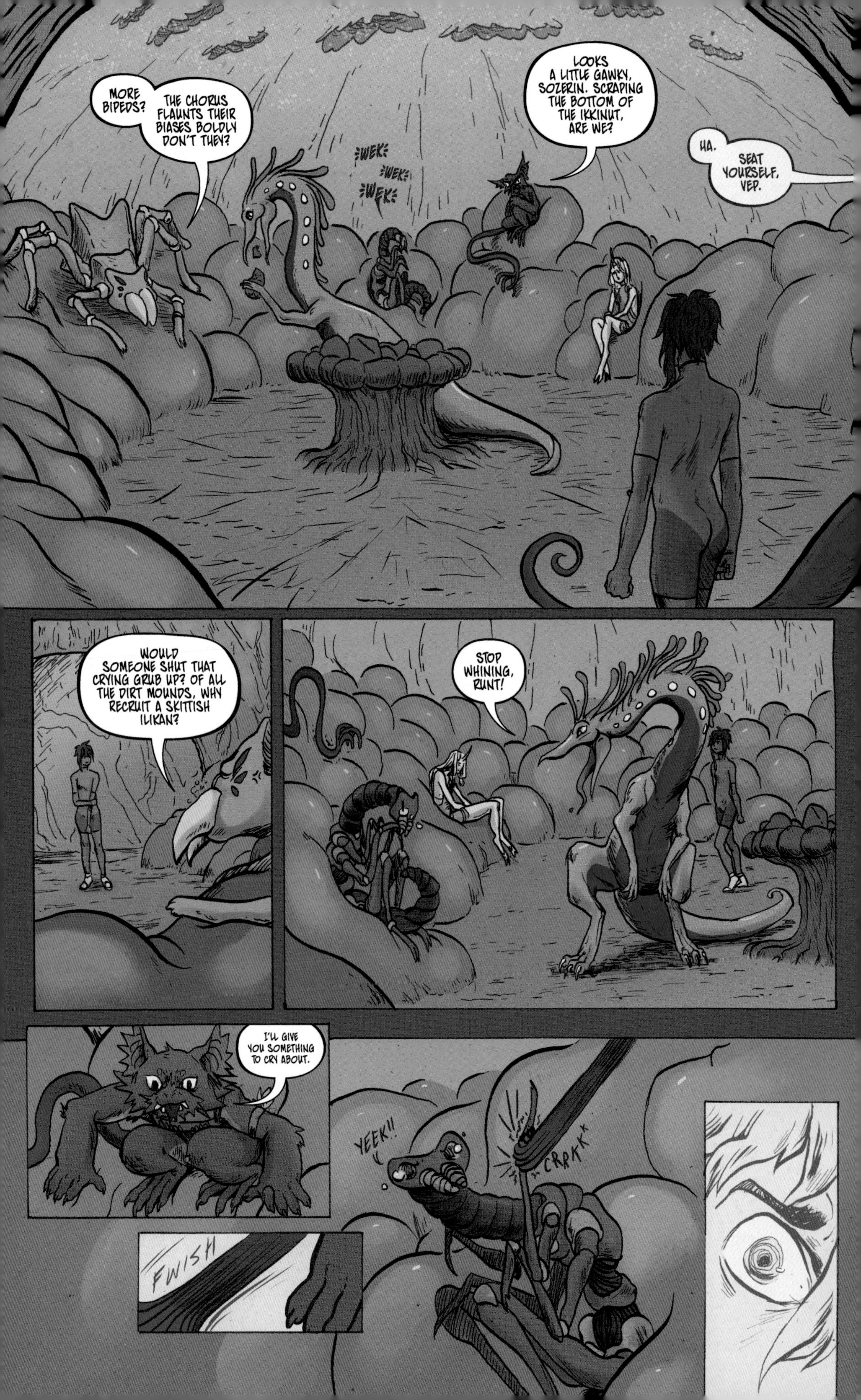
MORE BIPEDS?
THE CHORUS FLAUNTS THEIR BIASES BOLDLY DON'T THEY?
WEK WEK WEK
LOOKS A LITTLE GAWKY, SOZERIN. SCRAPING THE BOTTOM OF THE IKKINUT, ARE WE?
HA.
SEAT YOURSELF, VEP.
WOULD SOMEONE SHUT THAT CRYING GRUB UP? OF ALL THE DIRT MOUNDS, WHY RECRUIT A SKITTISH ILIKAN?
STOP WHINING, RUNT!
I'LL GIVE YOU SOMETHING TO CRY ABOUT.
FWISH
YEEK!!
CRAKK

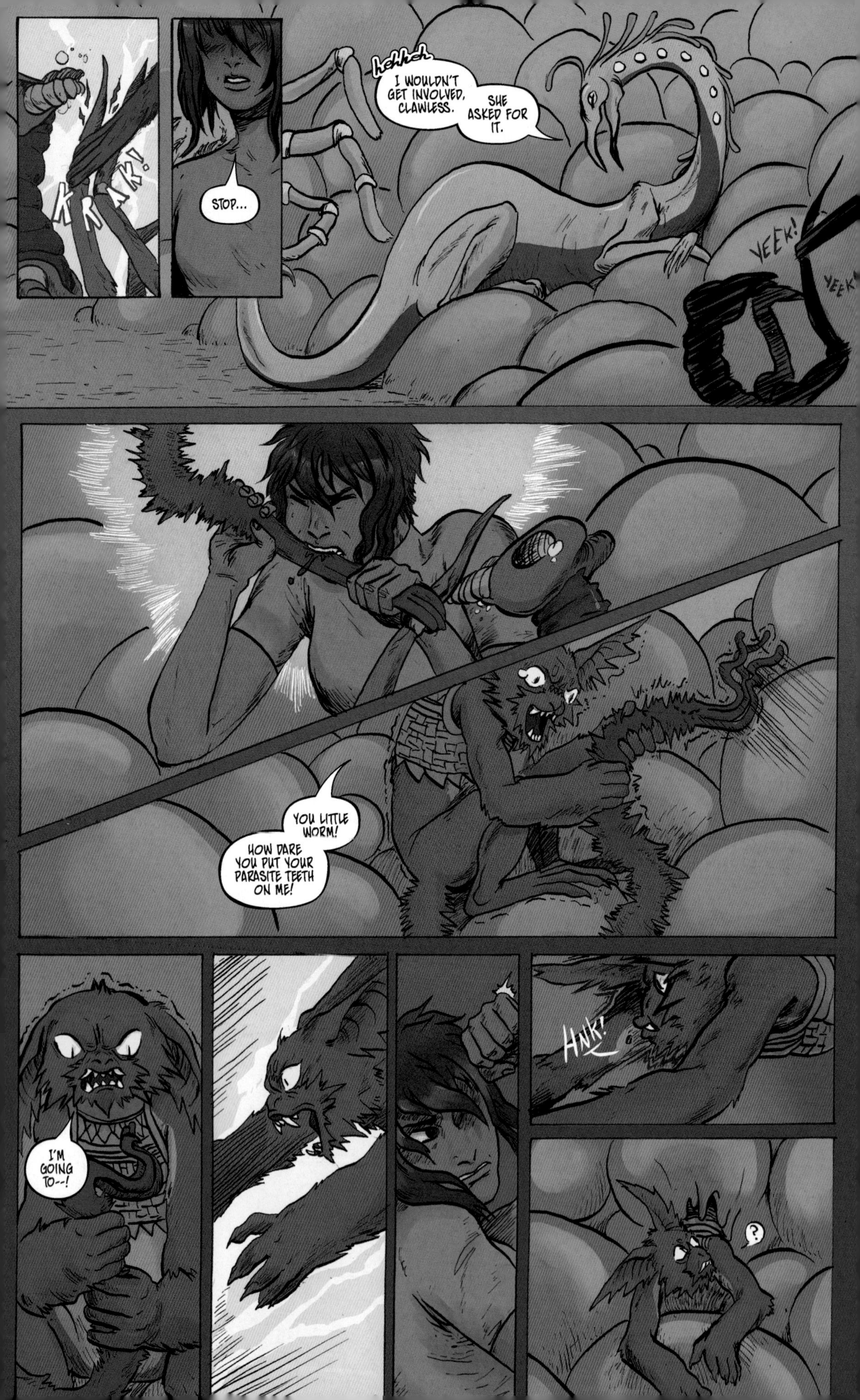
KRAK!
STOP...
hehheh
I WOULDN'T GET INVOLVED, CLAWLESS.
SHE ASKED FOR IT.
YEEK!
YEEK
YOU LITTLE WORM!
HOW DARE YOU PUT YOUR PARASITE TEETH ON ME!
I'M GOING TO--!
HNK!
?

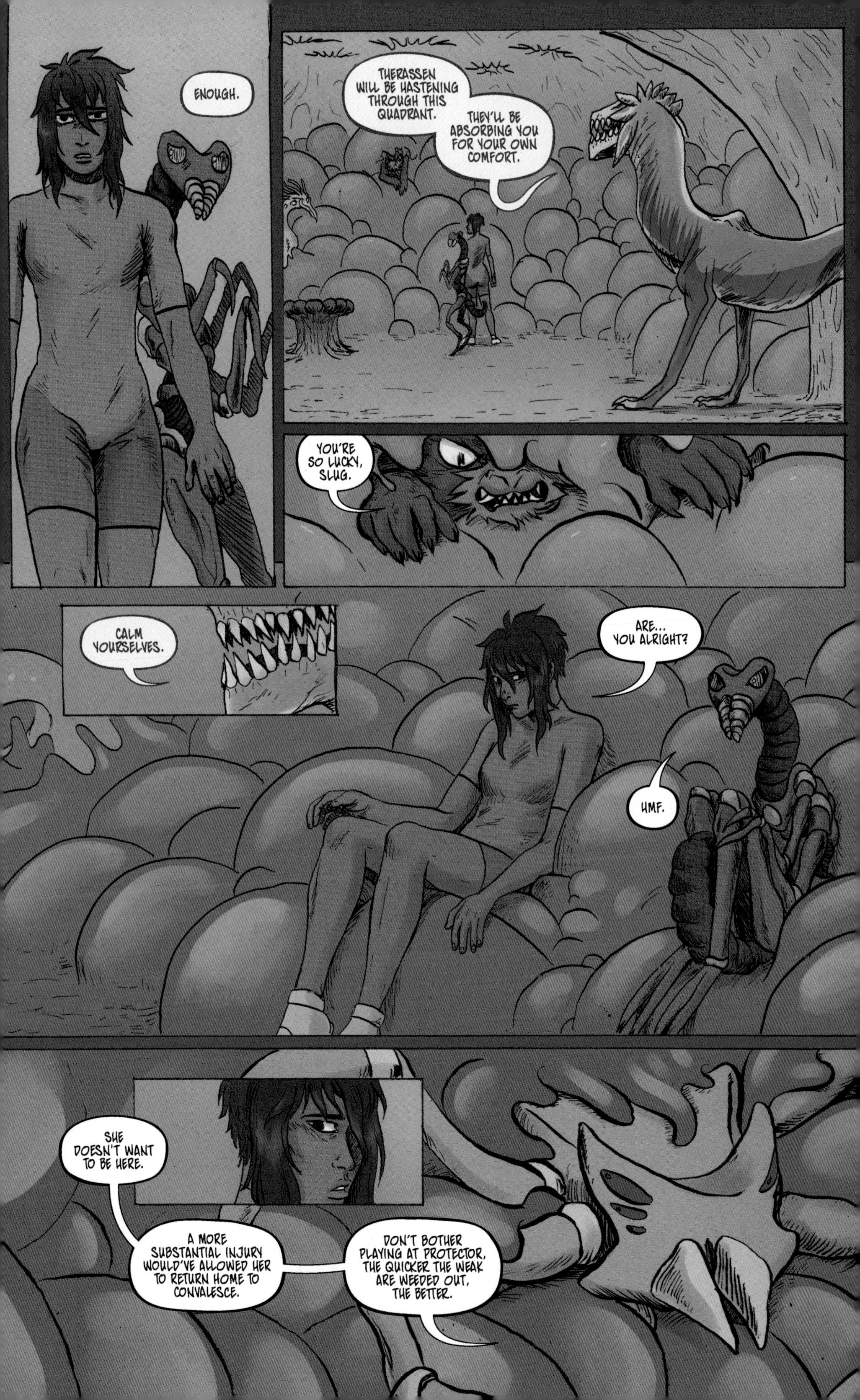
ENOUGH.
THERASSEN WILL BE HASTENING THROUGH THIS QUADRANT.
THEY'LL BE ABSORBING YOU FOR YOUR OWN COMFORT.
YOU'RE SO LUCKY, SLUG.
CALM YOURSELVES.
ARE... YOU ALRIGHT?
HMF.
SHE DOESN'T WANT TO BE HERE.
A MORE SUBSTANTIAL INJURY WOULD'VE ALLOWED HER TO RETURN HOME TO CONVALESCE.
DON'T BOTHER PLAYING AT PROTECTOR, THE QUICKER THE WEAK ARE WEEDED OUT, THE BETTER.

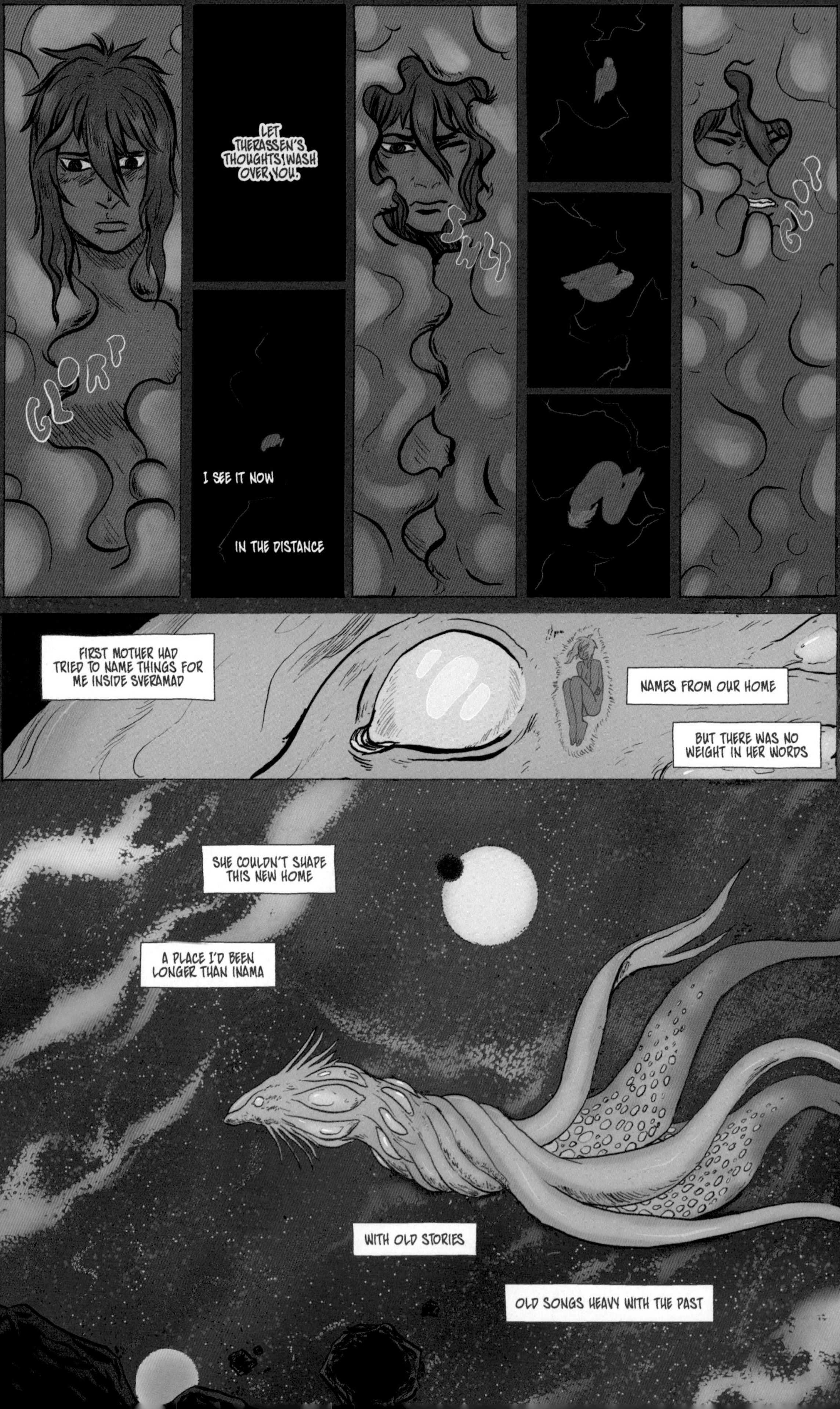

GLORP
LET THERASSEN'S THOUGHTS WASH OVER YOU.
I SEE IT NOW
IN THE DISTANCE
SHLP
GLOP
FIRST MOTHER HAD TRIED TO NAME THINGS FOR ME INSIDE SVERAMAD
NAMES FROM OUR HOME
BUT THERE WAS NO WEIGHT IN HER WORDS
SHE COULDN'T SHAPE THIS NEW HOME
A PLACE I'D BEEN LONGER THAN INAMA
WITH OLD STORIES
OLD SONGS HEAVY WITH THE PAST

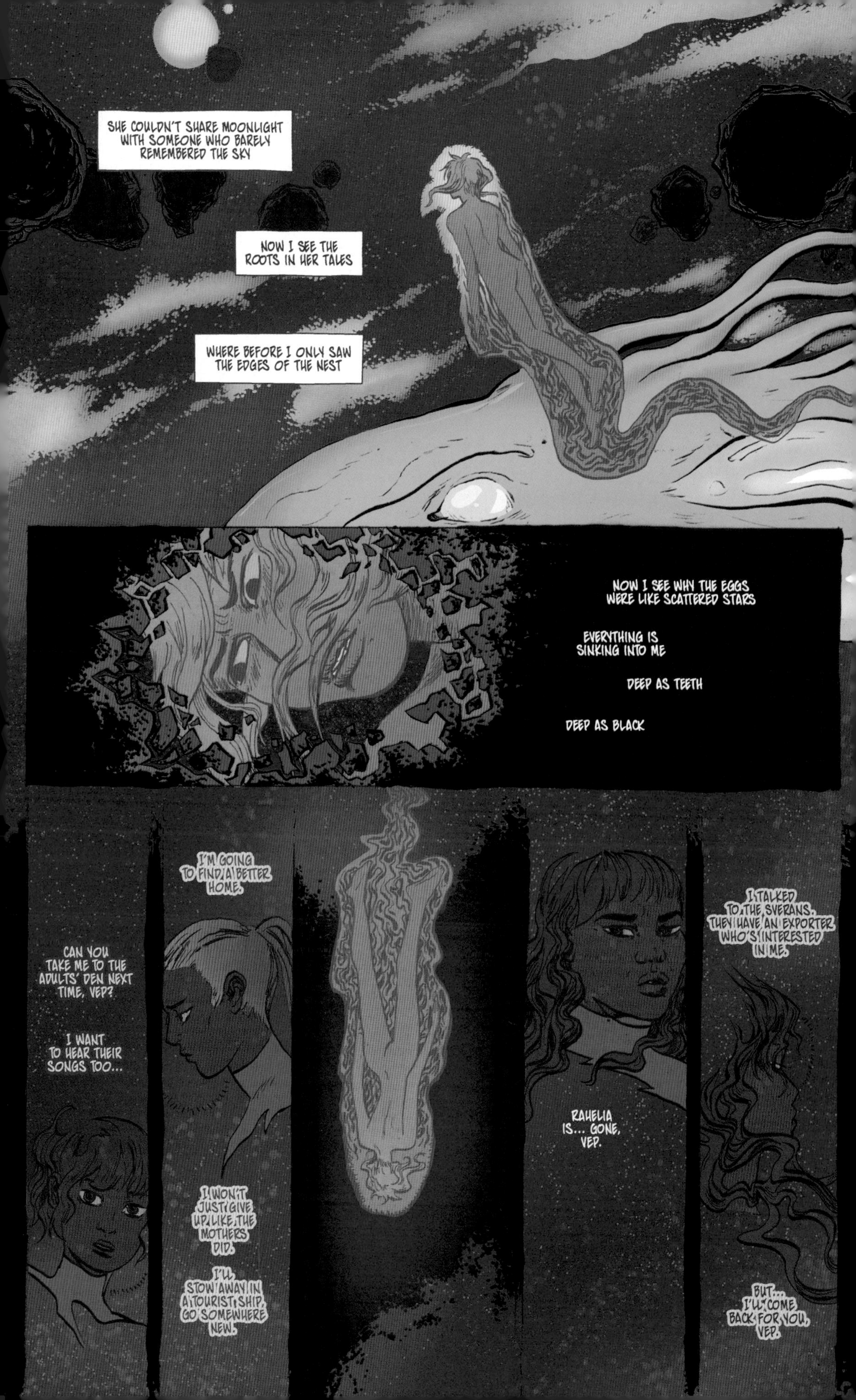
SHE COULDN'T SHARE MOONLIGHT WITH SOMEONE WHO BARELY REMEMBERED THE SKY
NOW I SEE THE ROOTS IN HER TALES
WHERE BEFORE I ONLY SAW THE EDGES OF THE NEST
NOW I SEE WHY THE EGGS WERE LIKE SCATTERED STARS
EVERYTHING IS SINKING INTO ME
DEEP AS TEETH
DEEP AS BLACK
CAN YOU TAKE ME TO THE ADULTS' DEN NEXT TIME, VEP?
I WANT TO HEAR THEIR SONGS TOO...
I'M GOING TO FIND A BETTER HOME.
I WON'T JUST GIVE UP LIKE THE MOTHERS DID.
I'LL STOW AWAY IN A TOURIST SHIP, GO SOMEWHERE NEW.
RAHELIA IS... GONE, VEP.
I TALKED TO THE SVERANS. THEY HAVE AN EXPORTER WHO'S INTERESTED IN ME.
BUT... I'LL COME BACK FOR YOU, VEP.

THERE HAS TO BE
SOMETHING MORE
OUT HERE

I CAN'T GO BACK TO
THEM EMPTY-HANDED

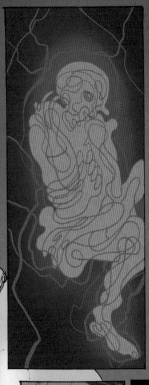

I WON'T

GO BACK

WITH NOTHING

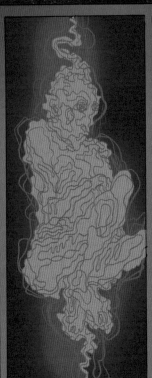

I'LL FIND US A
PLACE TO BE FREE

TO SING SONGS

TO SEE THE SKY

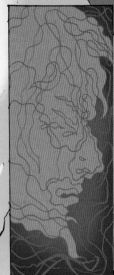

BE
STILL. WE'VE
ARRIVED.

THERASSEN
WILL RELEASE
YOU NOW.

YOU SHOULD
RESOLVE BACK TO
YOUR OWN BODY IN
A MOMENT.

GLUARGH

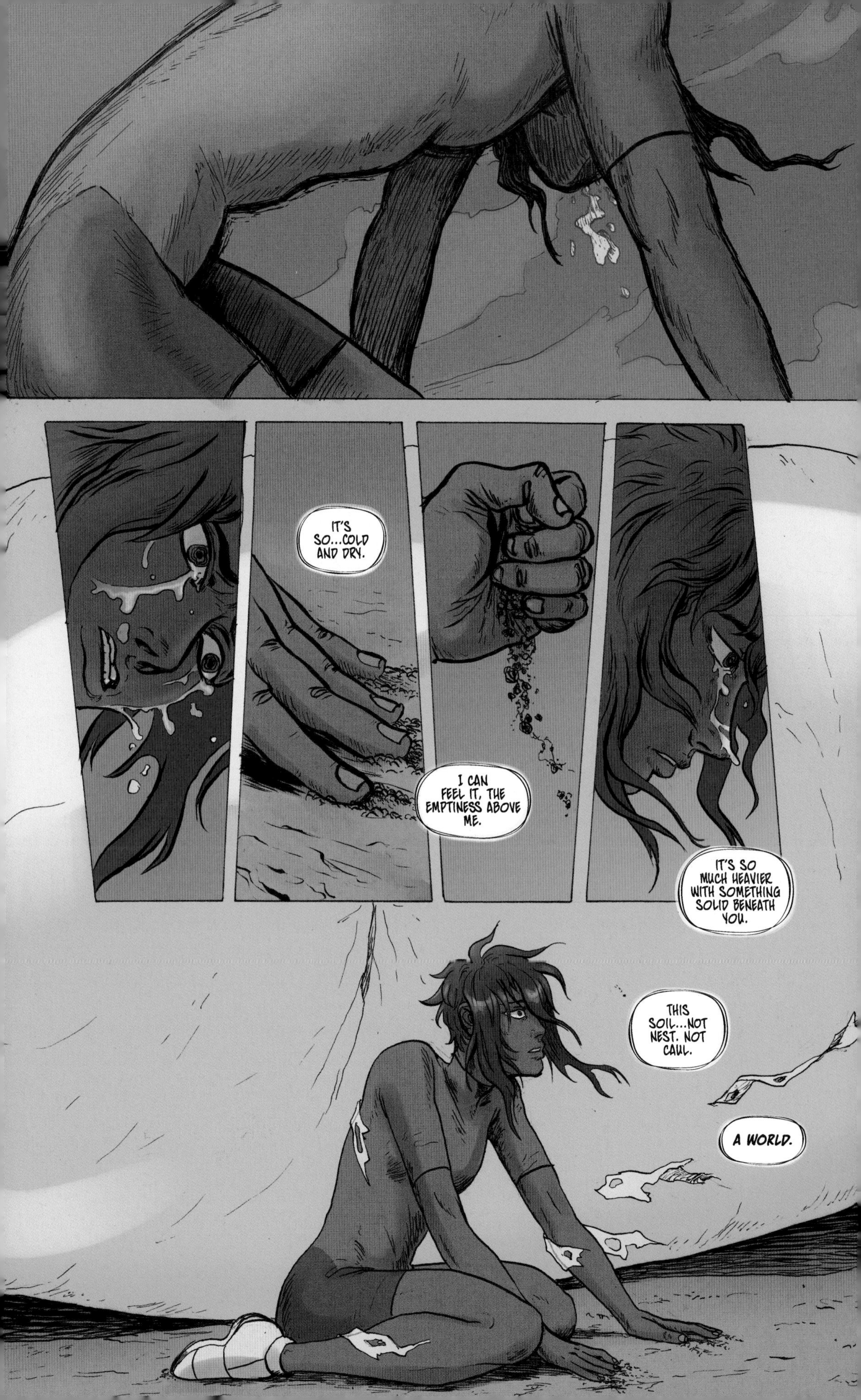
IT'S SO...COLD AND DRY.
I CAN FEEL IT, THE EMPTINESS ABOVE ME.
IT'S SO MUCH HEAVIER WITH SOMETHING SOLID BENEATH YOU.
THIS SOIL...NOT NEST. NOT CAUL.
A WORLD.

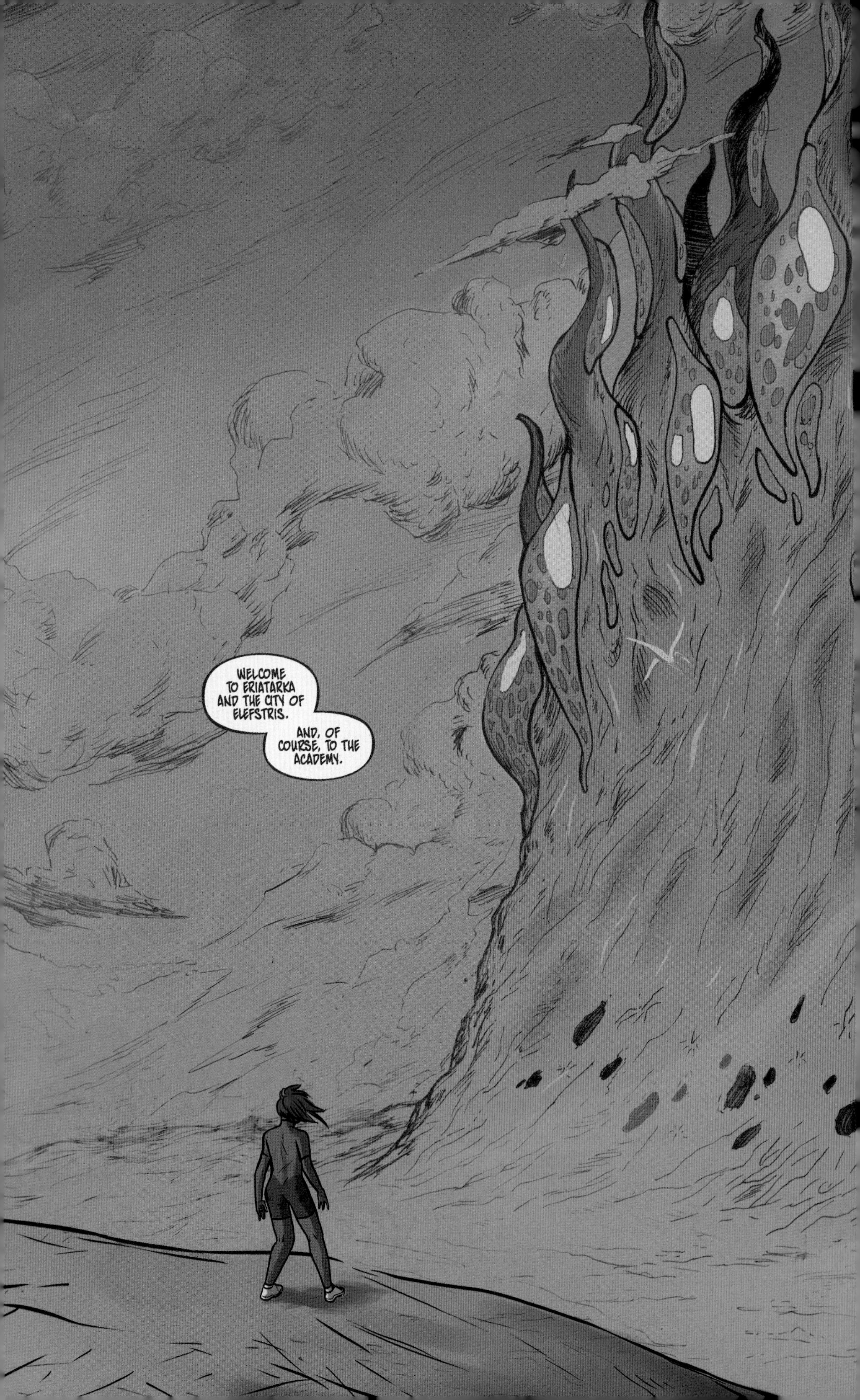
WELCOME TO ERIATARKA AND THE CITY OF ELEFSTRIS.
AND, OF COURSE, TO THE ACADEMY.

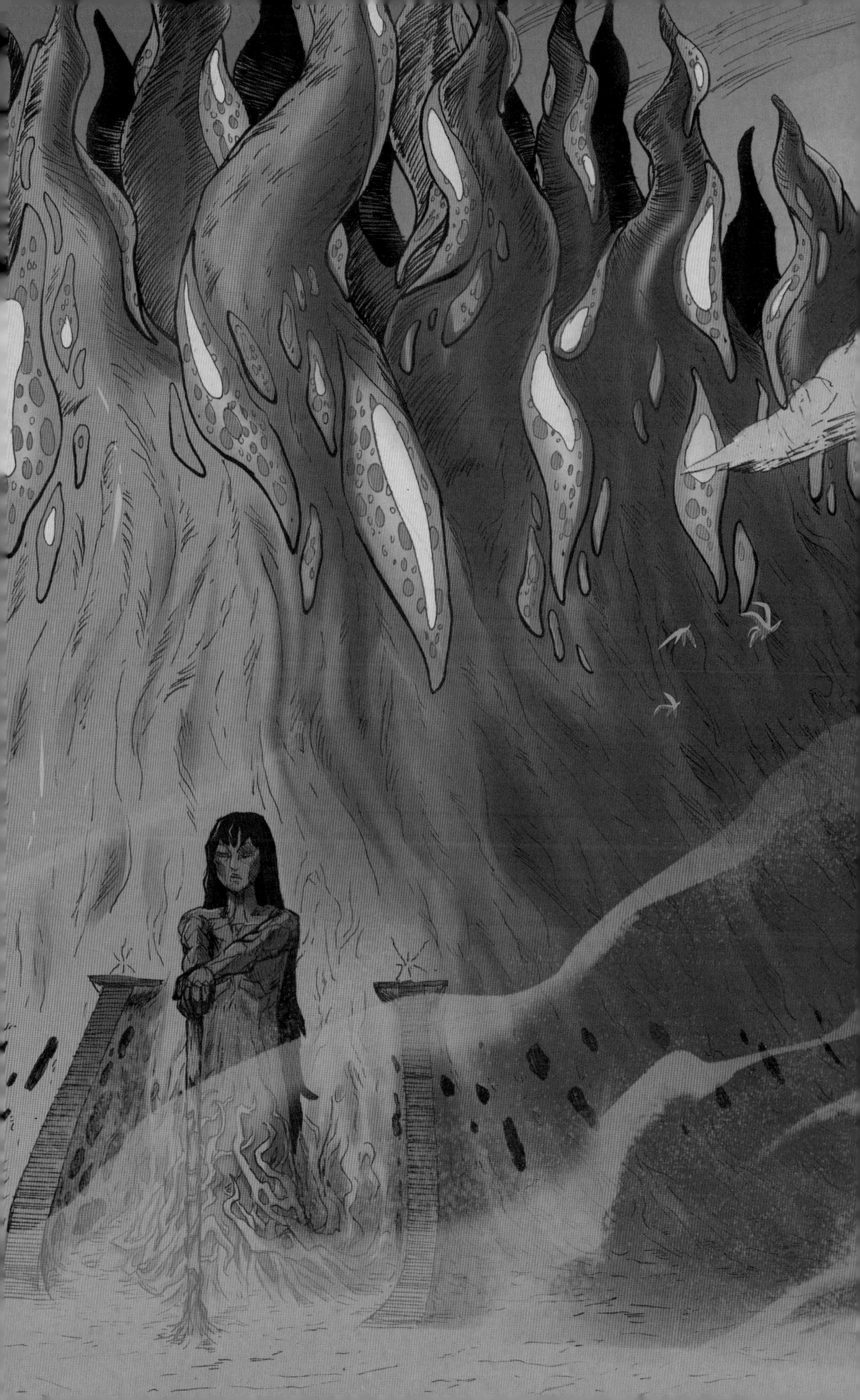

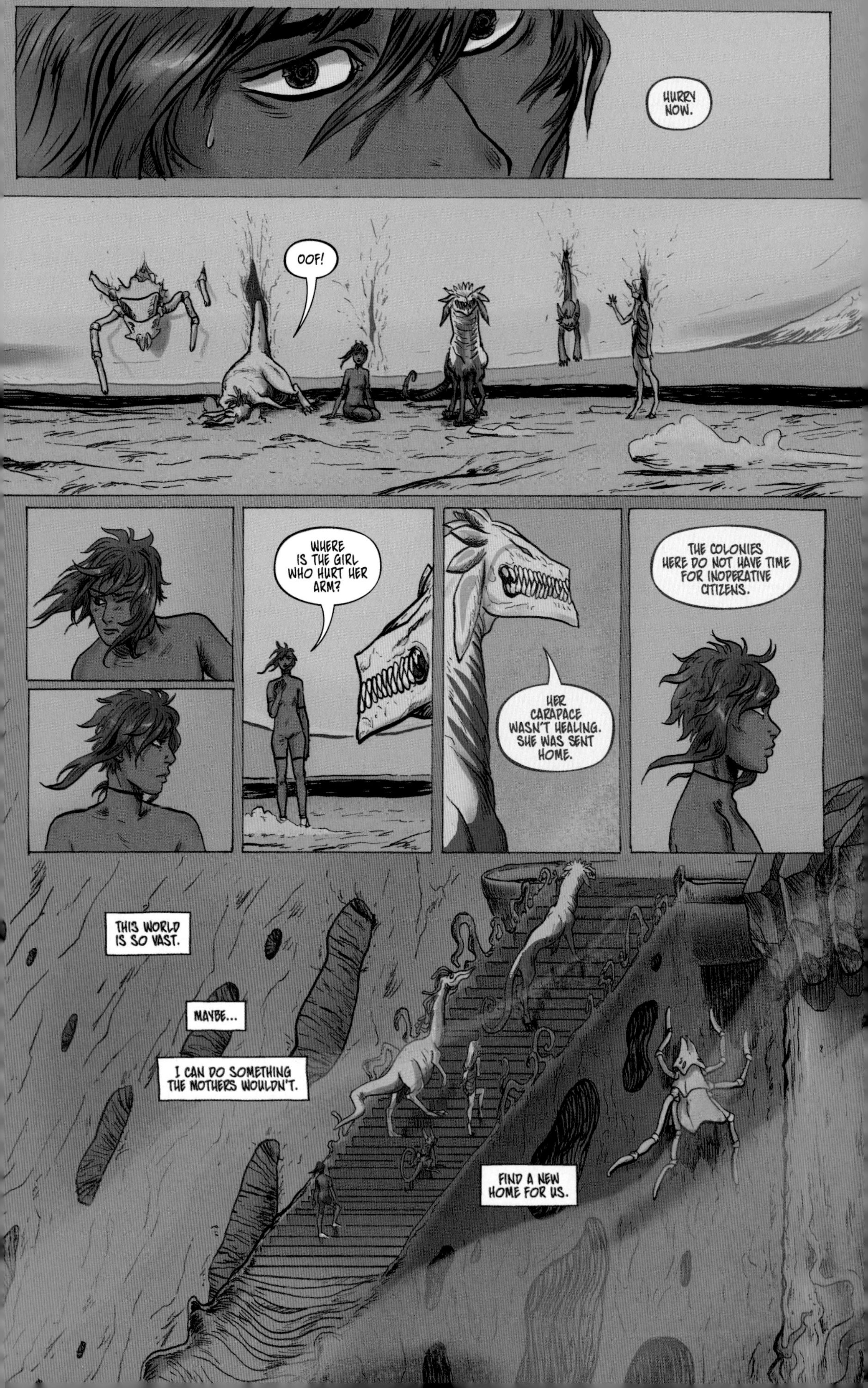
HURRY NOW.
OOF!
WHERE IS THE GIRL WHO HURT HER ARM?
HER CARAPACE WASN'T HEALING. SHE WAS SENT HOME.
THE COLONIES HERE DO NOT HAVE TIME FOR INOPERATIVE CITIZENS.
THIS WORLD IS SO VAST.
MAYBE...
I CAN DO SOMETHING THE MOTHERS WOULDN'T.
FIND A NEW HOME FOR US.

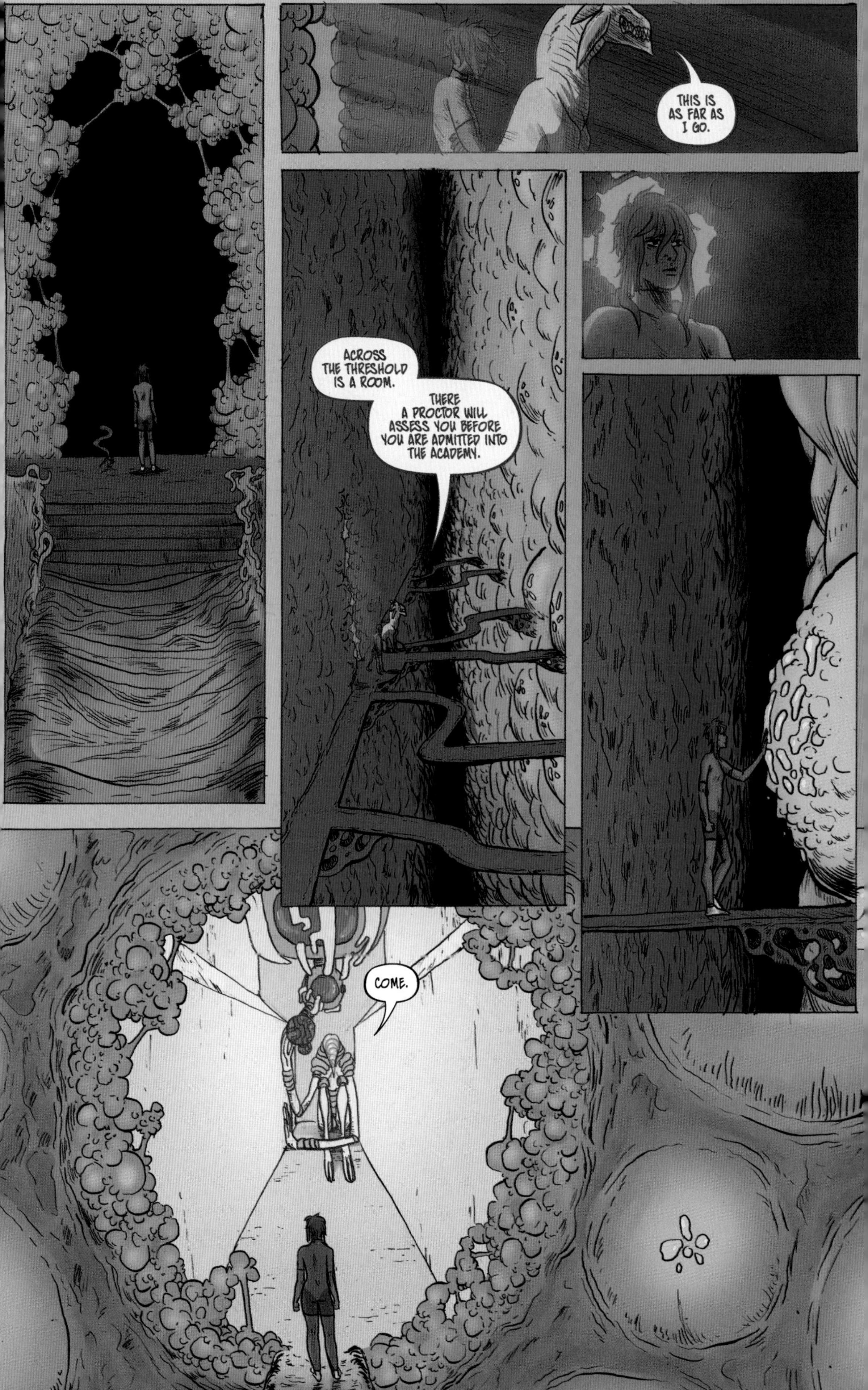
THIS IS AS FAR AS I GO.
ACROSS THE THRESHOLD IS A ROOM.
THERE A PROCTOR WILL ASSESS YOU BEFORE YOU ARE ADMITTED INTO THE ACADEMY.
COME.

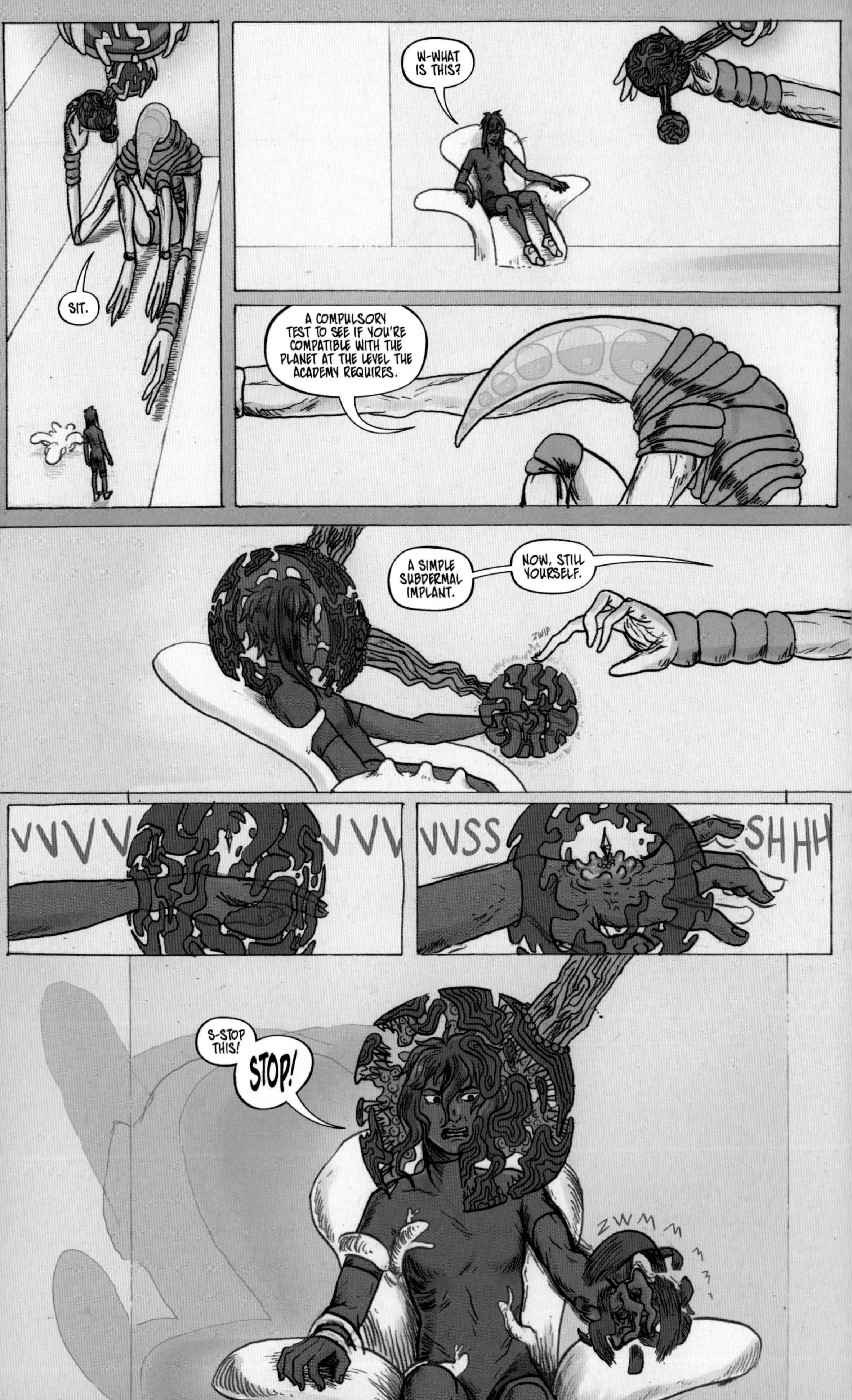
SIT.
W-WHAT IS THIS?
A COMPULSORY TEST TO SEE IF YOU'RE COMPATIBLE WITH THE PLANET AT THE LEVEL THE ACADEMY REQUIRES.
A SIMPLE SUBDERMAL IMPLANT.
NOW, STILL YOURSELF.
ZWIP
VVVV VVV
VVSS SHHH
S-STOP THIS!
STOP!
ZWMMM

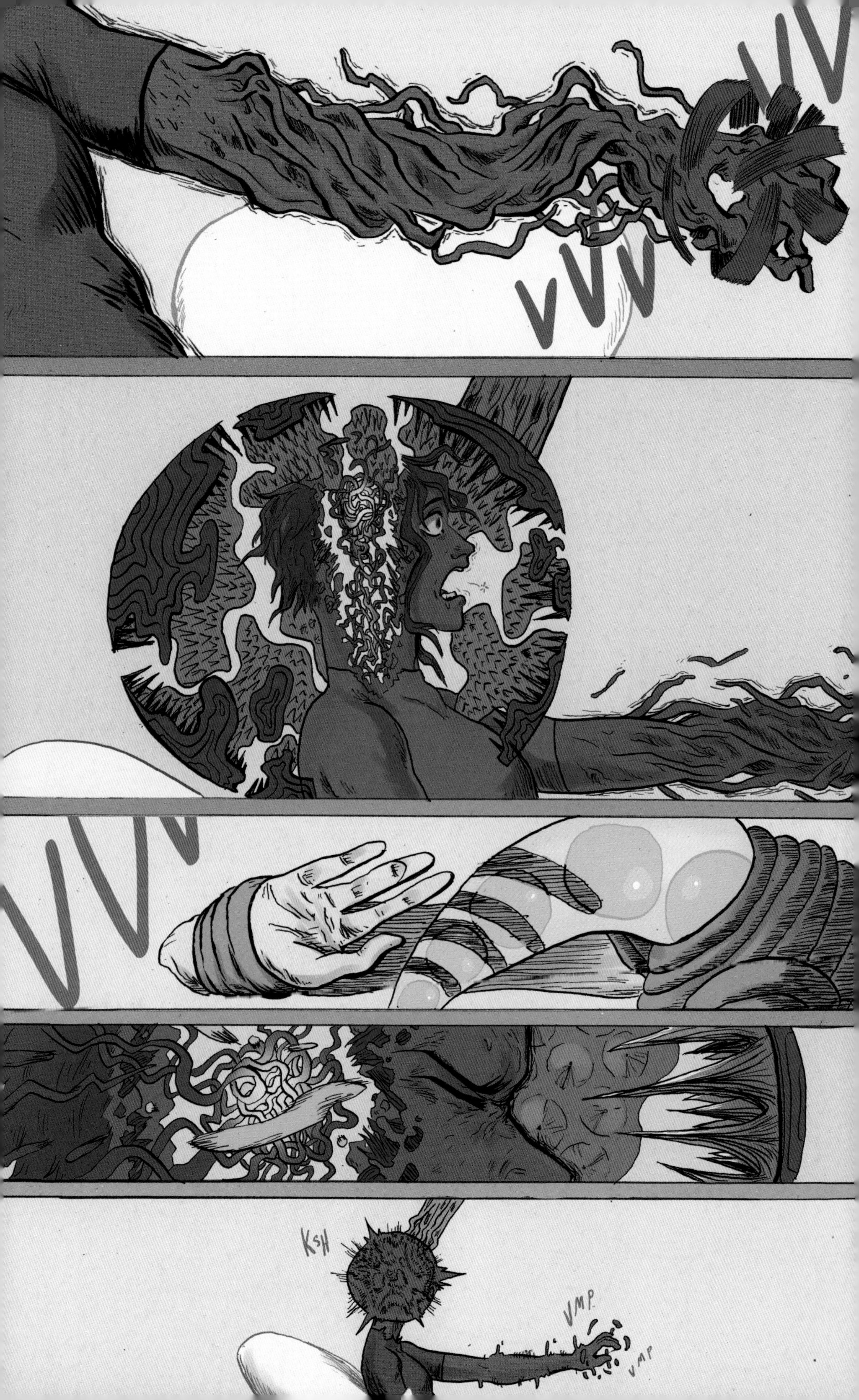
VVV
KSH
VMP.
VMP

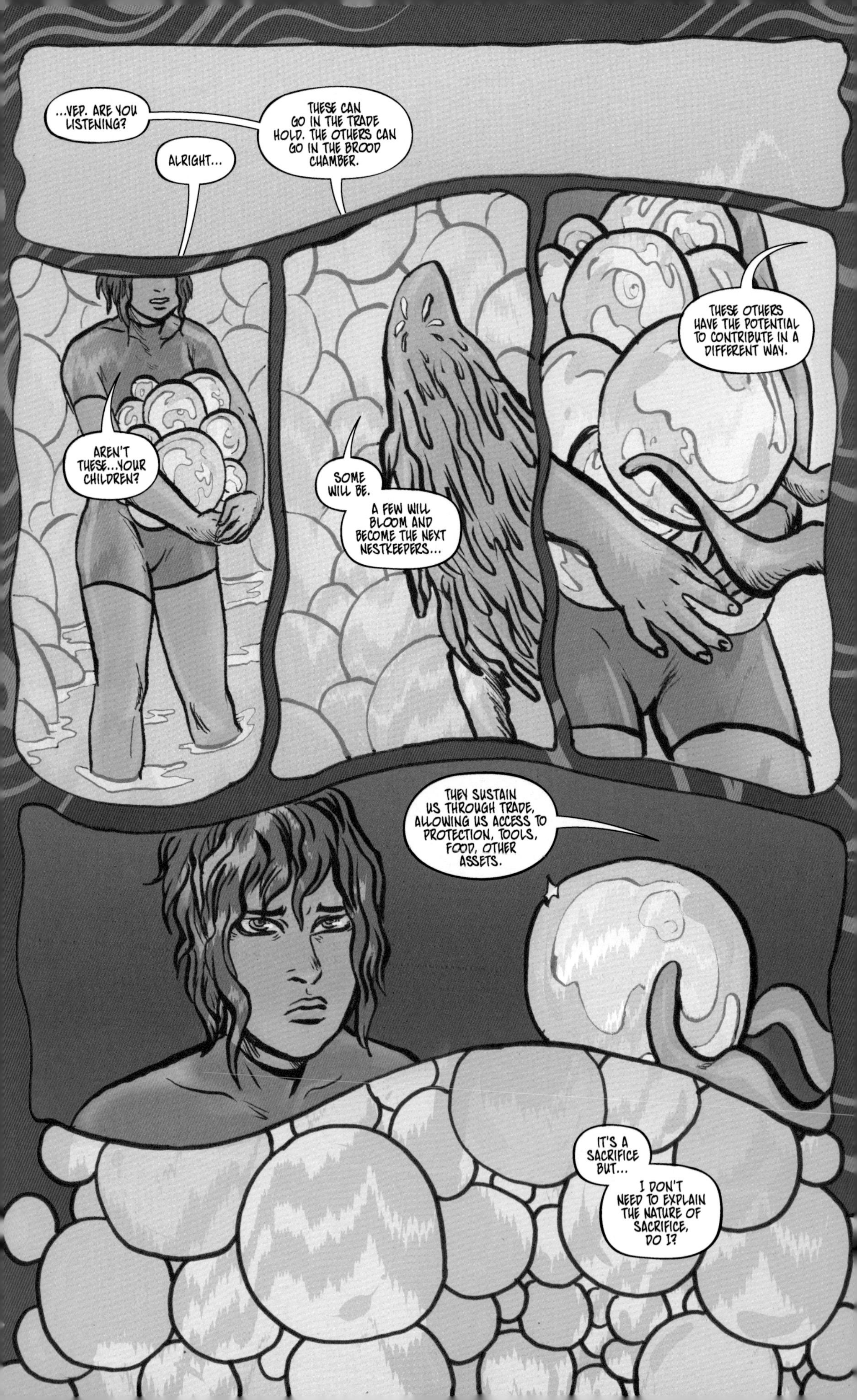
...YEP. ARE YOU LISTENING?
THESE CAN GO IN THE TRADE HOLD. THE OTHERS CAN GO IN THE BROOD CHAMBER.
ALRIGHT...
AREN'T THESE...YOUR CHILDREN?
SOME WILL BE.
A FEW WILL BLOOM AND BECOME THE NEXT NESTKEEPERS...
THESE OTHERS HAVE THE POTENTIAL TO CONTRIBUTE IN A DIFFERENT WAY.
THEY SUSTAIN US THROUGH TRADE, ALLOWING US ACCESS TO PROTECTION, TOOLS, FOOD, OTHER ASSETS.
IT'S A SACRIFICE BUT...
I DON'T NEED TO EXPLAIN THE NATURE OF SACRIFICE, DO I?

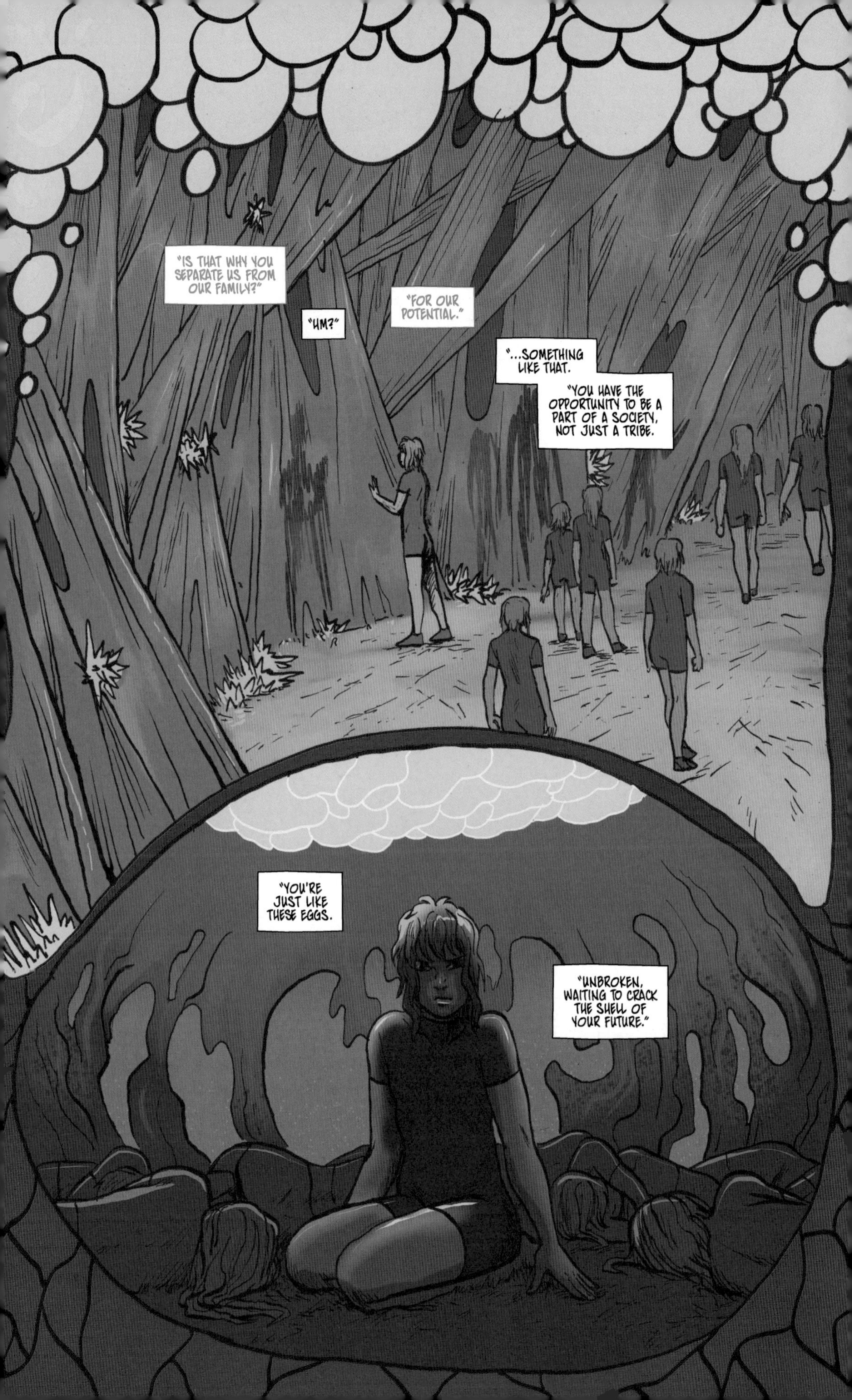
"IS THAT WHY YOU SEPARATE US FROM OUR FAMILY?"
"HM?"
"FOR OUR POTENTIAL."
"...SOMETHING LIKE THAT.
"YOU HAVE THE OPPORTUNITY TO BE A PART OF A SOCIETY, NOT JUST A TRIBE.
"YOU'RE JUST LIKE THESE EGGS.
"UNBROKEN, WAITING TO CRACK THE SHELL OF YOUR FUTURE."

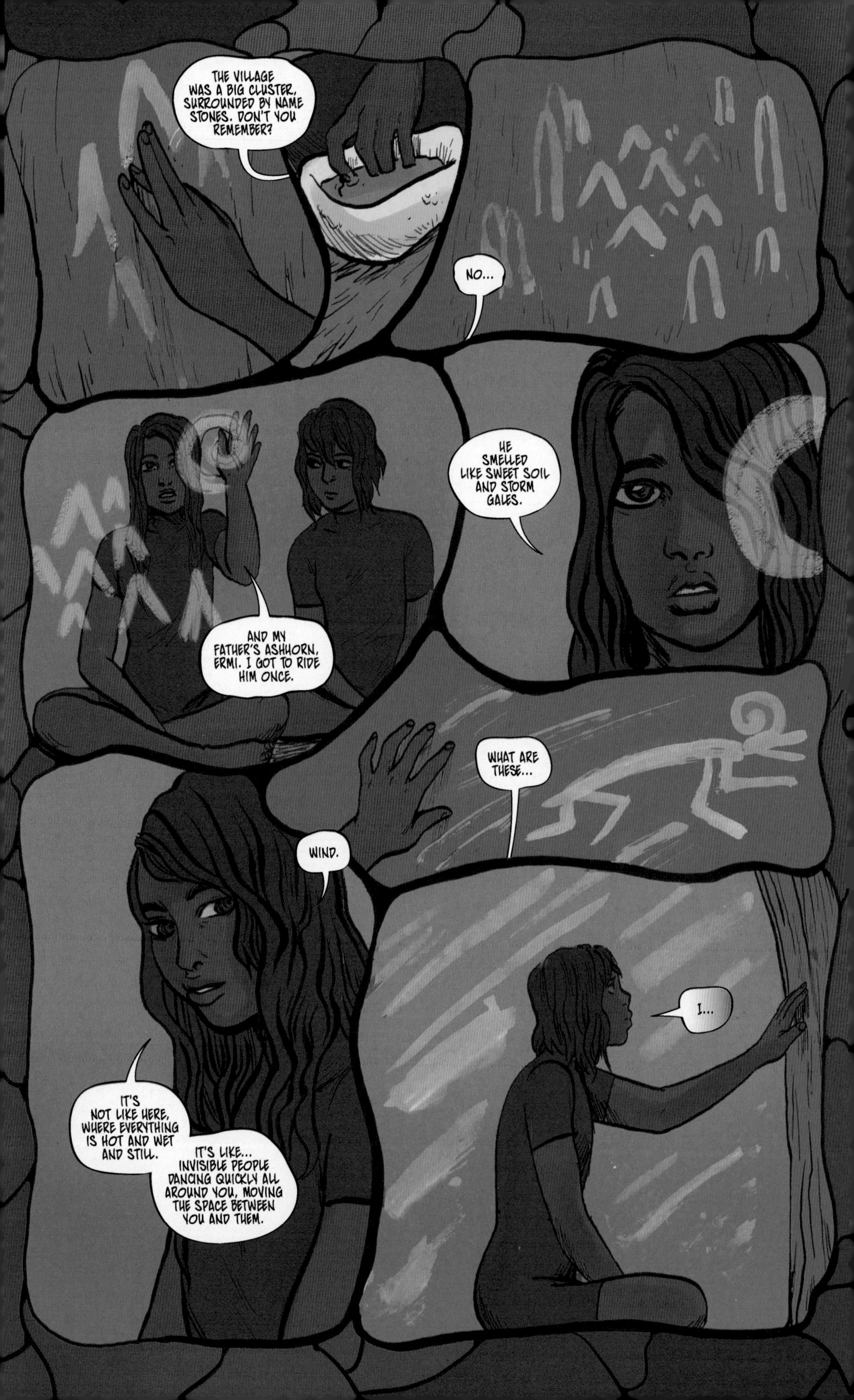
THE VILLAGE WAS A BIG CLUSTER, SURROUNDED BY NAME STONES. DON'T YOU REMEMBER?
NO...
HE SMELLED LIKE SWEET SOIL AND STORM GALES.
AND MY FATHER'S ASHHORN, ERMI. I GOT TO RIDE HIM ONCE.
WHAT ARE THESE...
WIND.
IT'S NOT LIKE HERE, WHERE EVERYTHING IS HOT AND WET AND STILL.
IT'S LIKE... INVISIBLE PEOPLE DANCING QUICKLY ALL AROUND YOU, MOVING THE SPACE BETWEEN YOU AND THEM.
I...

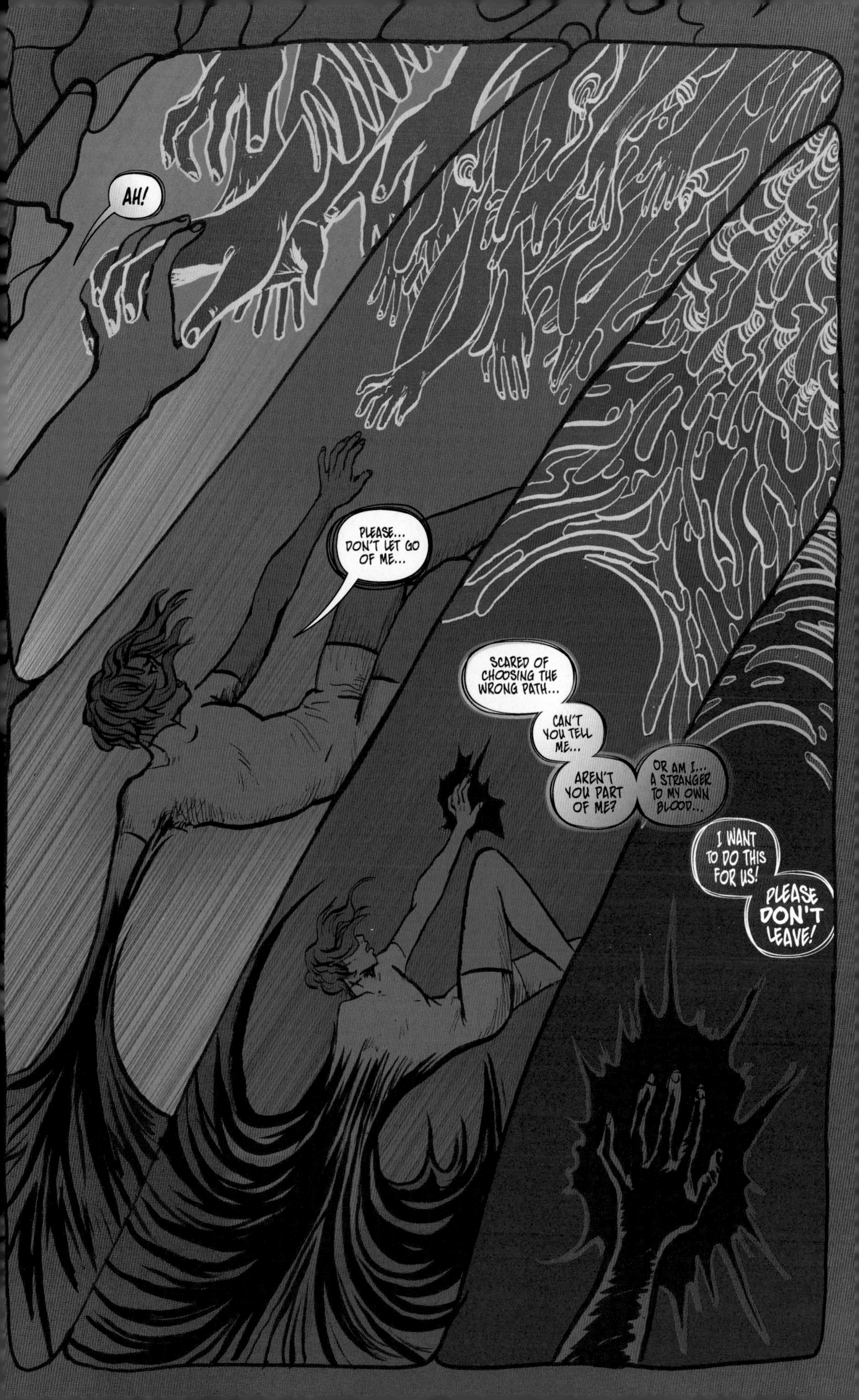
AH!
PLEASE... DON'T LET GO OF ME...
SCARED OF CHOOSING THE WRONG PATH...
CAN'T YOU TELL ME...
AREN'T YOU PART OF ME?
OR AM I... A STRANGER TO MY OWN BLOOD...
I WANT TO DO THIS FOR US!
PLEASE DON'T LEAVE!

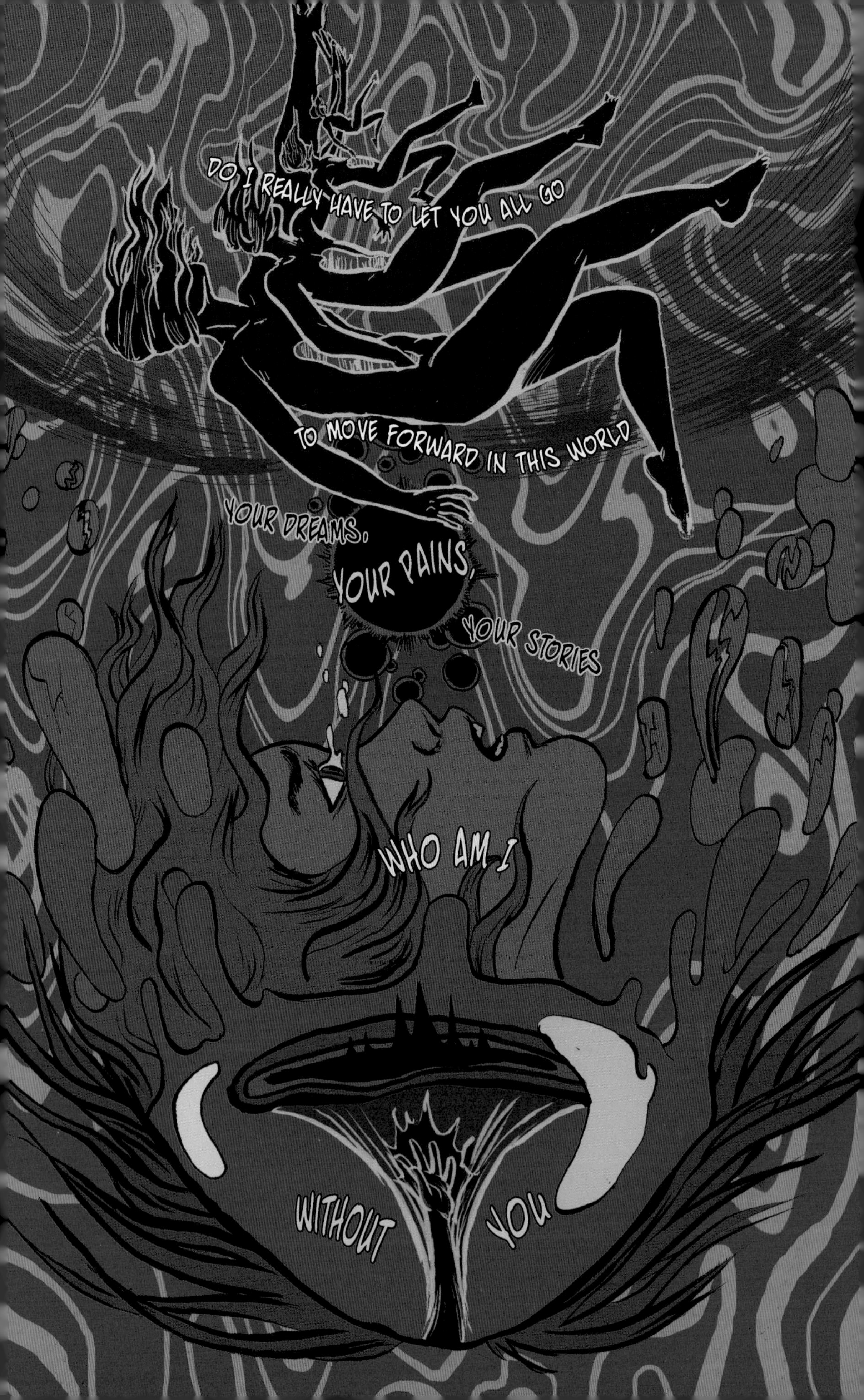
DO I REALLY HAVE TO LET YOU ALL GO
TO MOVE FORWARD IN THIS WORLD
YOUR DREAMS,
YOUR PAINS,
YOUR STORIES
WHO AM I
WITHOUT
YOU

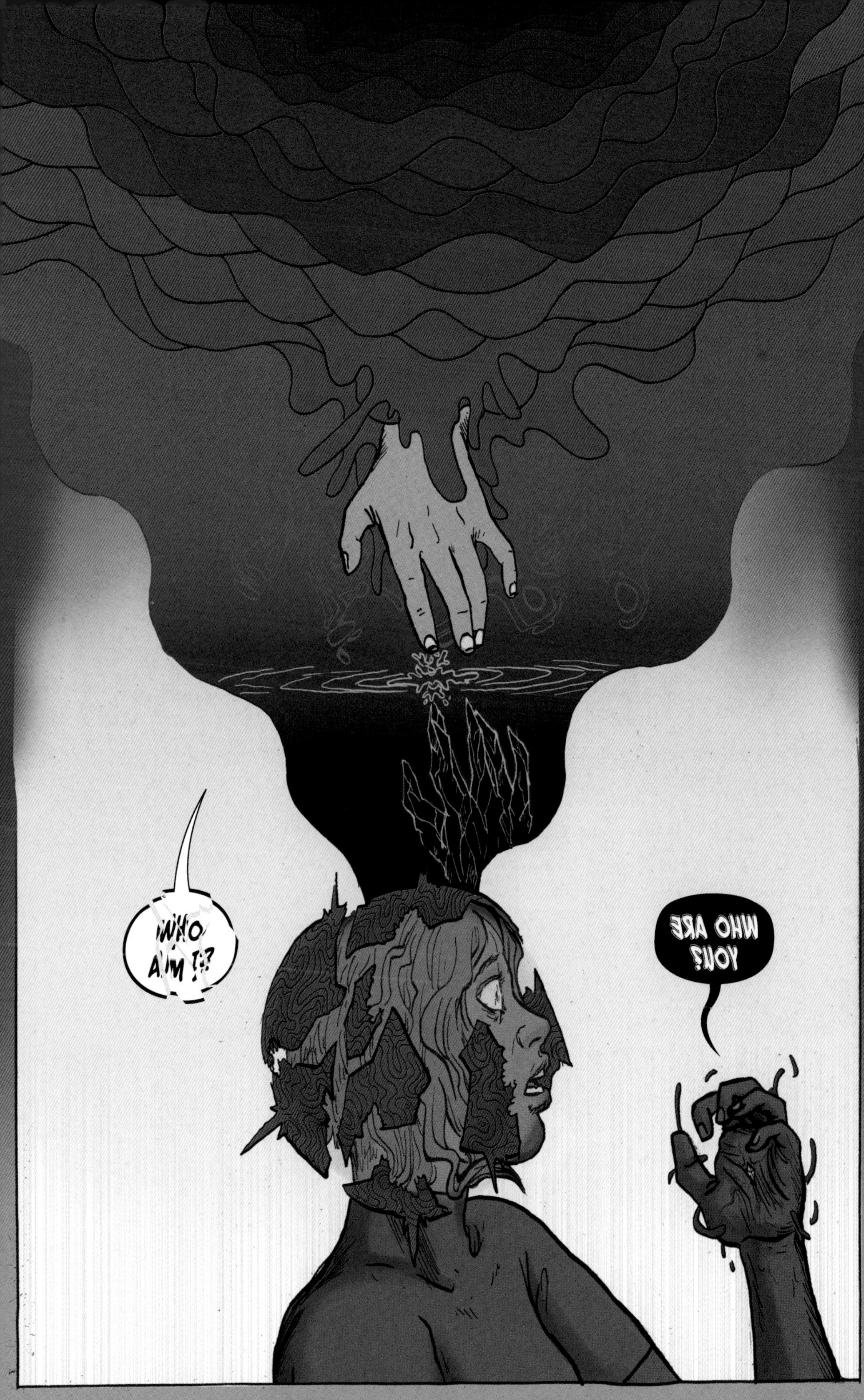
WHO AM I?
WHO ARE YOU?

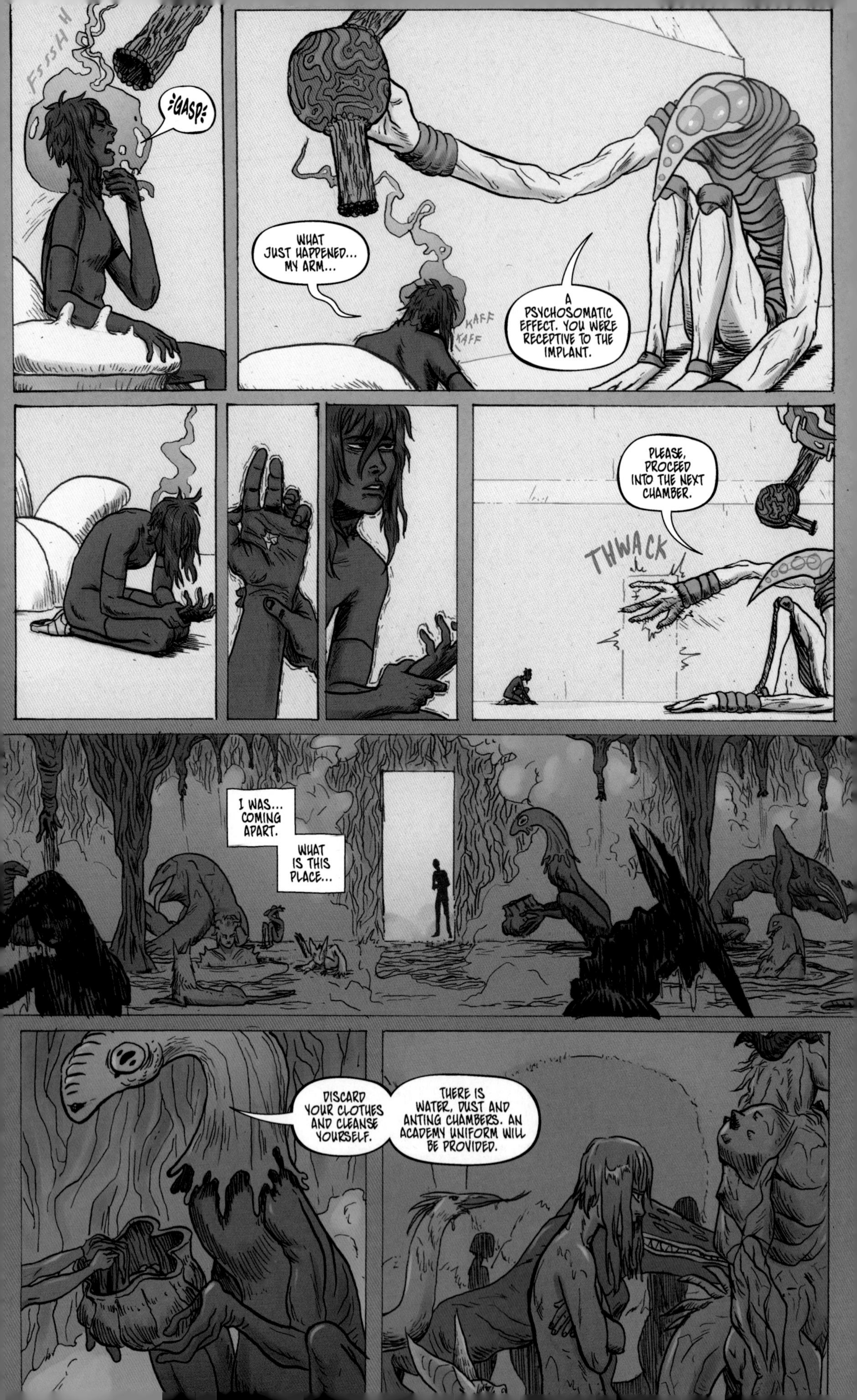
FSSSHH
GASP!
WHAT JUST HAPPENED... MY ARM...
KAFF KAFF
A PSYCHOSOMATIC EFFECT. YOU WERE RECEPTIVE TO THE IMPLANT.
PLEASE, PROCEED INTO THE NEXT CHAMBER.
THWACK
I WAS... COMING APART.
WHAT IS THIS PLACE...
DISCARD YOUR CLOTHES AND CLEANSE YOURSELF.
THERE IS WATER, DUST AND ANTING CHAMBERS. AN ACADEMY UNIFORM WILL BE PROVIDED.

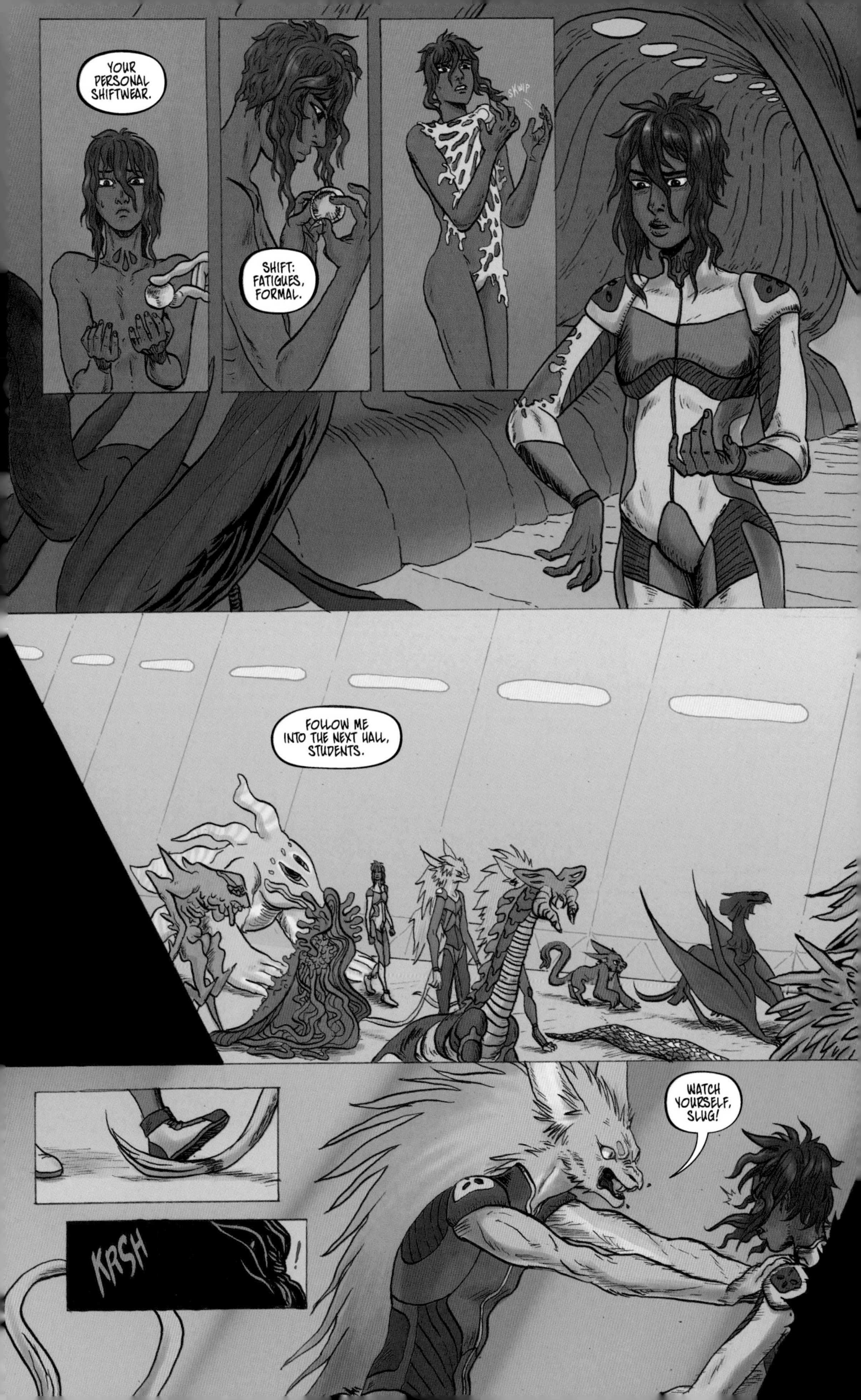
YOUR PERSONAL SHIFTWEAR.
SHIFT: FATIGUES, FORMAL.
SKWIP
FOLLOW ME INTO THE NEXT HALL, STUDENTS.
KRSH
!
WATCH YOURSELF, SLUG!

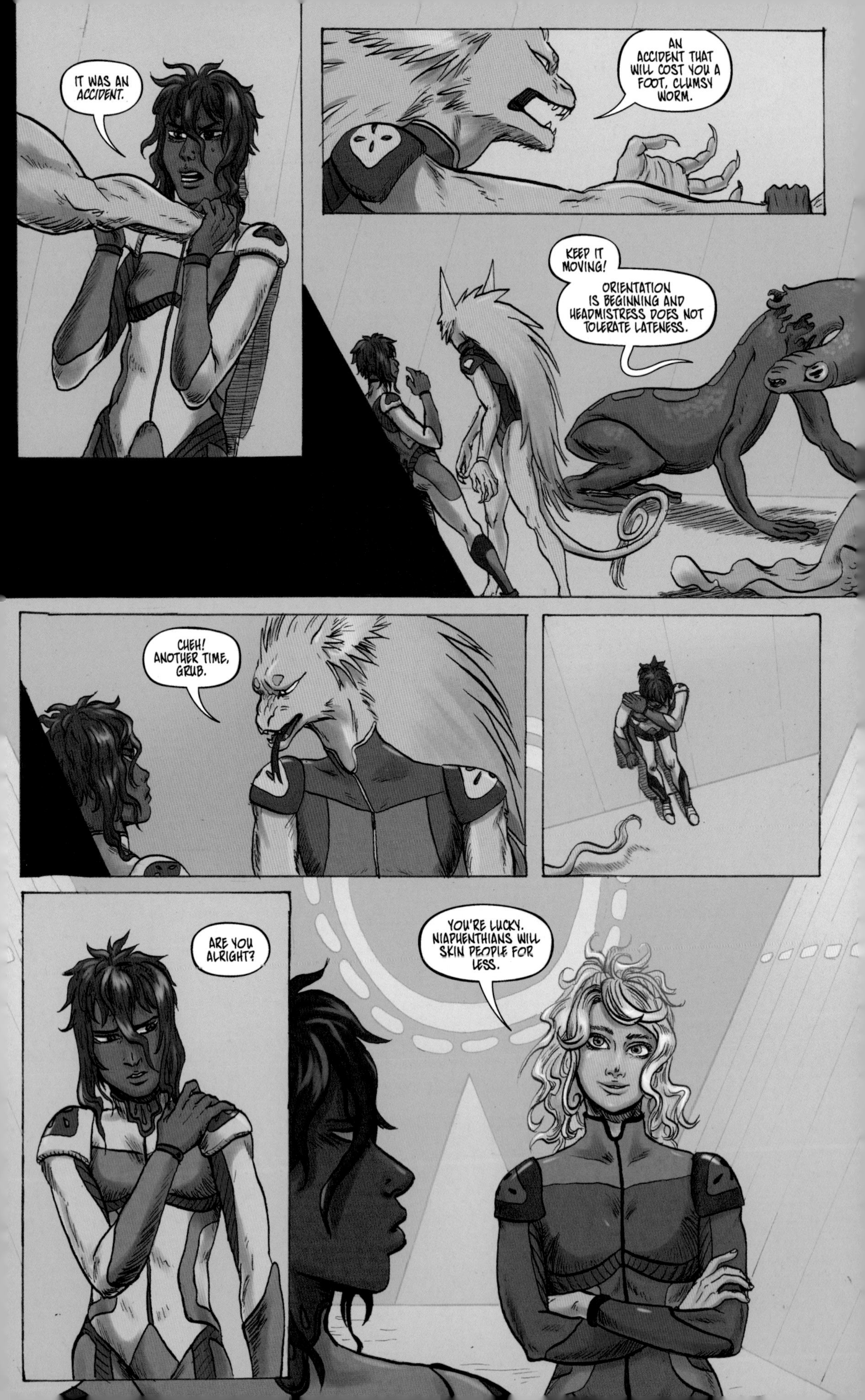
IT WAS AN ACCIDENT.
AN ACCIDENT THAT WILL COST YOU A FOOT, CLUMSY WORM.
KEEP IT MOVING!
ORIENTATION IS BEGINNING AND HEADMISTRESS DOES NOT TOLERATE LATENESS.
CHEH! ANOTHER TIME, GRUB.
ARE YOU ALRIGHT?
YOU'RE LUCKY. NIAPHENTHIANS WILL SKIN PEOPLE FOR LESS.

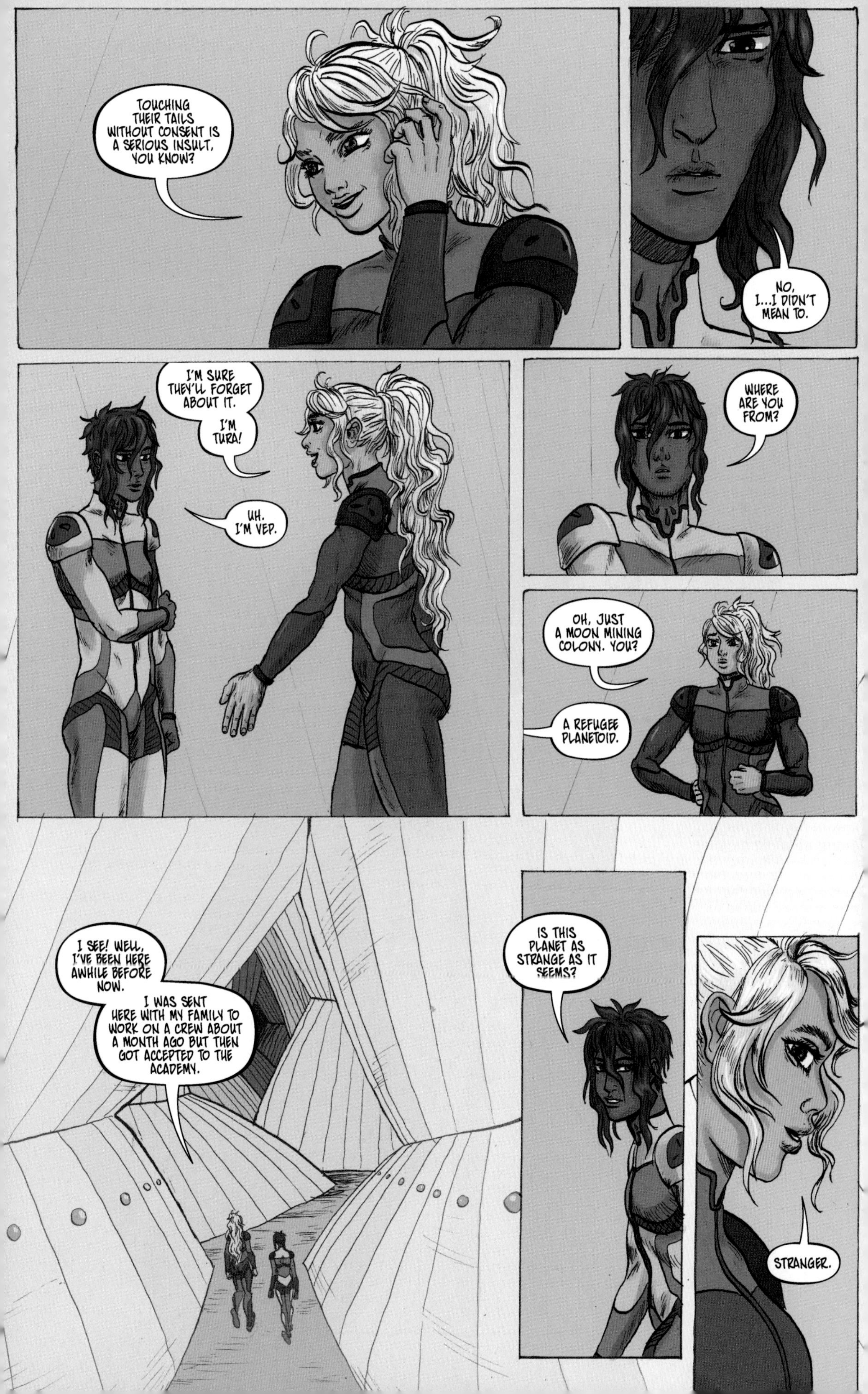
TOUCHING THEIR TAILS WITHOUT CONSENT IS A SERIOUS INSULT, YOU KNOW?
NO, I...I DIDN'T MEAN TO.
I'M SURE THEY'LL FORGET ABOUT IT.
I'M TURA!
UH. I'M VEP.
WHERE ARE YOU FROM?
OH, JUST A MOON MINING COLONY. YOU?
A REFUGEE PLANETOID.
I SEE! WELL, I'VE BEEN HERE AWHILE BEFORE NOW.
I WAS SENT HERE WITH MY FAMILY TO WORK ON A CREW ABOUT A MONTH AGO BUT THEN GOT ACCEPTED TO THE ACADEMY.
IS THIS PLANET AS STRANGE AS IT SEEMS?
STRANGER.

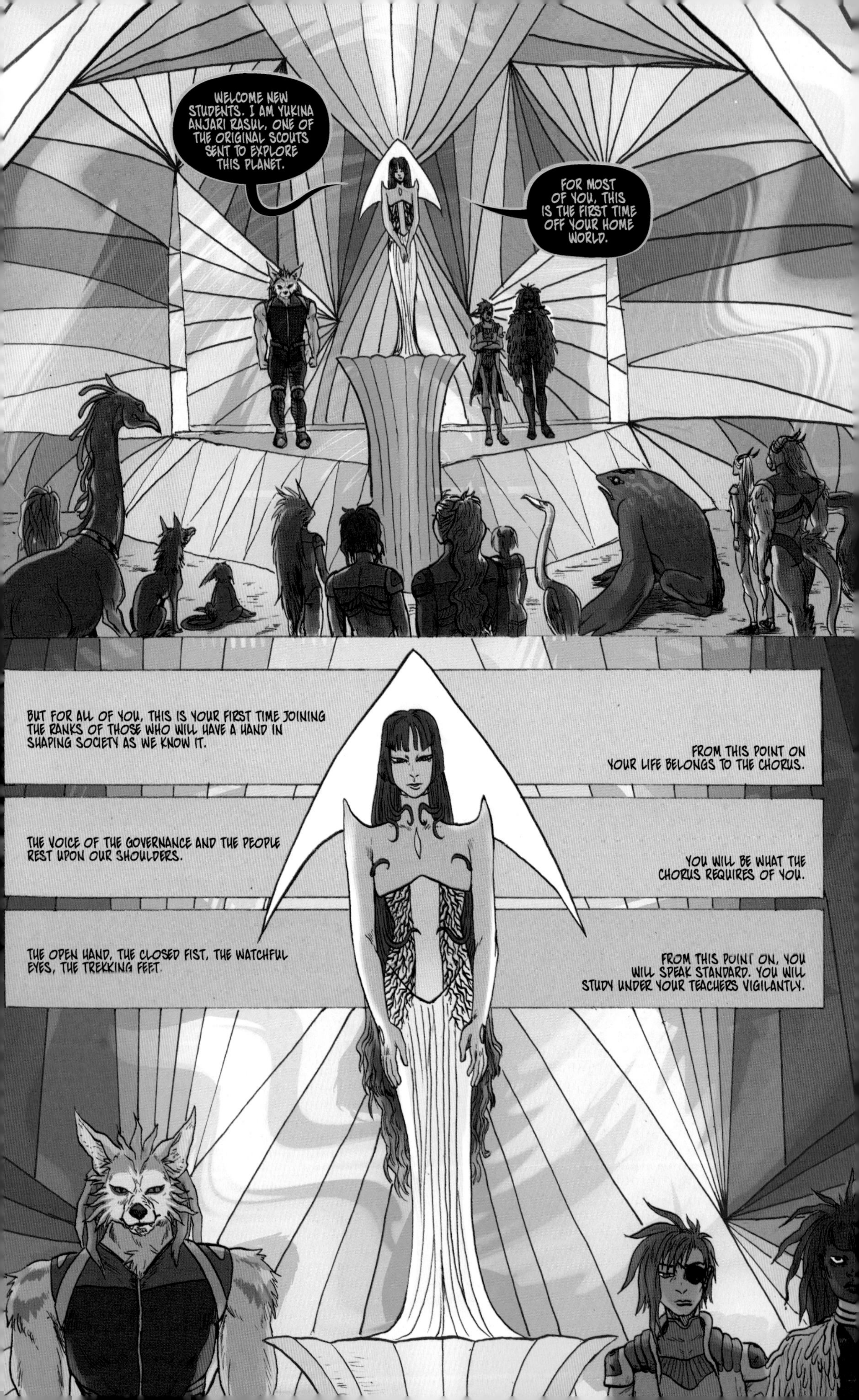
WELCOME NEW STUDENTS. I AM YUKINA ANJARI RASUL, ONE OF THE ORIGINAL SCOUTS SENT TO EXPLORE THIS PLANET.
FOR MOST OF YOU, THIS IS THE FIRST TIME OFF YOUR HOME WORLD.
BUT FOR ALL OF YOU, THIS IS YOUR FIRST TIME JOINING THE RANKS OF THOSE WHO WILL HAVE A HAND IN SHAPING SOCIETY AS WE KNOW IT.
FROM THIS POINT ON YOUR LIFE BELONGS TO THE CHORUS.
THE VOICE OF THE GOVERNANCE AND THE PEOPLE REST UPON OUR SHOULDERS.
YOU WILL BE WHAT THE CHORUS REQUIRES OF YOU.
THE OPEN HAND, THE CLOSED FIST, THE WATCHFUL EYES, THE TREKKING FEET.
FROM THIS POINT ON, YOU WILL SPEAK STANDARD. YOU WILL STUDY UNDER YOUR TEACHERS VIGILANTLY.

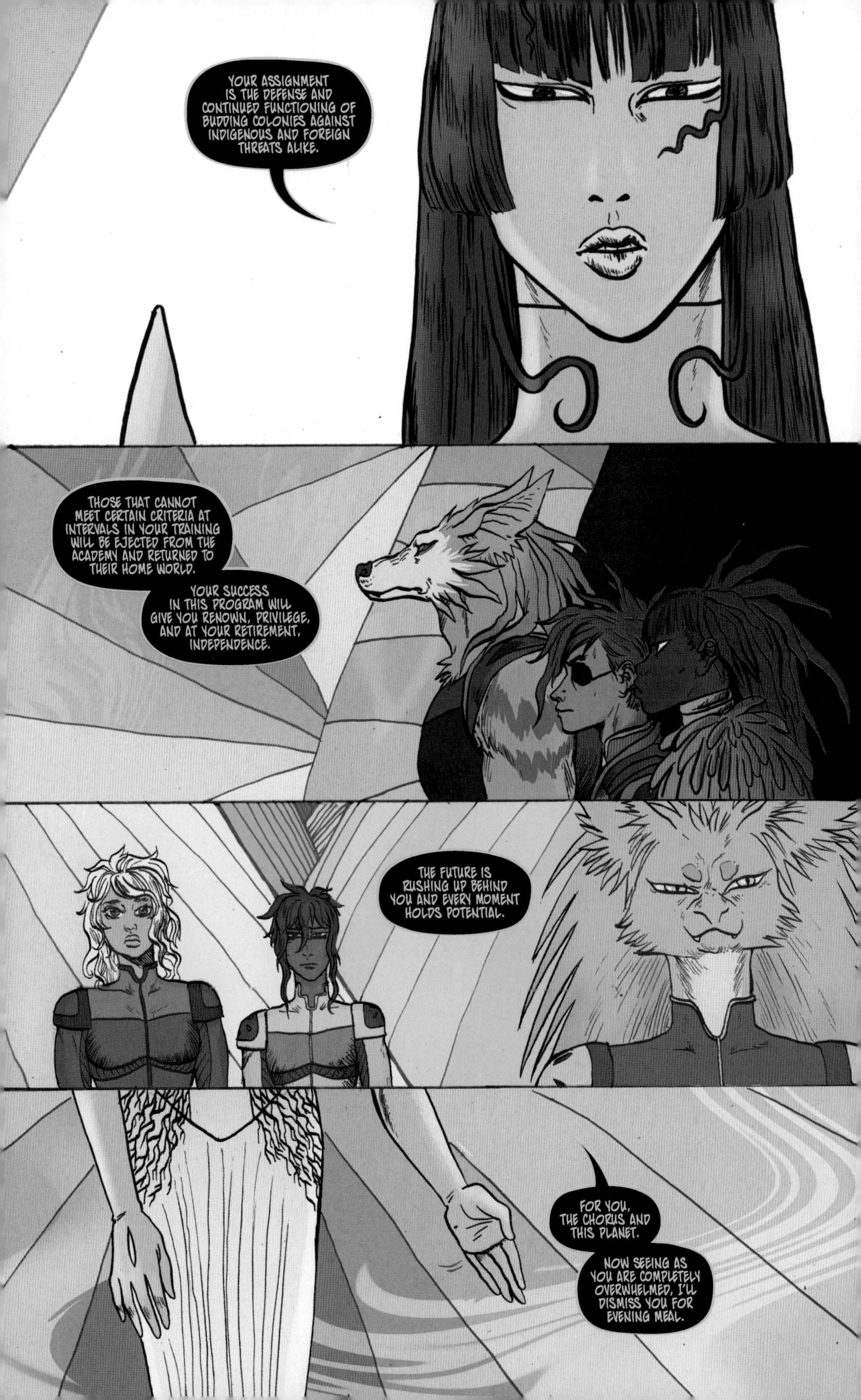
YOUR ASSIGNMENT IS THE DEFENSE AND CONTINUED FUNCTIONING OF BUDDING COLONIES AGAINST INDIGENOUS AND FOREIGN THREATS ALIKE.
THOSE THAT CANNOT MEET CERTAIN CRITERIA AT INTERVALS IN YOUR TRAINING WILL BE EJECTED FROM THE ACADEMY AND RETURNED TO THEIR HOME WORLD.
YOUR SUCCESS IN THIS PROGRAM WILL GIVE YOU RENOWN, PRIVILEGE, AND AT YOUR RETIREMENT, INDEPENDENCE.
THE FUTURE IS RUSHING UP BEHIND YOU AND EVERY MOMENT HOLDS POTENTIAL.
FOR YOU, THE CHORUS AND THIS PLANET.
NOW SEEING AS YOU ARE COMPLETELY OVERWHELMED, I'LL DISMISS YOU FOR EVENING MEAL.

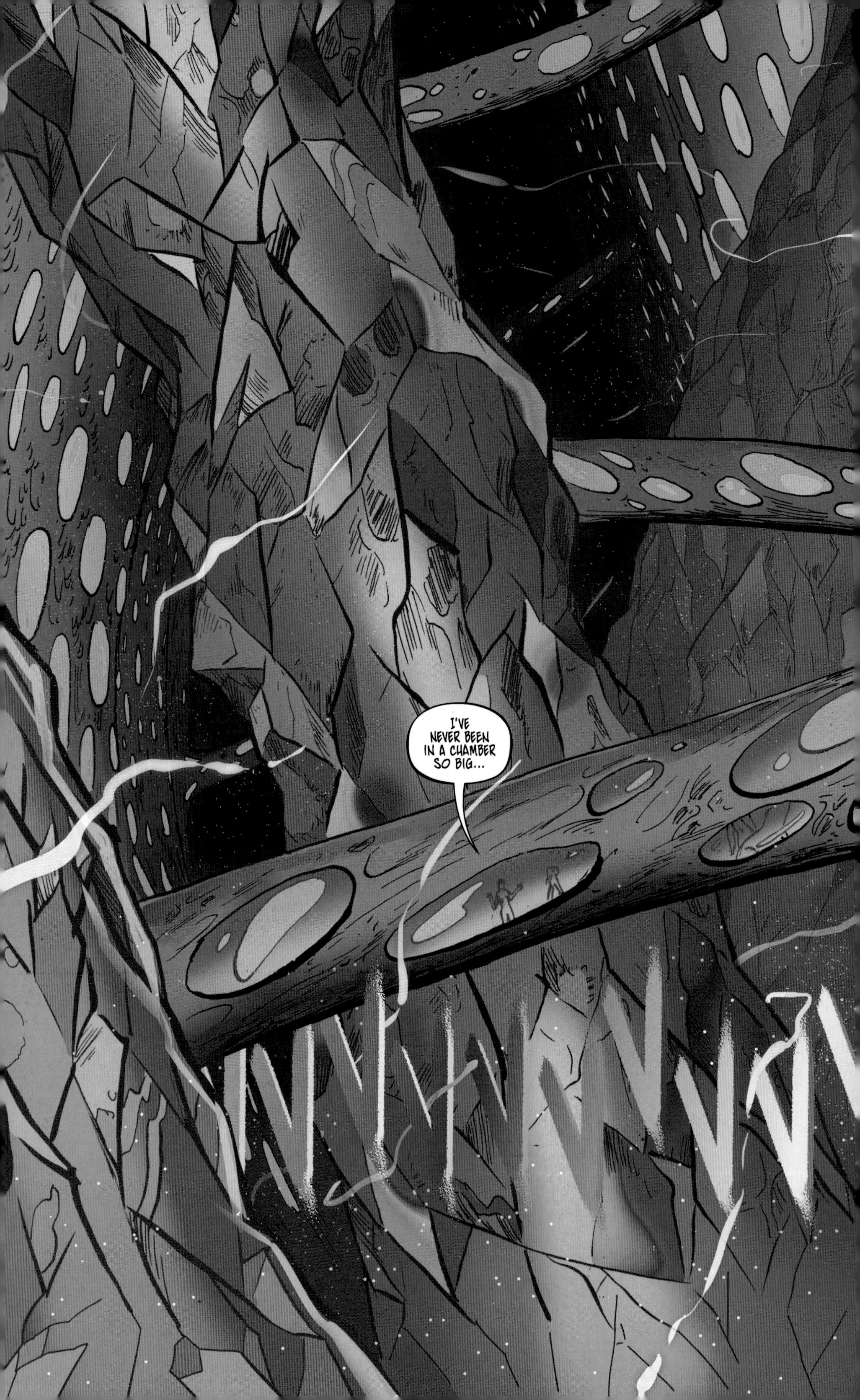
I'VE NEVER BEEN IN A CHAMBER SO BIG...

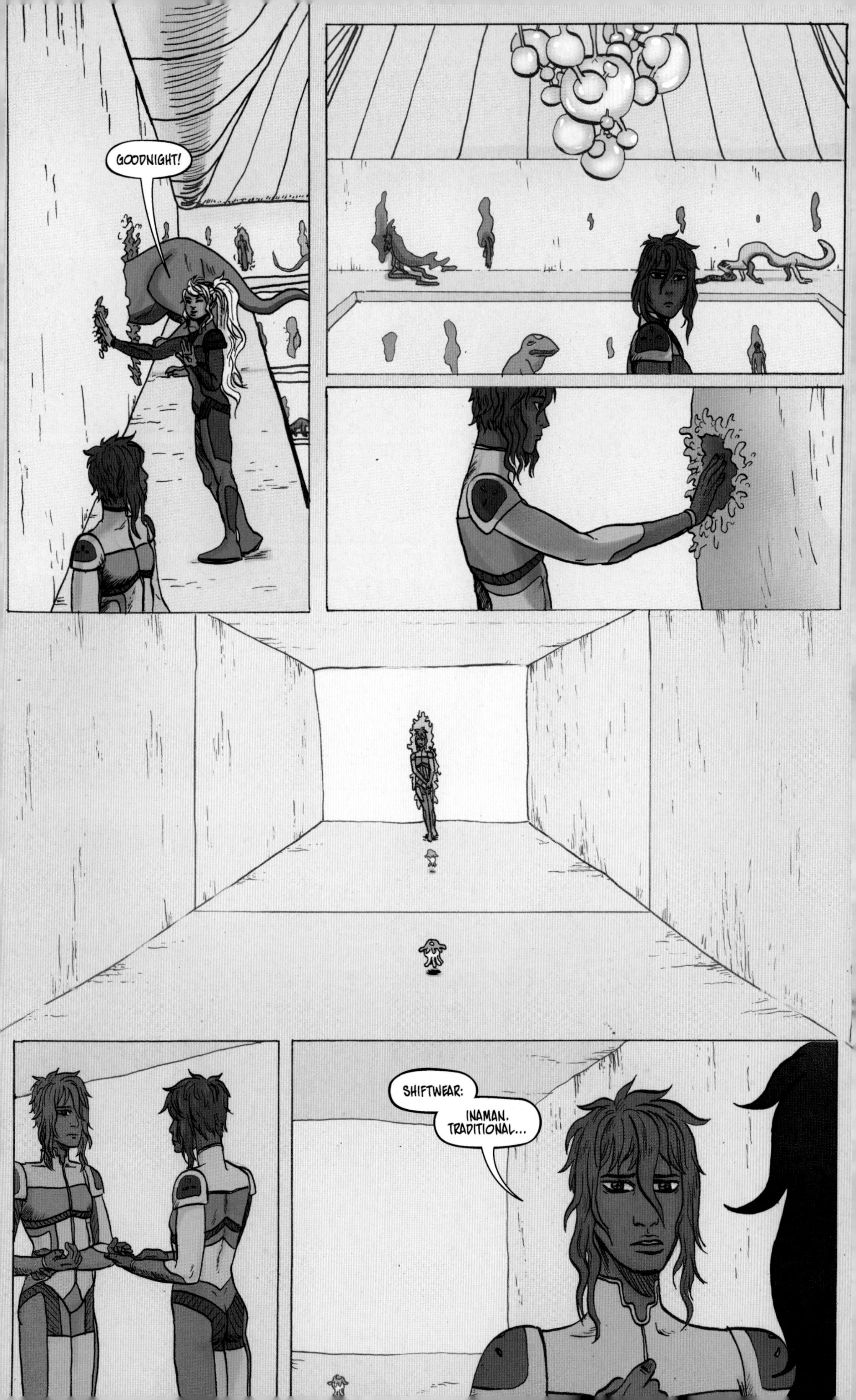
GOODNIGHT!
SHIFTWEAR:
INAMAN. TRADITIONAL...

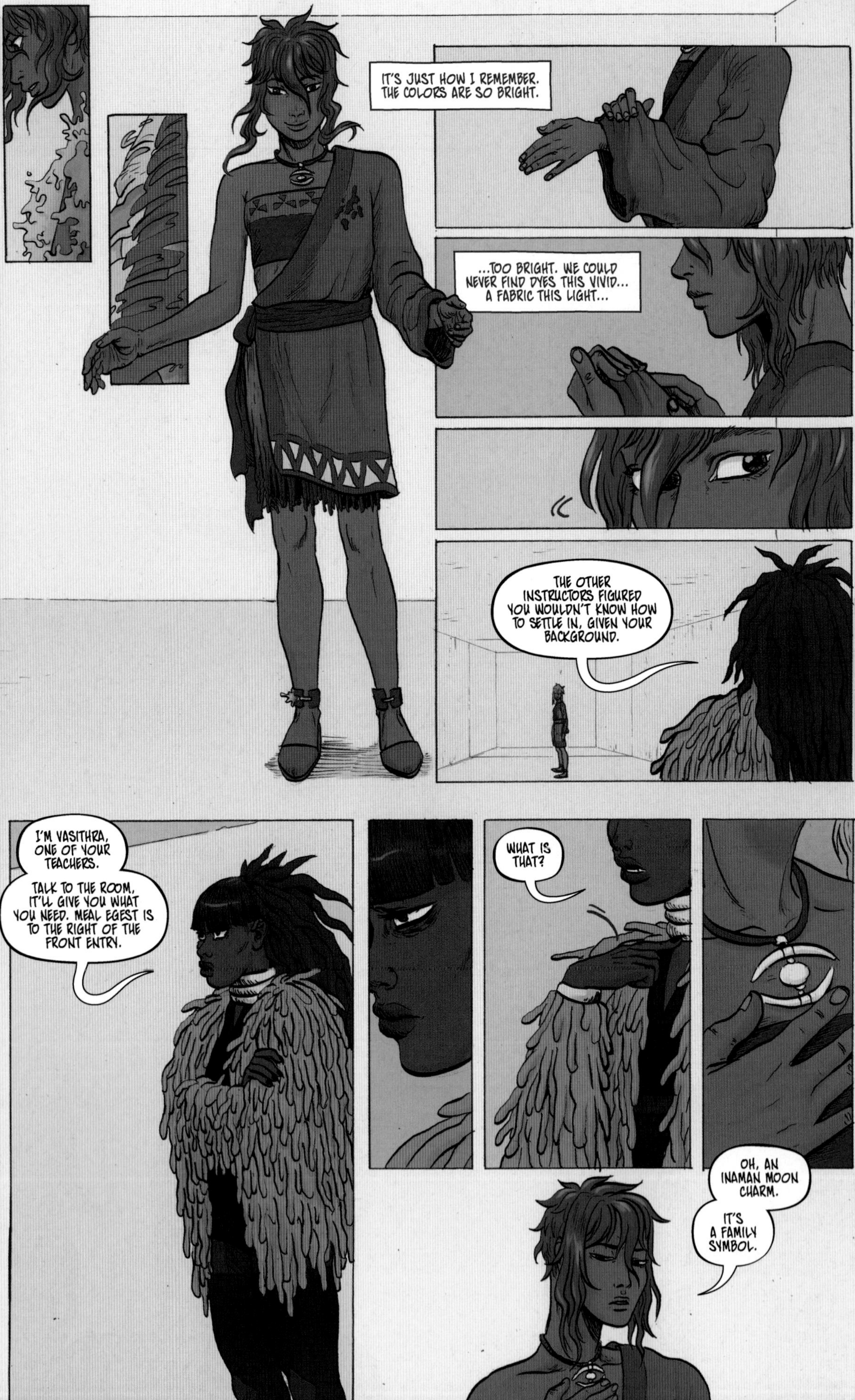
IT'S JUST HOW I REMEMBER. THE COLORS ARE SO BRIGHT.
...TOO BRIGHT. WE COULD NEVER FIND DYES THIS VIVID... A FABRIC THIS LIGHT...
THE OTHER INSTRUCTORS FIGURED YOU WOULDN'T KNOW HOW TO SETTLE IN, GIVEN YOUR BACKGROUND.
I'M VASITHRA, ONE OF YOUR TEACHERS.
TALK TO THE ROOM, IT'LL GIVE YOU WHAT YOU NEED. MEAL EGEST IS TO THE RIGHT OF THE FRONT ENTRY.
WHAT IS THAT?
OH, AN INAMAN MOON CHARM.
IT'S A FAMILY SYMBOL.

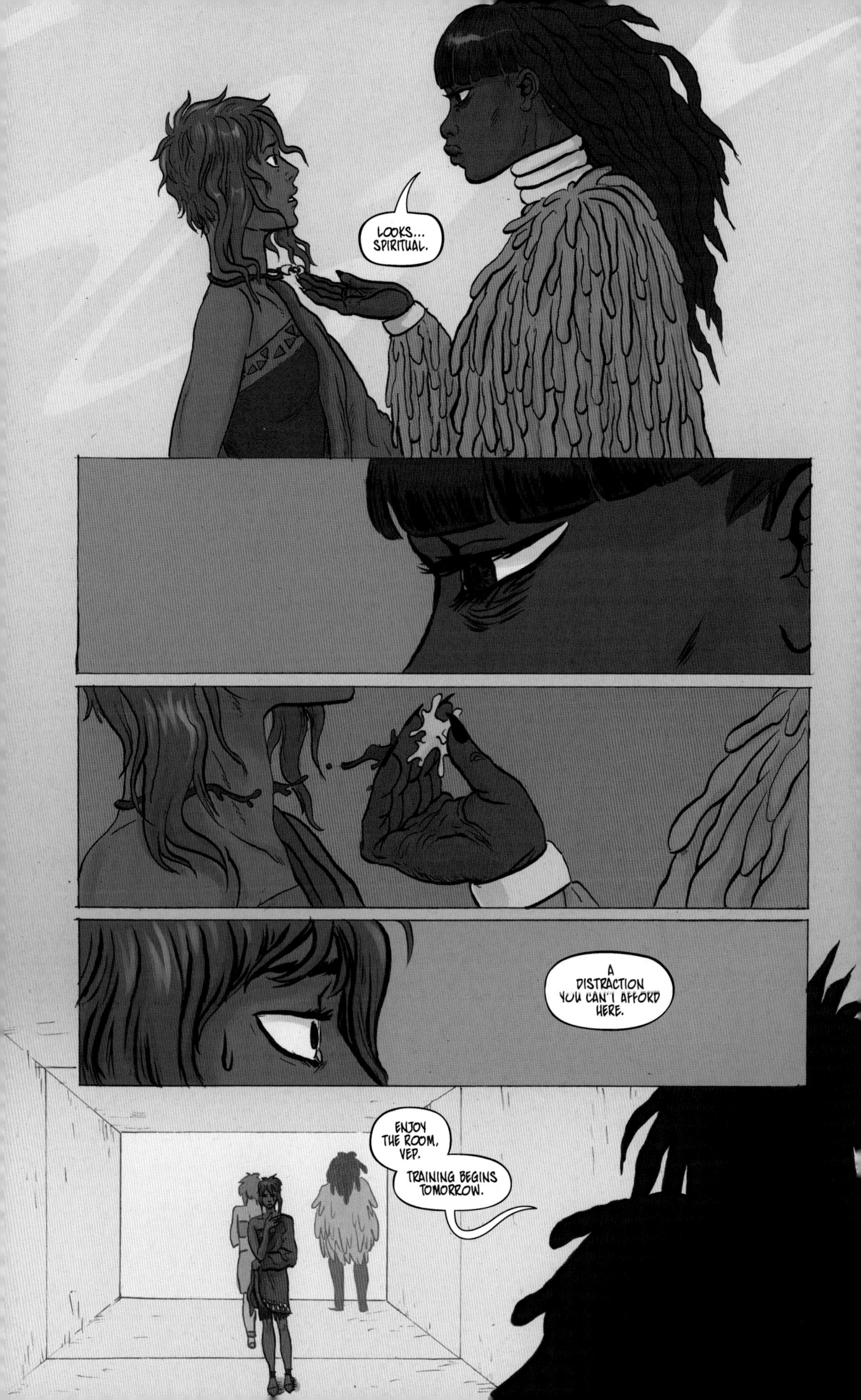
LOOKS... SPIRITUAL.
A DISTRACTION YOU CAN'T AFFORD HERE.
ENJOY THE ROOM, VEP.
TRAINING BEGINS TOMORROW.

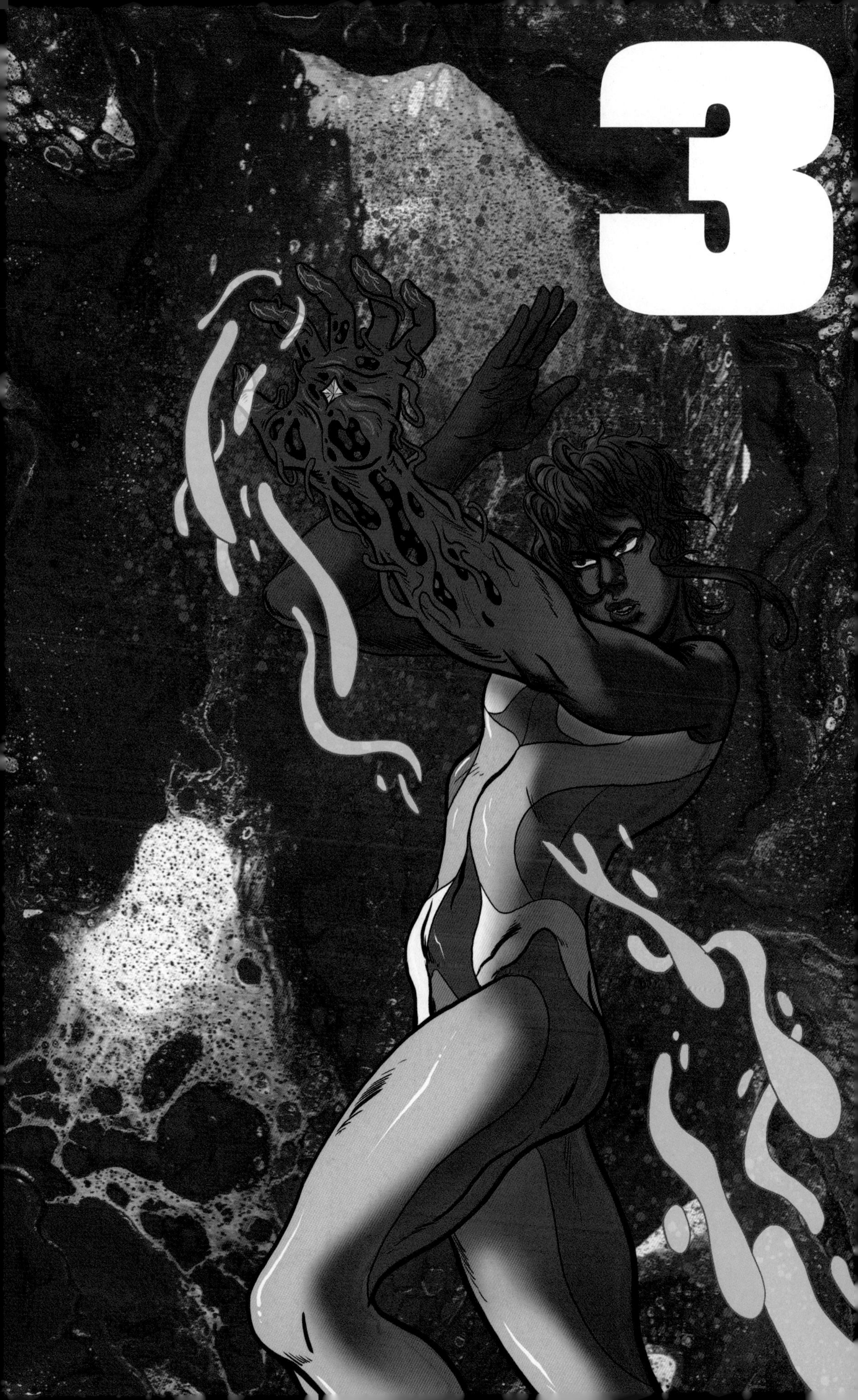
3

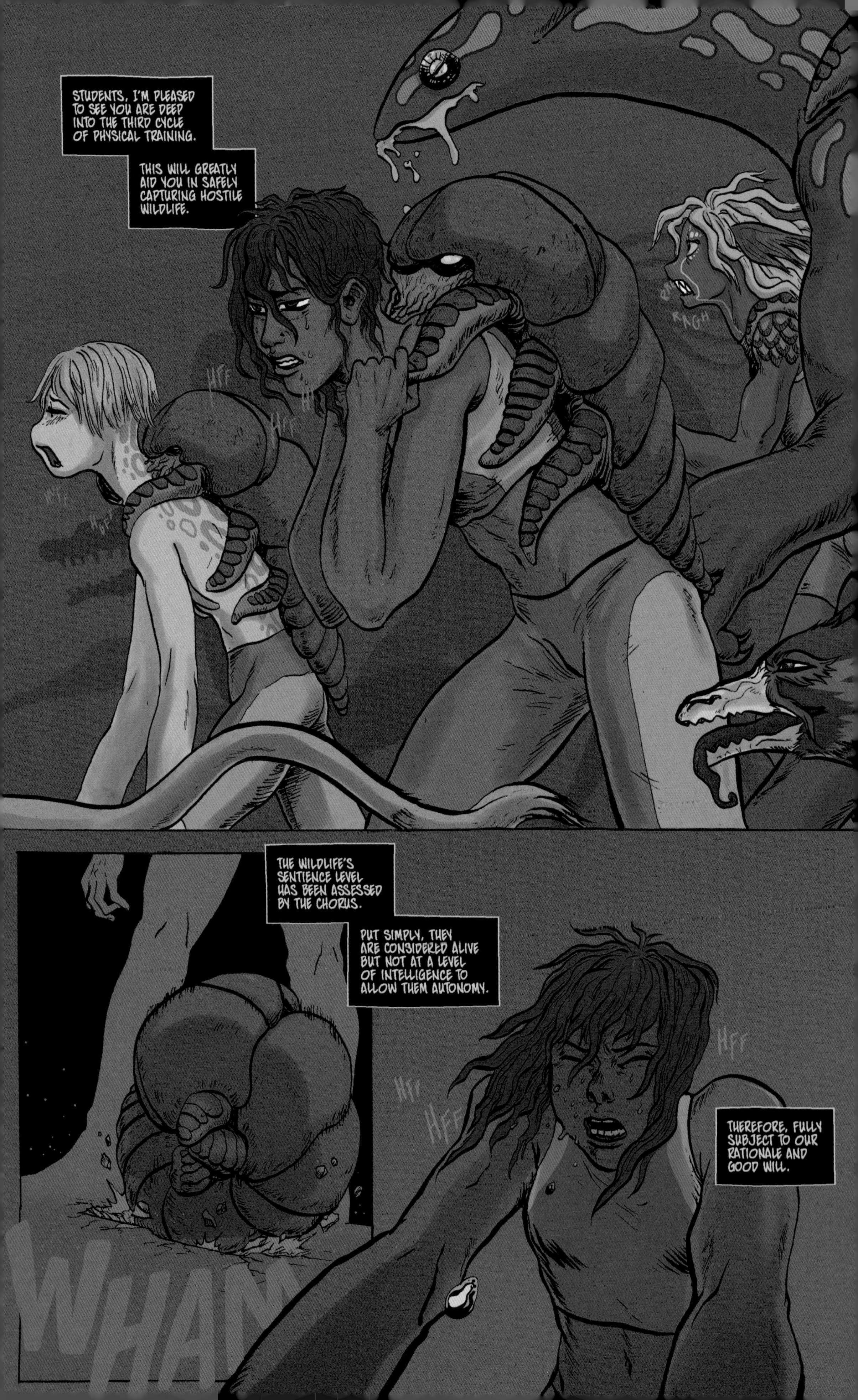
STUDENTS, I'M PLEASED TO SEE YOU ARE DEEP INTO THE THIRD CYCLE OF PHYSICAL TRAINING.
THIS WILL GREATLY AID YOU IN SAFELY CAPTURING HOSTILE WILDLIFE.
RAGH
HFF
HFF
HFF
HFF
THE WILDLIFE'S SENTIENCE LEVEL HAS BEEN ASSESSED BY THE CHORUS.
PUT SIMPLY, THEY ARE CONSIDERED ALIVE BUT NOT AT A LEVEL OF INTELLIGENCE TO ALLOW THEM AUTONOMY.
HFF
HFF
HFF
THEREFORE, FULLY SUBJECT TO OUR RATIONALE AND GOOD WILL.

THE MAIN FORM OF CONFLICT BETWEEN US AND THE WILDLIFE IS THEIR FORM OF META-PATHY COMMUNICATION.

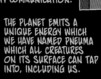

THE PLANET EMITS A UNIQUE ENERGY WHICH WE HAVE NAMED PNEUMA WHICH ALL CREATURES ON ITS SURFACE CAN TAP INTO, INCLUDING US.

THE NATIVE WILDLIFE USE THIS MAINLY TO COMMUNICATE OR DEFEND THEMSELVES,

USUALLY SENDING PRIMITIVE PROJECTIONS INTO ANOTHER MIND OR MANIPULATING PNEUMA IN PHYSICAL MANIFESTATIONS.

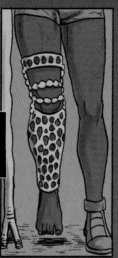

KEEP YOURSELF LIGHT. DON'T ANCHOR YOURSELF.

MANY OF YOUR OPPONENTS WILL BE LARGER THAN YOU.

USE YOUR SPEED AND THEIR WEIGHT AGAINST THEM.

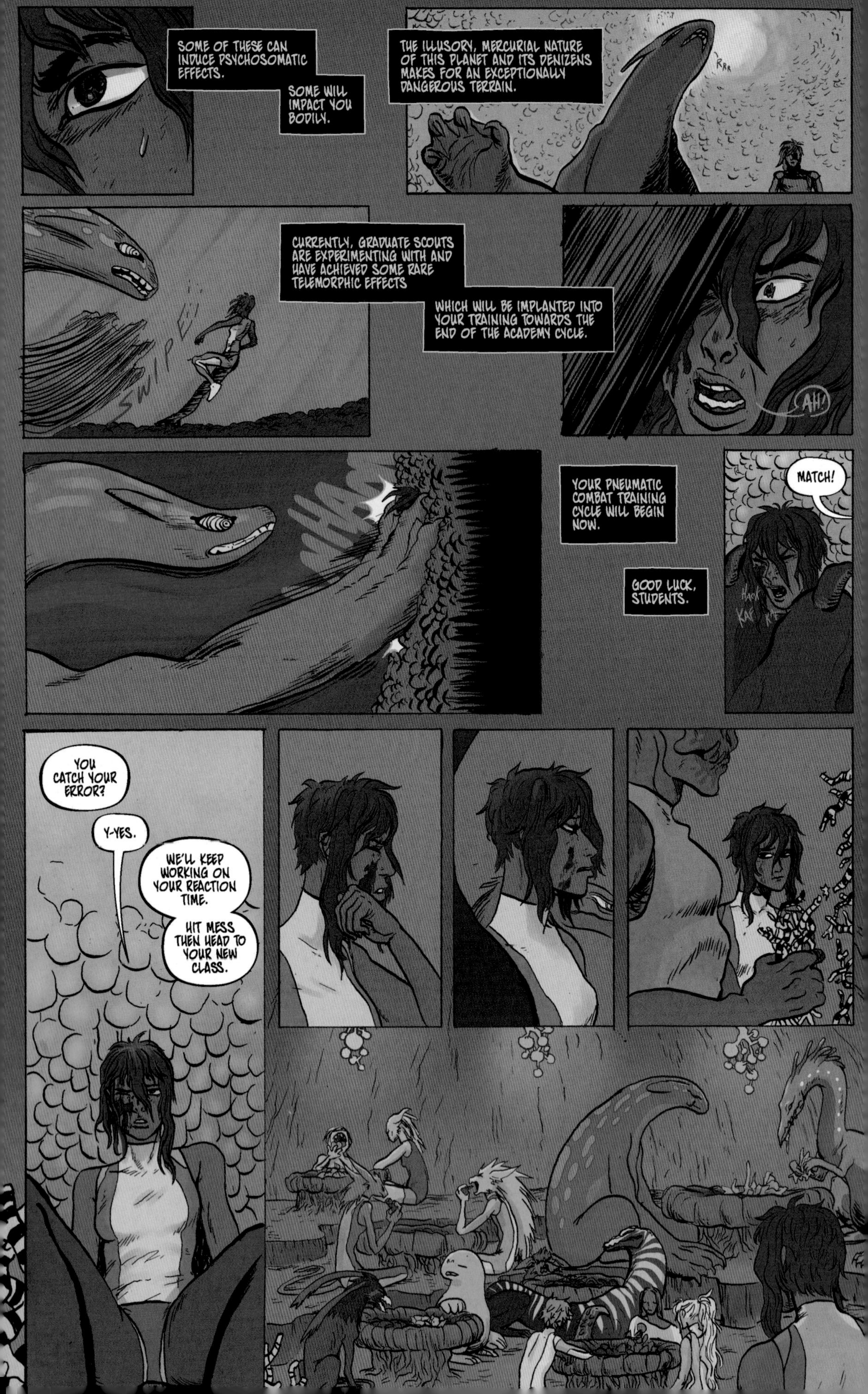

SOME OF THESE CAN INDUCE PSYCHOSOMATIC EFFECTS.
SOME WILL IMPACT YOU BODILY.
THE ILLUSORY, MERCURIAL NATURE OF THIS PLANET AND ITS DENIZENS MAKES FOR AN EXCEPTIONALLY DANGEROUS TERRAIN.
RRR
CURRENTLY, GRADUATE SCOUTS ARE EXPERIMENTING WITH AND HAVE ACHIEVED SOME RARE TELEMORPHIC EFFECTS
WHICH WILL BE IMPLANTED INTO YOUR TRAINING TOWARDS THE END OF THE ACADEMY CYCLE.
SWIPE!
AH!
YOUR PNEUMATIC COMBAT TRAINING CYCLE WILL BEGIN NOW.
GOOD LUCK, STUDENTS.
MATCH!
HACK
YOU CATCH YOUR ERROR?
Y-YES.
WE'LL KEEP WORKING ON YOUR REACTION TIME.
HIT MESS THEN HEAD TO YOUR NEW CLASS.

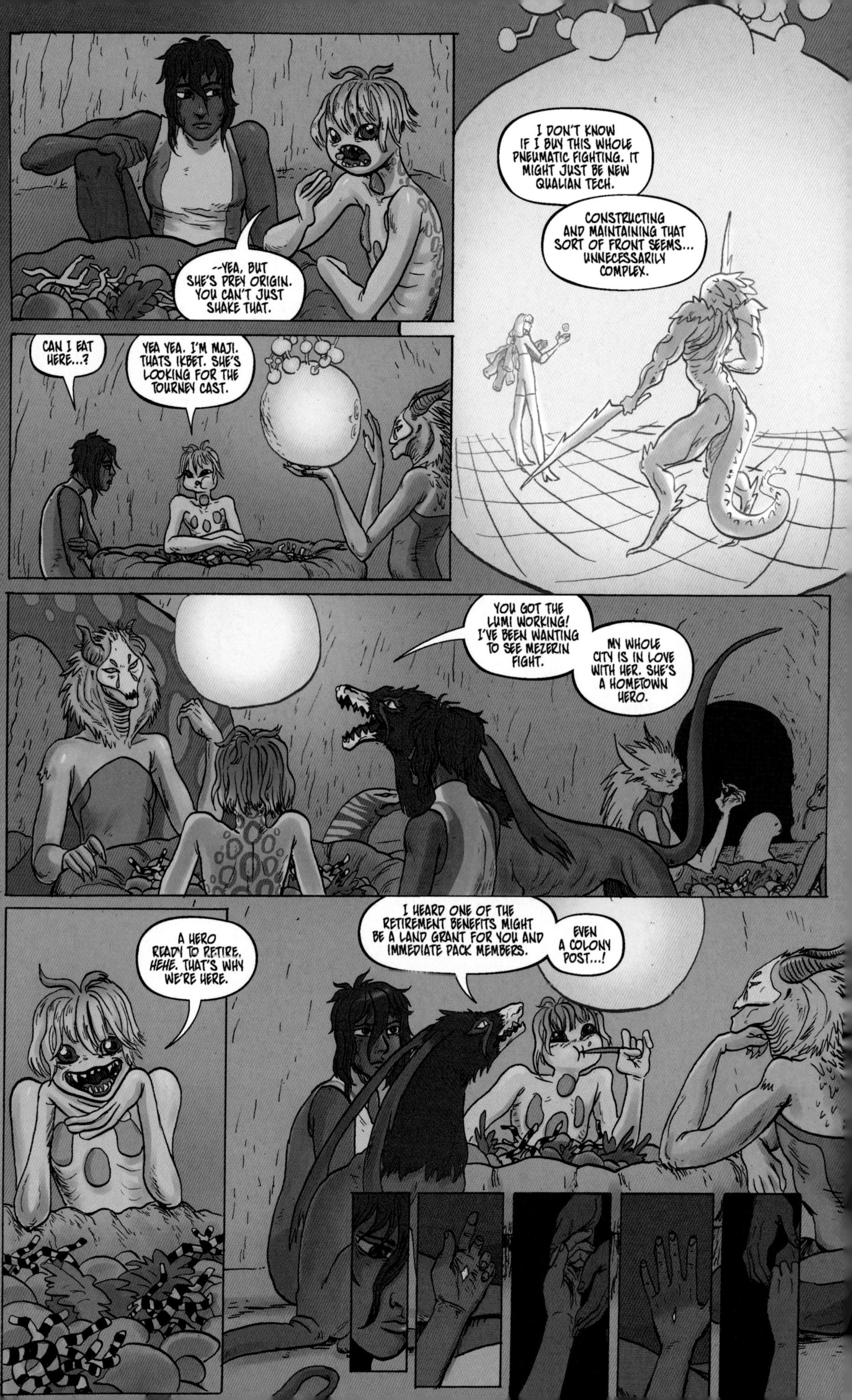
--YEA, BUT SHE'S PREY ORIGIN. YOU CAN'T JUST SHAKE THAT.
I DON'T KNOW IF I BUY THIS WHOLE PNEUMATIC FIGHTING. IT MIGHT JUST BE NEW QUALIAN TECH.
CONSTRUCTING AND MAINTAINING THAT SORT OF FRONT SEEMS... UNNECESSARILY COMPLEX.
CAN I EAT HERE...?
YEA YEA. I'M MAJI. THATS IKBET. SHE'S LOOKING FOR THE TOURNEY CAST.
YOU GOT THE LUMI WORKING! I'VE BEEN WANTING TO SEE MEZERIN FIGHT.
MY WHOLE CITY IS IN LOVE WITH HER. SHE'S A HOMETOWN HERO.
A HERO READY TO RETIRE. HEHE. THAT'S WHY WE'RE HERE.
I HEARD ONE OF THE RETIREMENT BENEFITS MIGHT BE A LAND GRANT FOR YOU AND IMMEDIATE PACK MEMBERS.
EVEN A COLONY POST...!

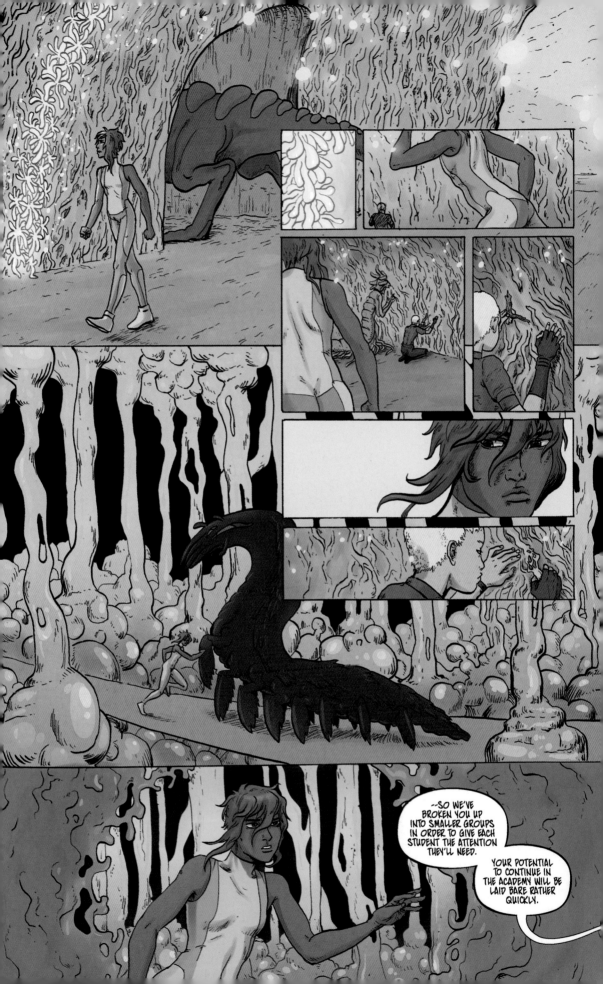

--SO WE'VE BROKEN YOU UP INTO SMALLER GROUPS IN ORDER TO GIVE EACH STUDENT THE ATTENTION THEY'LL NEED.

YOUR POTENTIAL TO CONTINUE IN THE ACADEMY WILL BE LAID BARE RATHER QUICKLY.

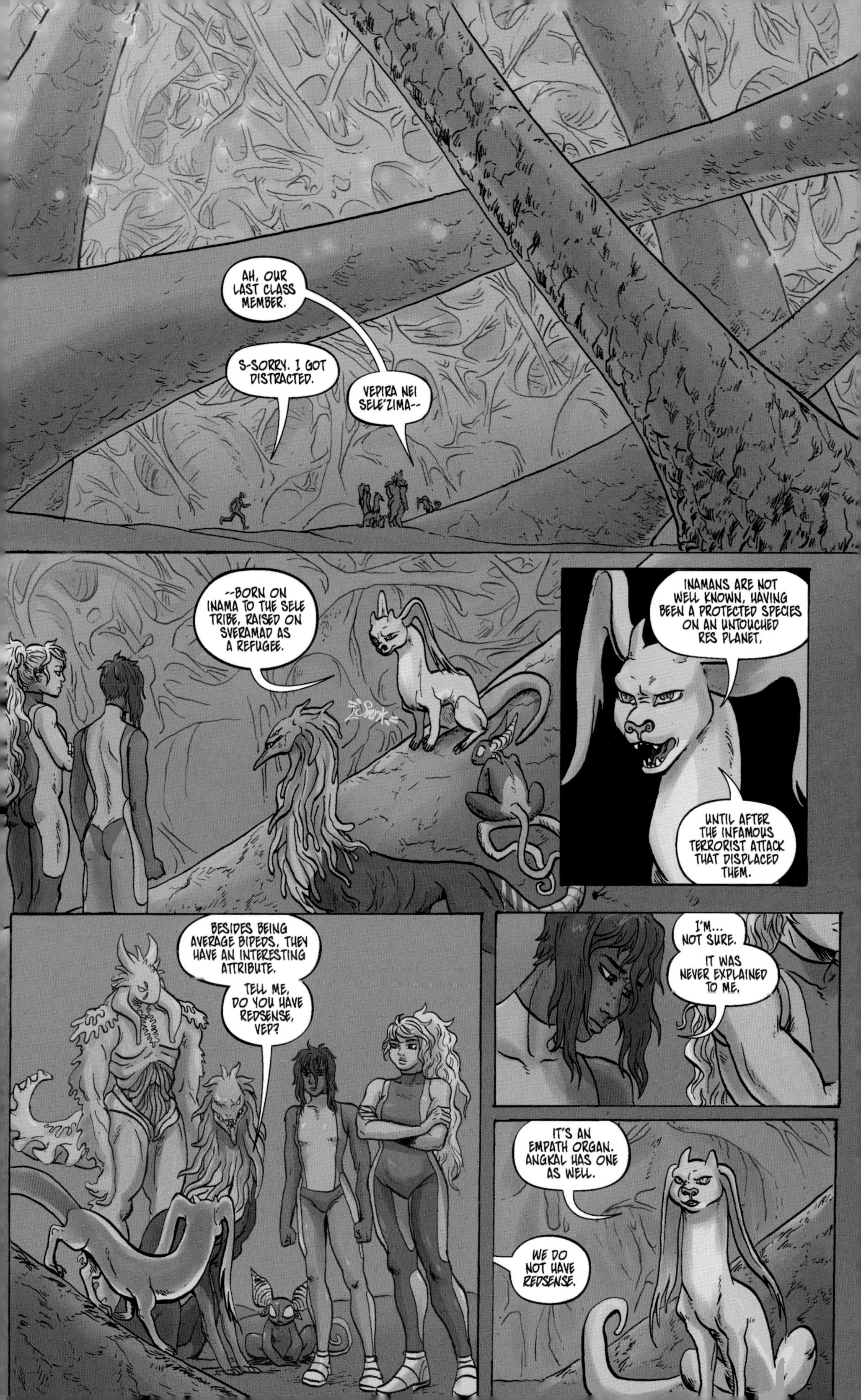
AH, OUR LAST CLASS MEMBER.
S-SORRY. I GOT DISTRACTED.
VEPIRA NEI SELE'ZIMA--
--BORN ON INAMA TO THE SELE TRIBE, RAISED ON SVERAMAD AS A REFUGEE.
SNORK
INAMANS ARE NOT WELL KNOWN, HAVING BEEN A PROTECTED SPECIES ON AN UNTOUCHED RES PLANET,
UNTIL AFTER THE INFAMOUS TERRORIST ATTACK THAT DISPLACED THEM.
BESIDES BEING AVERAGE BIPEDS, THEY HAVE AN INTERESTING ATTRIBUTE.
TELL ME, DO YOU HAVE REDSENSE, VEP?
I'M... NOT SURE.
IT WAS NEVER EXPLAINED TO ME.
IT'S AN EMPATH ORGAN. ANGKAL HAS ONE AS WELL.
WE DO NOT HAVE REDSENSE.

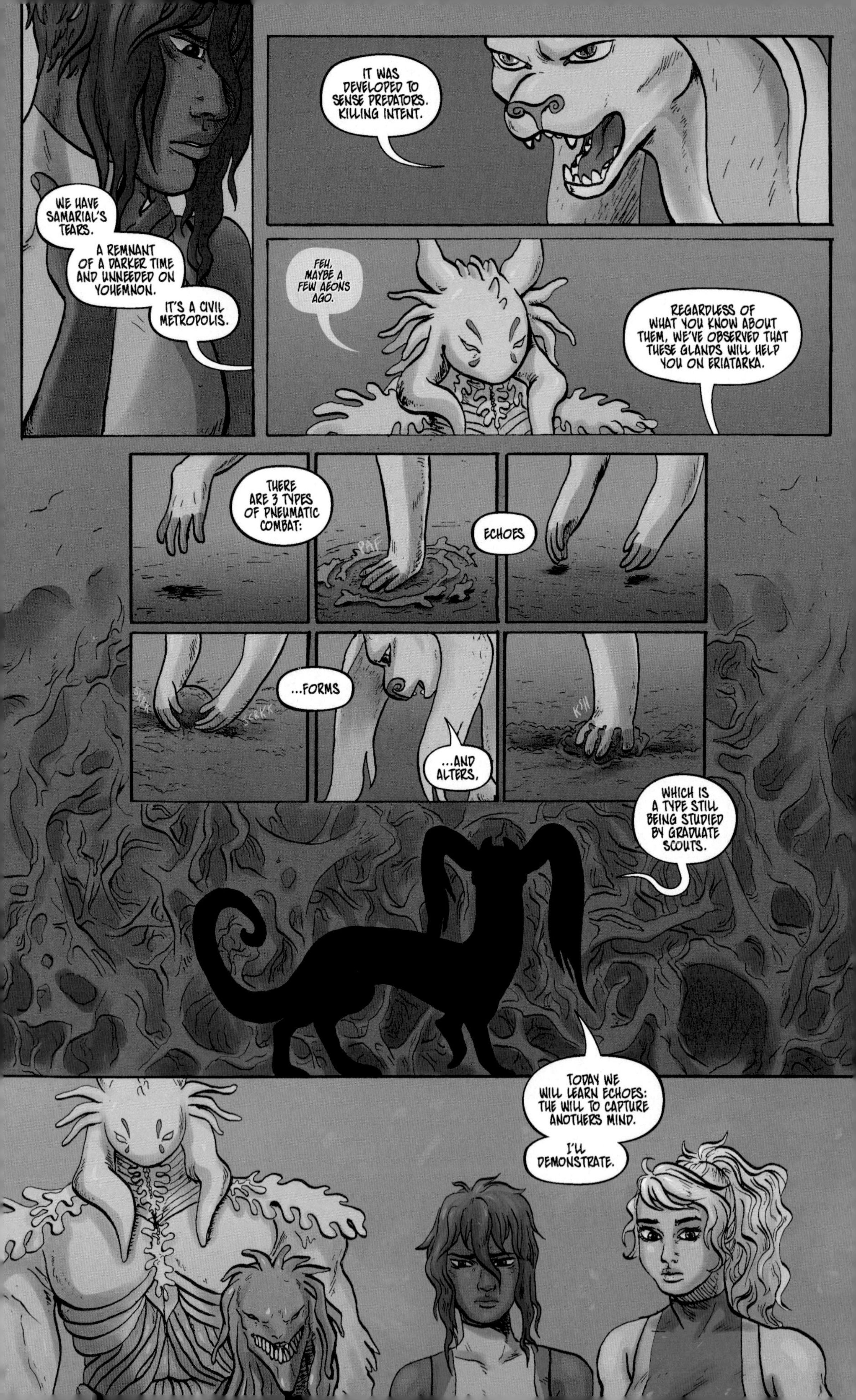
WE HAVE SAMARIAL'S TEARS.
A REMNANT OF A DARKER TIME AND UNNEEDED ON YOHEMNON.
IT'S A CIVIL METROPOLIS.
IT WAS DEVELOPED TO SENSE PREDATORS. KILLING INTENT.
FEH, MAYBE A FEW AEONS AGO.
REGARDLESS OF WHAT YOU KNOW ABOUT THEM, WE'VE OBSERVED THAT THESE GLANDS WILL HELP YOU ON ERIATARKA.
THERE ARE 3 TYPES OF PNEUMATIC COMBAT:
PAF
ECHOES
SKRK
SCRKK
...FORMS
...AND ALTERS,
KSH
WHICH IS A TYPE STILL BEING STUDIED BY GRADUATE SCOUTS.
TODAY WE WILL LEARN ECHOES: THE WILL TO CAPTURE ANOTHERS MIND.
I'LL DEMONSTRATE.

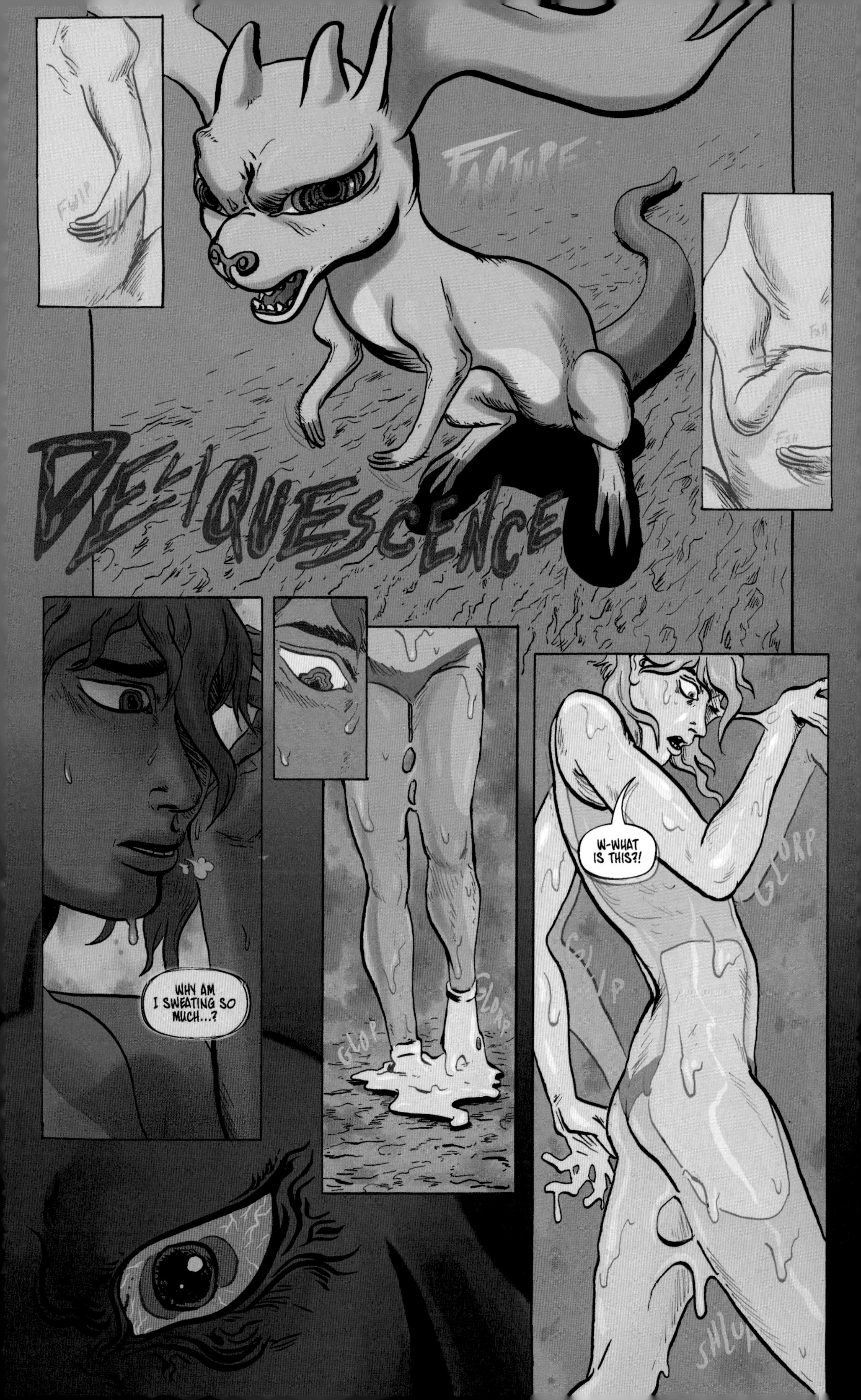
FWIP
DELIQUESCENCE
FSH
FSH
WHY AM I SWEATING SO MUCH...?
GLORP
GLORP
W-WHAT IS THIS?!

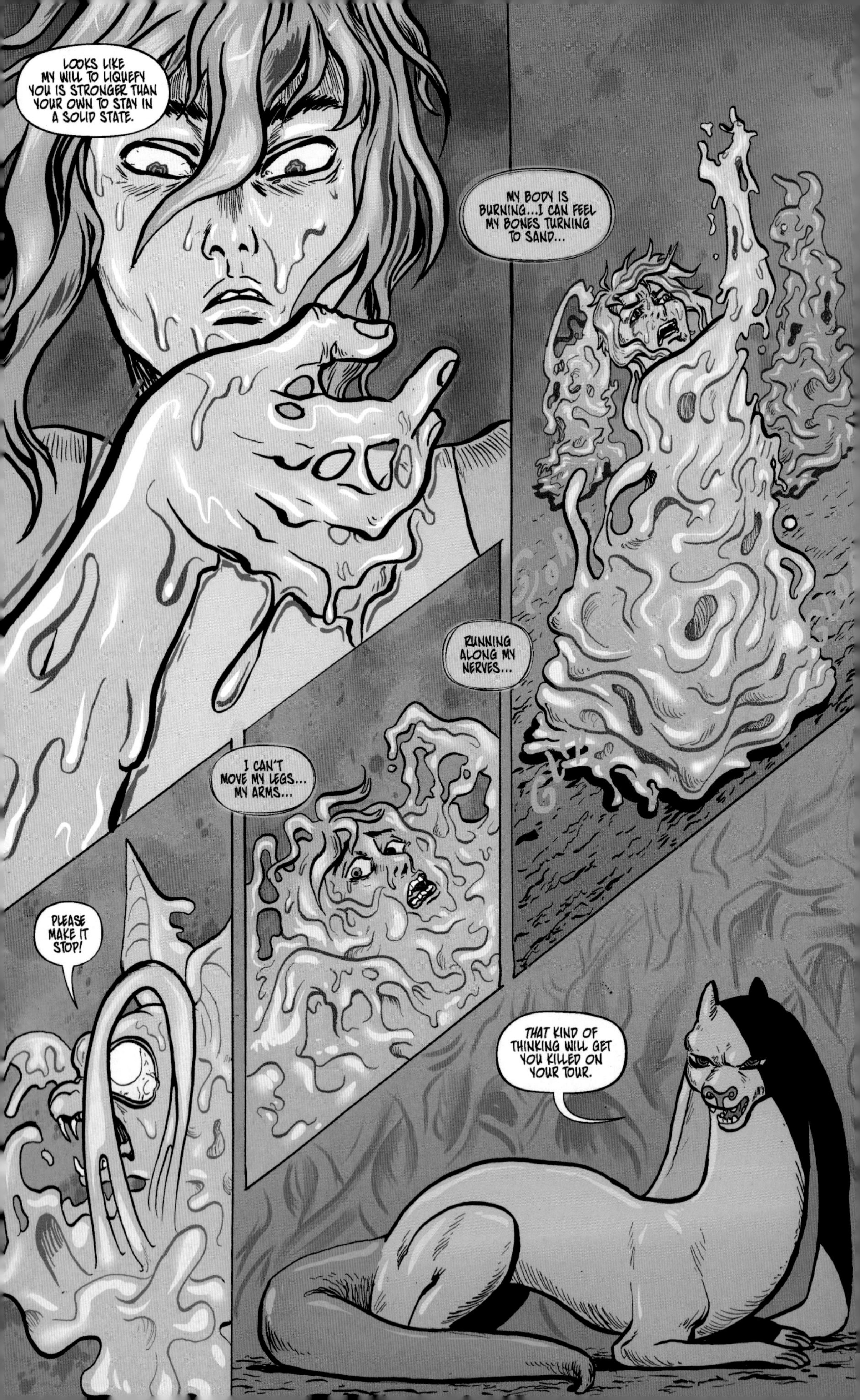
LOOKS LIKE MY WILL TO LIQUEFY YOU IS STRONGER THAN YOUR OWN TO STAY IN A SOLID STATE.
MY BODY IS BURNING...I CAN FEEL MY BONES TURNING TO SAND...
RUNNING ALONG MY NERVES...
I CAN'T MOVE MY LEGS... MY ARMS...
PLEASE MAKE IT STOP!
THAT KIND OF THINKING WILL GET YOU KILLED ON YOUR TOUR.

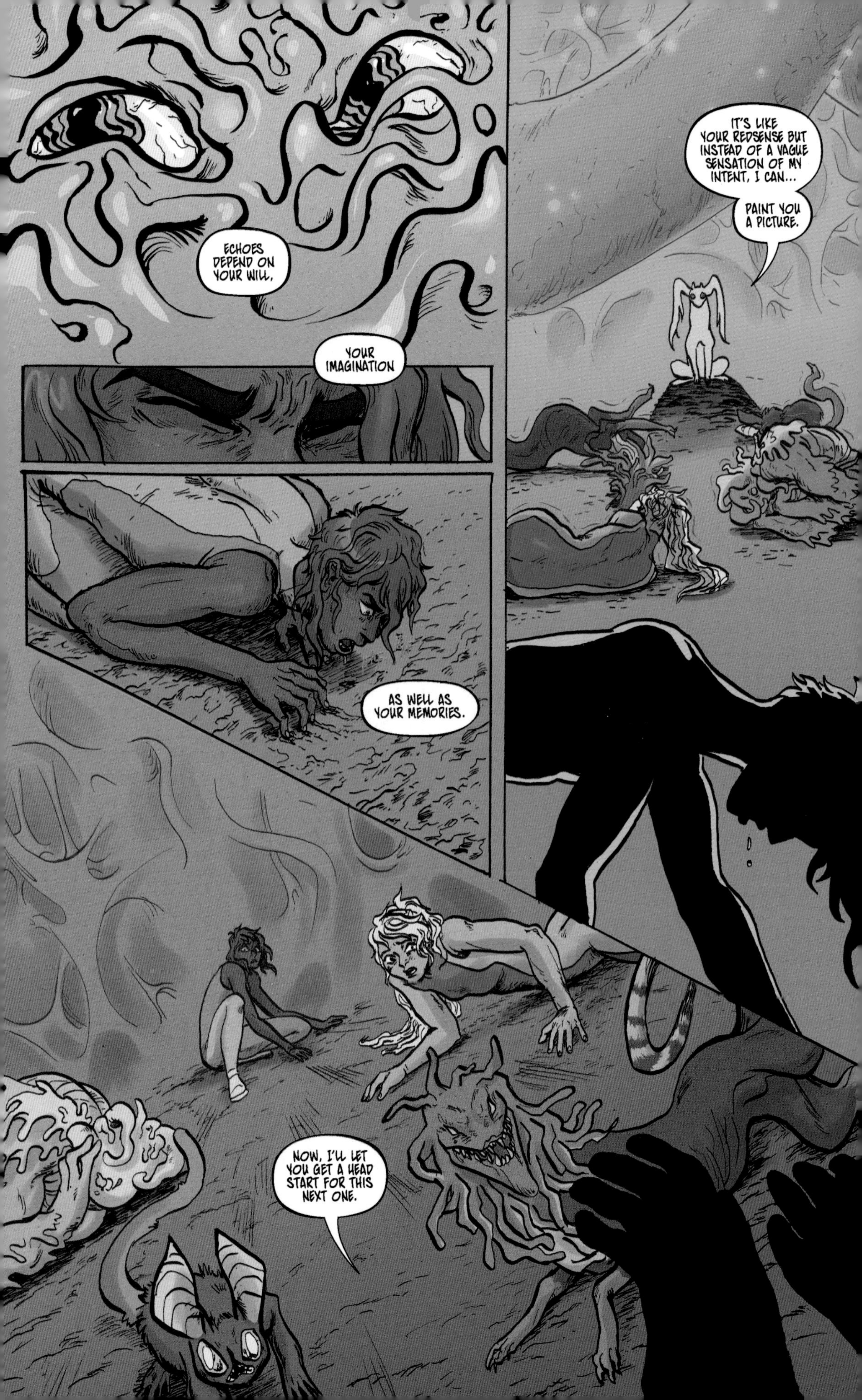
ECHOES DEPEND ON YOUR WILL,
YOUR IMAGINATION
AS WELL AS YOUR MEMORIES.
IT'S LIKE YOUR REDSENSE BUT INSTEAD OF A VAGUE SENSATION OF MY INTENT, I CAN...
PAINT YOU A PICTURE.
NOW, I'LL LET YOU GET A HEAD START FOR THIS NEXT ONE.

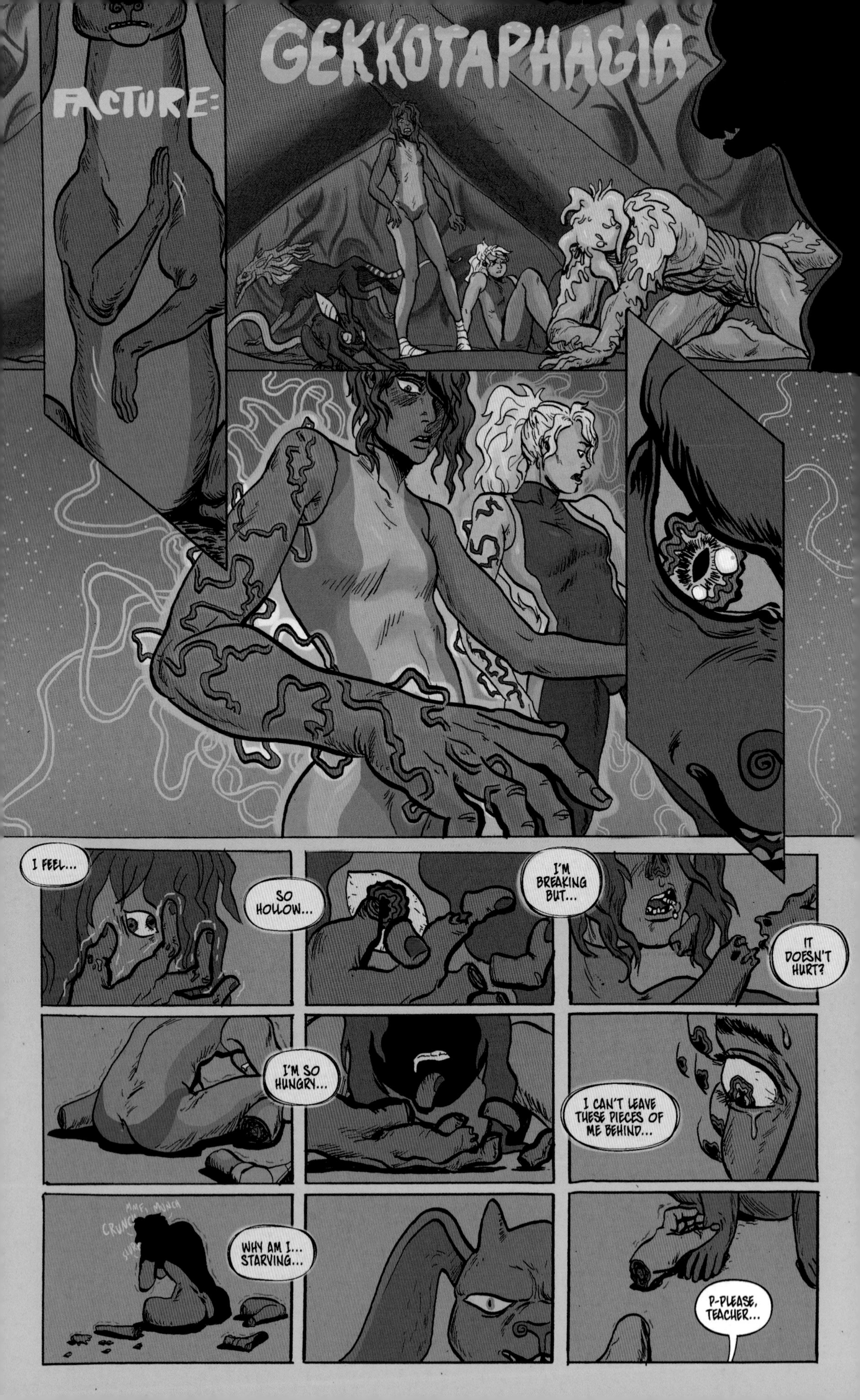
FACTURE:
GEKKOTAPHAGIA
I FEEL...
SO HOLLOW...
I'M BREAKING BUT...
IT DOESN'T HURT?
I'M SO HUNGRY...
I CAN'T LEAVE THESE PIECES OF ME BEHIND...
MMF, MUNCH
WHY AM I... STARVING...
P-PLEASE, TEACHER...

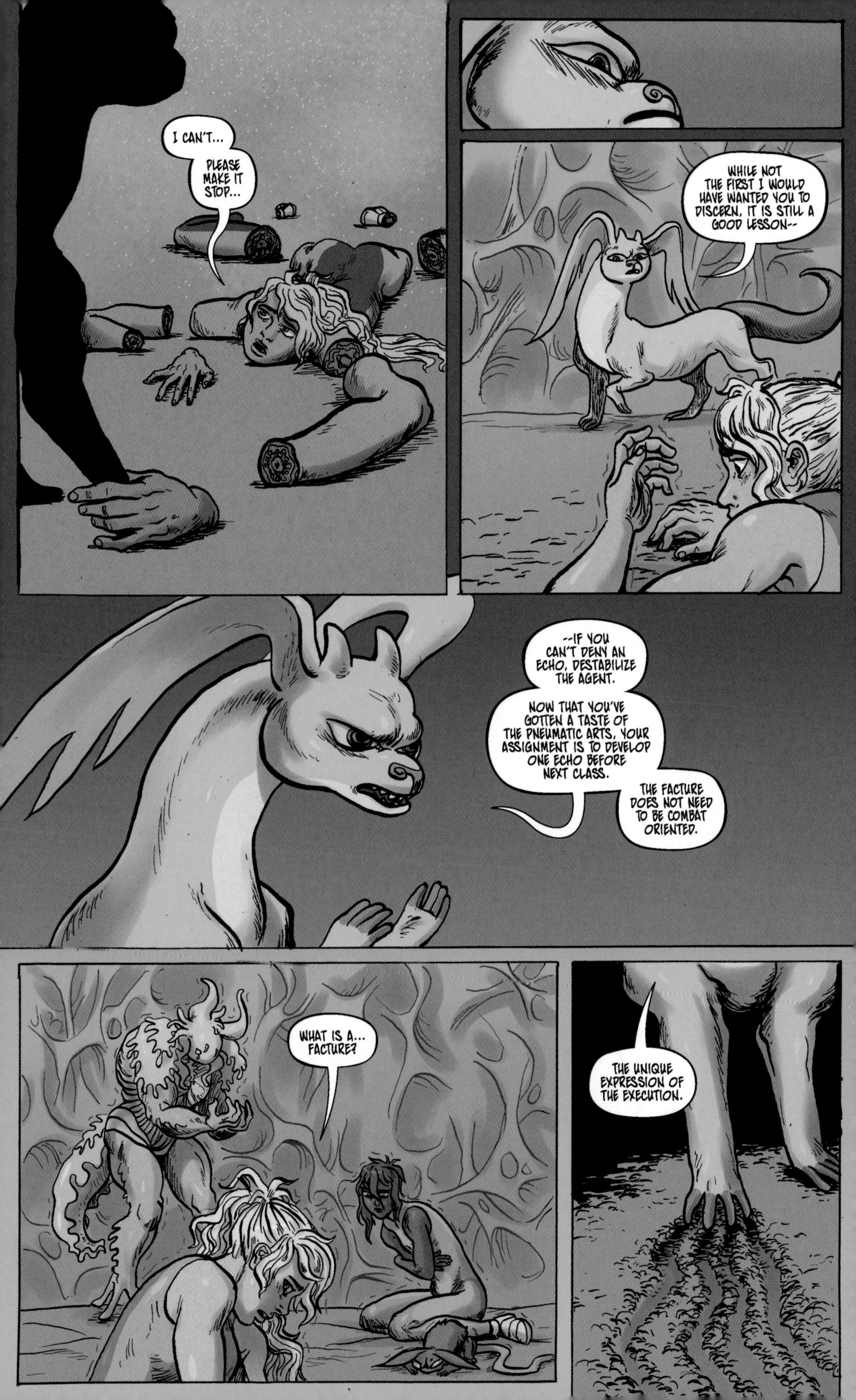
I CAN'T...
PLEASE MAKE IT STOP...
WHILE NOT THE FIRST I WOULD HAVE WANTED YOU TO DISCERN, IT IS STILL A GOOD LESSON--
--IF YOU CAN'T DENY AN ECHO, DESTABILIZE THE AGENT.
NOW THAT YOU'VE GOTTEN A TASTE OF THE PNEUMATIC ARTS, YOUR ASSIGNMENT IS TO DEVELOP ONE ECHO BEFORE NEXT CLASS.
THE FACTURE DOES NOT NEED TO BE COMBAT ORIENTED.
WHAT IS A... FACTURE?
THE UNIQUE EXPRESSION OF THE EXECUTION.

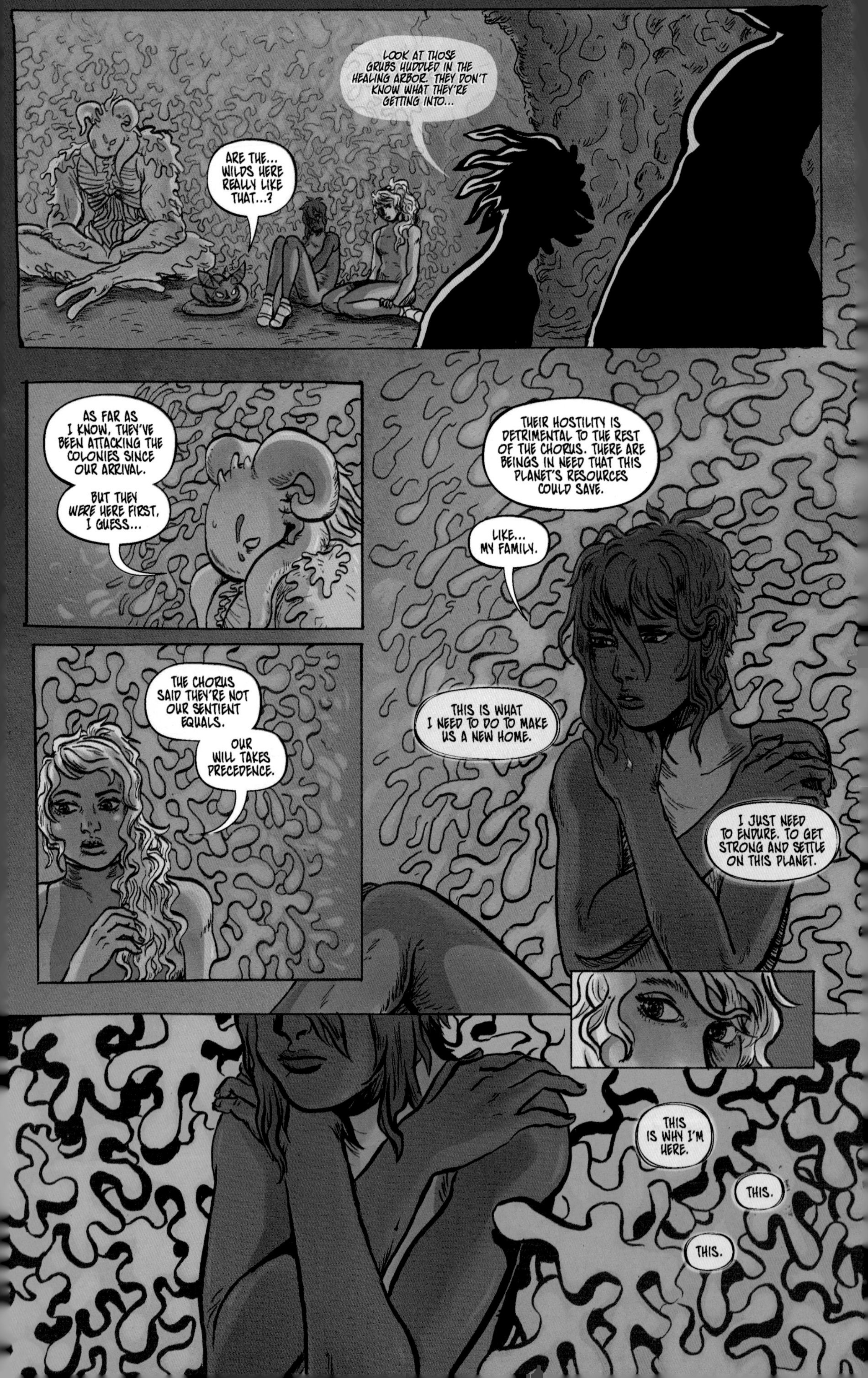

LOOK AT THOSE GRUBS HUDDLED IN THE HEALING ARBOR. THEY DON'T KNOW WHAT THEY'RE GETTING INTO...
ARE THE... WILDS HERE REALLY LIKE THAT...?
AS FAR AS I KNOW, THEY'VE BEEN ATTACKING THE COLONIES SINCE OUR ARRIVAL.
BUT THEY WERE HERE FIRST, I GUESS...
THEIR HOSTILITY IS DETRIMENTAL TO THE REST OF THE CHORUS. THERE ARE BEINGS IN NEED THAT THIS PLANET'S RESOURCES COULD SAVE.
LIKE... MY FAMILY.
THE CHORUS SAID THEY'RE NOT OUR SENTIENT EQUALS.
OUR WILL TAKES PRECEDENCE.
THIS IS WHAT I NEED TO DO TO MAKE US A NEW HOME.
I JUST NEED TO ENDURE. TO GET STRONG AND SETTLE ON THIS PLANET.
THIS IS WHY I'M HERE.
THIS.
THIS.

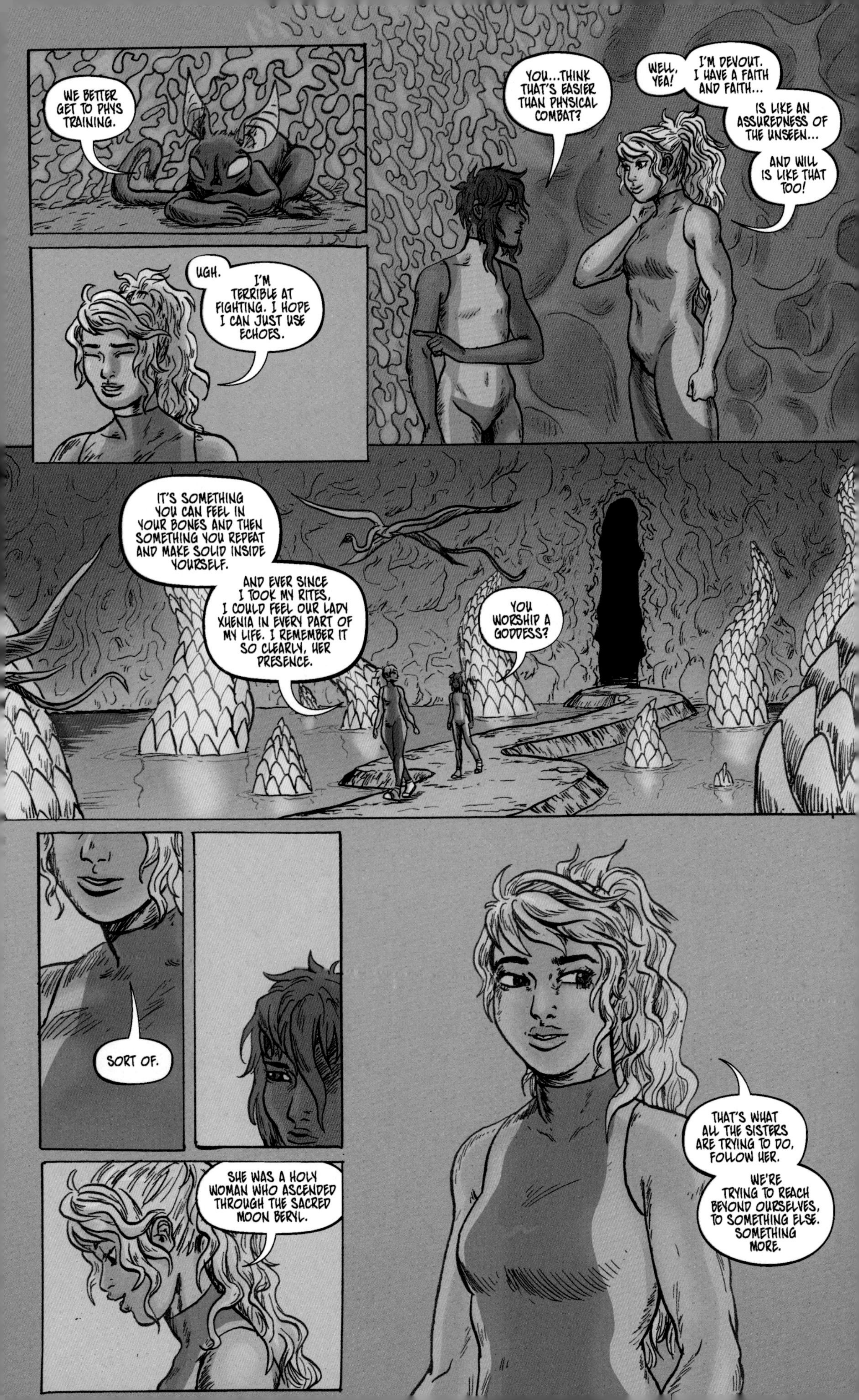
WE BETTER GET TO PHYS TRAINING.
UGH.
I'M TERRIBLE AT FIGHTING. I HOPE I CAN JUST USE ECHOES.
YOU...THINK THAT'S EASIER THAN PHYSICAL COMBAT?
WELL, YEA!
I'M DEVOUT. I HAVE A FAITH AND FAITH...
IS LIKE AN ASSUREDNESS OF THE UNSEEN...
AND WILL IS LIKE THAT TOO!
IT'S SOMETHING YOU CAN FEEL IN YOUR BONES AND THEN SOMETHING YOU REPEAT AND MAKE SOLID INSIDE YOURSELF.
AND EVER SINCE I TOOK MY RITES, I COULD FEEL OUR LADY XHENIA IN EVERY PART OF MY LIFE. I REMEMBER IT SO CLEARLY, HER PRESENCE.
YOU WORSHIP A GODDESS?
SORT OF.
SHE WAS A HOLY WOMAN WHO ASCENDED THROUGH THE SACRED MOON BERYL.
THAT'S WHAT ALL THE SISTERS ARE TRYING TO DO, FOLLOW HER.
WE'RE TRYING TO REACH BEYOND OURSELVES, TO SOMETHING ELSE. SOMETHING MORE.

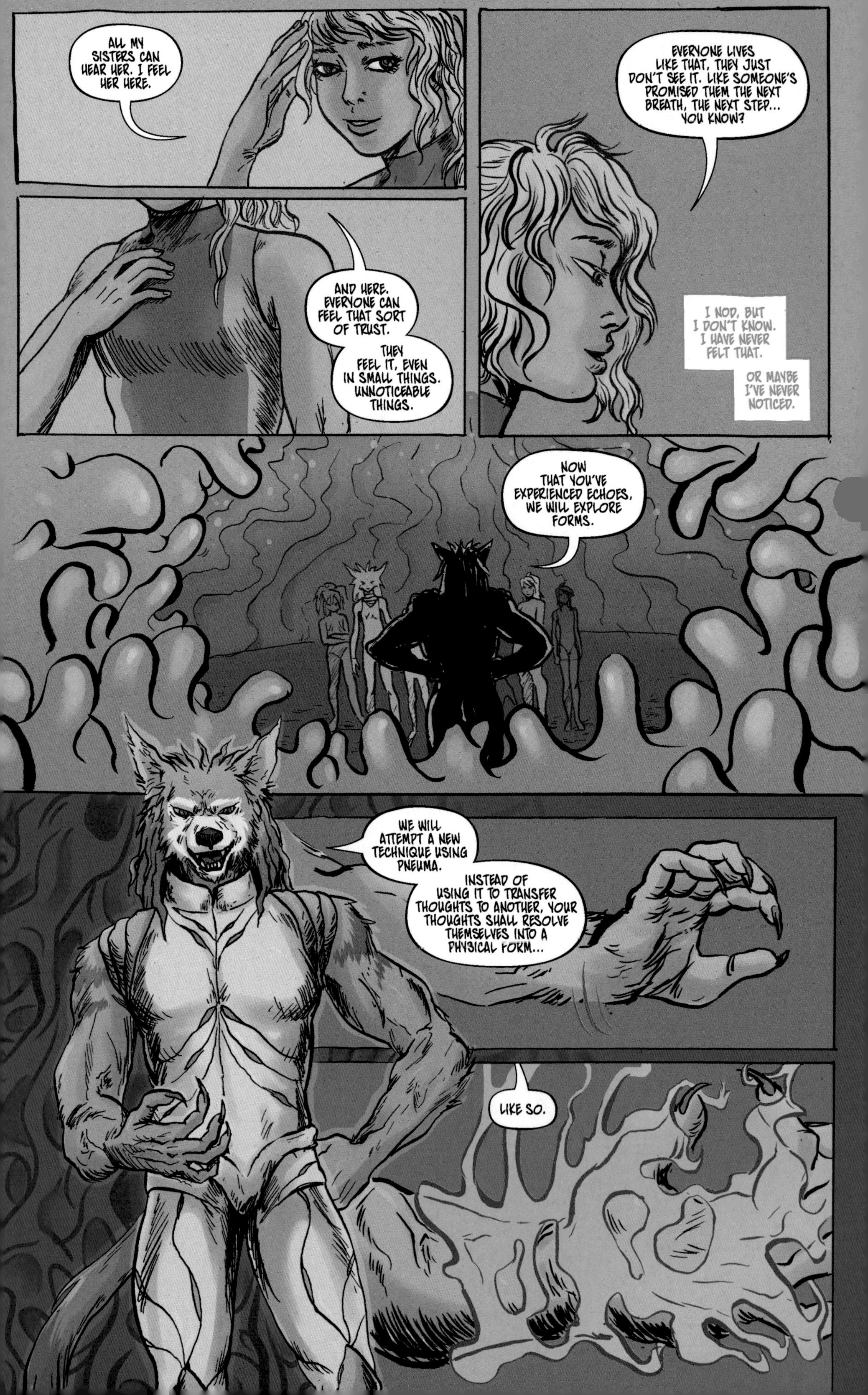
ALL MY SISTERS CAN HEAR HER. I FEEL HER HERE.
AND HERE. EVERYONE CAN FEEL THAT SORT OF TRUST.
THEY FEEL IT, EVEN IN SMALL THINGS. UNNOTICEABLE THINGS.
EVERYONE LIVES LIKE THAT, THEY JUST DON'T SEE IT. LIKE SOMEONE'S PROMISED THEM THE NEXT BREATH, THE NEXT STEP... YOU KNOW?
I NOD, BUT I DON'T KNOW. I HAVE NEVER FELT THAT.
OR MAYBE I'VE NEVER NOTICED.
NOW THAT YOU'VE EXPERIENCED ECHOES, WE WILL EXPLORE FORMS.
WE WILL ATTEMPT A NEW TECHNIQUE USING PNEUMA.
INSTEAD OF USING IT TO TRANSFER THOUGHTS TO ANOTHER, YOUR THOUGHTS SHALL RESOLVE THEMSELVES INTO A PHYSICAL FORM...
LIKE SO.

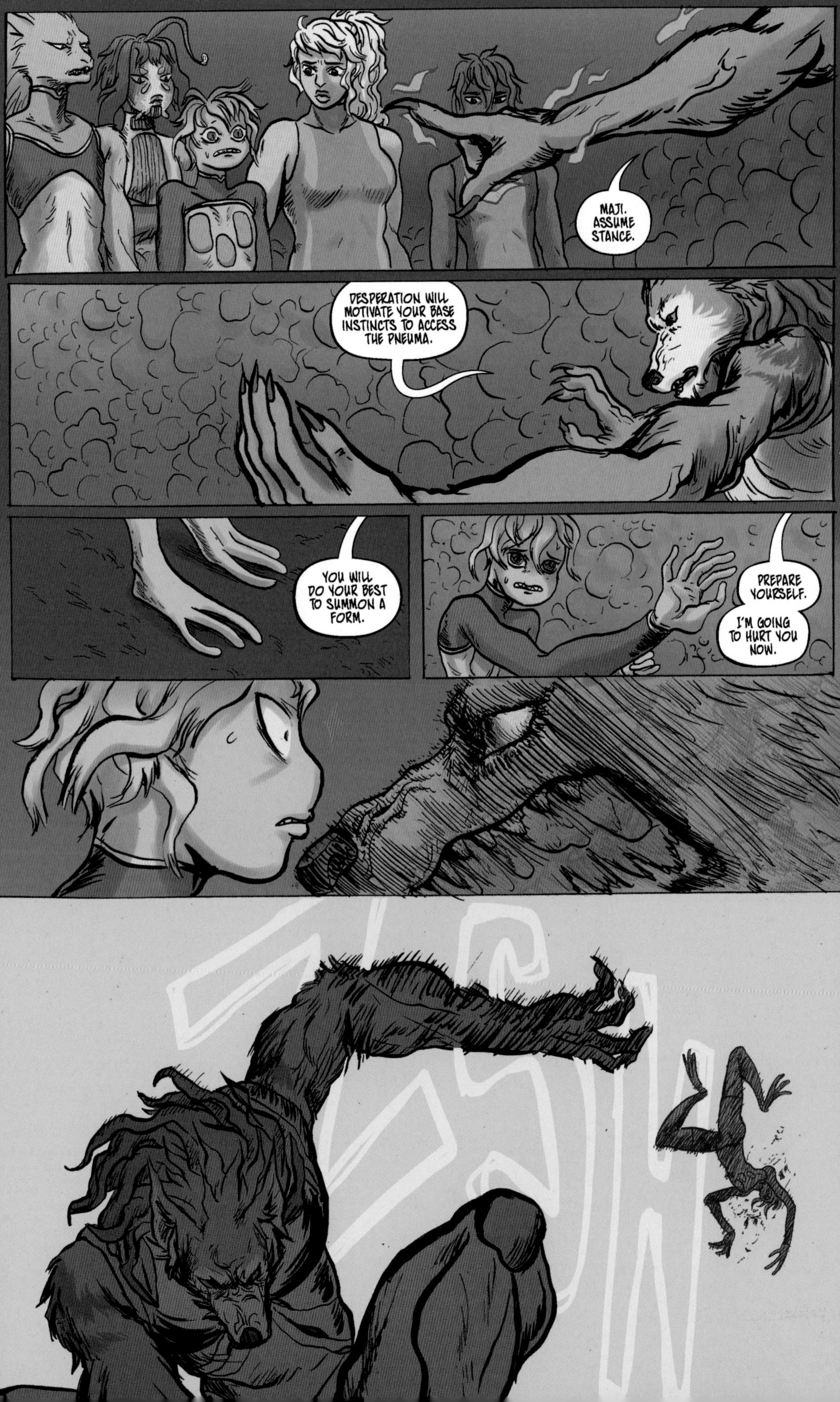
MAJI. ASSUME STANCE.
DESPERATION WILL MOTIVATE YOUR BASE INSTINCTS TO ACCESS THE PNEUMA.
YOU WILL DO YOUR BEST TO SUMMON A FORM.
PREPARE YOURSELF.
I'M GOING TO HURT YOU NOW.
FWSH

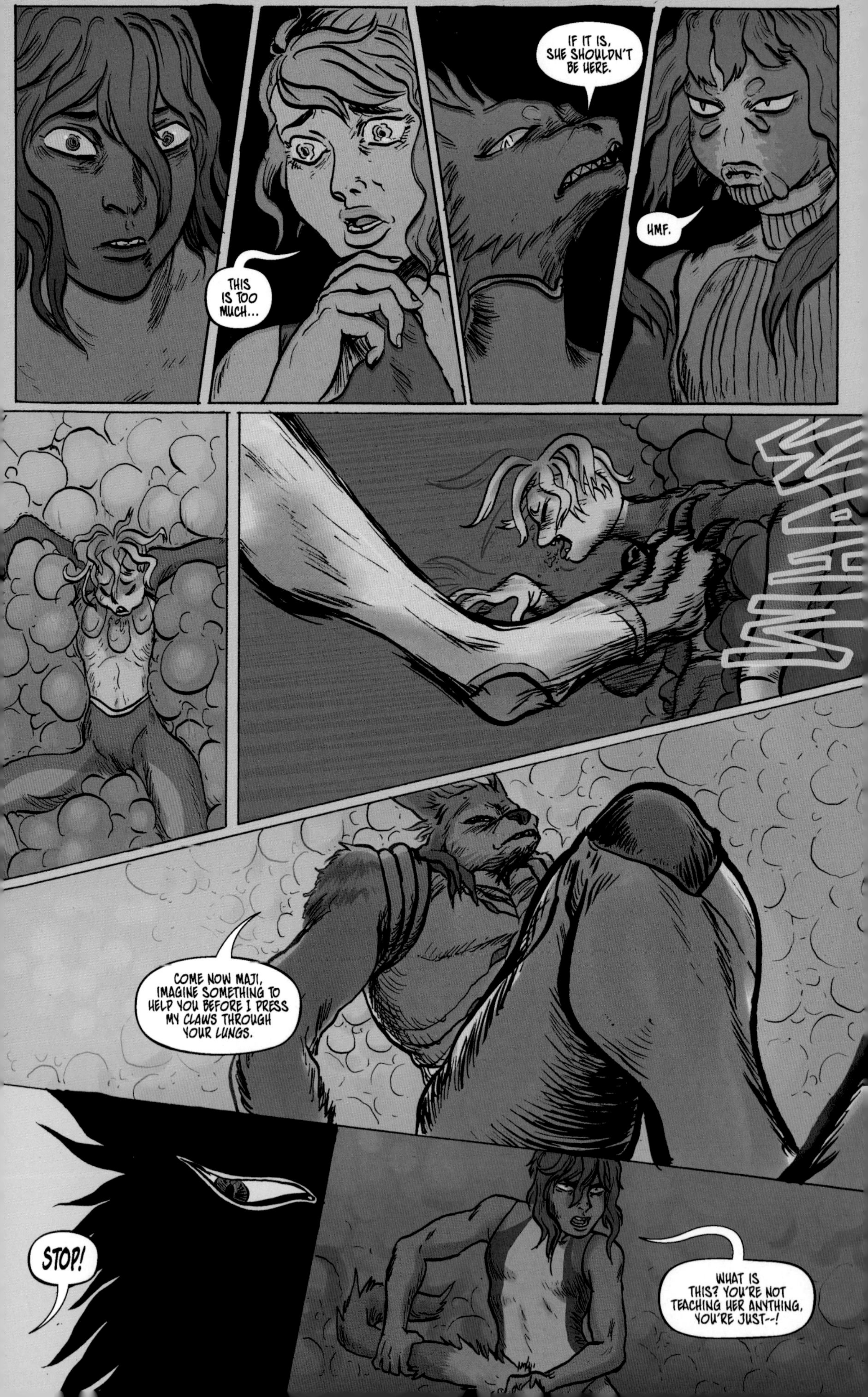
THIS IS TOO MUCH...
IF IT IS, SHE SHOULDN'T BE HERE.
UMF.
COME NOW MAJI, IMAGINE SOMETHING TO HELP YOU BEFORE I PRESS MY *CLAWS* THROUGH YOUR *LUNGS.*
STOP!
WHAT IS THIS? YOU'RE NOT TEACHING HER ANYTHING, YOU'RE JUST--!

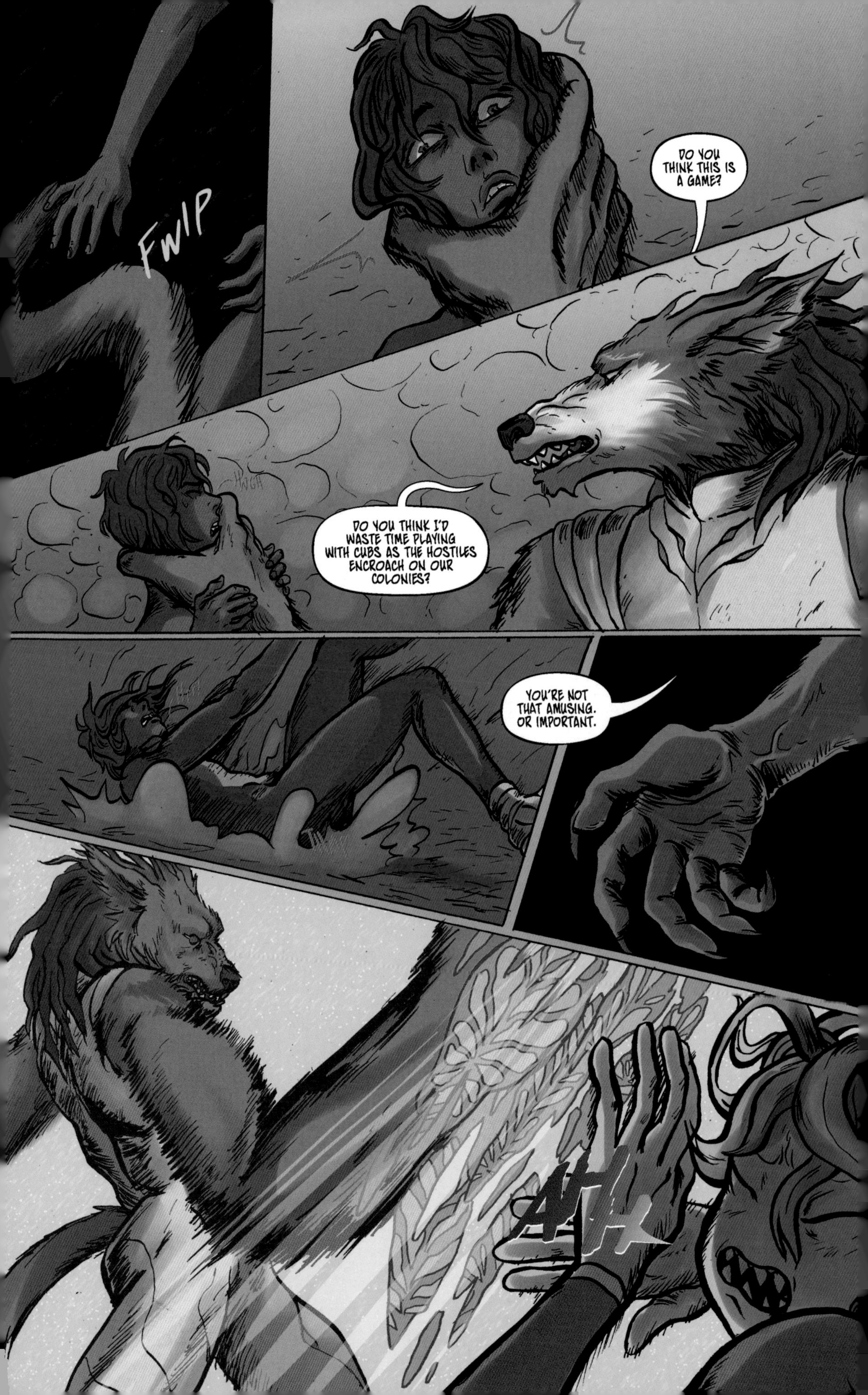
FWIP
DO YOU THINK THIS IS A GAME?
HNGH
DO YOU THINK I'D WASTE TIME PLAYING WITH CUBS AS THE HOSTILES ENCROACH ON OUR COLONIES?
YOU'RE NOT THAT AMUSING. OR IMPORTANT.
AHH

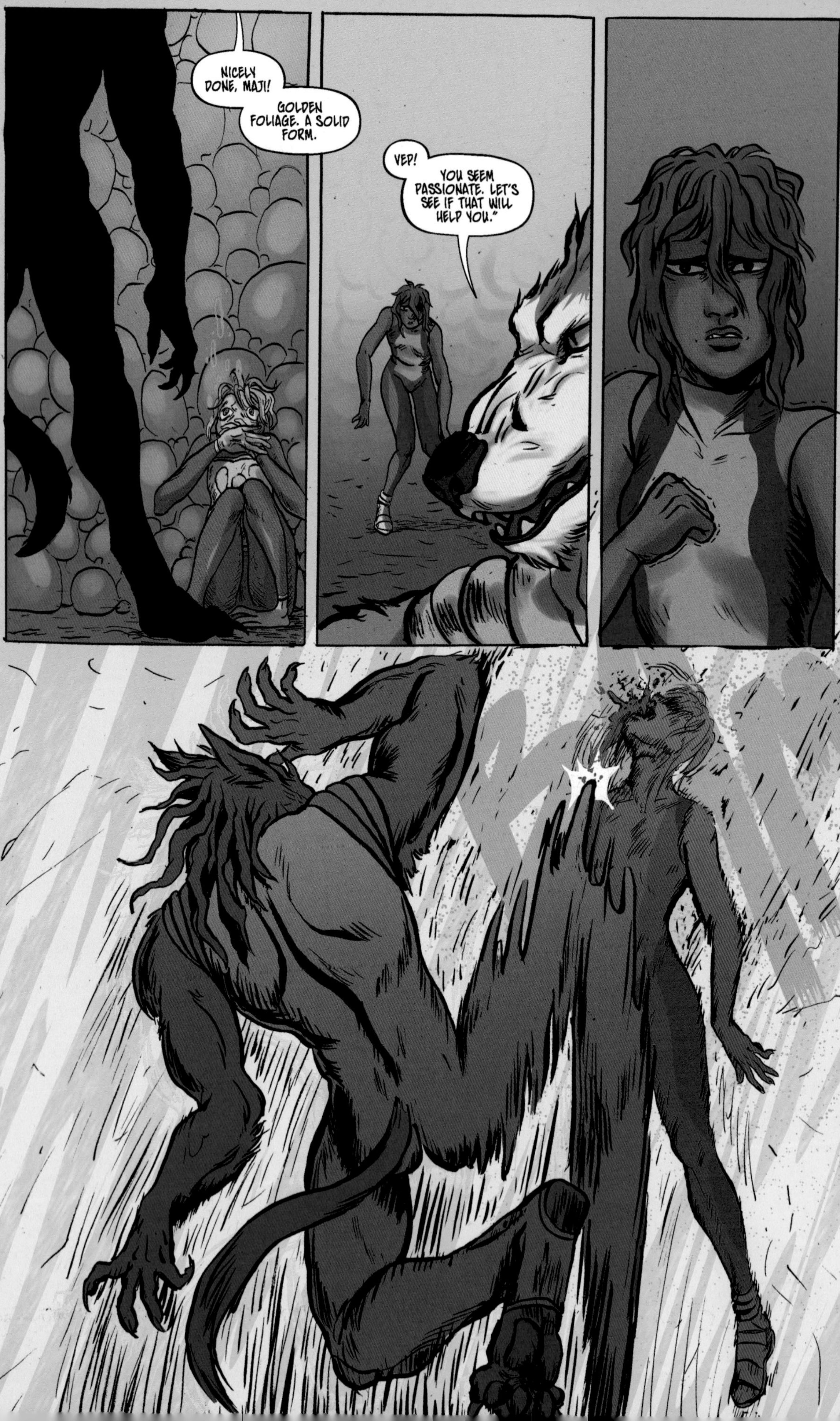
NICELY DONE, MAJI!
GOLDEN FOLIAGE. A SOLID FORM.
YEP!
YOU SEEM PASSIONATE. LET'S SEE IF THAT WILL HELP YOU."

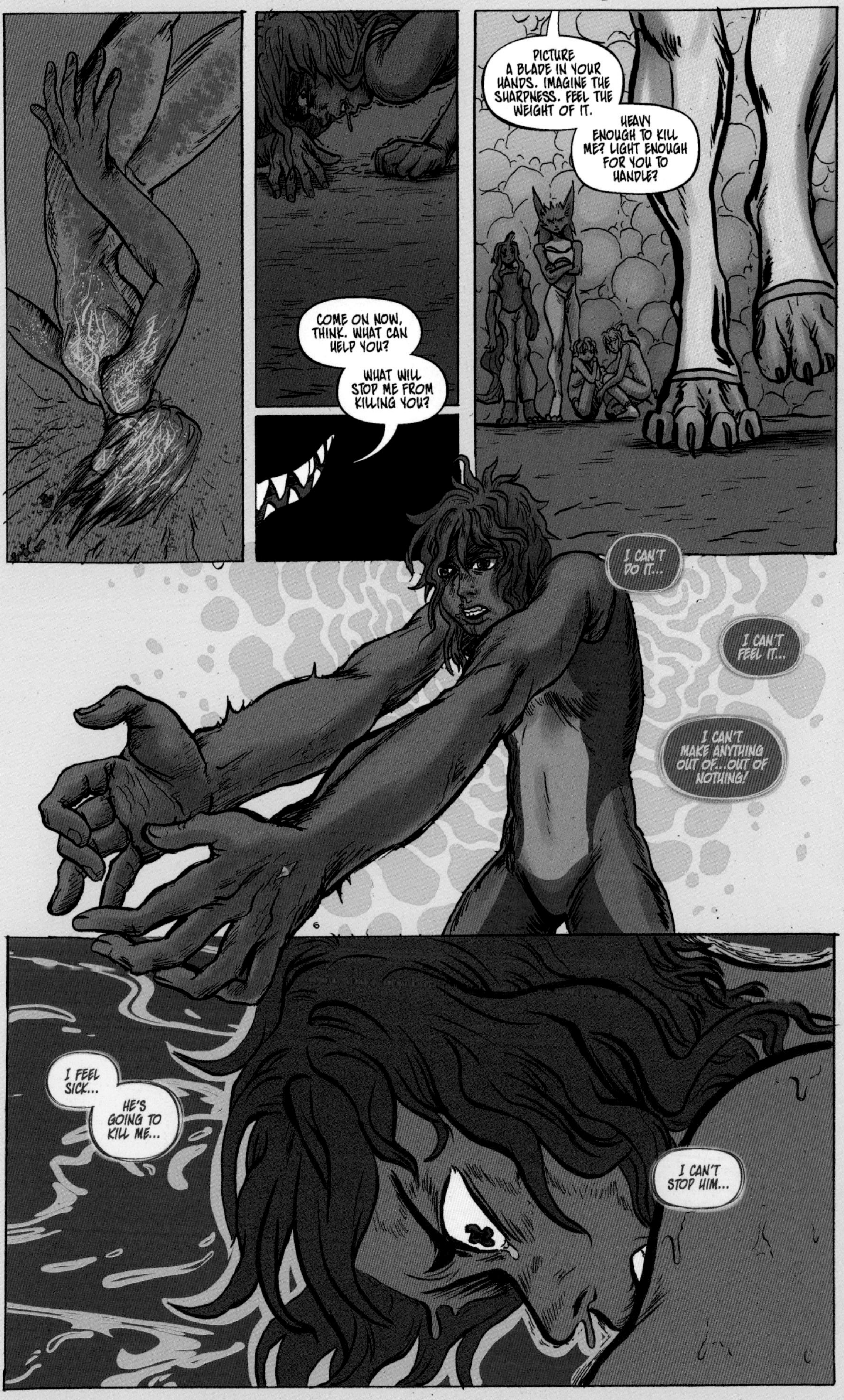
COME ON NOW, THINK. WHAT CAN HELP YOU?
WHAT WILL STOP ME FROM KILLING YOU?
PICTURE A BLADE IN YOUR HANDS. IMAGINE THE SHARPNESS. FEEL THE WEIGHT OF IT.
HEAVY ENOUGH TO KILL ME? LIGHT ENOUGH FOR YOU TO HANDLE?
I CAN'T DO IT...
I CAN'T FEEL IT...
I CAN'T MAKE ANYTHING OUT OF...OUT OF NOTHING!
I FEEL SICK...
HE'S GOING TO KILL ME...
I CAN'T STOP HIM...

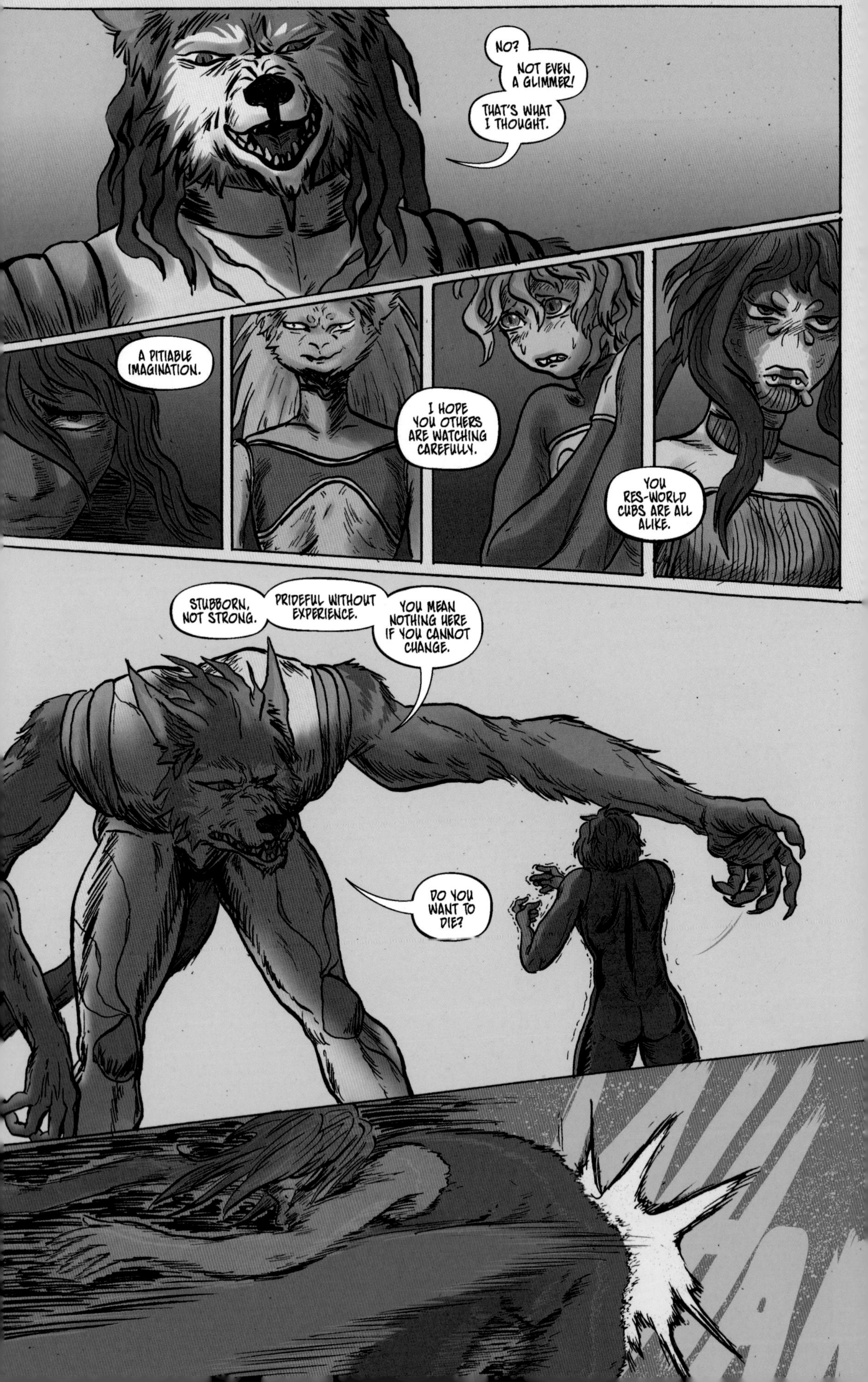
NO?
NOT EVEN A GLIMMER!
THAT'S WHAT I THOUGHT.
A PITIABLE IMAGINATION.
I HOPE YOU OTHERS ARE WATCHING CAREFULLY.
YOU RES-WORLD CUBS ARE ALL ALIKE.
STUBBORN, NOT STRONG.
PRIDEFUL WITHOUT EXPERIENCE.
YOU MEAN NOTHING HERE IF YOU CANNOT CHANGE.
DO YOU WANT TO DIE?

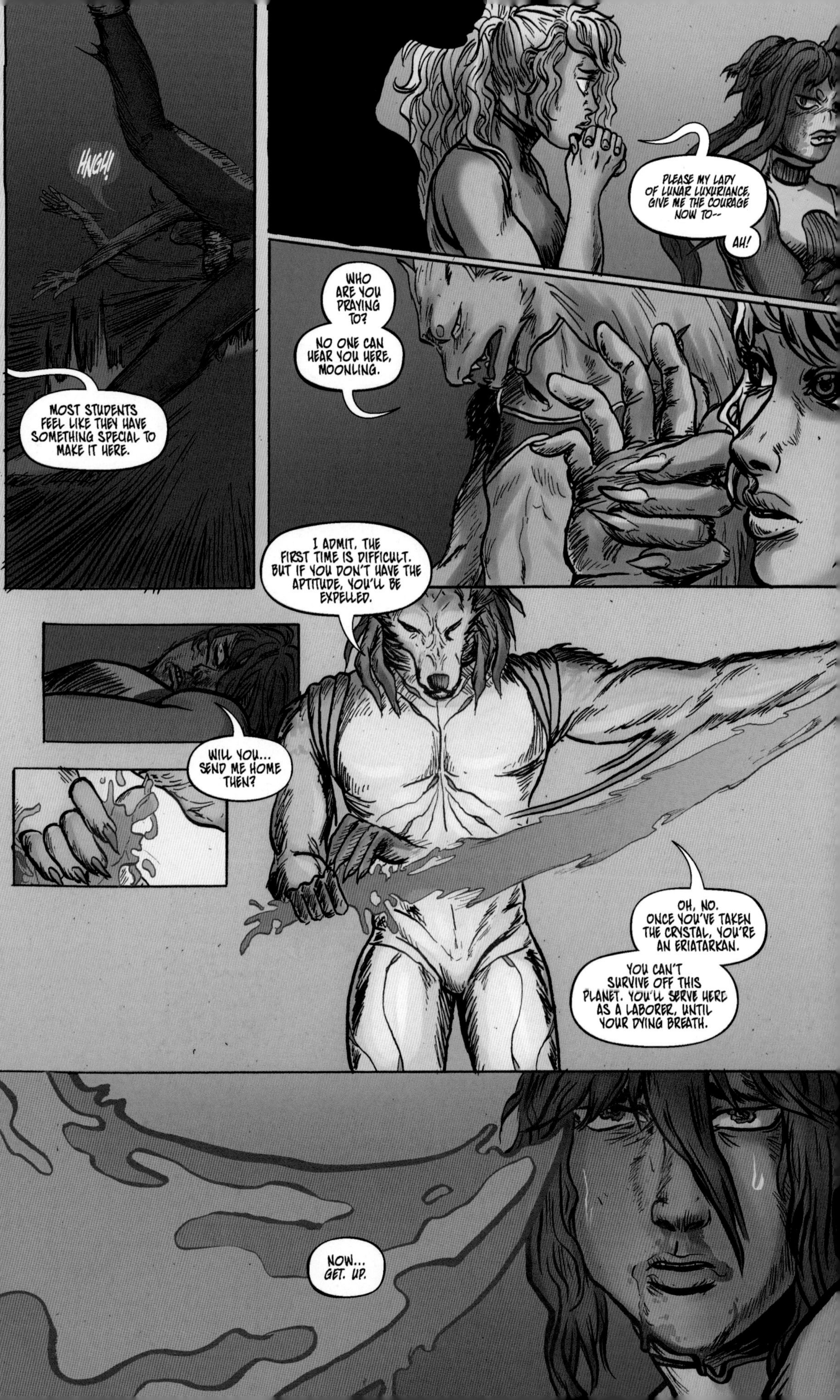
HNGH!
PLEASE MY LADY OF LUNAR LUXURIANCE, GIVE ME THE COURAGE NOW TO--
AH!
MOST STUDENTS FEEL LIKE THEY HAVE SOMETHING SPECIAL TO MAKE IT HERE.
WHO ARE YOU PRAYING TO?
NO ONE CAN HEAR YOU HERE, MOONLING.
I ADMIT, THE FIRST TIME IS DIFFICULT. BUT IF YOU DON'T HAVE THE APTITUDE, YOU'LL BE EXPELLED.
WILL YOU... SEND ME HOME THEN?
OH, NO. ONCE YOU'VE TAKEN THE CRYSTAL, YOU'RE AN ERIATARKAN.
YOU CAN'T SURVIVE OFF THIS PLANET. YOU'LL SERVE HERE AS A LABORER, UNTIL YOUR DYING BREATH.
NOW... GET. UP.

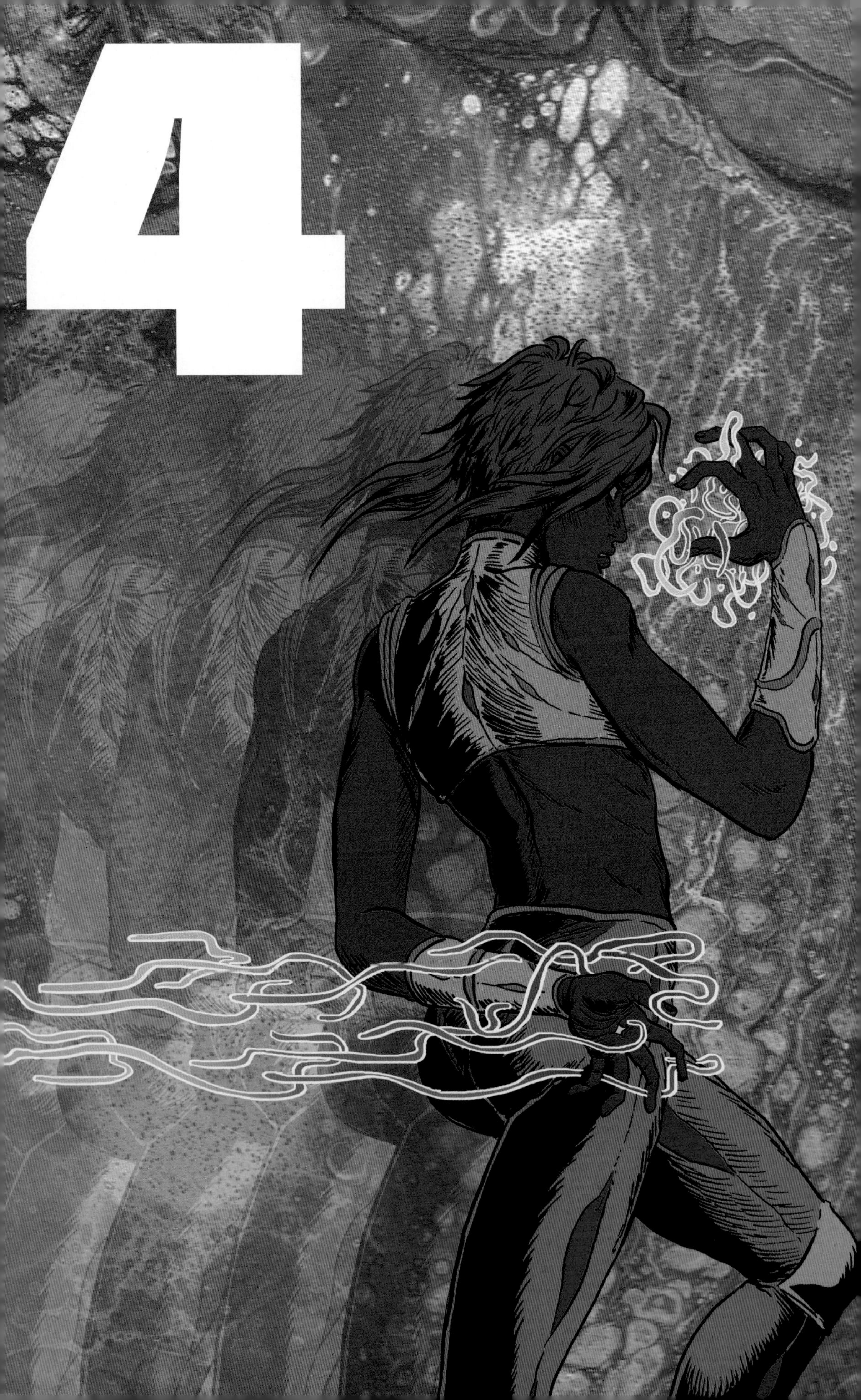
4

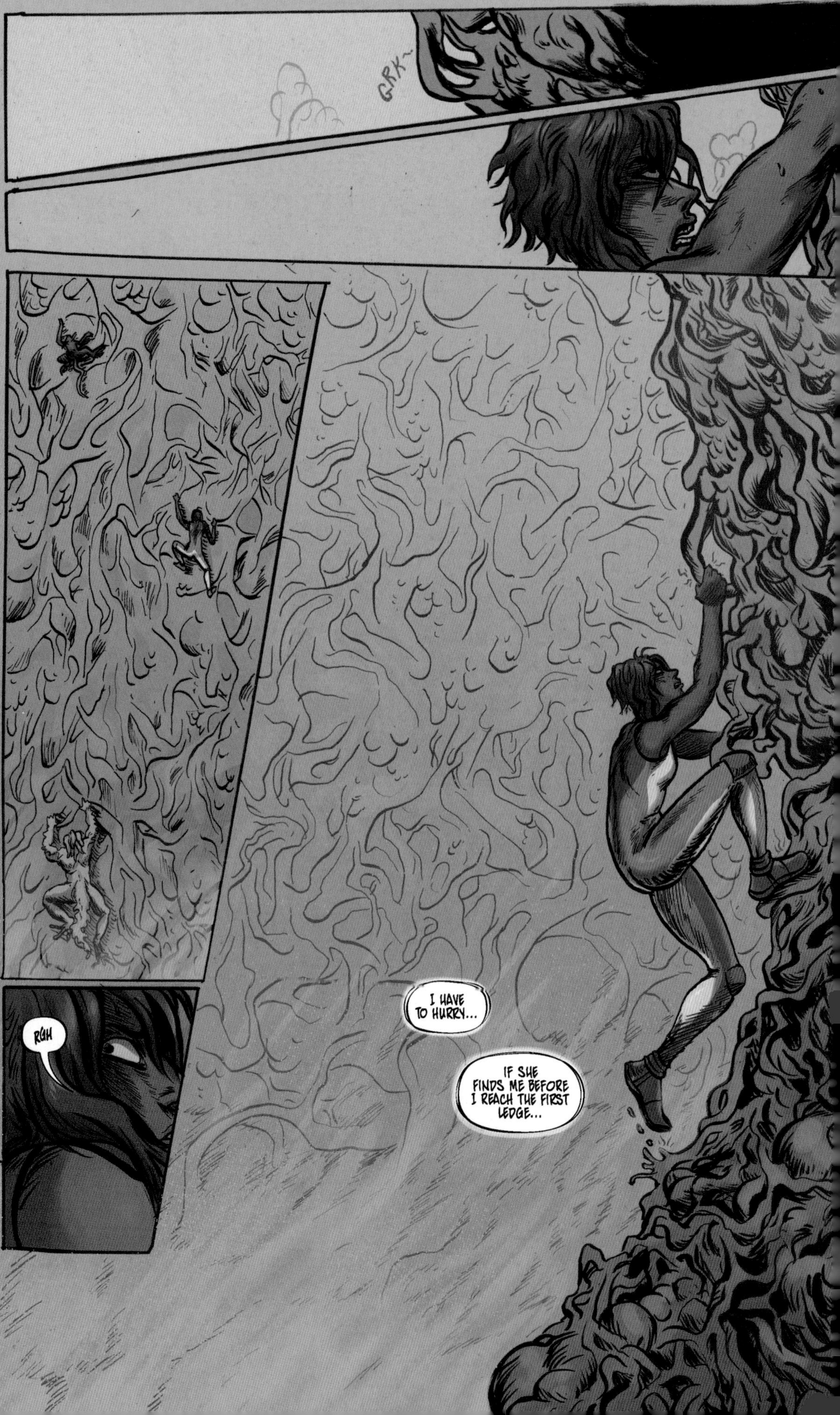
GRK~
RGH
I HAVE TO HURRY...
IF SHE FINDS ME BEFORE I REACH THE FIRST LEDGE...

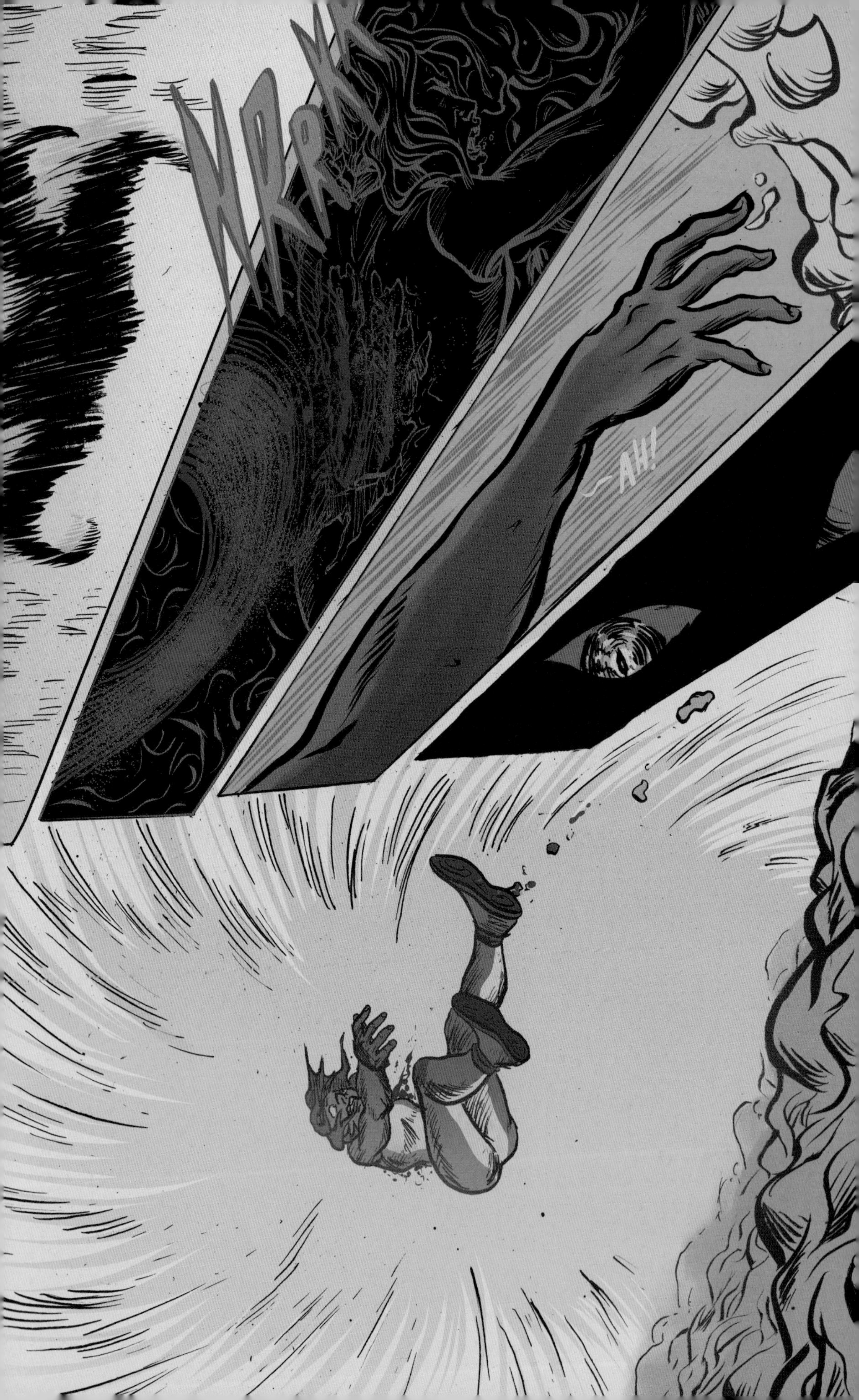
—AH!

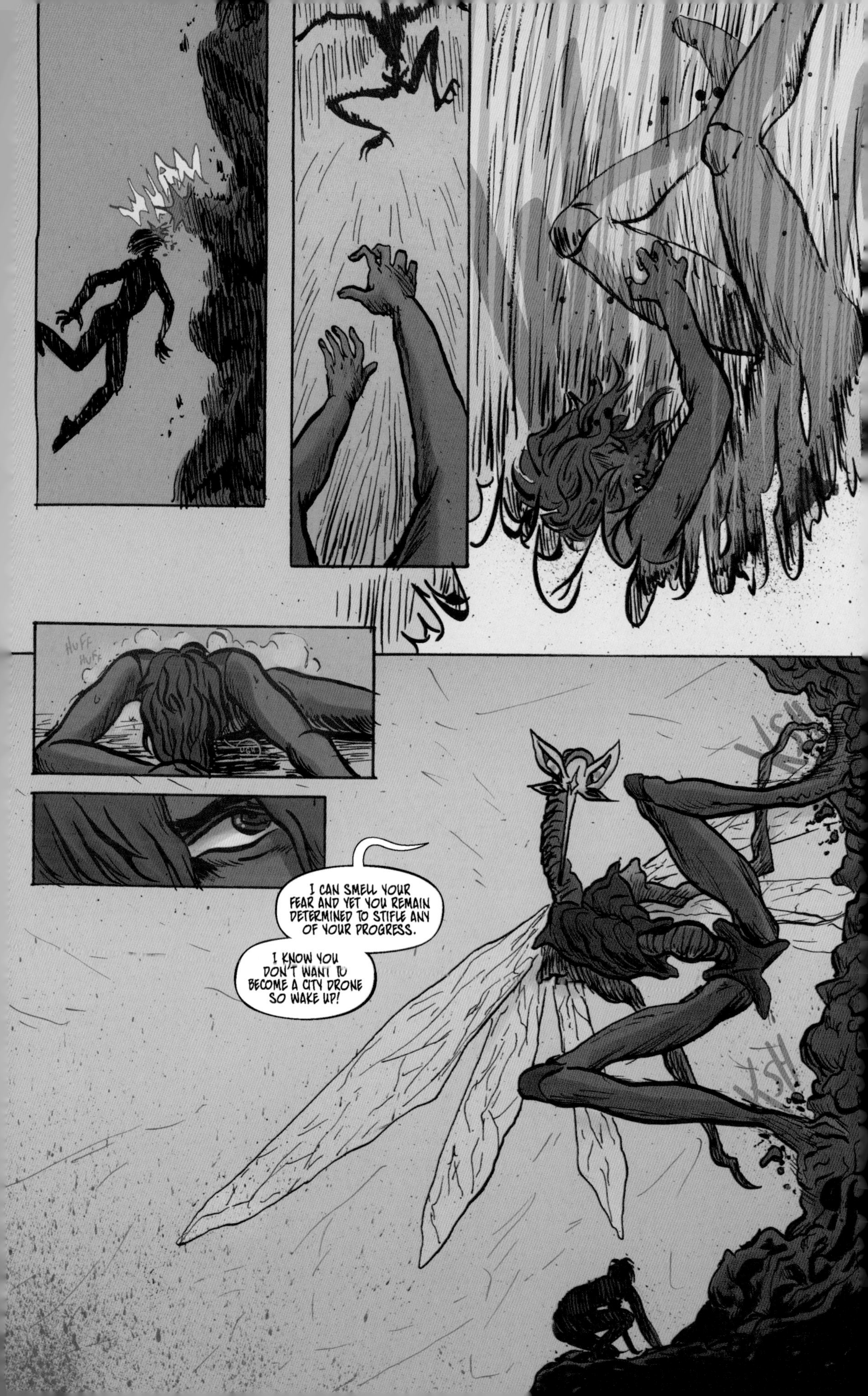
WUMM
HUFF HUFF
I CAN SMELL YOUR FEAR AND YET YOU REMAIN DETERMINED TO STIFLE ANY OF YOUR PROGRESS.
I KNOW YOU DON'T WANT TO BECOME A CITY DRONE SO WAKE UP!
KSH
KSH

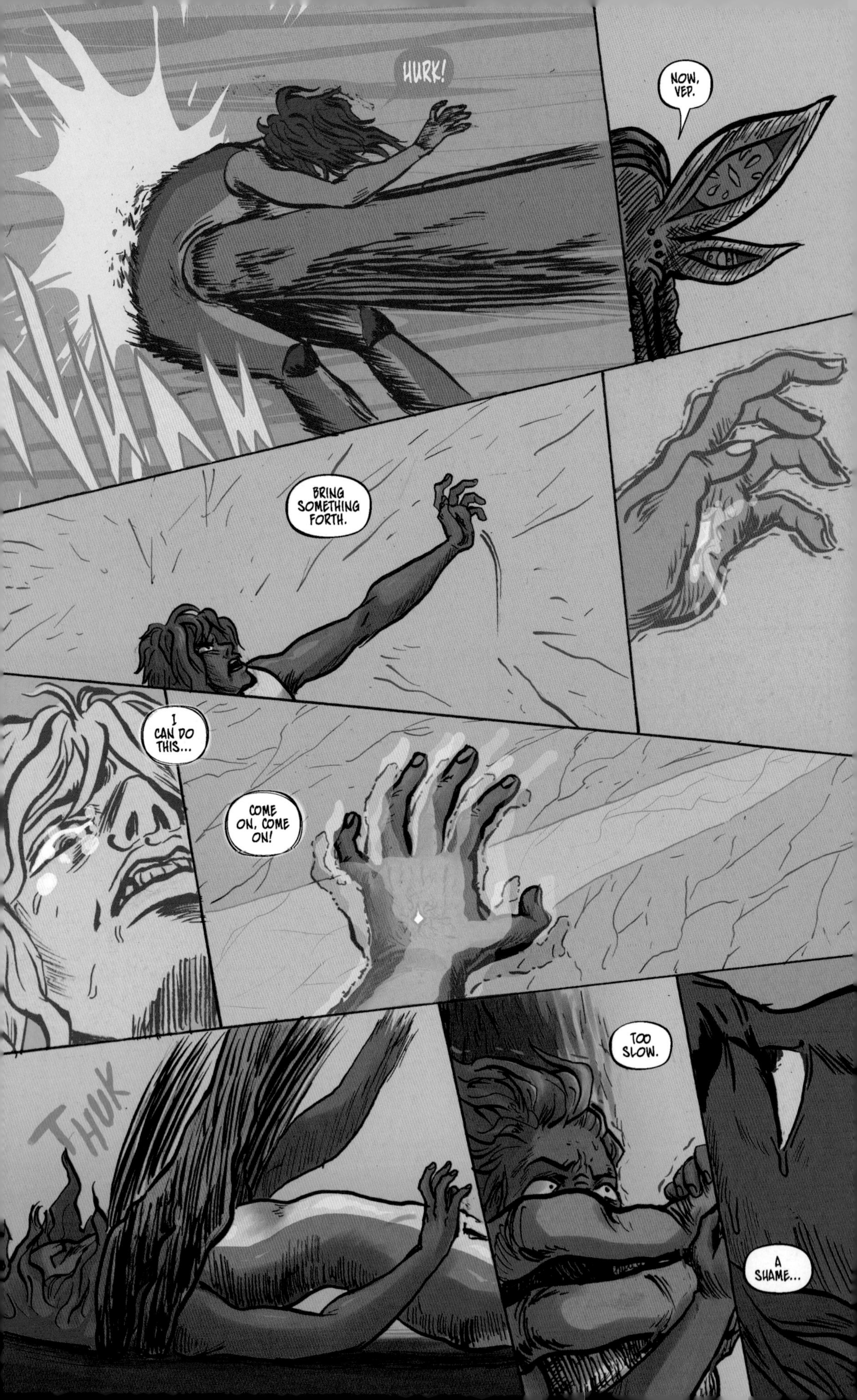

HURK!
NOW, VEP.
BRING SOMETHING FORTH.
I CAN DO THIS...
COME ON, COME ON!
THUK
TOO SLOW.
A SHAME...

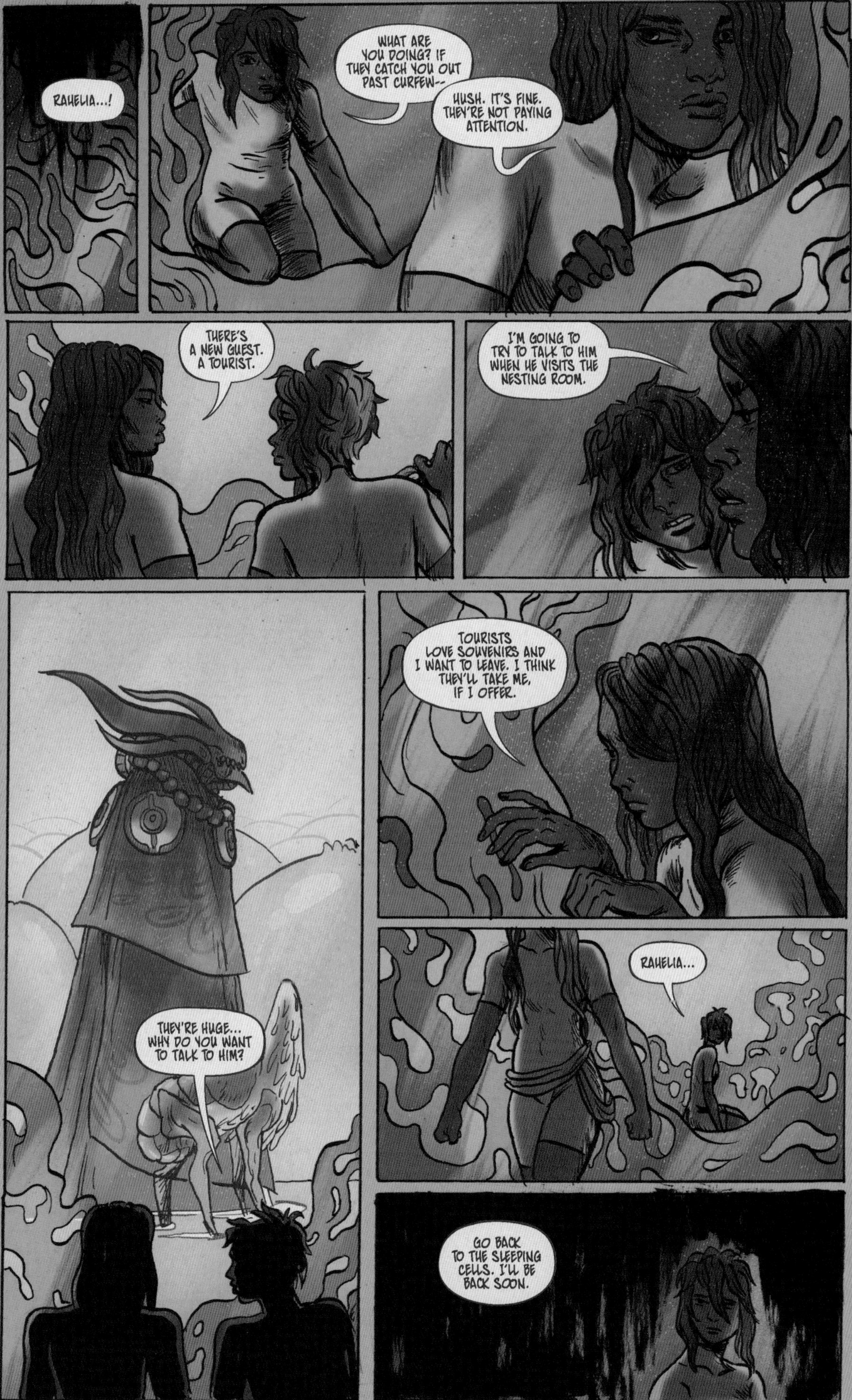
RAHELIA...!
WHAT ARE YOU DOING? IF THEY CATCH YOU OUT PAST CURFEW--
HUSH. IT'S FINE. THEY'RE NOT PAYING ATTENTION.
THERE'S A NEW GUEST. A TOURIST.
I'M GOING TO TRY TO TALK TO HIM WHEN HE VISITS THE NESTING ROOM.
THEY'RE HUGE... WHY DO YOU WANT TO TALK TO HIM?
TOURISTS LOVE SOUVENIRS AND I WANT TO LEAVE. I THINK THEY'LL TAKE ME, IF I OFFER.
RAHELIA...
GO BACK TO THE SLEEPING CELLS. I'LL BE BACK SOON.

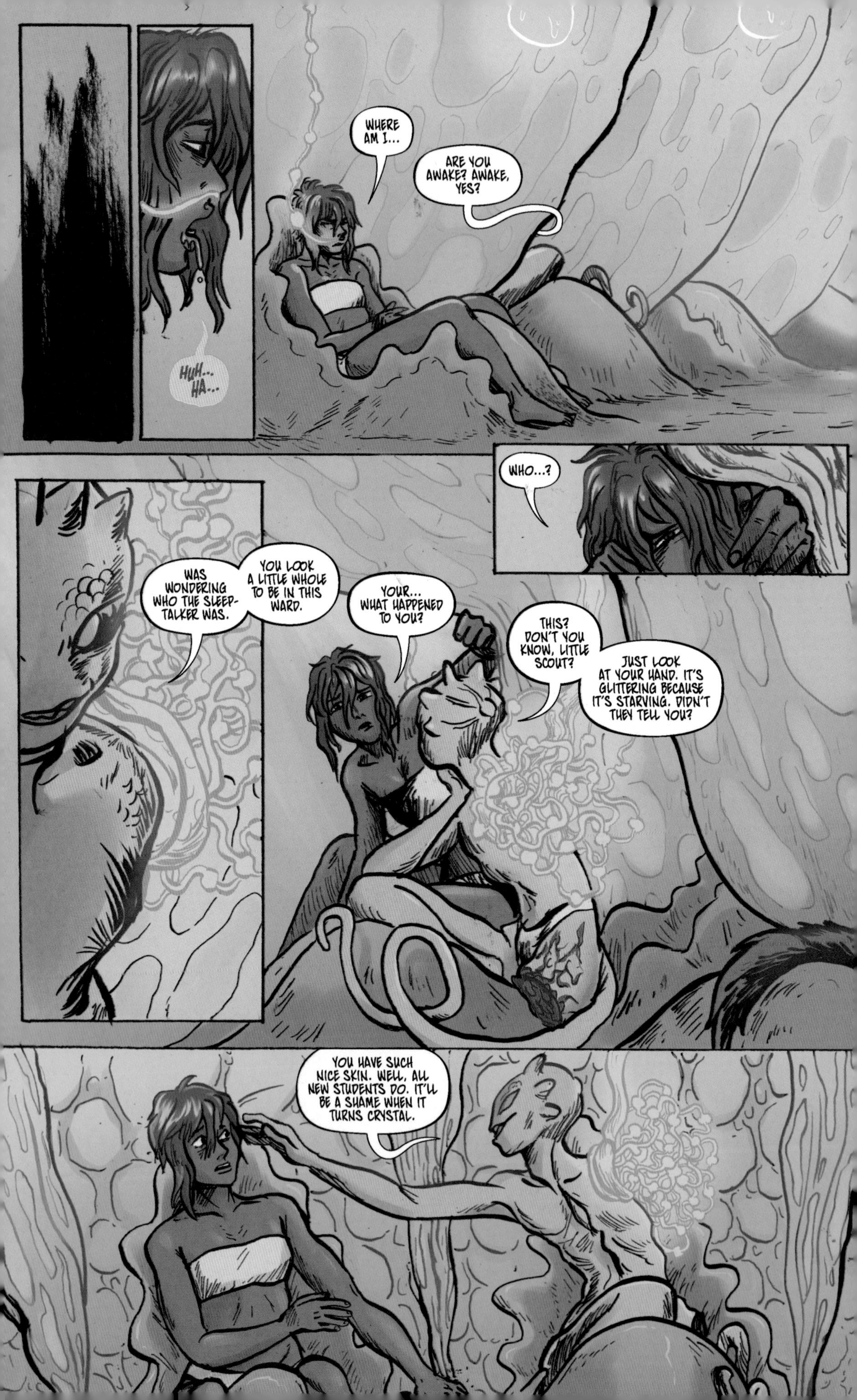
HUH... HA...
WHERE AM I...
ARE YOU AWAKE? AWAKE, YES?
WHO...?
WAS WONDERING WHO THE SLEEP-TALKER WAS.
YOU LOOK A LITTLE WHOLE TO BE IN THIS WARD.
YOUR... WHAT HAPPENED TO YOU?
THIS? DON'T YOU KNOW, LITTLE SCOUT?
JUST LOOK AT YOUR HAND. IT'S GLITTERING BECAUSE IT'S STARVING. DIDN'T THEY TELL YOU?
YOU HAVE SUCH NICE SKIN. WELL, ALL NEW STUDENTS DO. IT'LL BE A SHAME WHEN IT TURNS CRYSTAL.

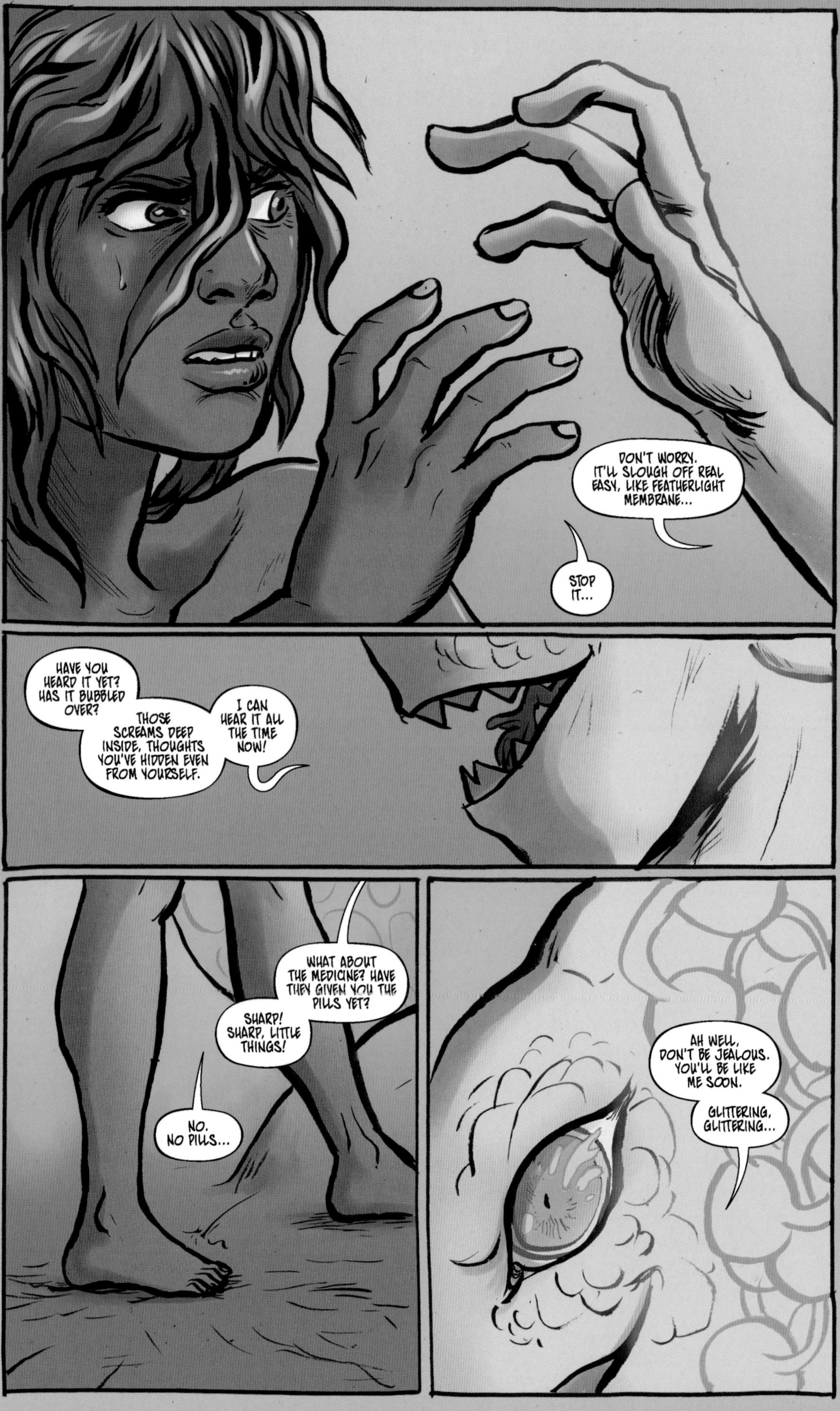
DON'T WORRY. IT'LL SLOUGH OFF REAL EASY, LIKE FEATHERLIGHT MEMBRANE...
STOP IT...
HAVE YOU HEARD IT YET? HAS IT BUBBLED OVER?
THOSE SCREAMS DEEP INSIDE, THOUGHTS YOU'VE HIDDEN EVEN FROM YOURSELF.
I CAN HEAR IT ALL THE TIME NOW!
WHAT ABOUT THE MEDICINE? HAVE THEY GIVEN YOU THE PILLS YET?
SHARP! SHARP, LITTLE THINGS!
NO. NO PILLS...
AH WELL, DON'T BE JEALOUS. YOU'LL BE LIKE ME SOON.
GLITTERING, GLITTERING...

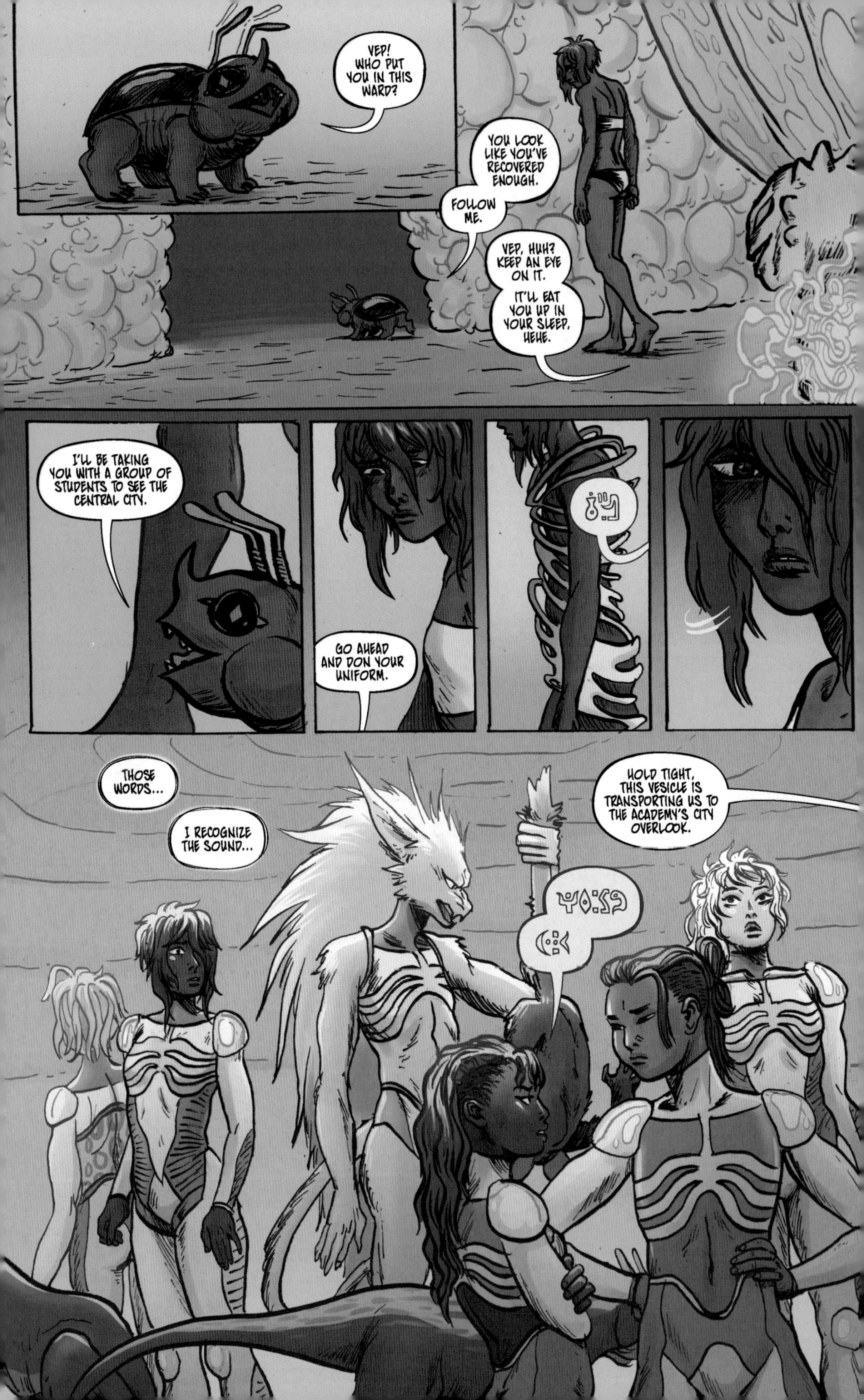
VEP! WHO PUT YOU IN THIS WARD?
YOU LOOK LIKE YOU'VE RECOVERED ENOUGH.
FOLLOW ME.
VEP, HUH? KEEP AN EYE ON IT.
IT'LL EAT YOU UP IN YOUR SLEEP, HEHE.
I'LL BE TAKING YOU WITH A GROUP OF STUDENTS TO SEE THE CENTRAL CITY.
GO AHEAD AND DON YOUR UNIFORM.
THOSE WORDS...
I RECOGNIZE THE SOUND...
HOLD TIGHT, THIS VESICLE IS TRANSPORTING US TO THE ACADEMY'S CITY OVERLOOK.

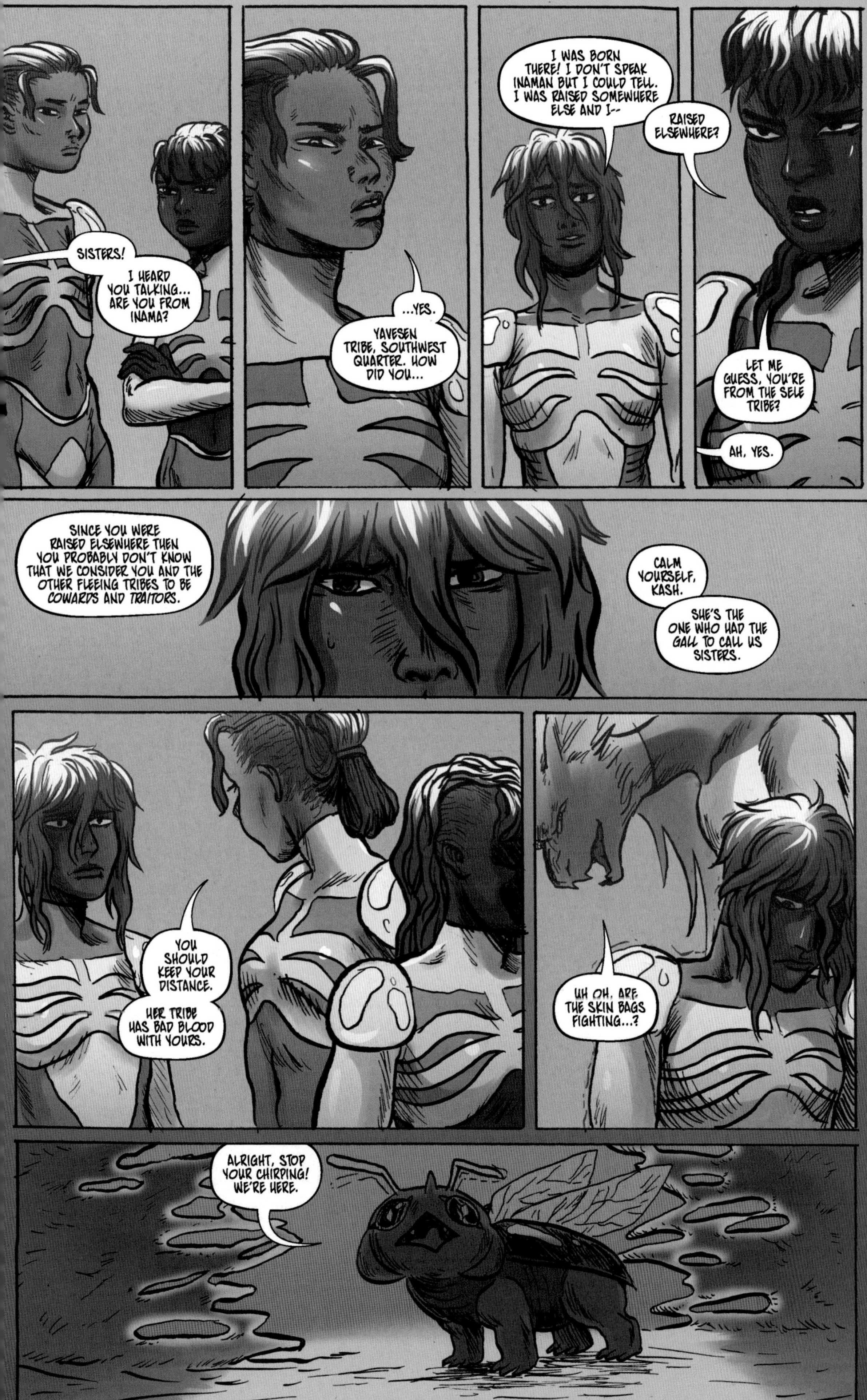
SISTERS!
I HEARD YOU TALKING... ARE YOU FROM INAMA?
...YES.
YAVESEN TRIBE, SOUTHWEST QUARTER. HOW DID YOU...
I WAS BORN THERE! I DON'T SPEAK INAMAN BUT I COULD TELL. I WAS RAISED SOMEWHERE ELSE AND I--
RAISED ELSEWHERE?
LET ME GUESS, YOU'RE FROM THE SELE TRIBE?
AH, YES.
SINCE YOU WERE RAISED ELSEWHERE THEN YOU PROBABLY DON'T KNOW THAT WE CONSIDER YOU AND THE OTHER FLEEING TRIBES TO BE COWARDS AND TRAITORS.
CALM YOURSELF, KASH.
SHE'S THE ONE WHO HAD THE GALL TO CALL US SISTERS.
YOU SHOULD KEEP YOUR DISTANCE.
HER TRIBE HAS BAD BLOOD WITH YOURS.
UH OH. ARE THE SKIN BAGS FIGHTING...?
ALRIGHT, STOP YOUR CHIRPING! WE'RE HERE.

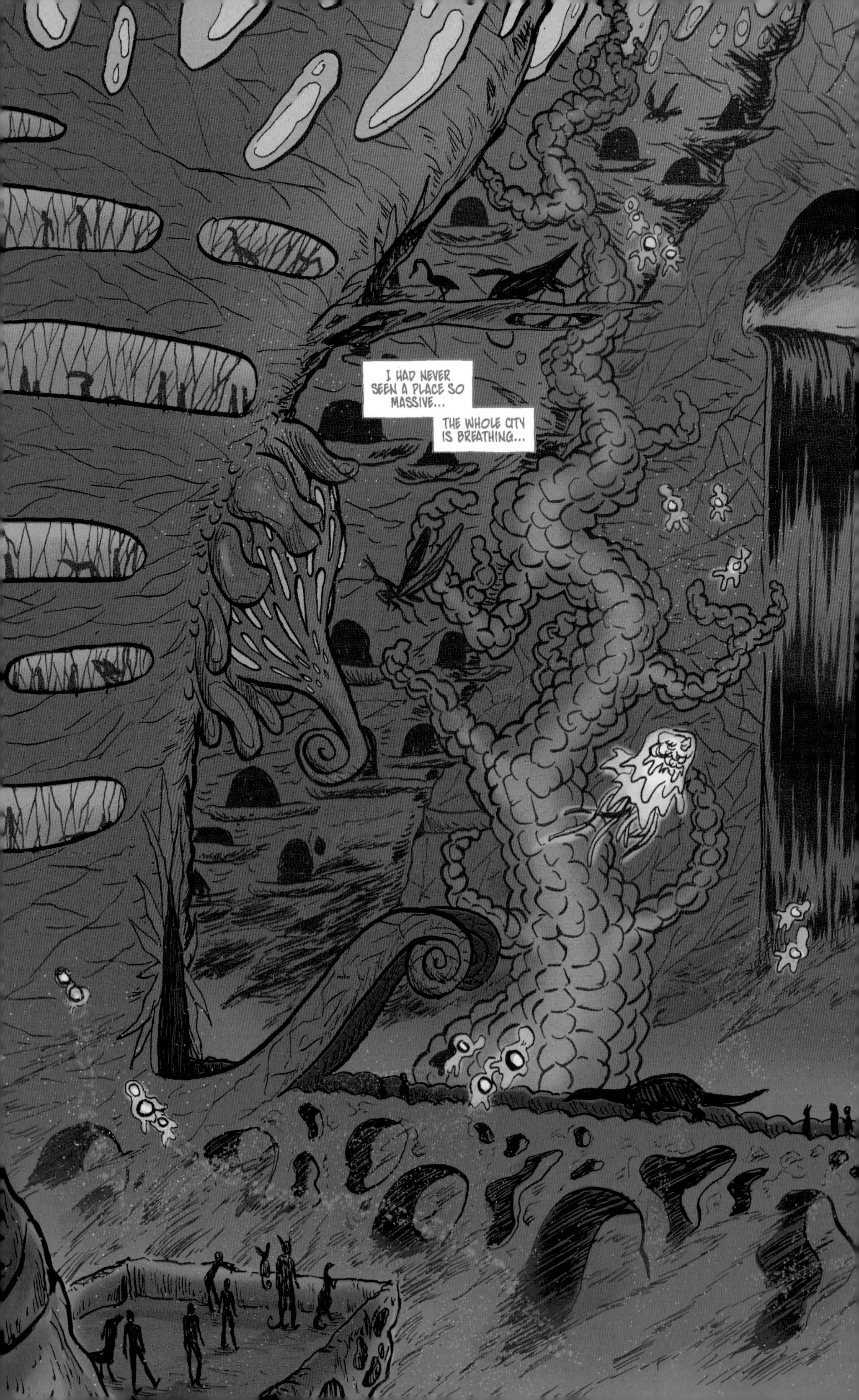
I HAD NEVER SEEN A PLACE SO MASSIVE...
THE WHOLE CITY IS BREATHING...

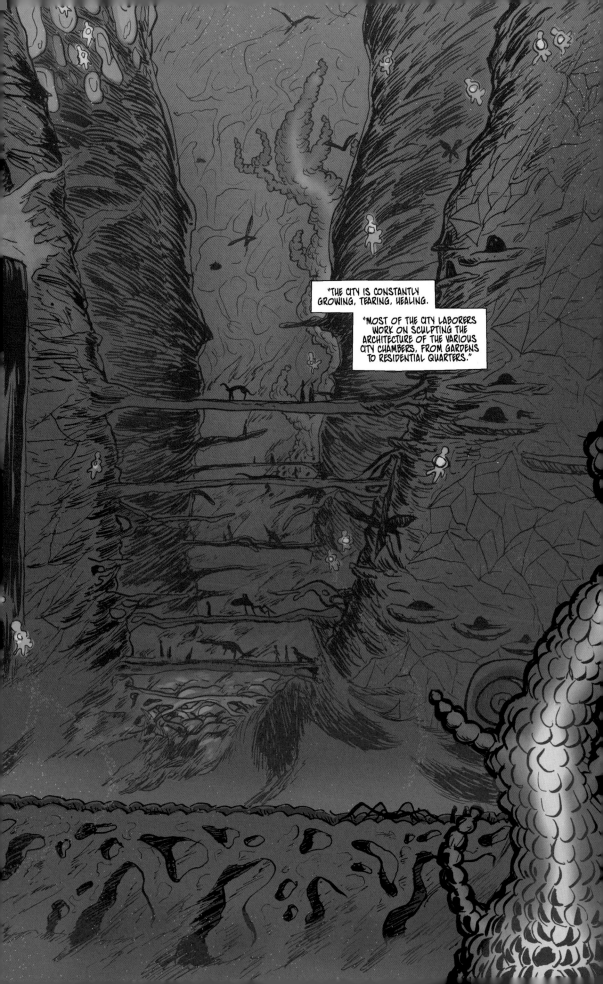

"THE CITY IS CONSTANTLY GROWING, TEARING, HEALING.

"MOST OF THE CITY LABORERS WORK ON SCULPTING THE ARCHITECTURE OF THE VARIOUS CITY CHAMBERS, FROM GARDENS TO RESIDENTIAL QUARTERS."

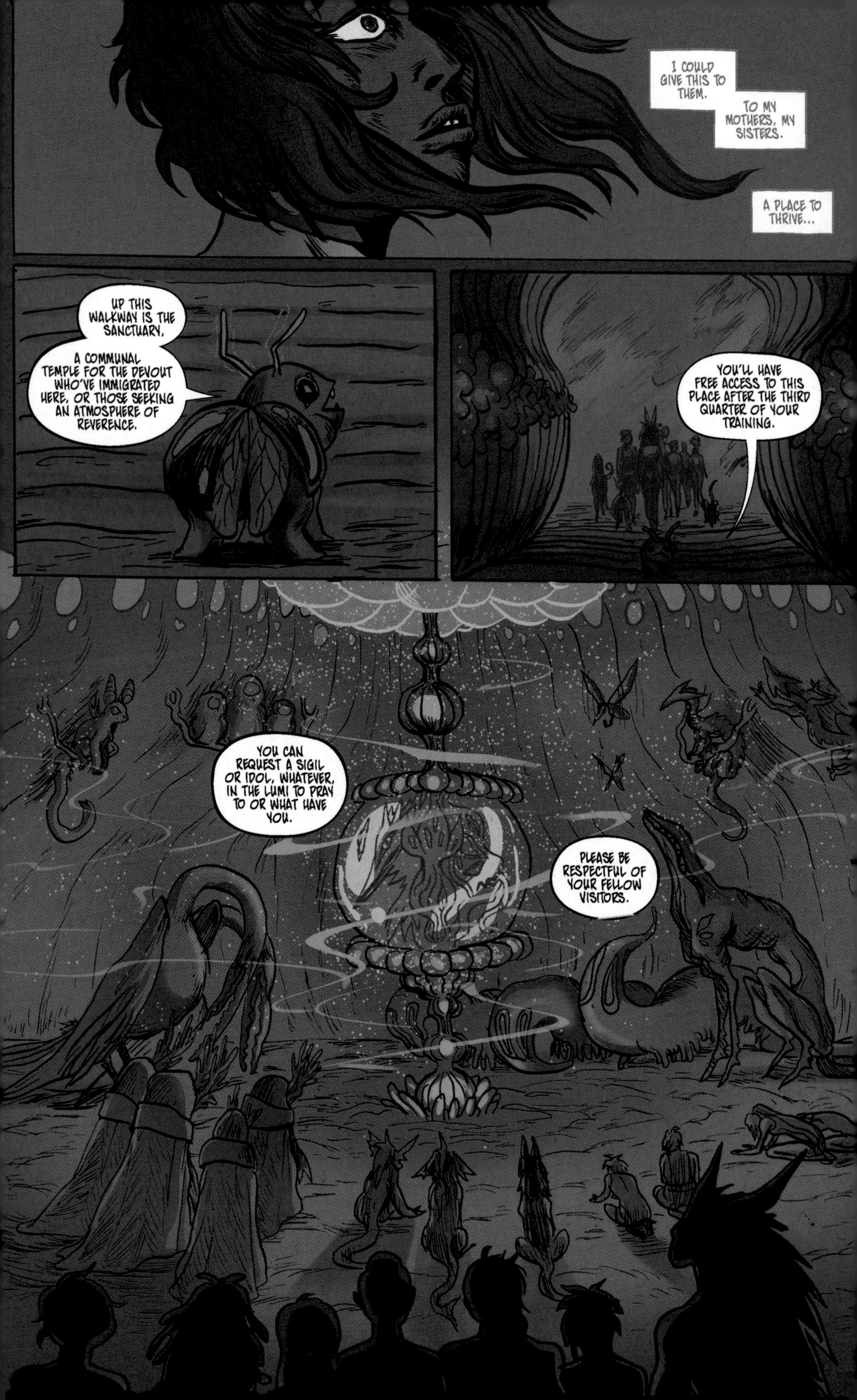
I COULD GIVE THIS TO THEM.
TO MY MOTHERS, MY SISTERS.
A PLACE TO THRIVE...
UP THIS WALKWAY IS THE SANCTUARY,
A COMMUNAL TEMPLE FOR THE DEVOUT WHO'VE IMMIGRATED HERE, OR THOSE SEEKING AN ATMOSPHERE OF REVERENCE.
YOU'LL HAVE FREE ACCESS TO THIS PLACE AFTER THE THIRD QUARTER OF YOUR TRAINING.
YOU CAN REQUEST A SIGIL OR IDOL, WHATEVER, IN THE LUMI TO PRAY TO OR WHAT HAVE YOU.
PLEASE BE RESPECTFUL OF YOUR FELLOW VISITORS.

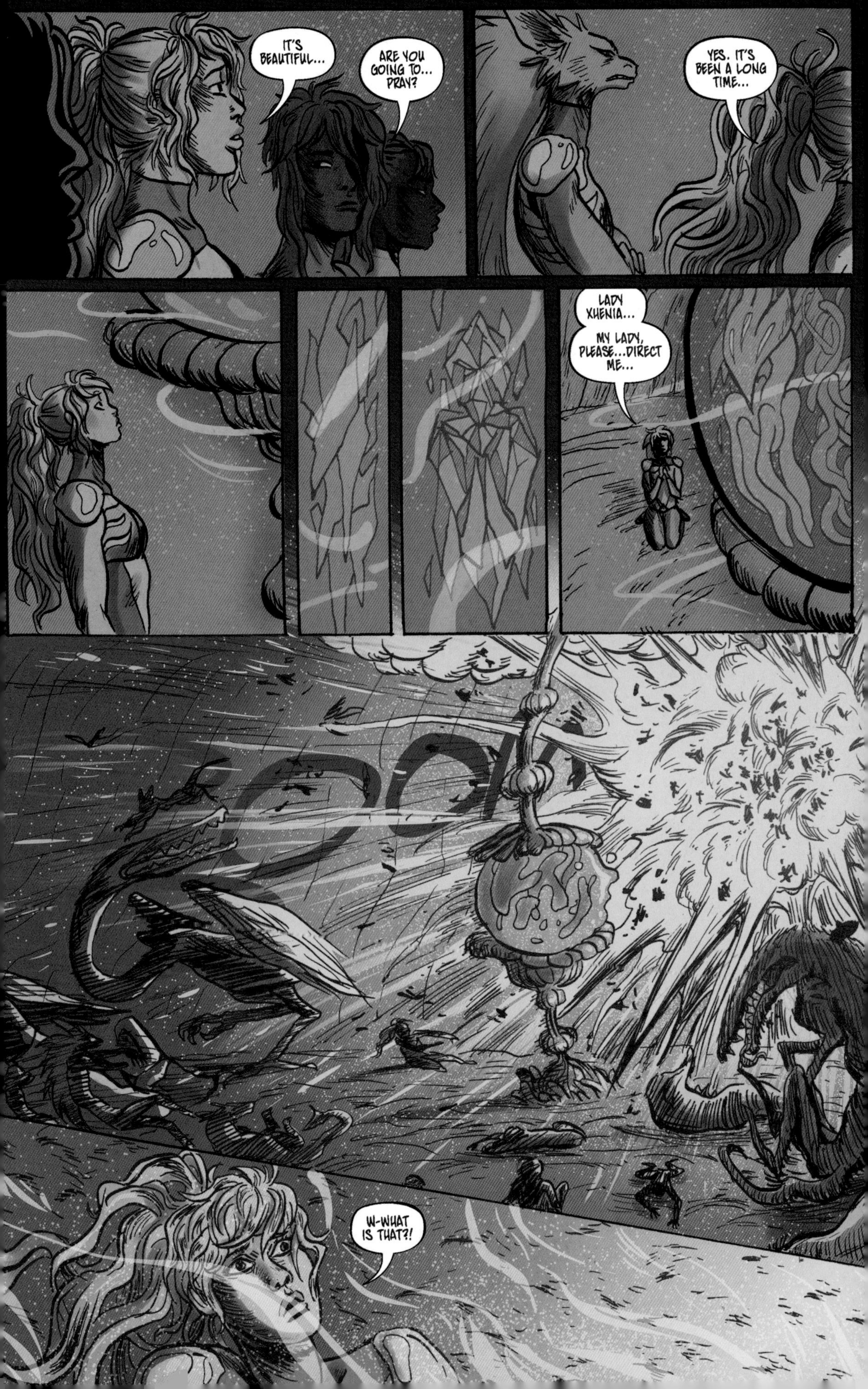
IT'S BEAUTIFUL...
ARE YOU GOING TO... PRAY?
YES. IT'S BEEN A LONG TIME...
LADY XHENIA...
MY LADY, PLEASE...DIRECT ME...
W-WHAT IS THAT?!

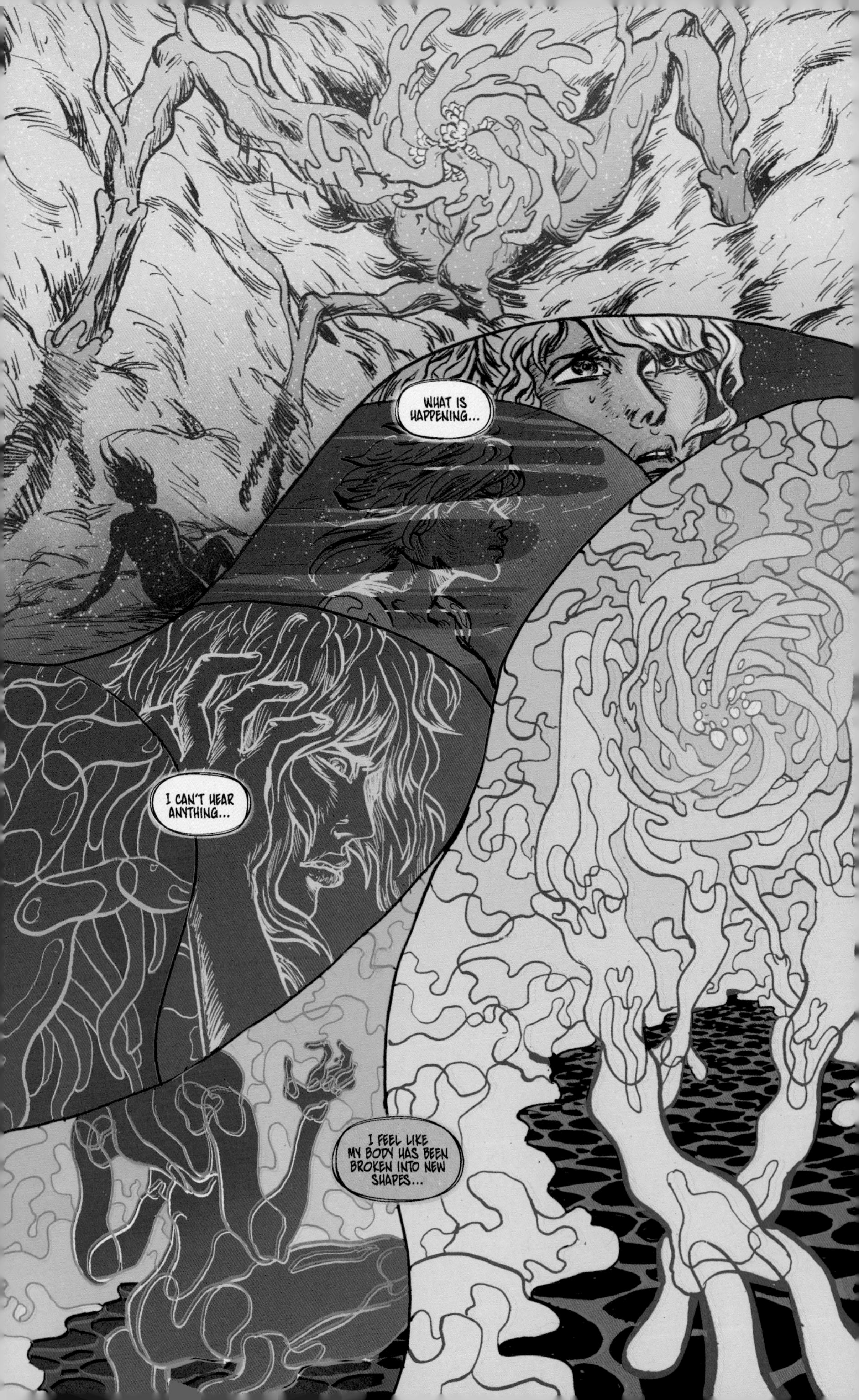
WHAT IS HAPPENING...
I CAN'T HEAR ANYTHING...
I FEEL LIKE MY BODY HAS BEEN BROKEN INTO NEW SHAPES...

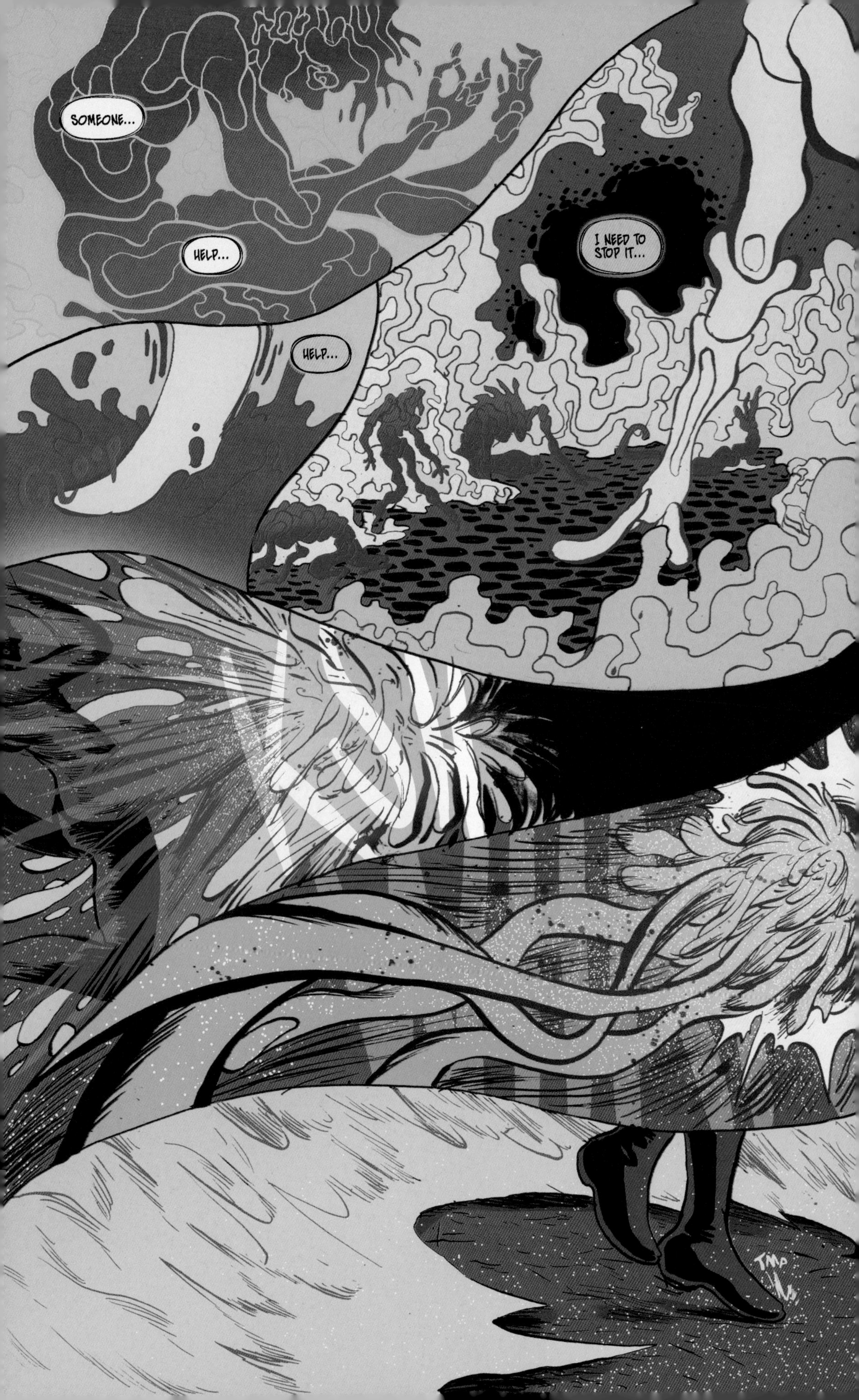
SOMEONE...
HELP...
HELP...
I NEED TO STOP IT...

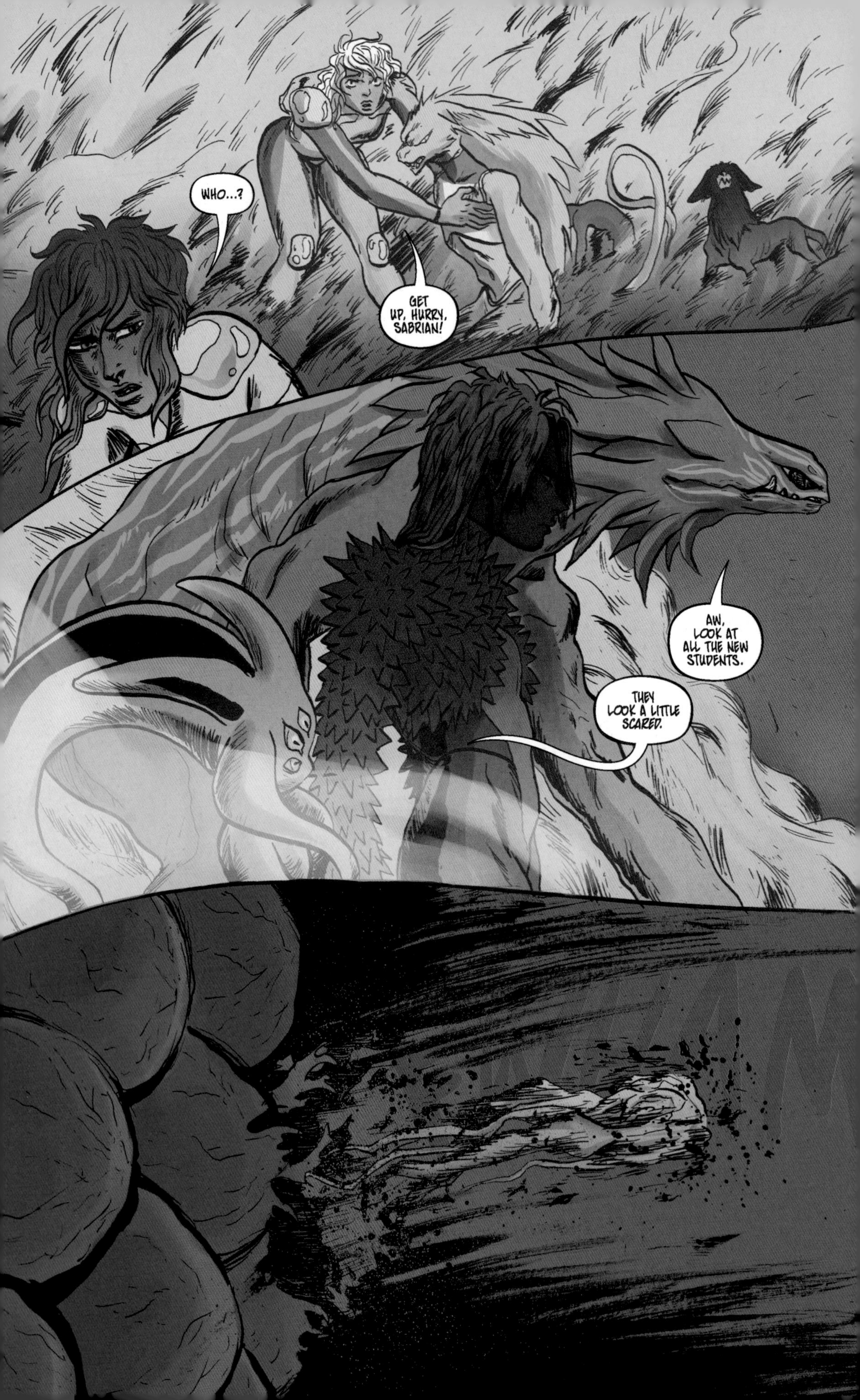
WHO...?
GET UP, HURRY, SABRIAN!
AW, LOOK AT ALL THE NEW STUDENTS.
THEY LOOK A LITTLE SCARED.

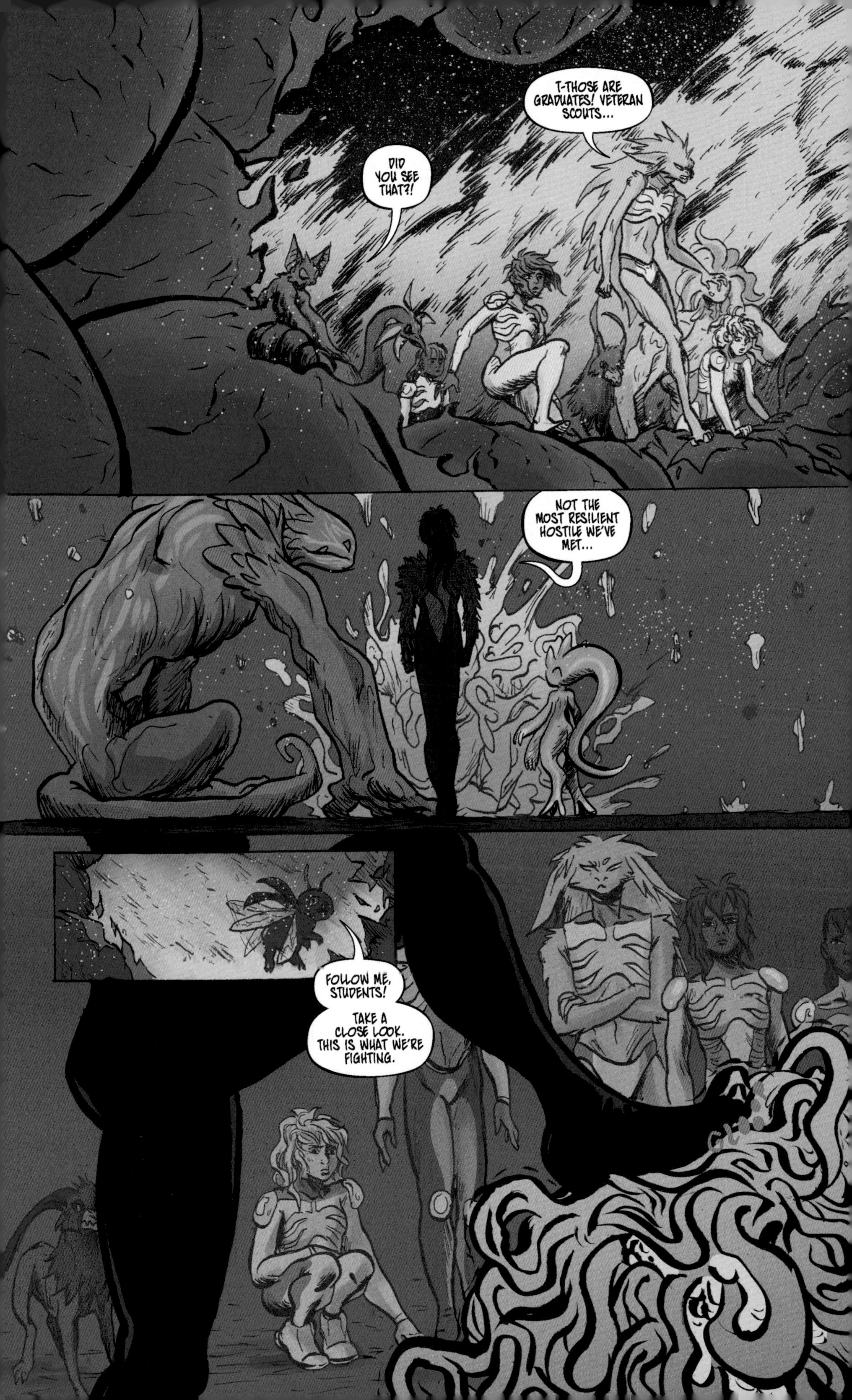
T-THOSE ARE GRADUATES! VETERAN SCOUTS...
DID YOU SEE THAT?!
NOT THE MOST RESILIENT HOSTILE WE'VE MET...
FOLLOW ME, STUDENTS!
TAKE A CLOSE LOOK. THIS IS WHAT WE'RE FIGHTING.

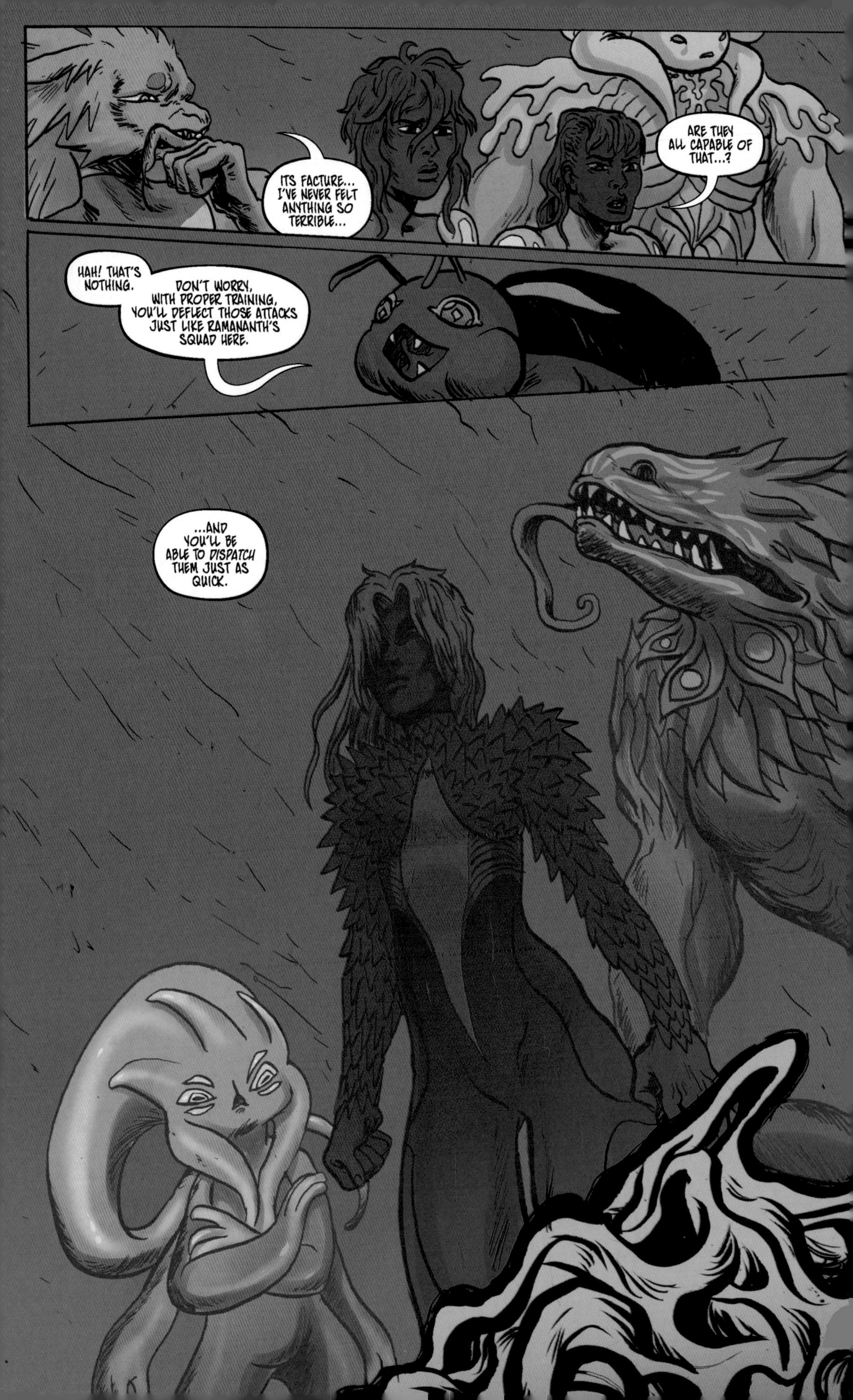
ITS FACTURE... I'VE NEVER FELT ANYTHING SO TERRIBLE...
ARE THEY ALL CAPABLE OF THAT...?
HAH! THAT'S NOTHING.
DON'T WORRY, WITH PROPER TRAINING, YOU'LL DEFLECT THOSE ATTACKS JUST LIKE RAMANANTH'S SQUAD HERE.
...AND YOU'LL BE ABLE TO DISPATCH THEM JUST AS QUICK.

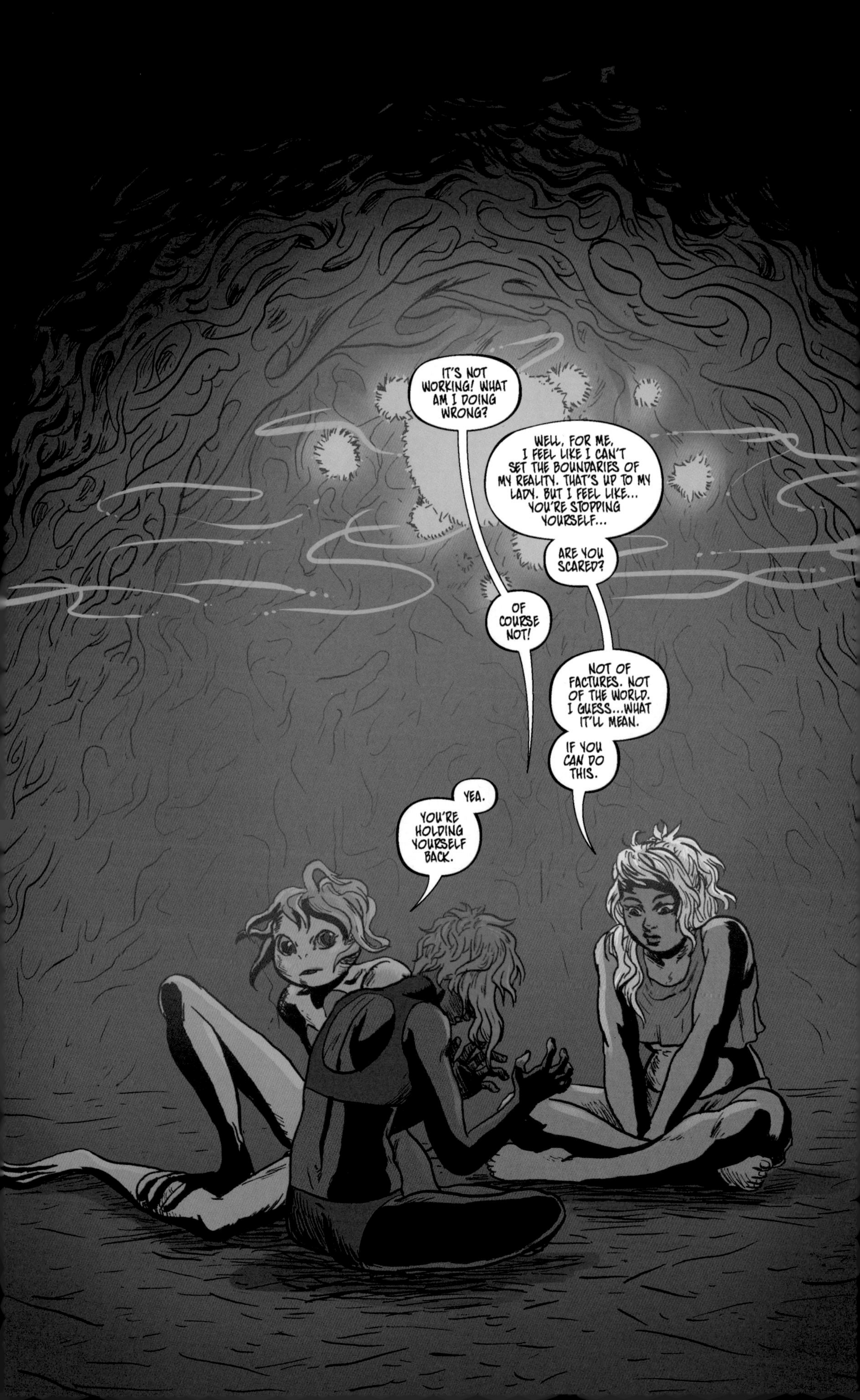
IT'S NOT WORKING! WHAT AM I DOING WRONG?
WELL, FOR ME, I FEEL LIKE I CAN'T SET THE BOUNDARIES OF MY REALITY. THAT'S UP TO MY LADY. BUT I FEEL LIKE... YOU'RE STOPPING YOURSELF...
ARE YOU SCARED?
OF COURSE NOT!
NOT OF FACTURES. NOT OF THE WORLD. I GUESS...WHAT IT'LL MEAN.
IF YOU CAN DO THIS.
YEA.
YOU'RE HOLDING YOURSELF BACK.

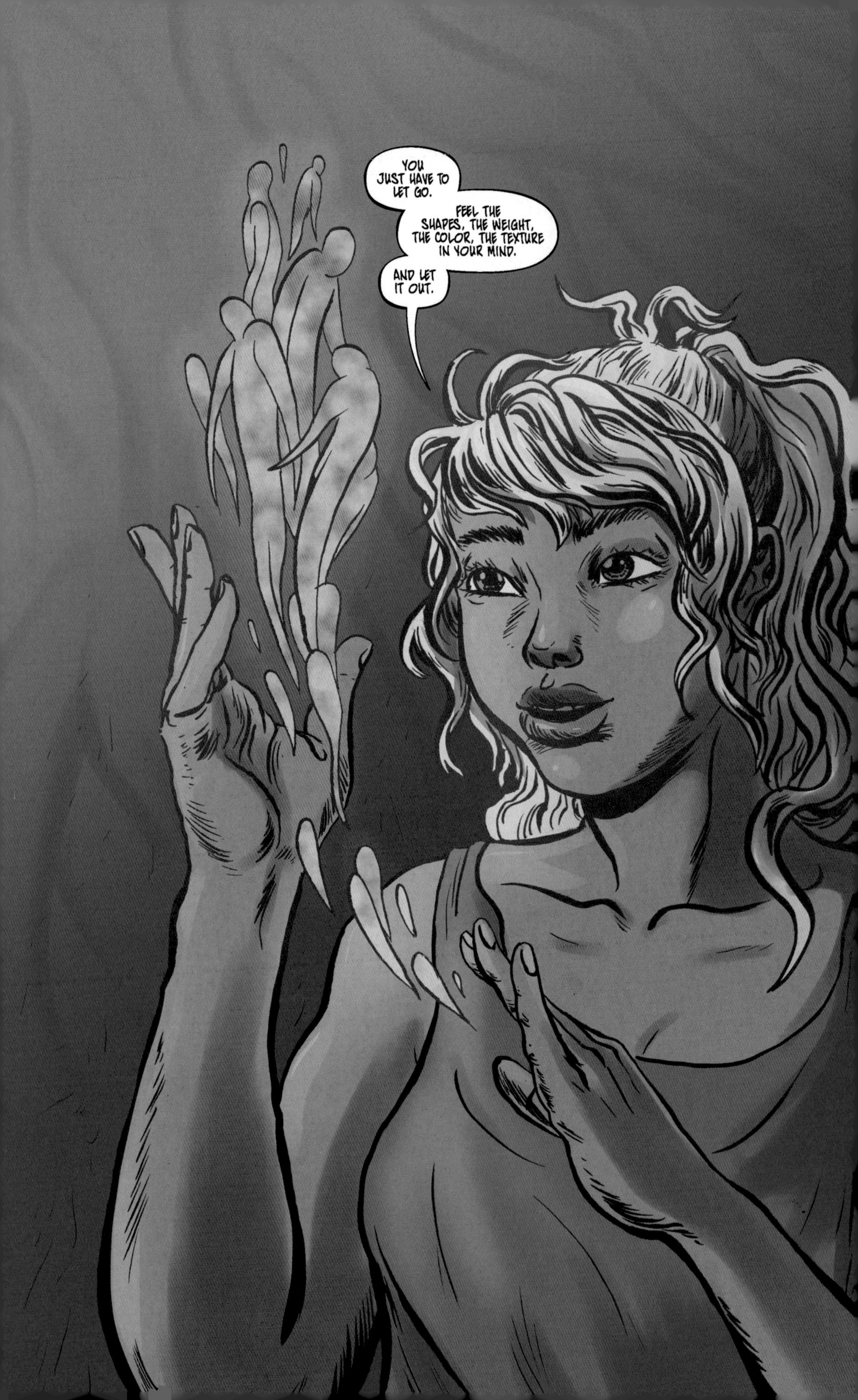
YOU JUST HAVE TO LET GO.
FEEL THE SHAPES, THE WEIGHT, THE COLOR, THE TEXTURE IN YOUR MIND.
AND LET IT OUT.

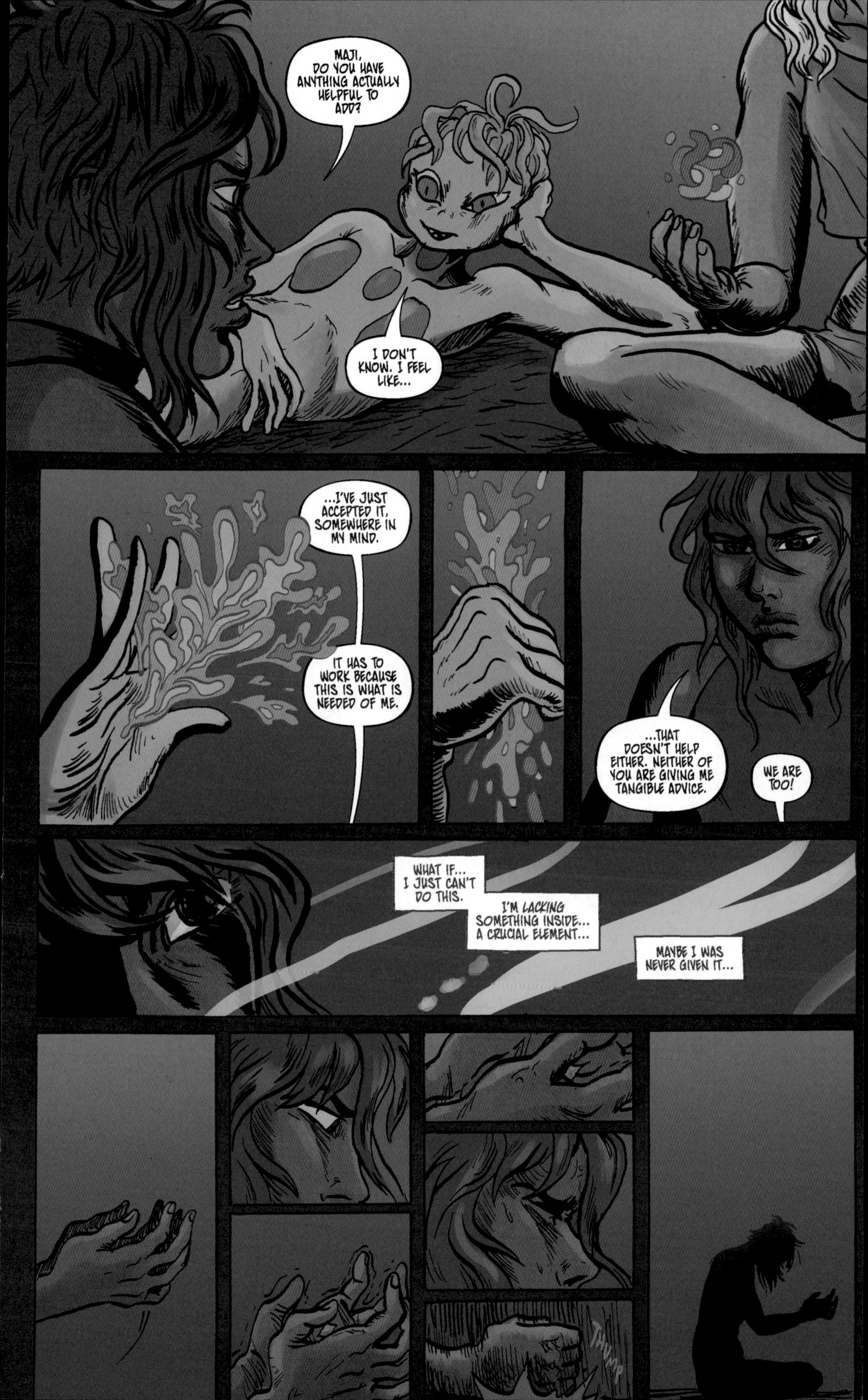
MAJI, DO YOU HAVE ANYTHING ACTUALLY HELPFUL TO ADD?
I DON'T KNOW. I FEEL LIKE...
...I'VE JUST ACCEPTED IT, SOMEWHERE IN MY MIND.
IT HAS TO WORK BECAUSE THIS IS WHAT IS NEEDED OF ME.
...THAT DOESN'T HELP EITHER. NEITHER OF YOU ARE GIVING ME TANGIBLE ADVICE.
WE ARE TOO!
WHAT IF... I JUST CAN'T DO THIS.
I'M LACKING SOMETHING INSIDE... A CRUCIAL ELEMENT...
MAYBE I WAS NEVER GIVEN IT...
THUMP

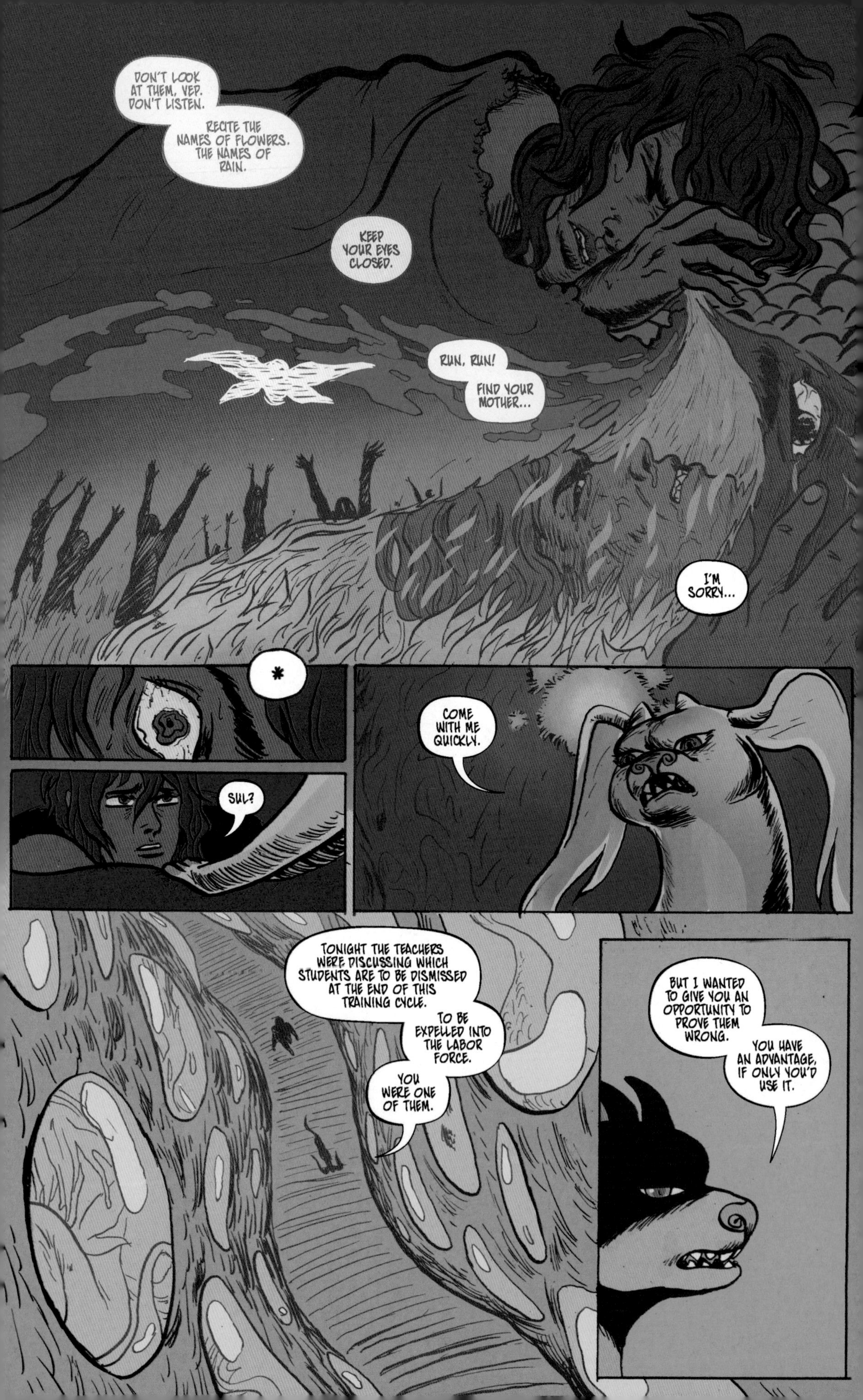
DON'T LOOK AT THEM, VEP. DON'T LISTEN.
RECITE THE NAMES OF FLOWERS. THE NAMES OF RAIN.
KEEP YOUR EYES CLOSED.
RUN, RUN!
FIND YOUR MOTHER...
I'M SORRY...
*
SUL?
COME WITH ME QUICKLY.
TONIGHT THE TEACHERS WERE DISCUSSING WHICH STUDENTS ARE TO BE DISMISSED AT THE END OF THIS TRAINING CYCLE.
TO BE EXPELLED INTO THE LABOR FORCE.
YOU WERE ONE OF THEM.
BUT I WANTED TO GIVE YOU AN OPPORTUNITY TO PROVE THEM WRONG.
YOU HAVE AN ADVANTAGE, IF ONLY YOU'D USE IT.

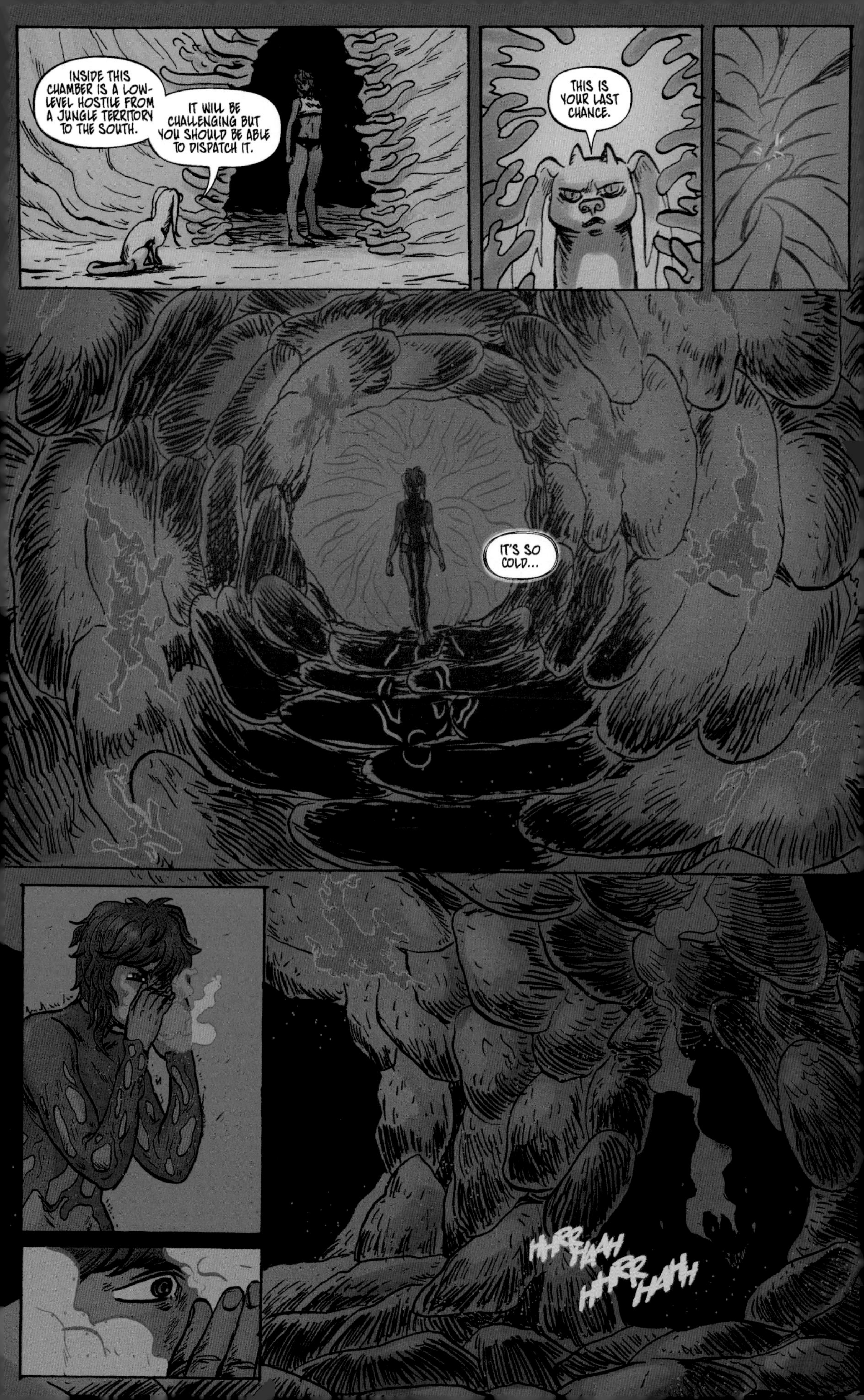
INSIDE THIS CHAMBER IS A LOW-LEVEL HOSTILE FROM A JUNGLE TERRITORY TO THE SOUTH.
IT WILL BE CHALLENGING BUT YOU SHOULD BE ABLE TO DISPATCH IT.
THIS IS YOUR LAST CHANCE.
IT'S SO COLD...
HHRR HAAH HHRR HAAH

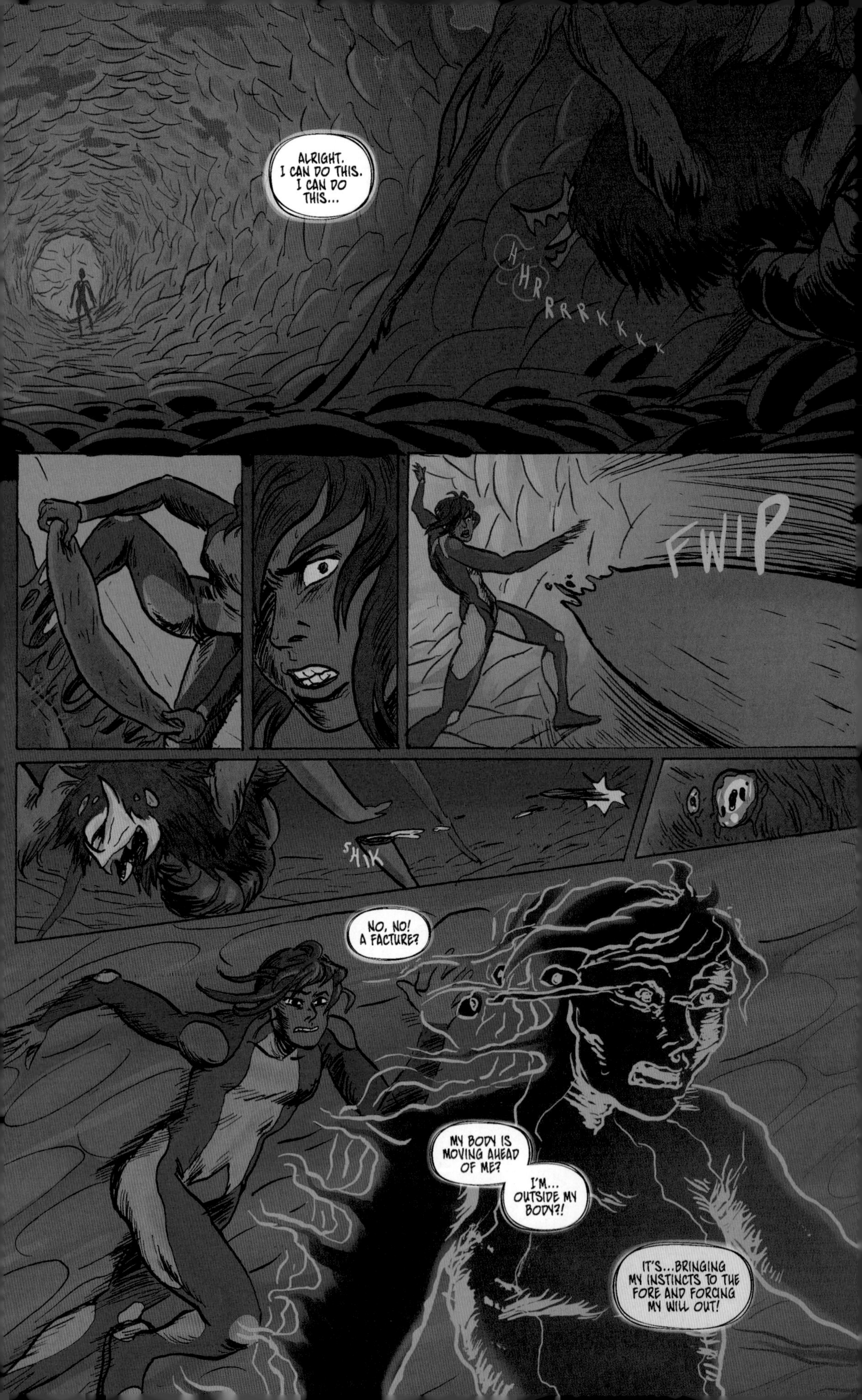
ALRIGHT. I CAN DO THIS. I CAN DO THIS...
HHRRRRKKKKK
FWIP
SHIK
NO, NO! A FACTURE?
MY BODY IS MOVING AHEAD OF ME?
I'M... OUTSIDE MY BODY?!
IT'S...BRINGING MY INSTINCTS TO THE FORE AND FORCING MY WILL OUT!

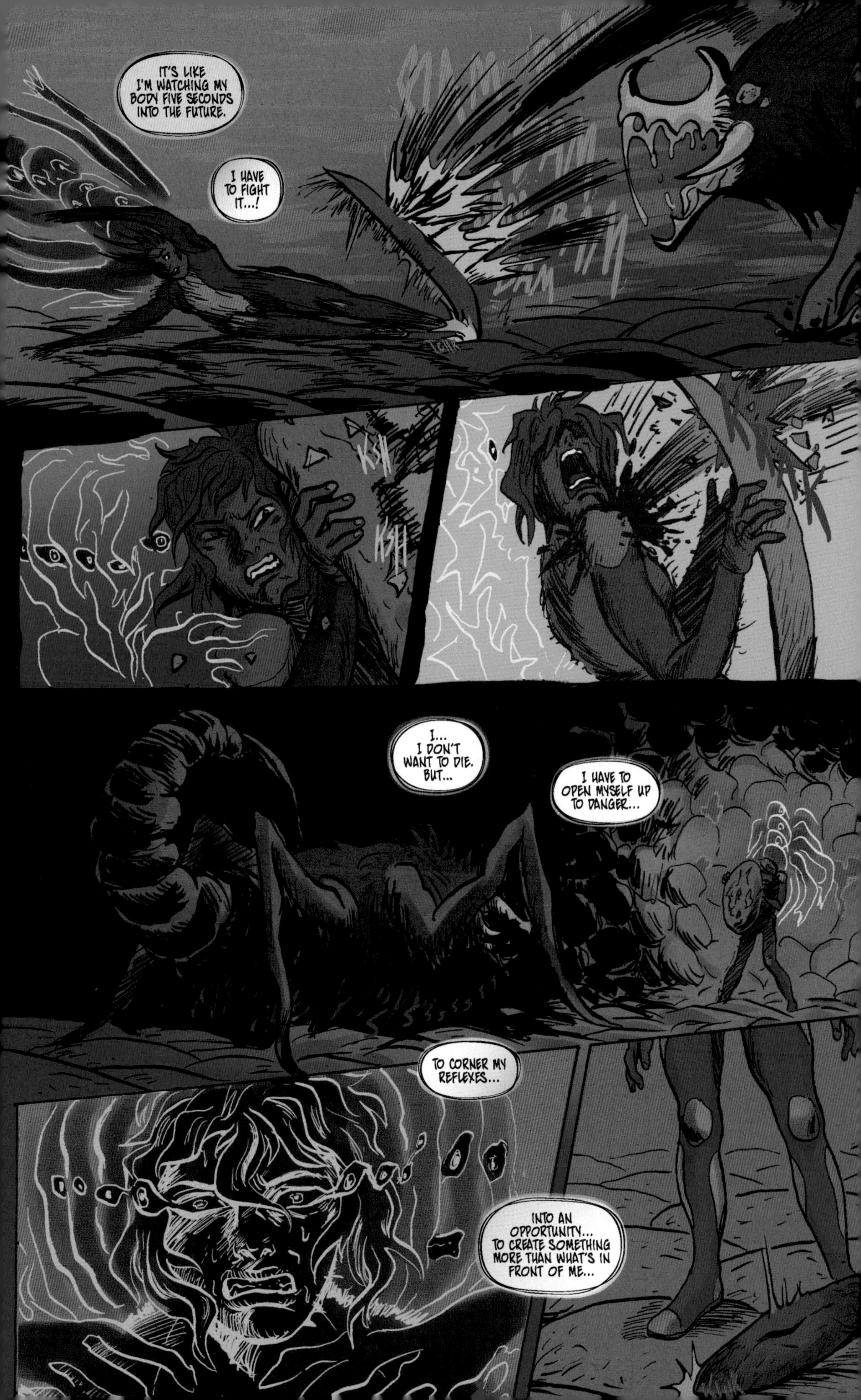
IT'S LIKE I'M WATCHING MY BODY FIVE SECONDS INTO THE FUTURE.
I HAVE TO FIGHT IT...!
KSH
KSH
I... I DON'T WANT TO DIE. BUT...
I HAVE TO OPEN MYSELF UP TO DANGER...
TO CORNER MY REFLEXES...
INTO AN OPPORTUNITY... TO CREATE SOMETHING MORE THAN WHAT'S IN FRONT OF ME...

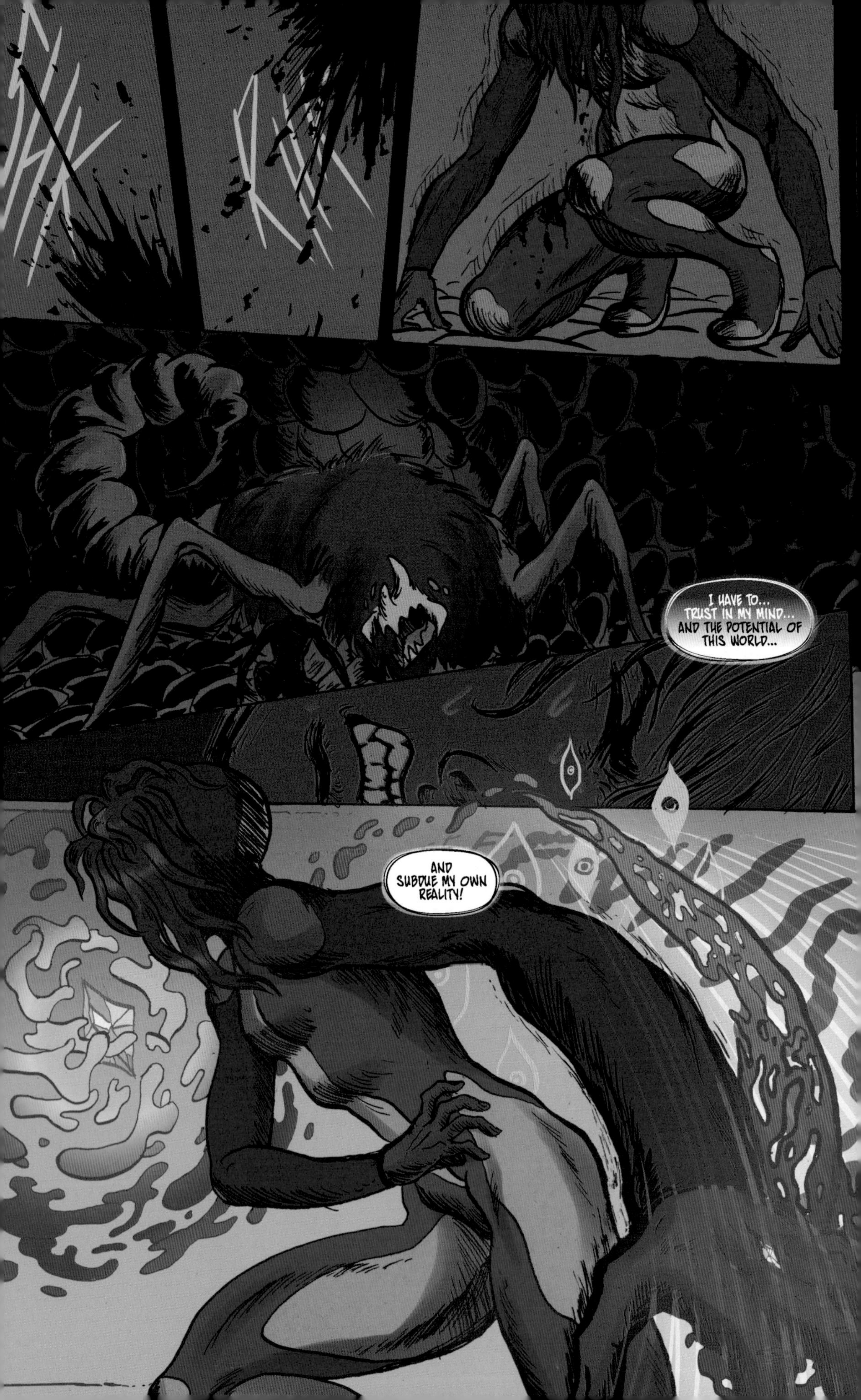
I HAVE TO... TRUST IN MY MIND... AND THE POTENTIAL OF THIS WORLD...
AND SUBDUE MY OWN REALITY!

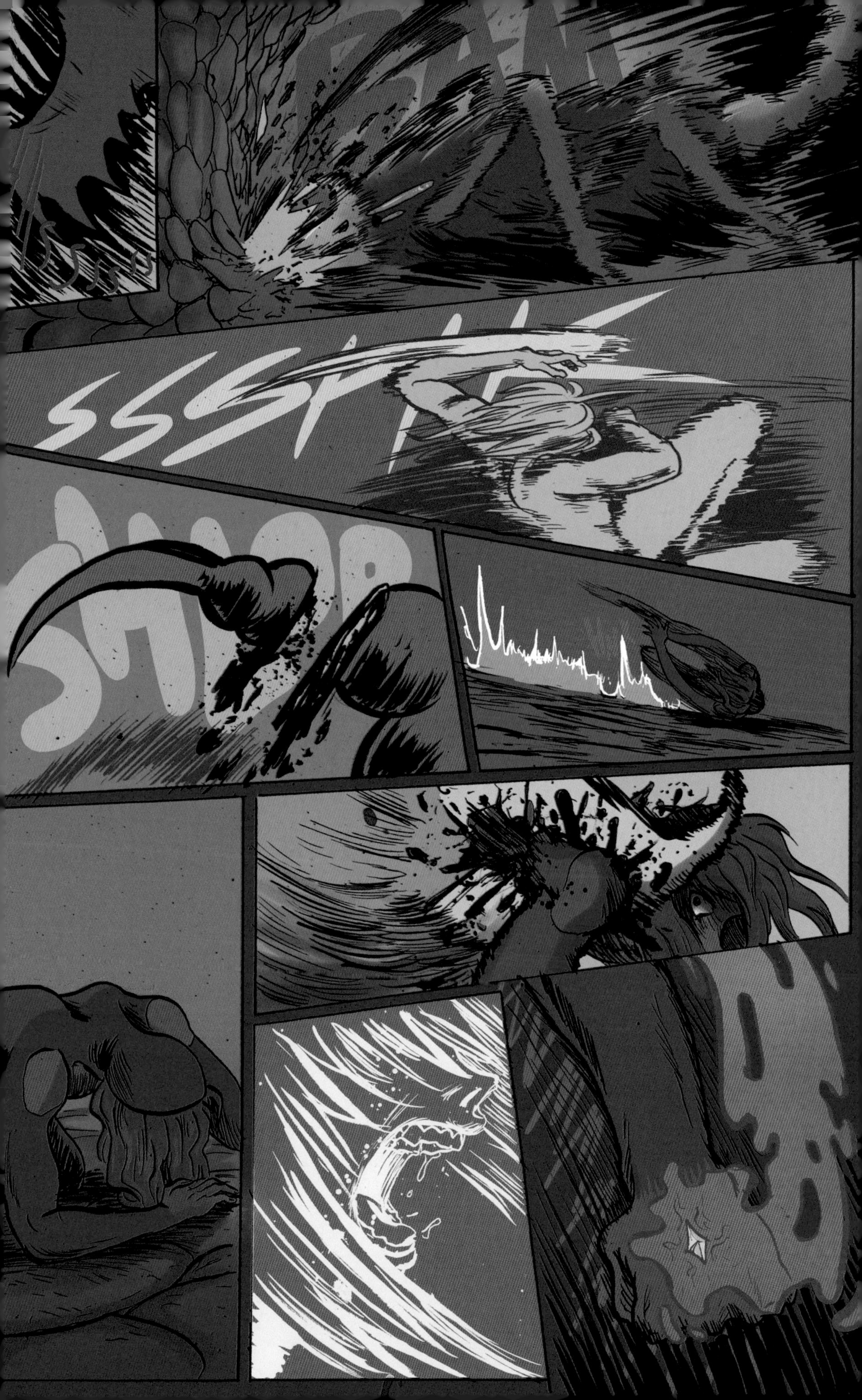
HSSSSSS

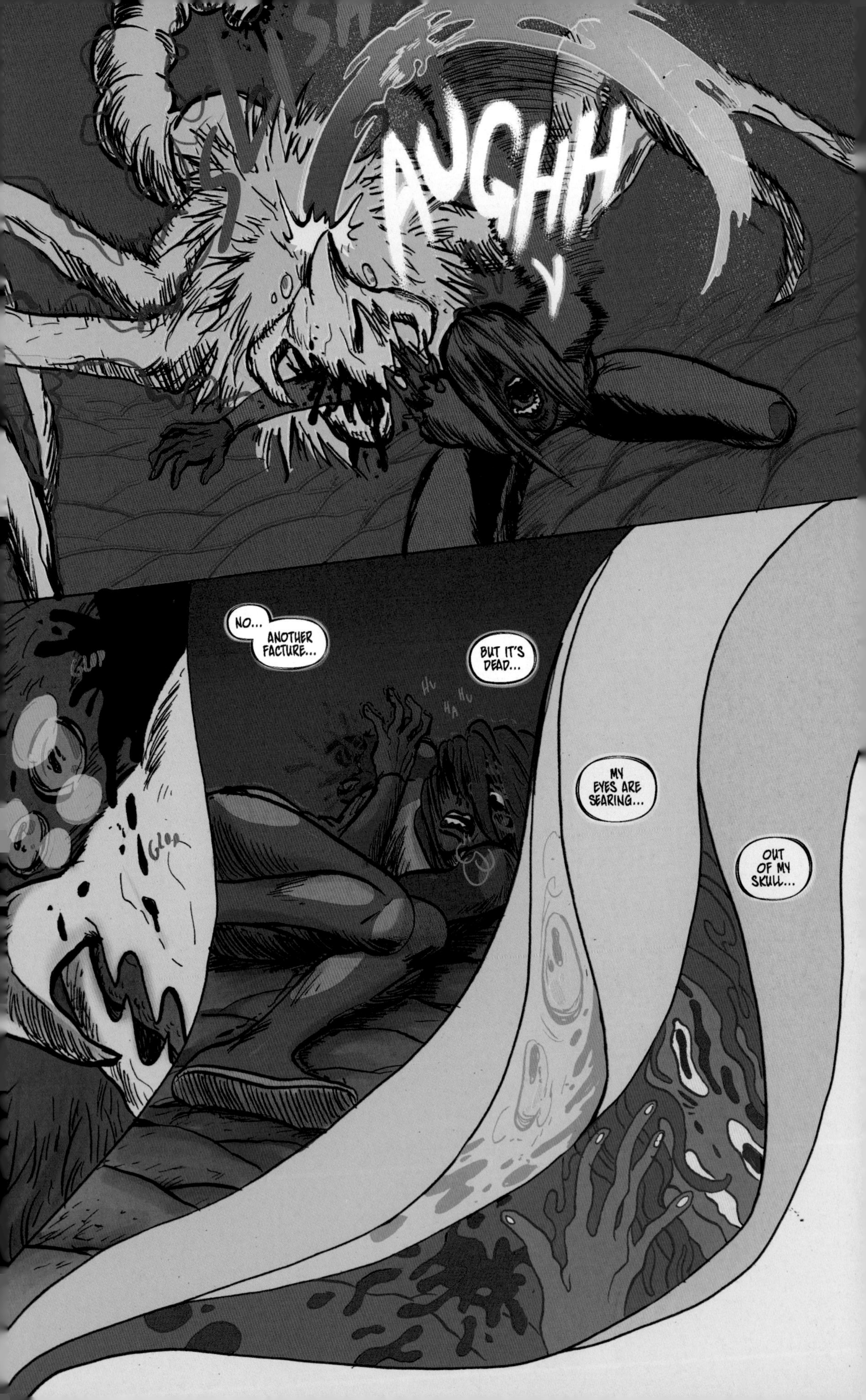
AUGHH
NO... ANOTHER FACTURE...
BUT IT'S DEAD...
MY EYES ARE SEARING...
OUT OF MY SKULL...

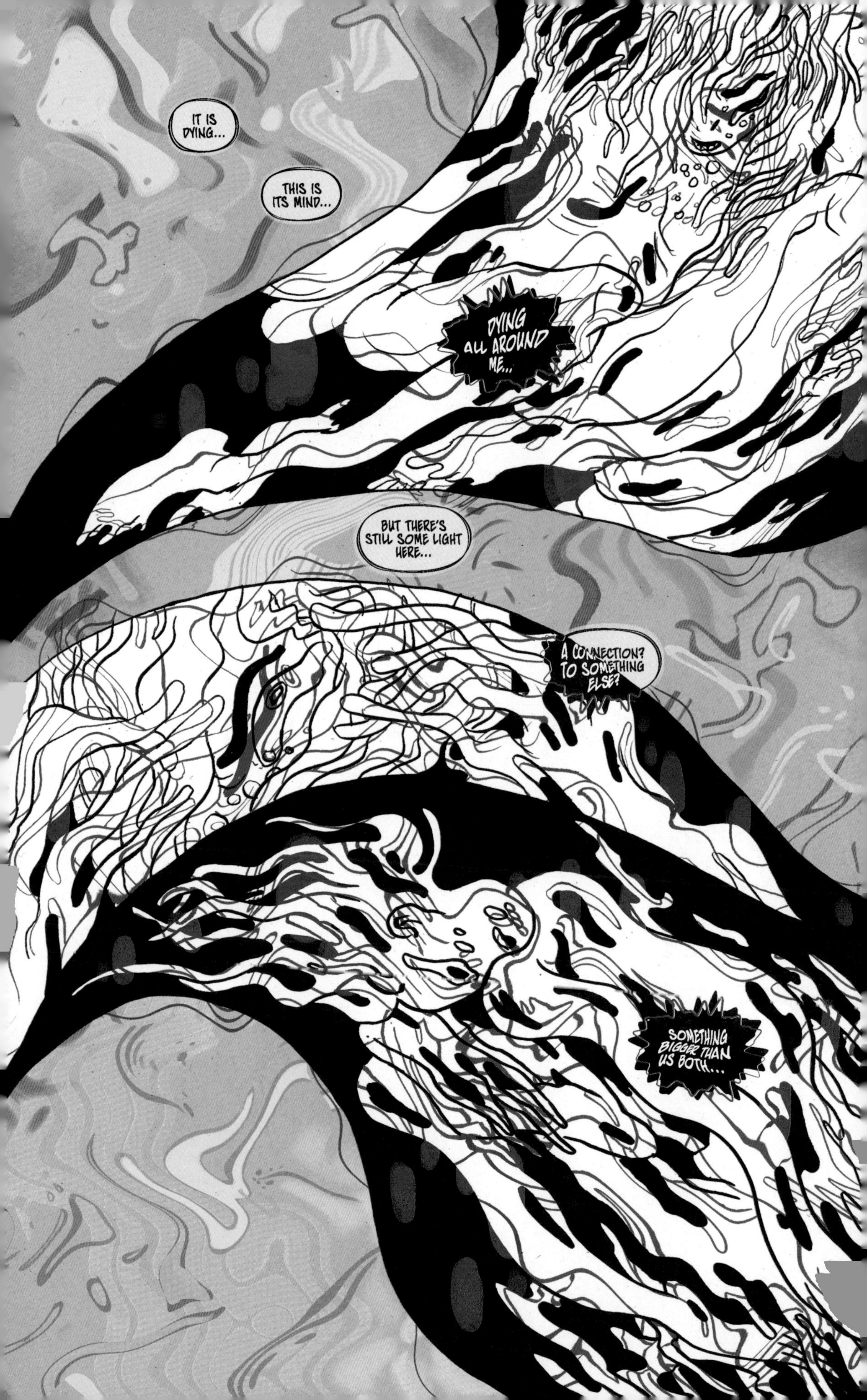
IT IS DYING...
THIS IS ITS MIND...
DYING ALL AROUND ME...
BUT THERE'S STILL SOME LIGHT HERE...
A CONNECTION? TO SOMETHING ELSE?
SOMETHING BIGGER THAN US BOTH...

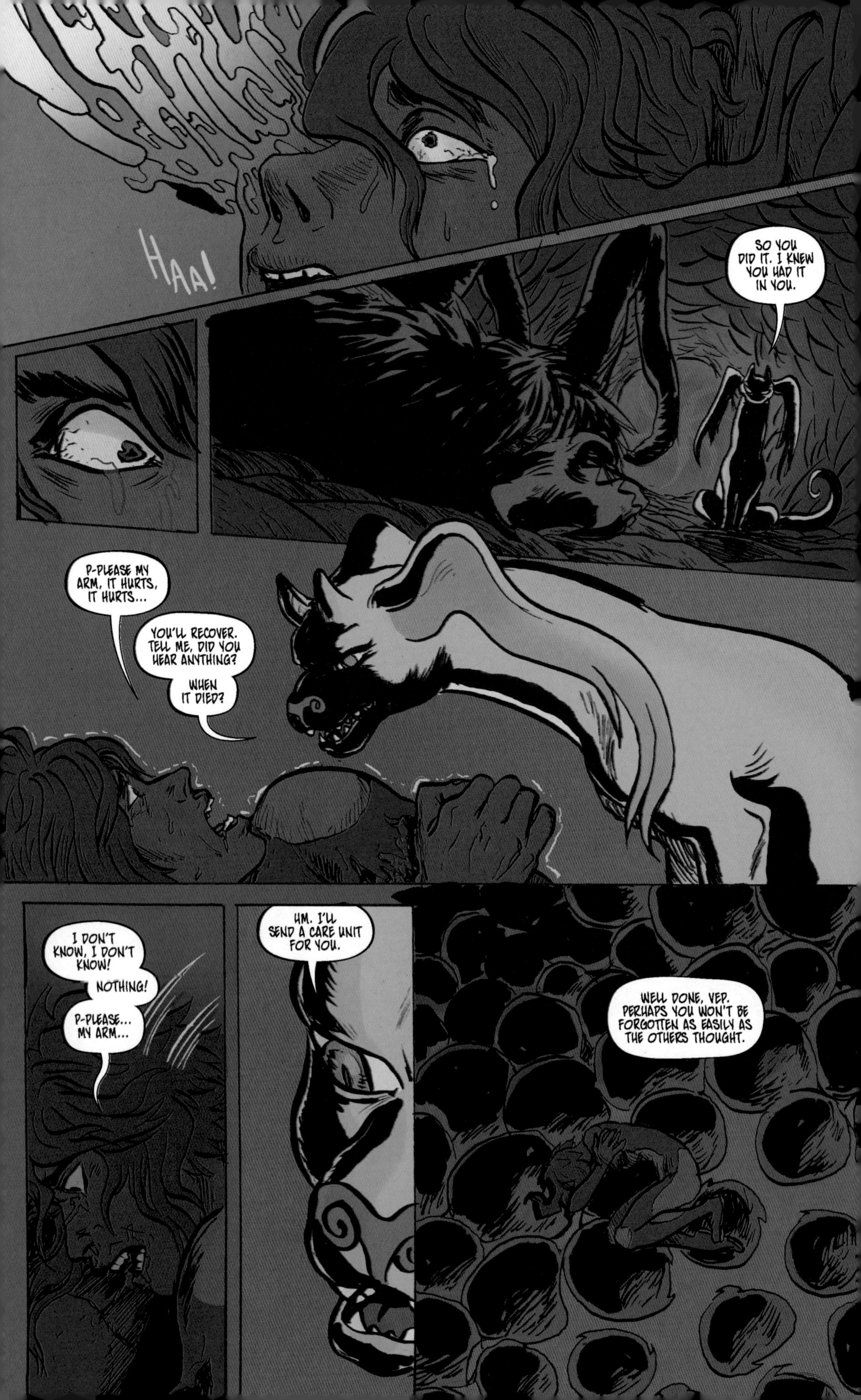
HAA!
SO YOU DID IT. I KNEW YOU HAD IT IN YOU.
P-PLEASE MY ARM, IT HURTS, IT HURTS...
YOU'LL RECOVER. TELL ME, DID YOU HEAR ANYTHING?
WHEN IT DIED?
I DON'T KNOW, I DON'T KNOW!
NOTHING!
P-PLEASE... MY ARM...
HM. I'LL SEND A CARE UNIT FOR YOU.
WELL DONE, VEP. PERHAPS YOU WON'T BE FORGOTTEN AS EASILY AS THE OTHERS THOUGHT.

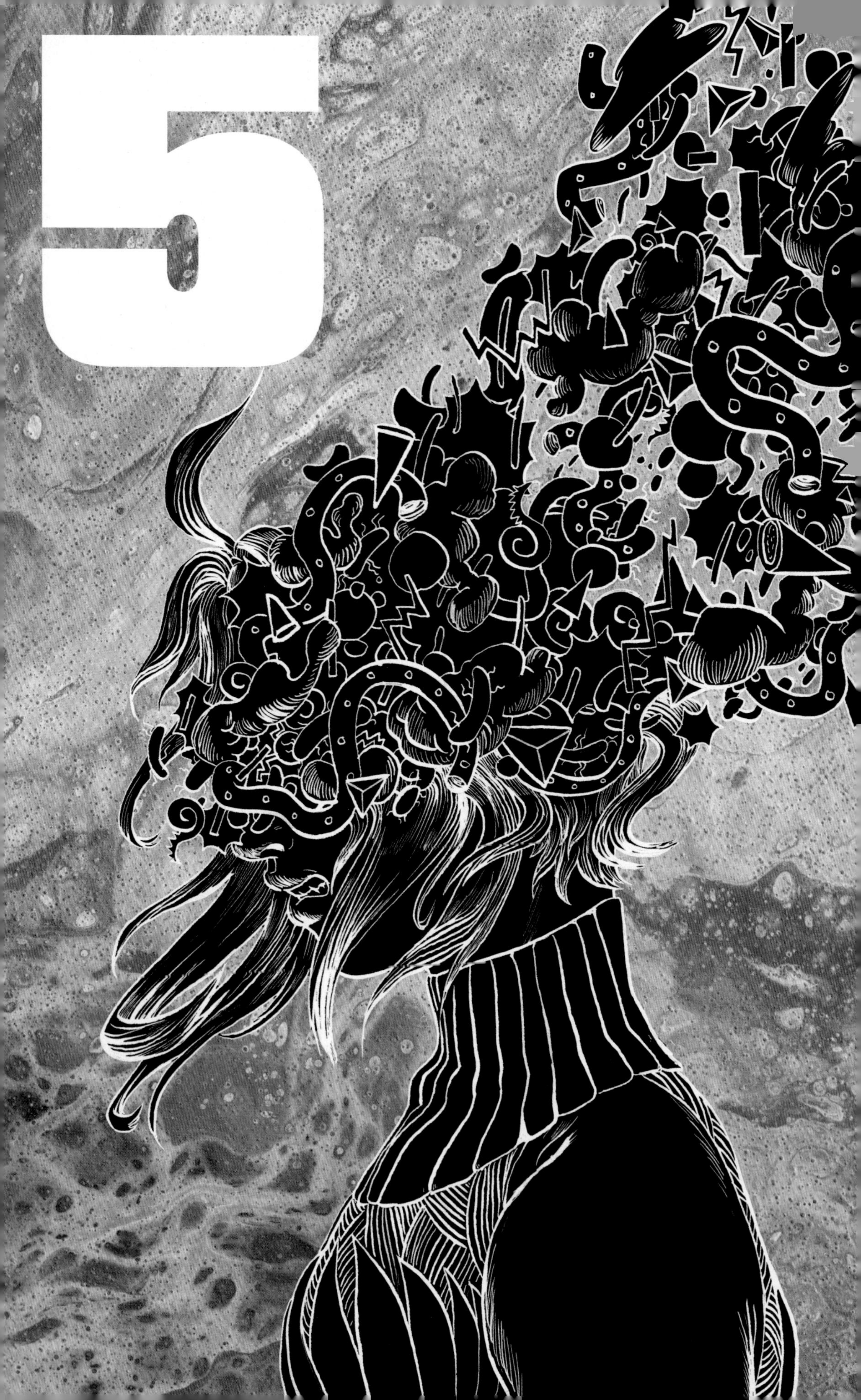
5

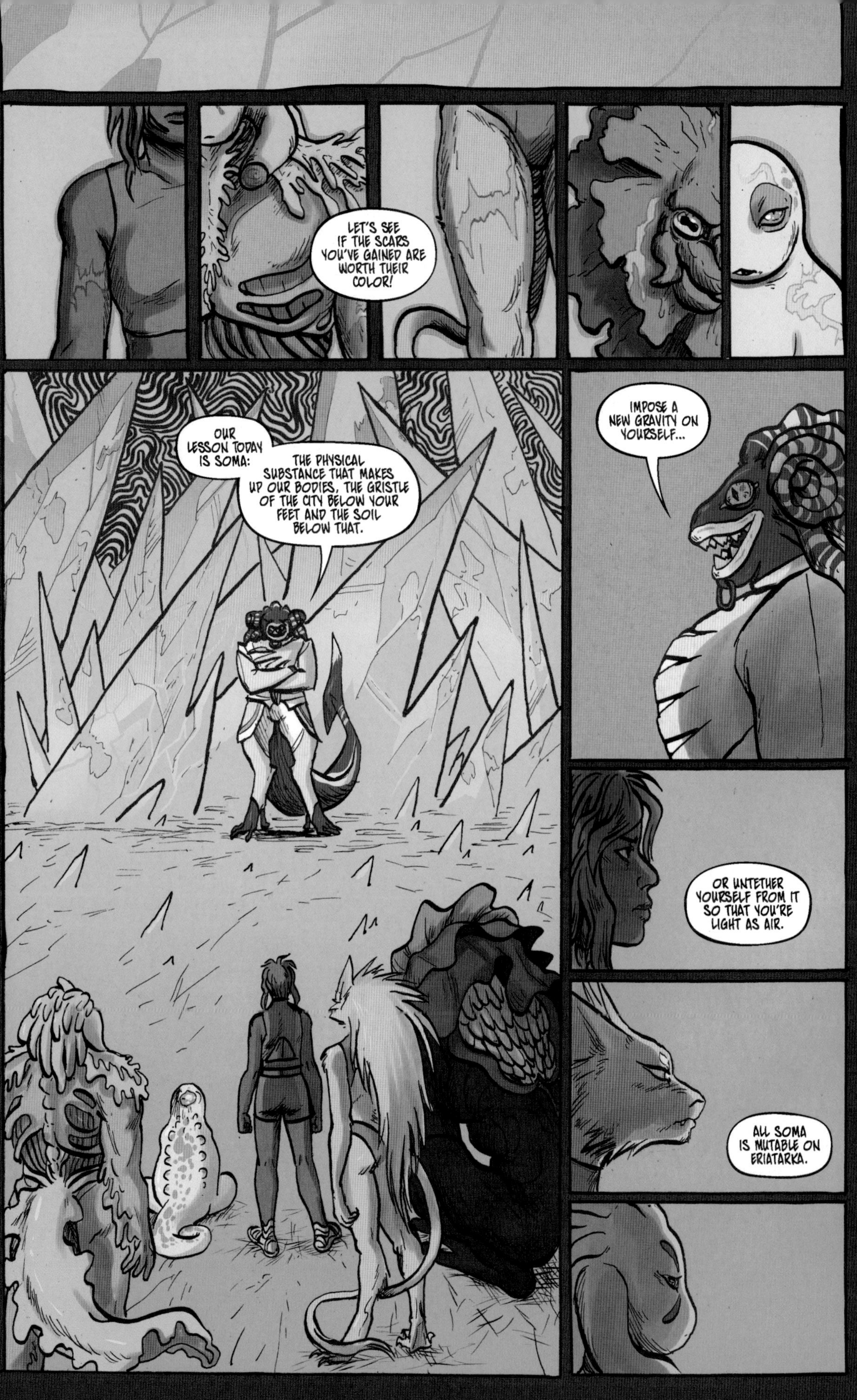
LET'S SEE IF THE SCARS YOU'VE GAINED ARE WORTH THEIR COLOR!
OUR LESSON TODAY IS SOMA:
THE PHYSICAL SUBSTANCE THAT MAKES UP OUR BODIES, THE GRISTLE OF THE CITY BELOW YOUR FEET AND THE SOIL BELOW THAT.
IMPOSE A NEW GRAVITY ON YOURSELF...
OR UNTETHER YOURSELF FROM IT SO THAT YOU'RE LIGHT AS AIR.
ALL SOMA IS MUTABLE ON ERIATARKA.

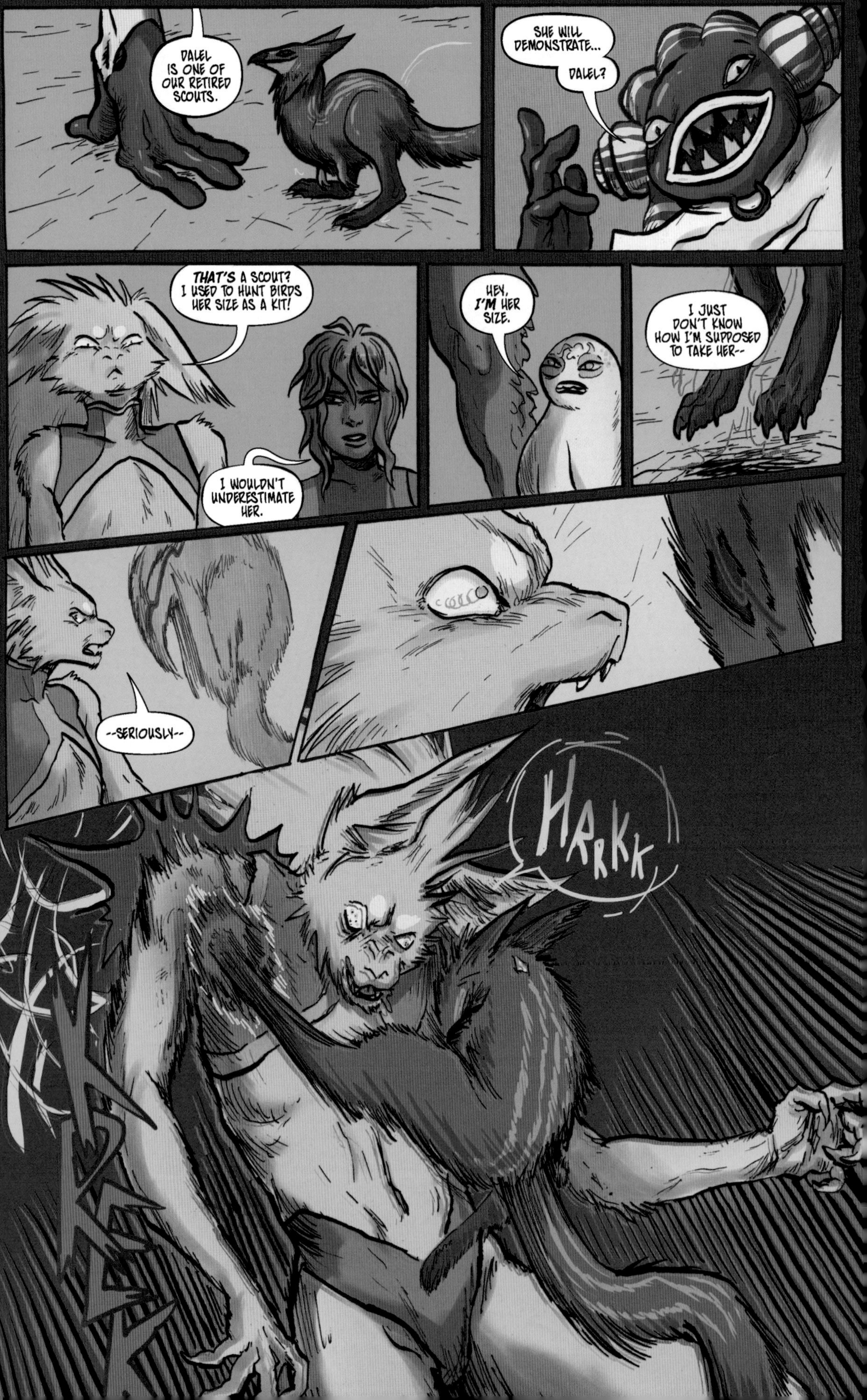
DALEL IS ONE OF OUR RETIRED SCOUTS.
SHE WILL DEMONSTRATE...
DALEL?
THAT'S A SCOUT? I USED TO HUNT BIRDS HER SIZE AS A KIT!
I WOULDN'T UNDERESTIMATE HER.
HEY, I'M HER SIZE.
I JUST DON'T KNOW HOW I'M SUPPOSED TO TAKE HER--
--SERIOUSLY--
HRKK

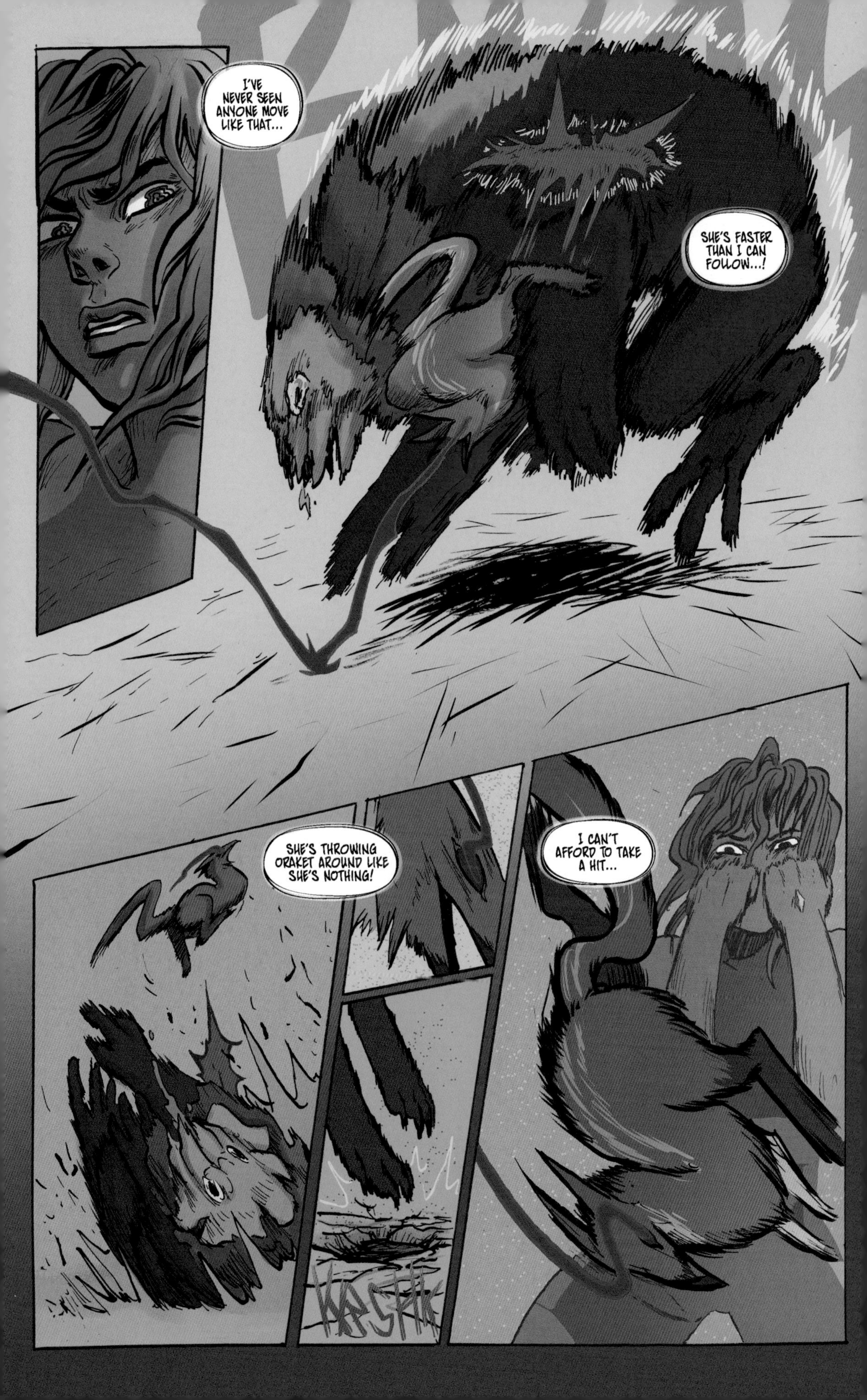
I'VE NEVER SEEN ANYONE MOVE LIKE THAT...
SHE'S FASTER THAN I CAN FOLLOW...!
SHE'S THROWING ORAKET AROUND LIKE SHE'S NOTHING!
KRSHK
I CAN'T AFFORD TO TAKE A HIT...

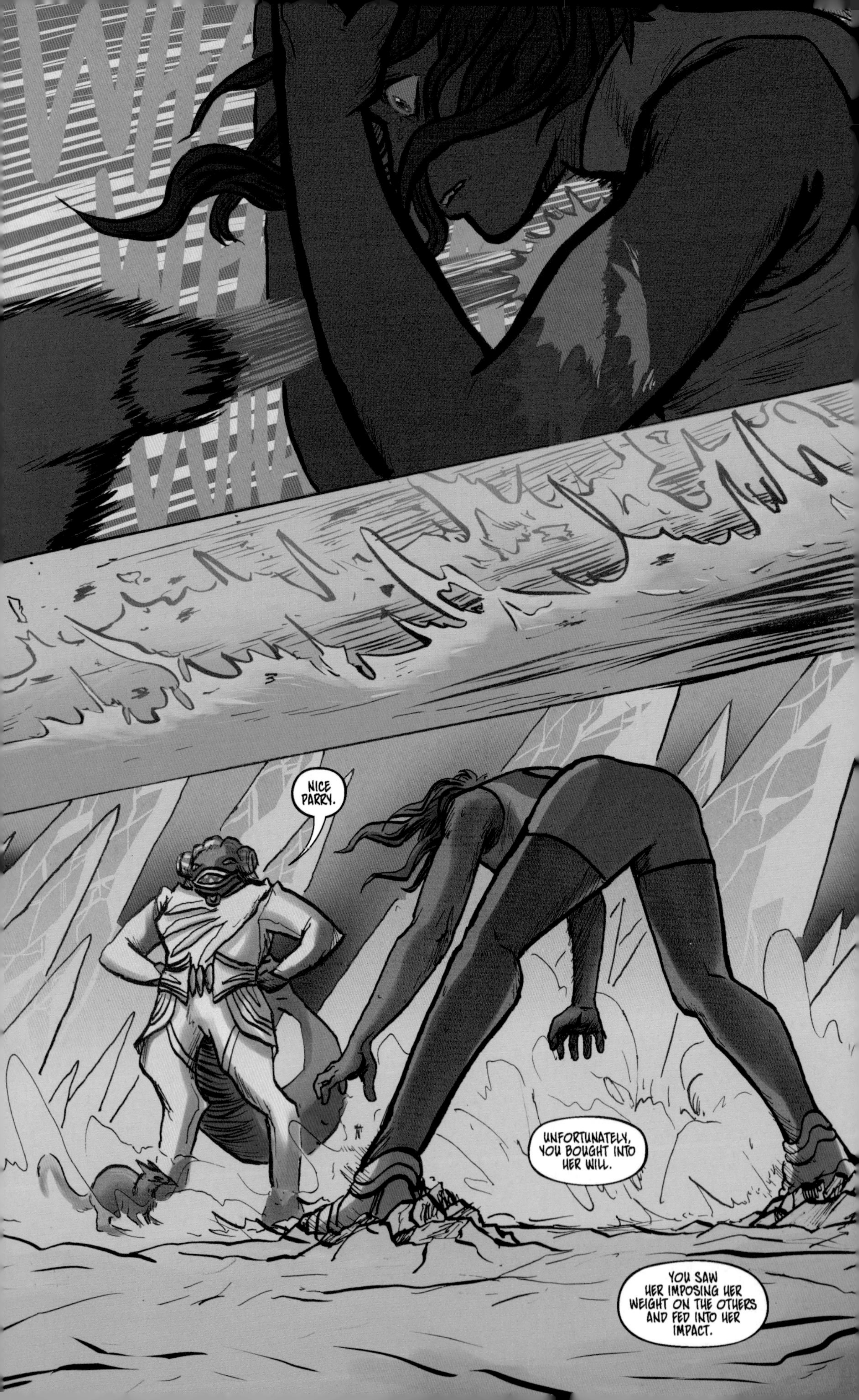
NICE PARRY.
UNFORTUNATELY, YOU BOUGHT INTO HER WILL.
YOU SAW HER IMPOSING HER WEIGHT ON THE OTHERS AND FED INTO HER IMPACT.

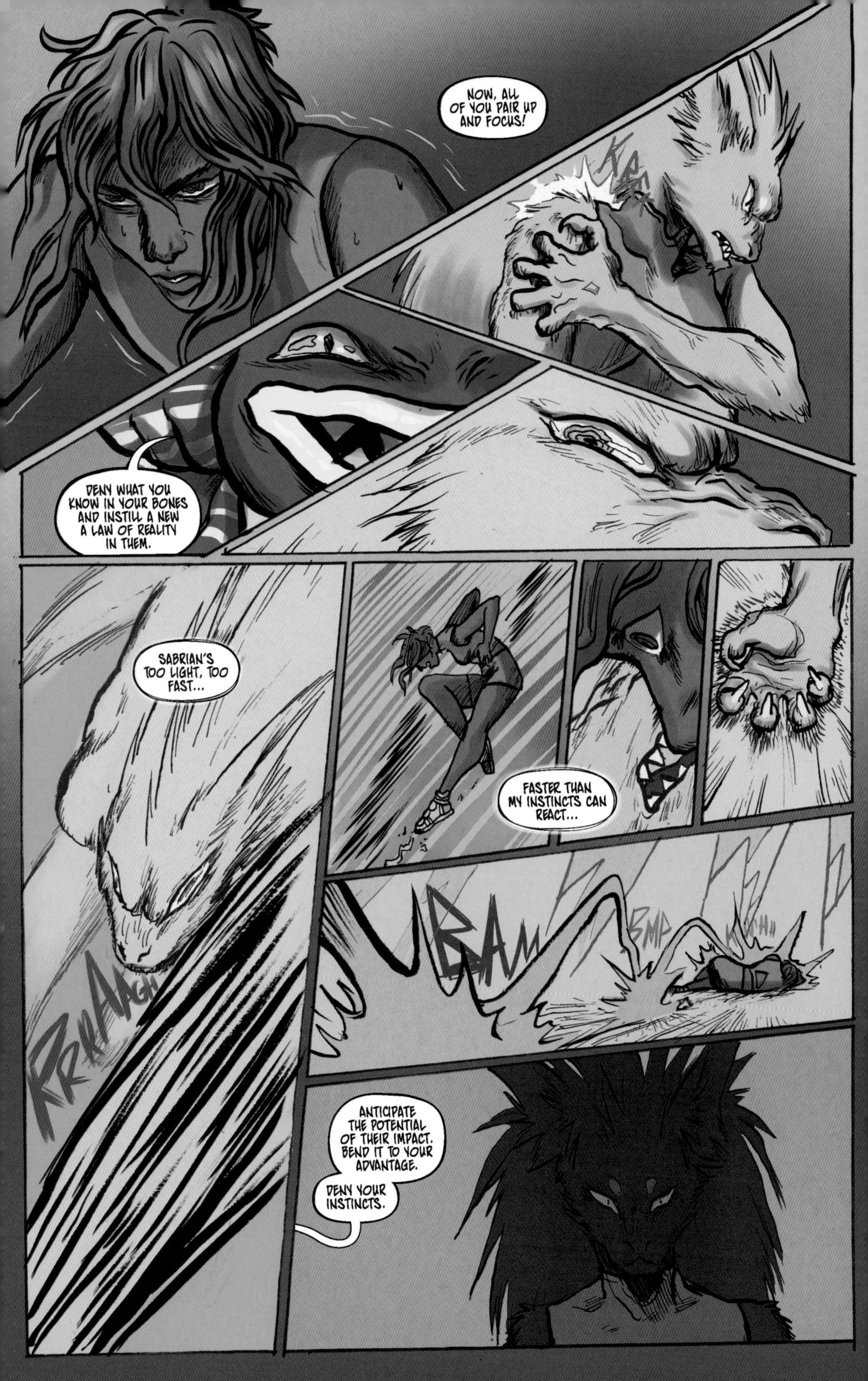
NOW, ALL OF YOU PAIR UP AND FOCUS!
DENY WHAT YOU KNOW IN YOUR BONES AND INSTILL A NEW A LAW OF REALITY IN THEM.
SABRIAN'S TOO LIGHT, TOO FAST...
FASTER THAN MY INSTINCTS CAN REACT...
BAM
BMP
ANTICIPATE THE POTENTIAL OF THEIR IMPACT. BEND IT TO YOUR ADVANTAGE.
DENY YOUR INSTINCTS.

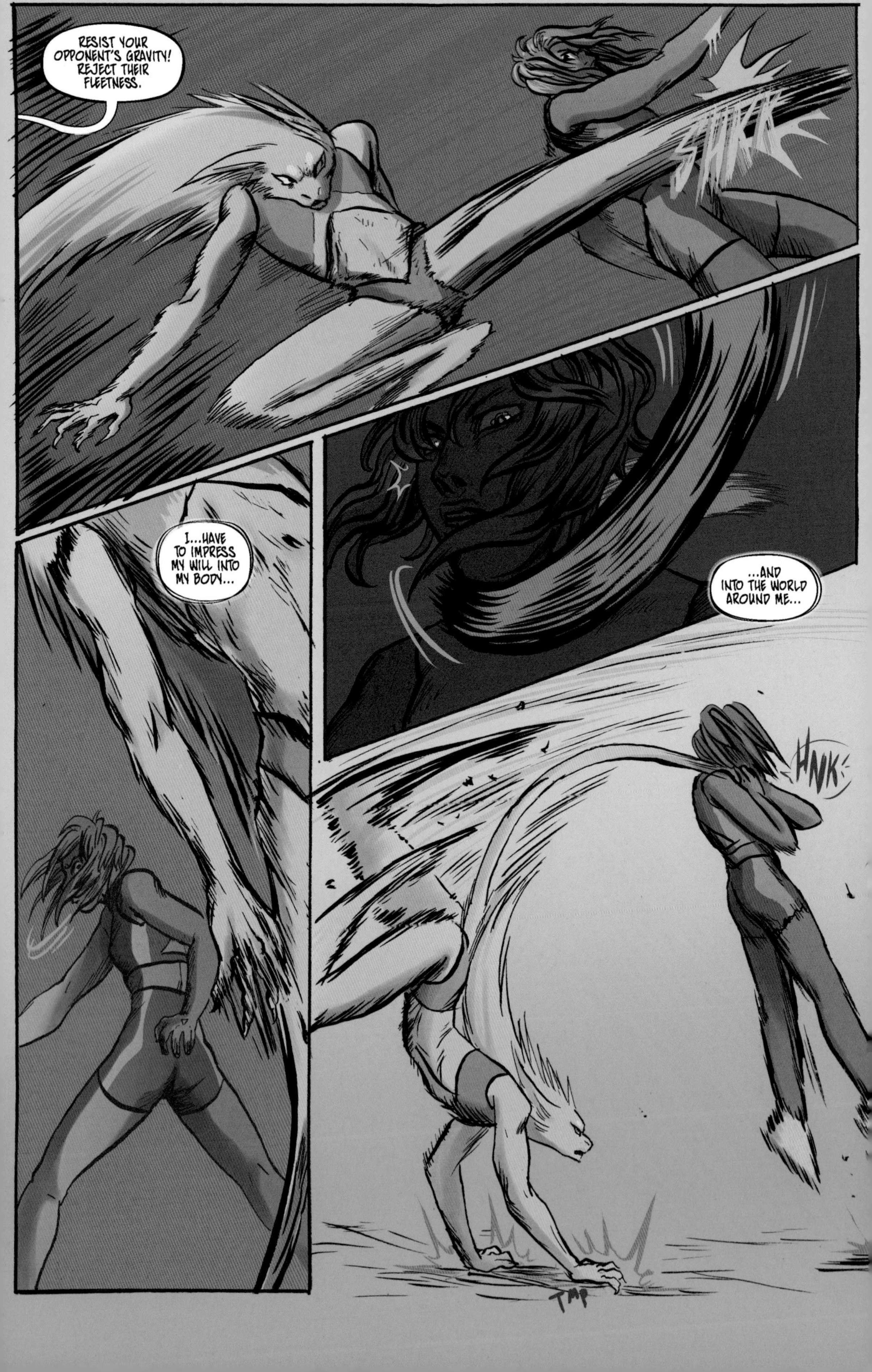

RESIST YOUR OPPONENT'S GRAVITY! REJECT THEIR FLEETNESS.
SHKK
I...HAVE TO IMPRESS MY WILL INTO MY BODY...
...AND INTO THE WORLD AROUND ME...
HNK!
TAP

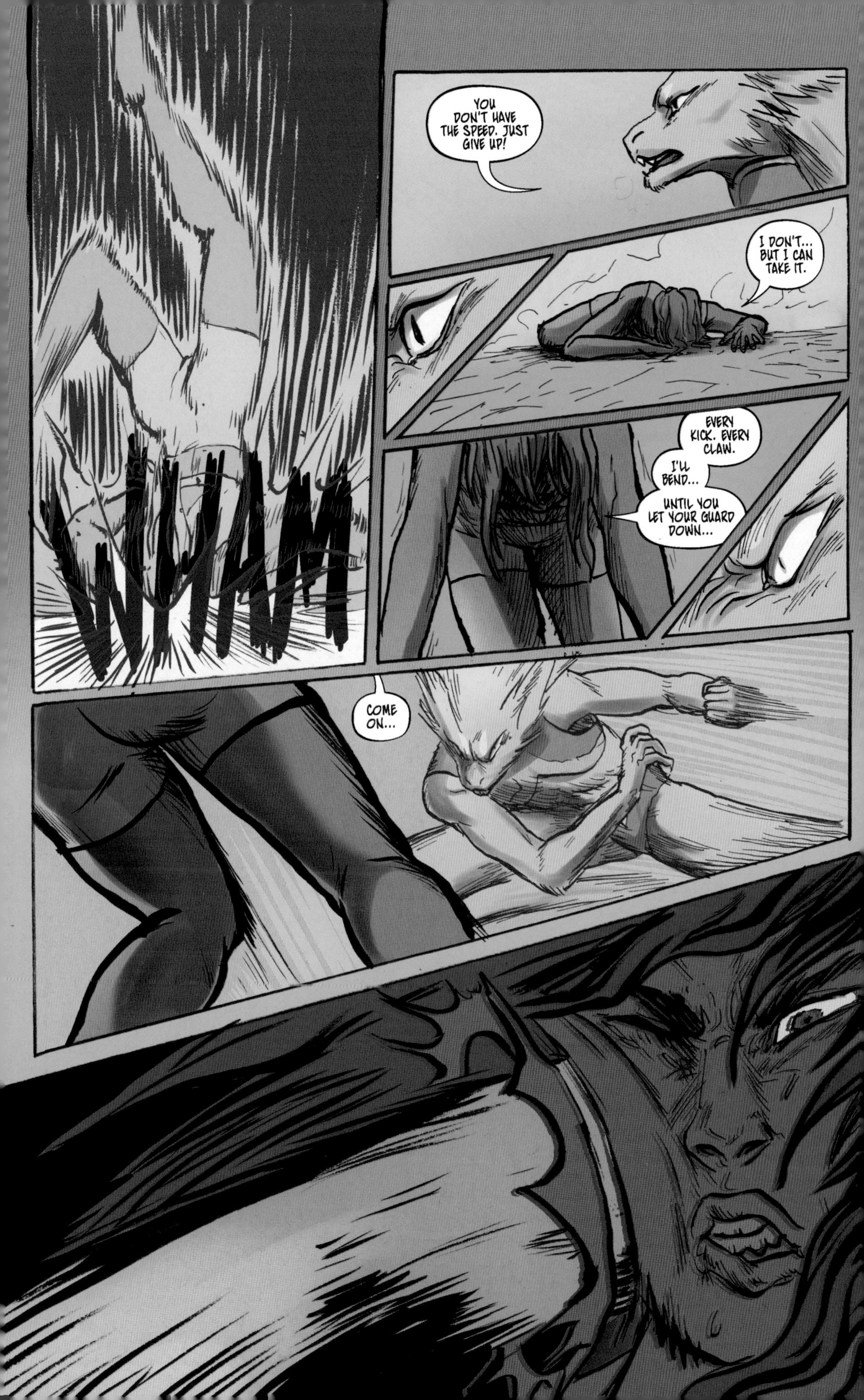
WHAM
YOU DON'T HAVE THE SPEED. JUST GIVE UP!
I DON'T... BUT I CAN TAKE IT.
EVERY KICK. EVERY CLAW.
I'LL BEND...
UNTIL YOU LET YOUR GUARD DOWN...
COME ON...

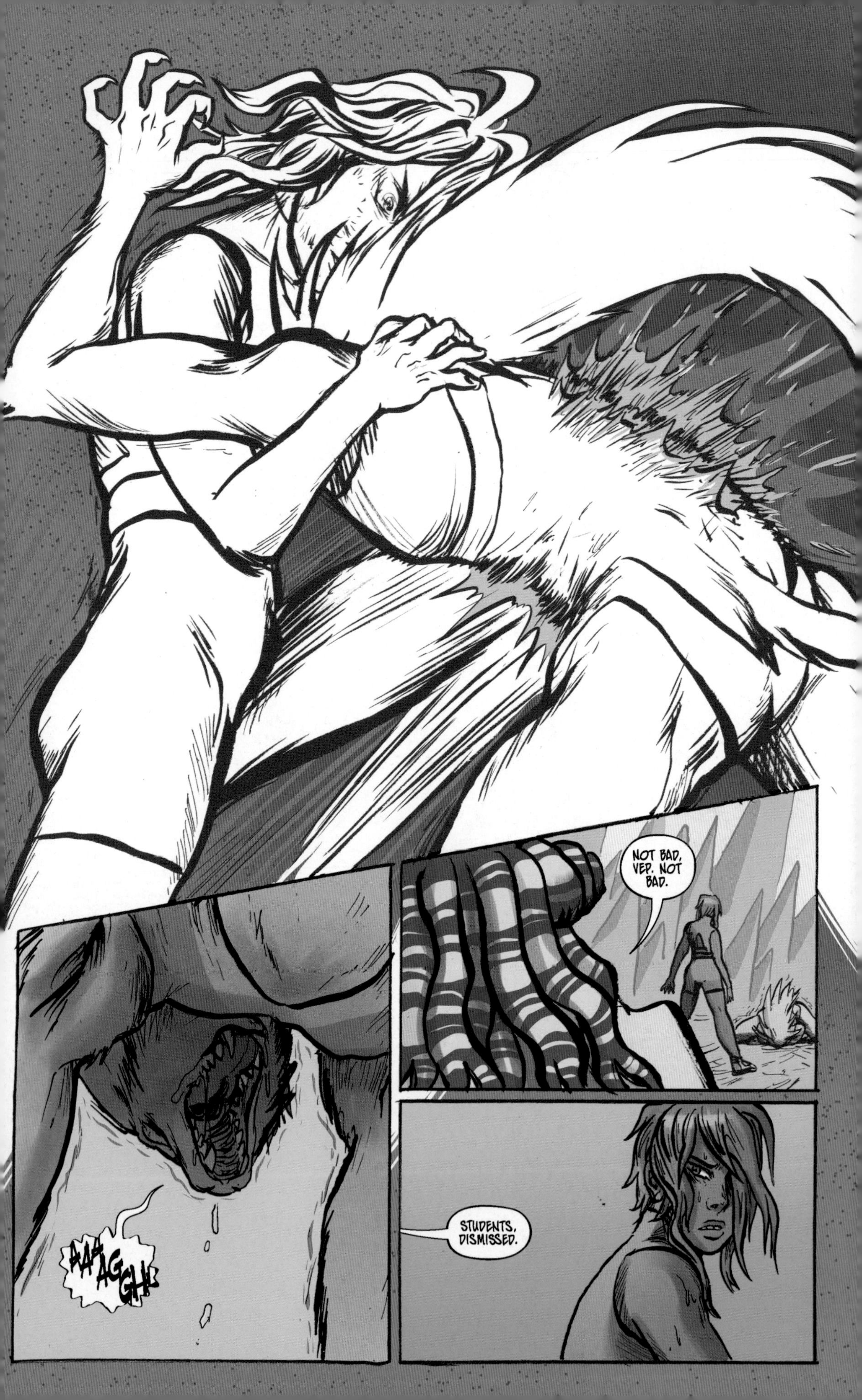
AAAAGGH!
NOT BAD, VEP. NOT BAD.
STUDENTS, DISMISSED.

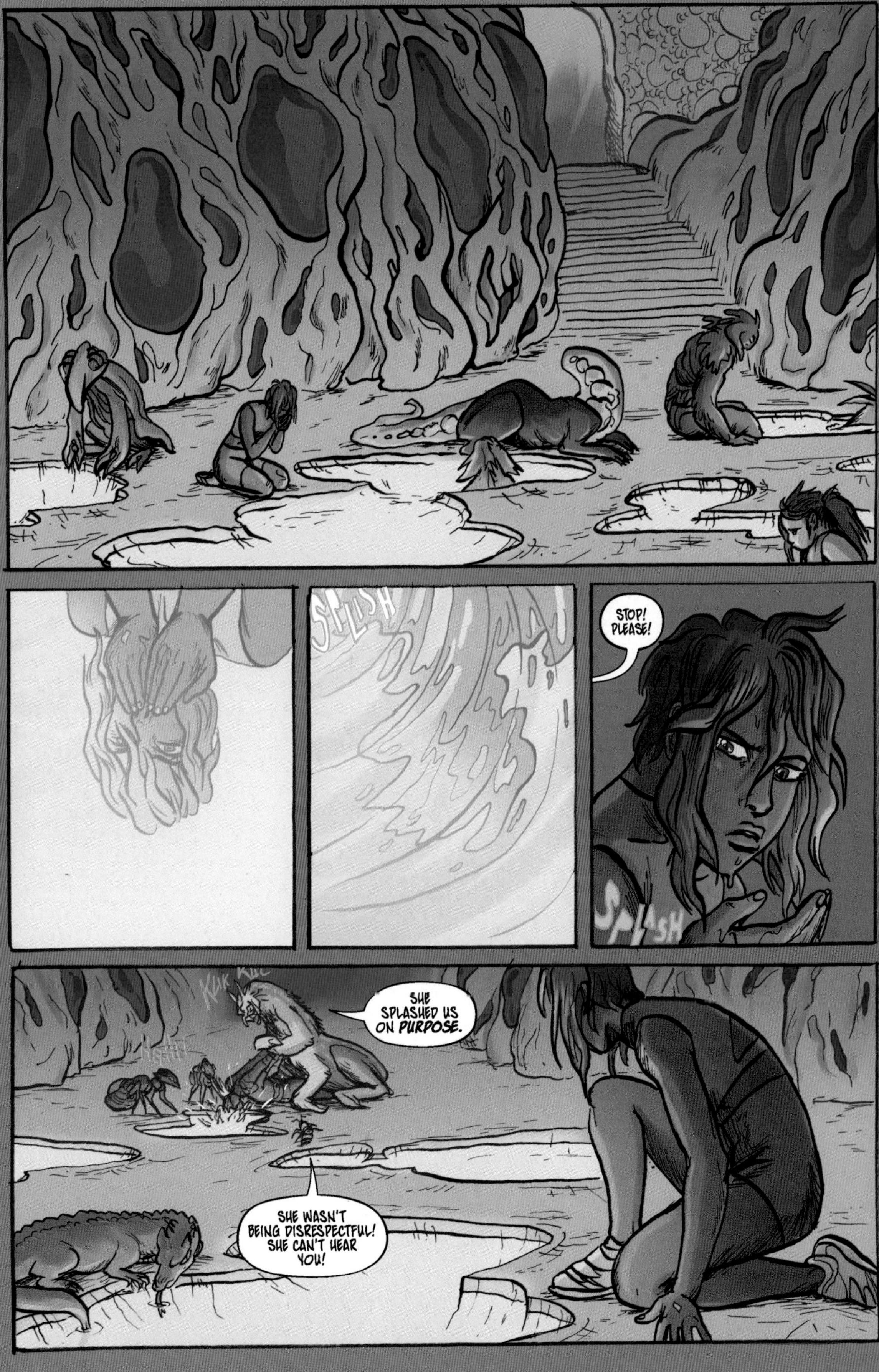
SPLASH
STOP! PLEASE!
SPLASH
SHE SPLASHED US ON PURPOSE.
SHE WASN'T BEING DISRESPECTFUL! SHE CAN'T HEAR YOU!

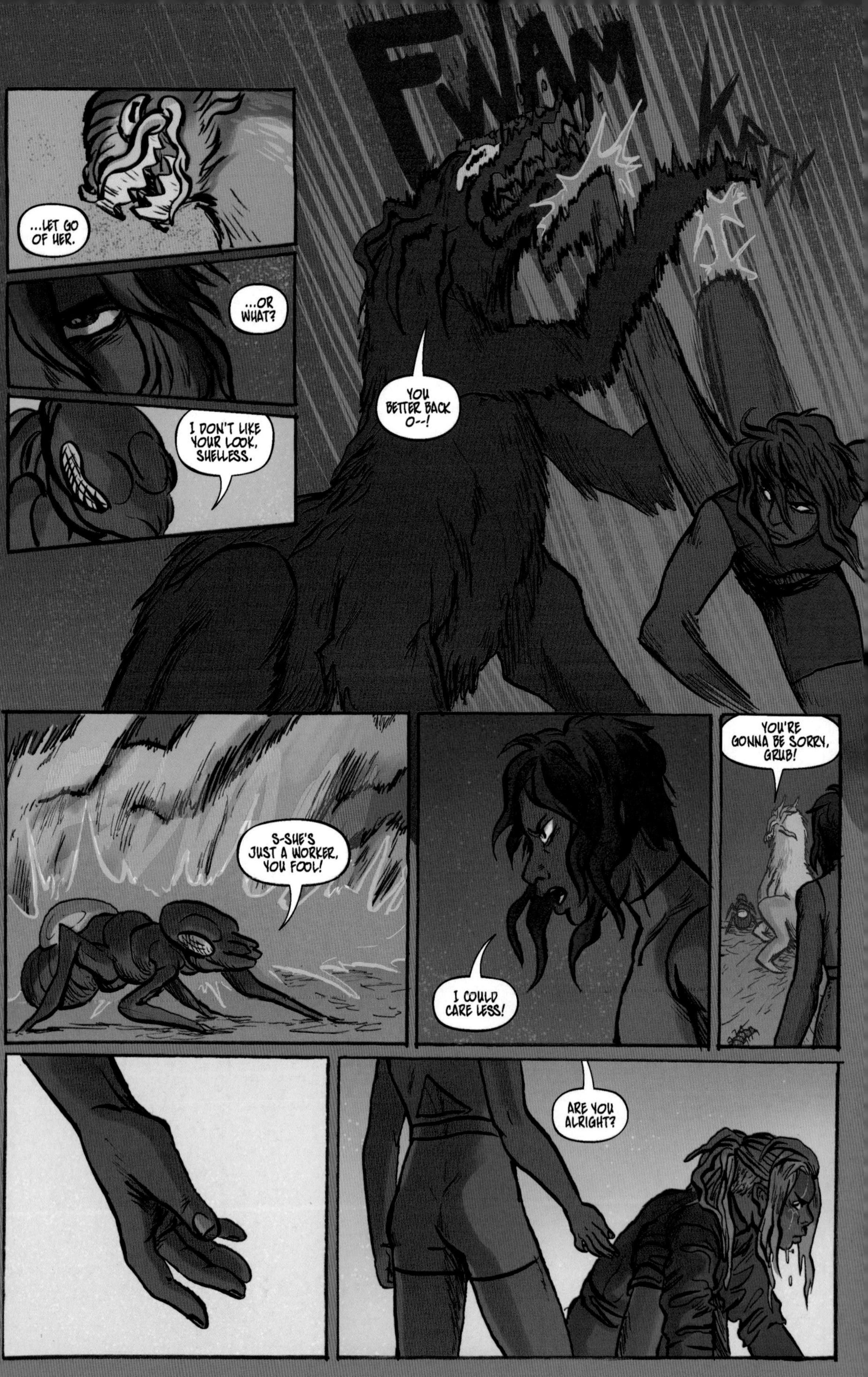
FWAM
KRASH
...LET GO OF HER.
...OR WHAT?
I DON'T LIKE YOUR LOOK, SHELLESS.
YOU BETTER BACK O--!
S-SHE'S JUST A WORKER, YOU FOOL!
I COULD CARE LESS!
YOU'RE GONNA BE SORRY, GRUB!
ARE YOU ALRIGHT?

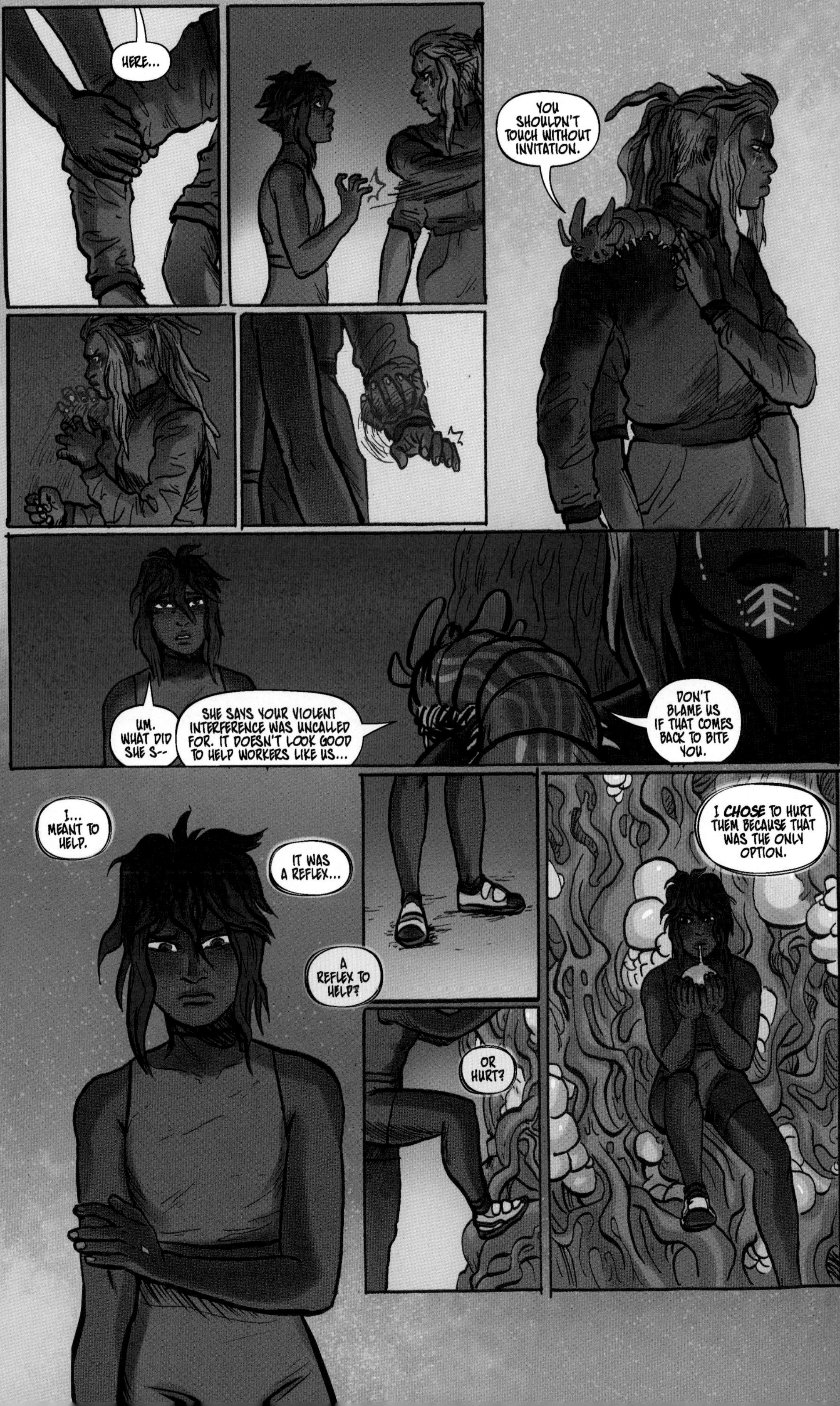
HERE...
YOU SHOULDN'T TOUCH WITHOUT INVITATION.
UM. WHAT DID SHE S--
SHE SAYS YOUR VIOLENT INTERFERENCE WAS UNCALLED FOR. IT DOESN'T LOOK GOOD TO HELP WORKERS LIKE US...
DON'T BLAME US IF THAT COMES BACK TO BITE YOU.
I... MEANT TO HELP.
IT WAS A REFLEX...
A REFLEX TO HELP?
OR HURT?
I CHOSE TO HURT THEM BECAUSE THAT WAS THE ONLY OPTION.

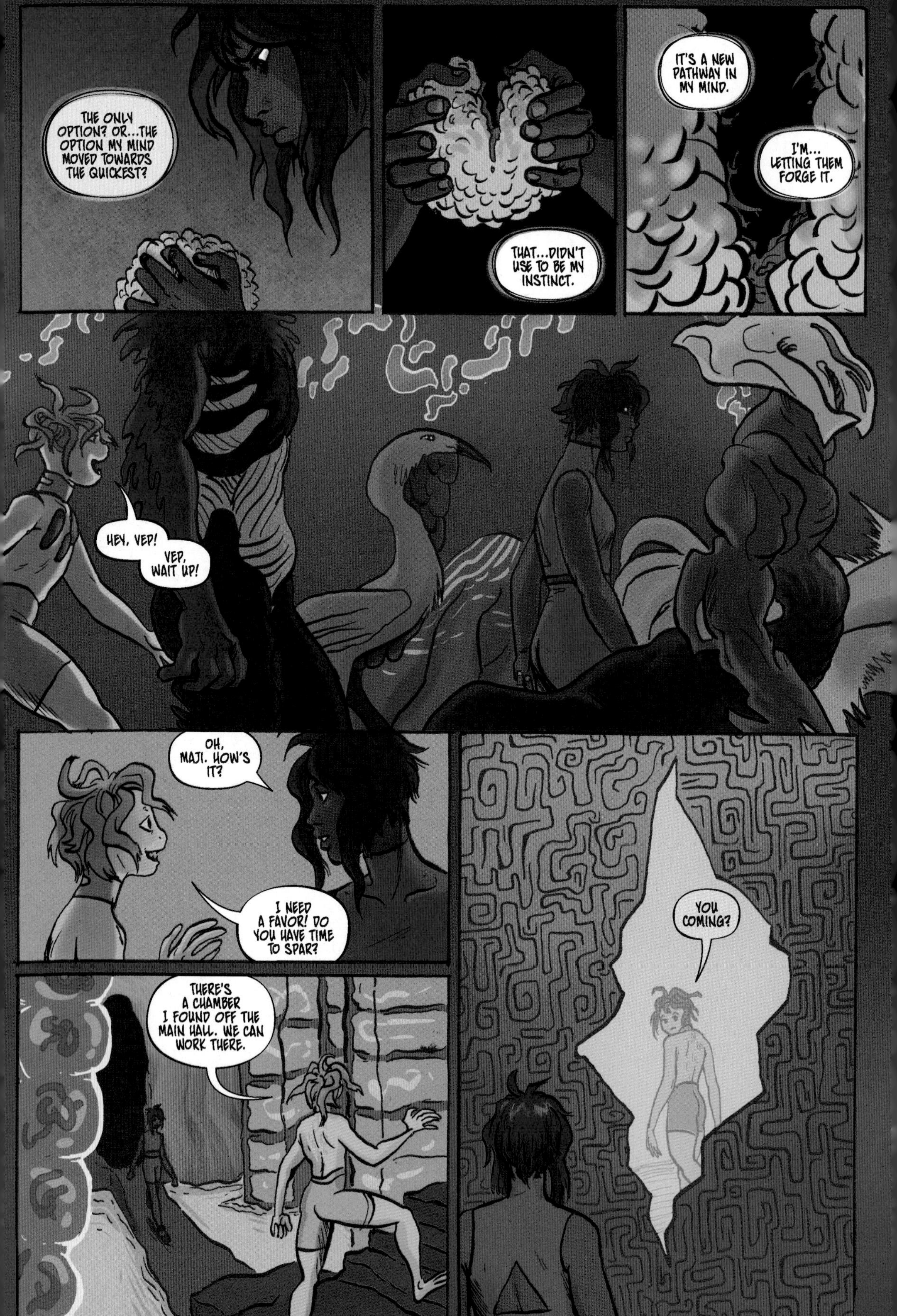
THE ONLY OPTION? OR...THE OPTION MY MIND MOVED TOWARDS THE QUICKEST?
THAT...DIDN'T USE TO BE MY INSTINCT.
IT'S A NEW PATHWAY IN MY MIND.
I'M... LETTING THEM FORGE IT.
HEY, VEP!
VEP, WAIT UP!
OH, MAJI. HOW'S IT?
I NEED A FAVOR! DO YOU HAVE TIME TO SPAR?
THERE'S A CHAMBER I FOUND OFF THE MAIN HALL. WE CAN WORK THERE.
YOU COMING?

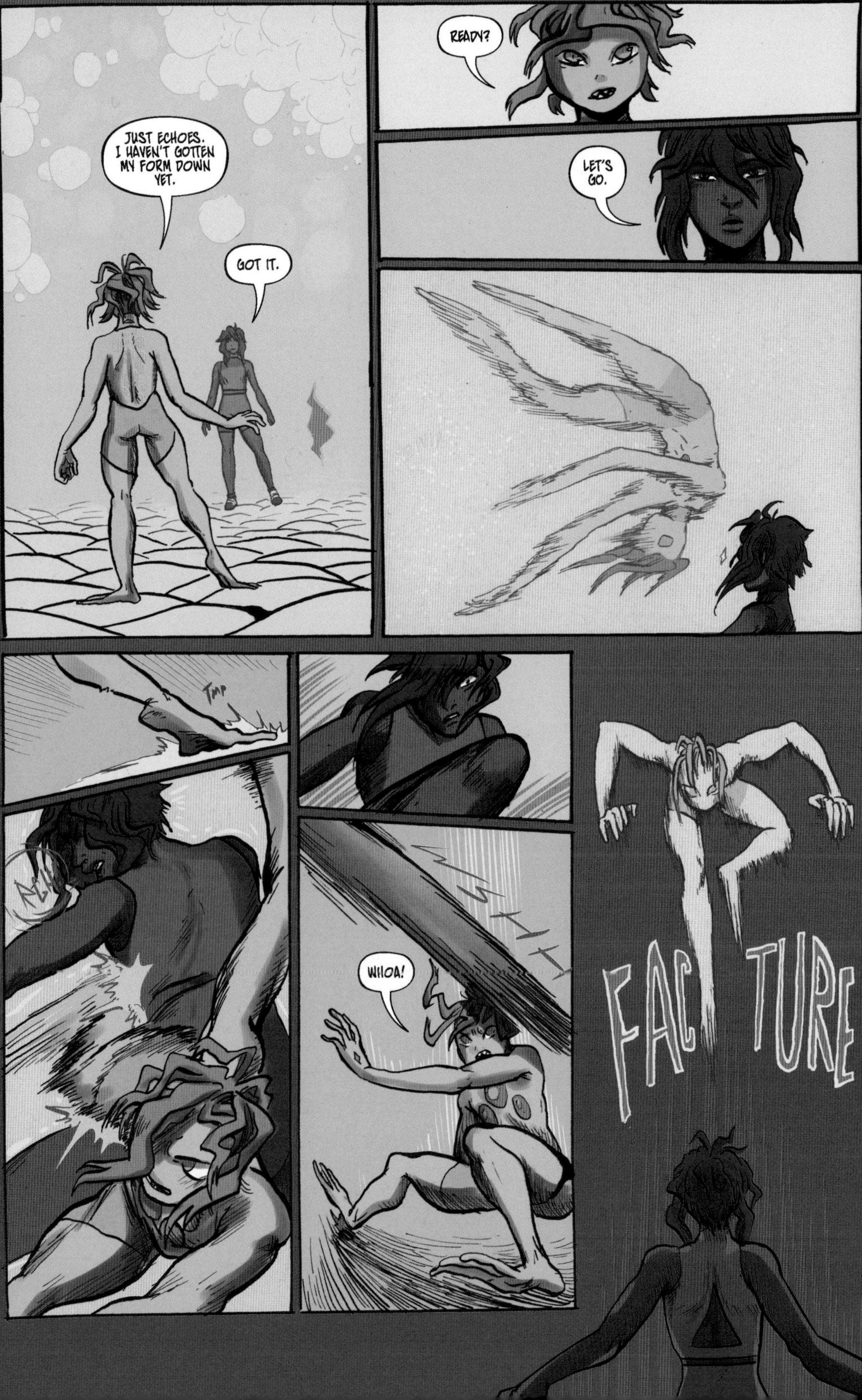

JUST ECHOES. I HAVEN'T GOTTEN MY FORM DOWN YET.
GOT IT.
READY?
LET'S GO.
TMP
WHOA!
FAC TURE

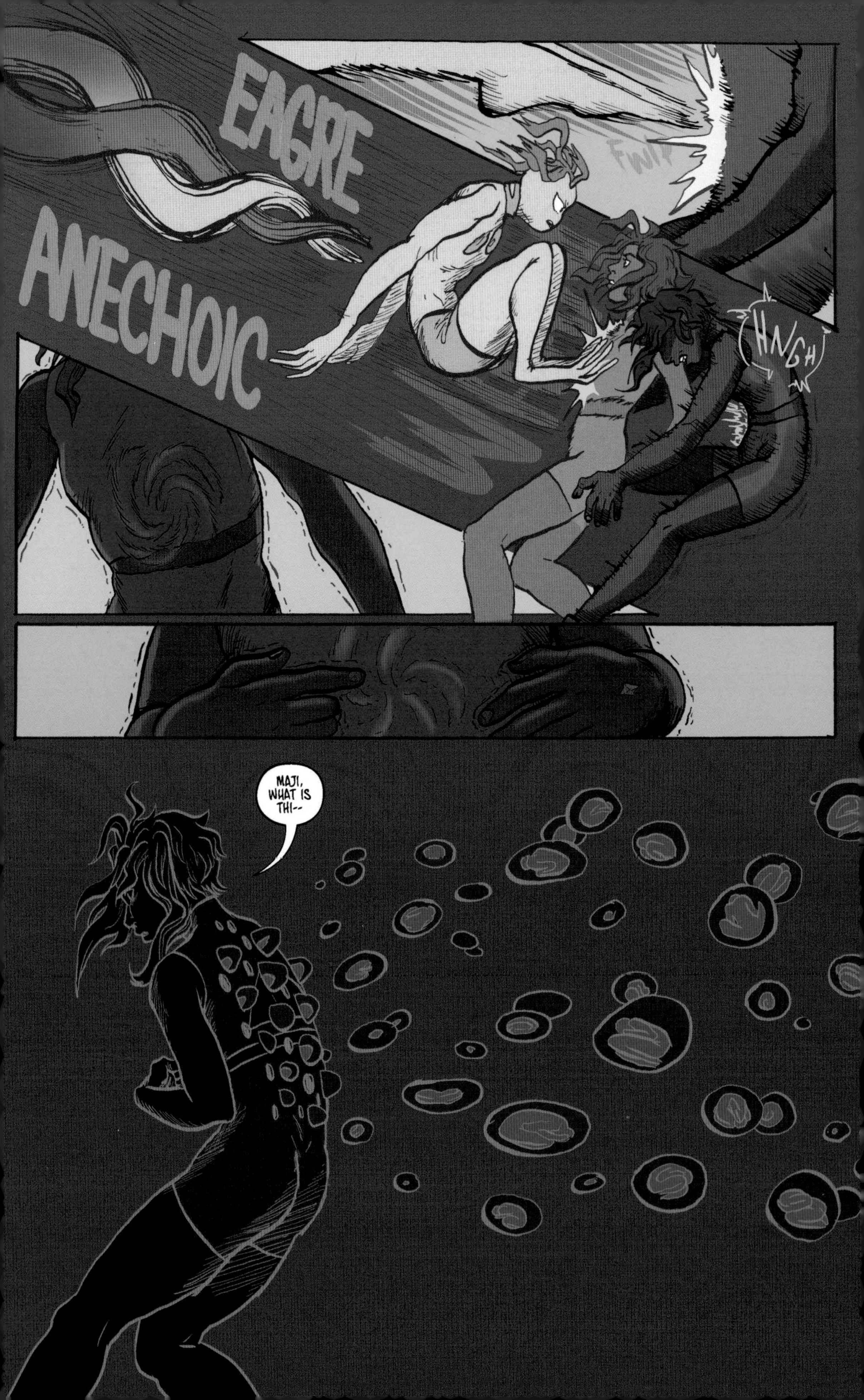
EAGRE
ANECHOIC
HNGH
MAJI, WHAT IS THI--

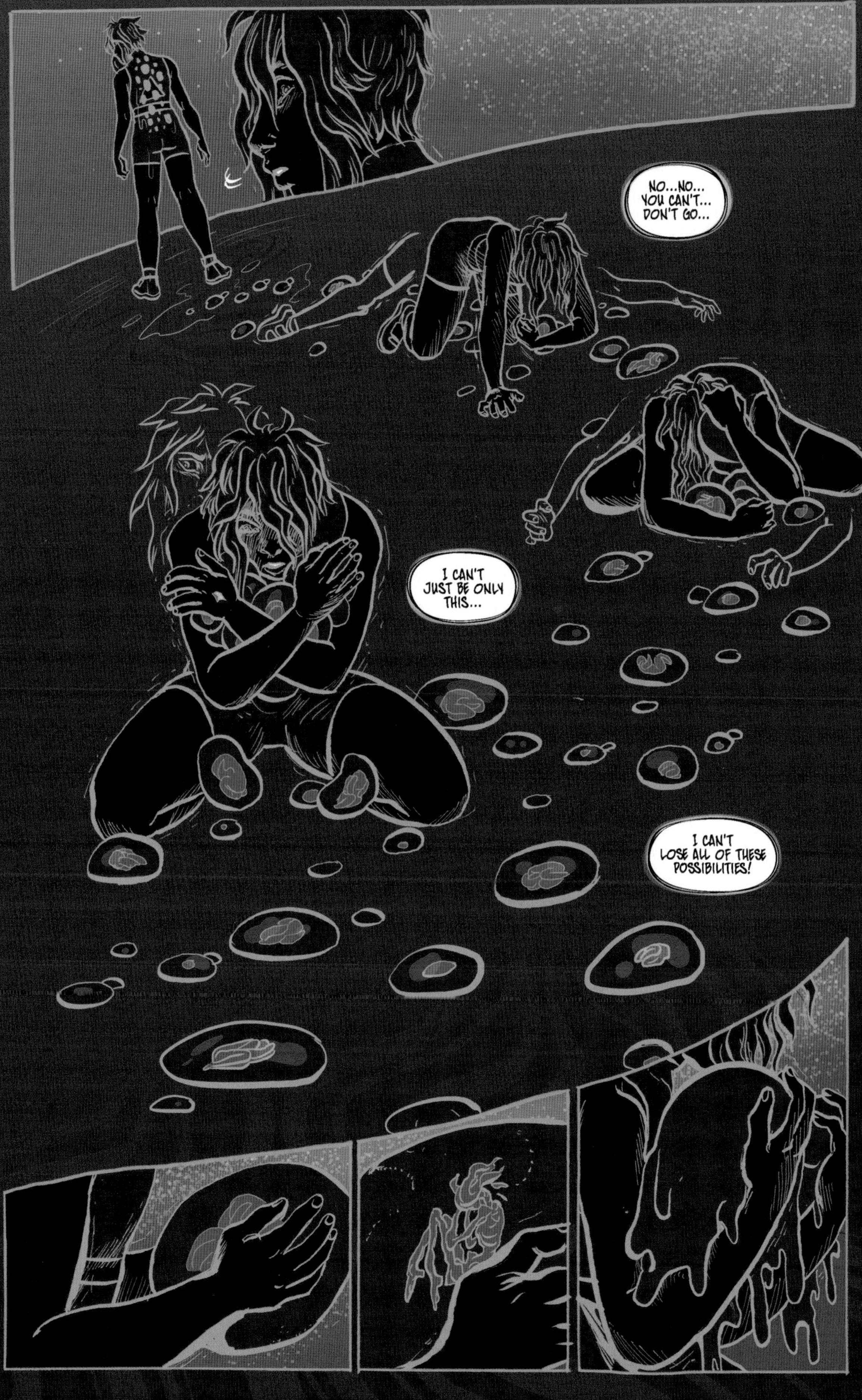
NO...NO... YOU CAN'T... DON'T GO...
I CAN'T JUST BE ONLY THIS...
I CAN'T LOSE ALL OF THESE POSSIBILITIES!

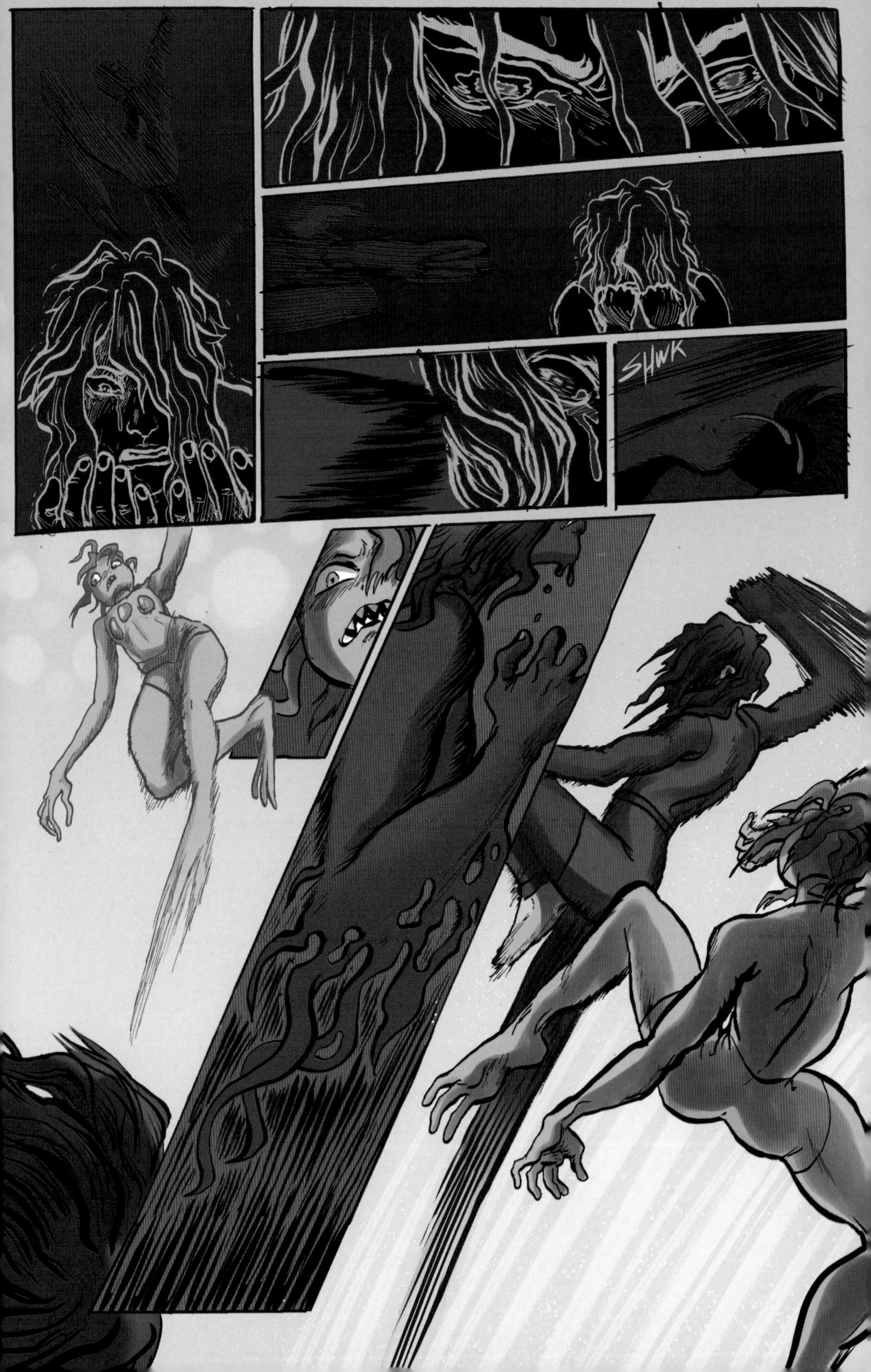
SHWK

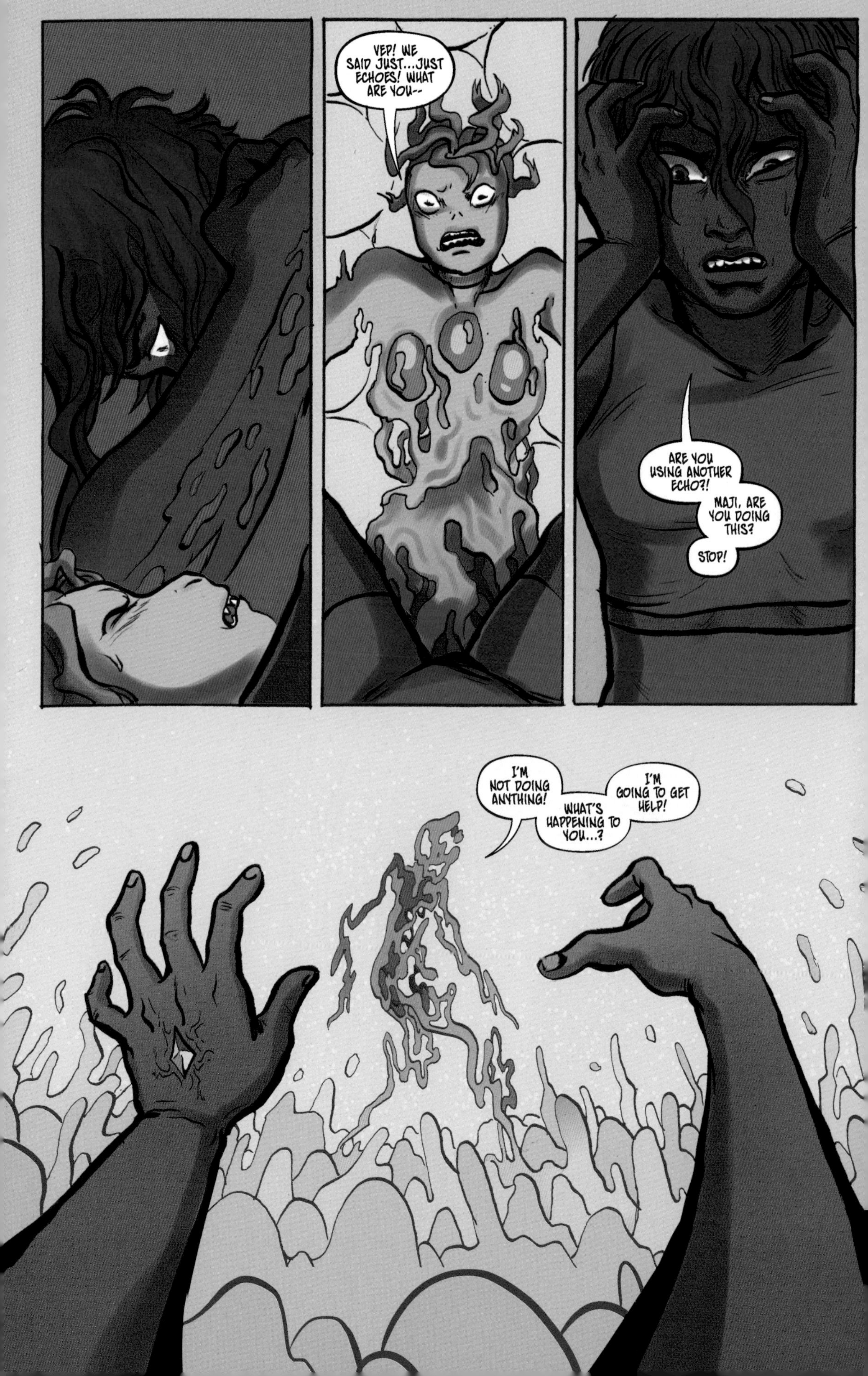
YEP! WE SAID JUST...JUST ECHOES! WHAT ARE YOU--
ARE YOU USING ANOTHER ECHO?!
MAJI, ARE YOU DOING THIS?
STOP!
I'M NOT DOING ANYTHING!
WHAT'S HAPPENING TO YOU...?
I'M GOING TO GET HELP!

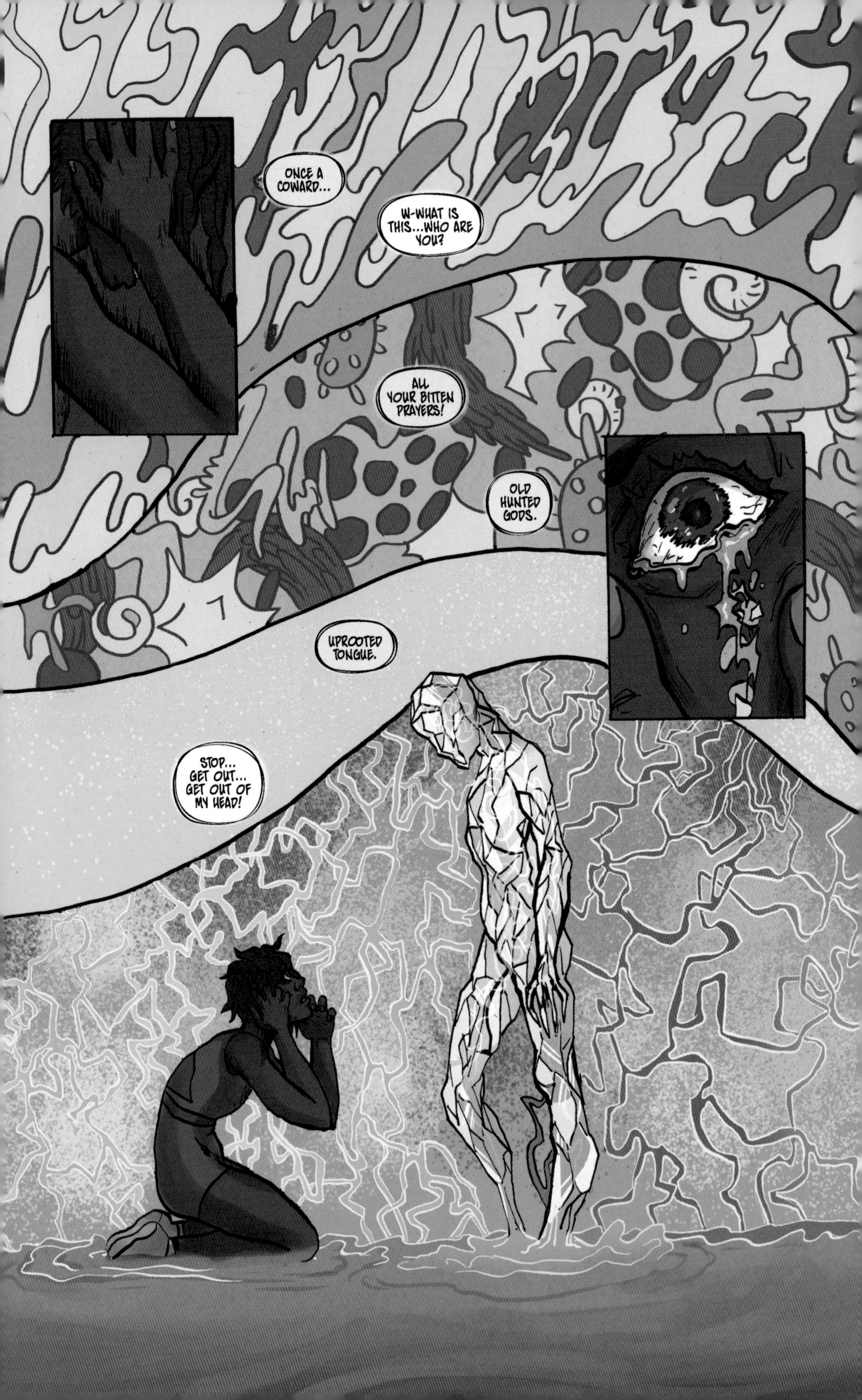
ONCE A COWARD...
W-WHAT IS THIS...WHO ARE YOU?
ALL YOUR BITTEN PRAYERS!
OLD HUNTED GODS.
UPROOTED TONGUE.
STOP... GET OUT... GET OUT OF MY HEAD!

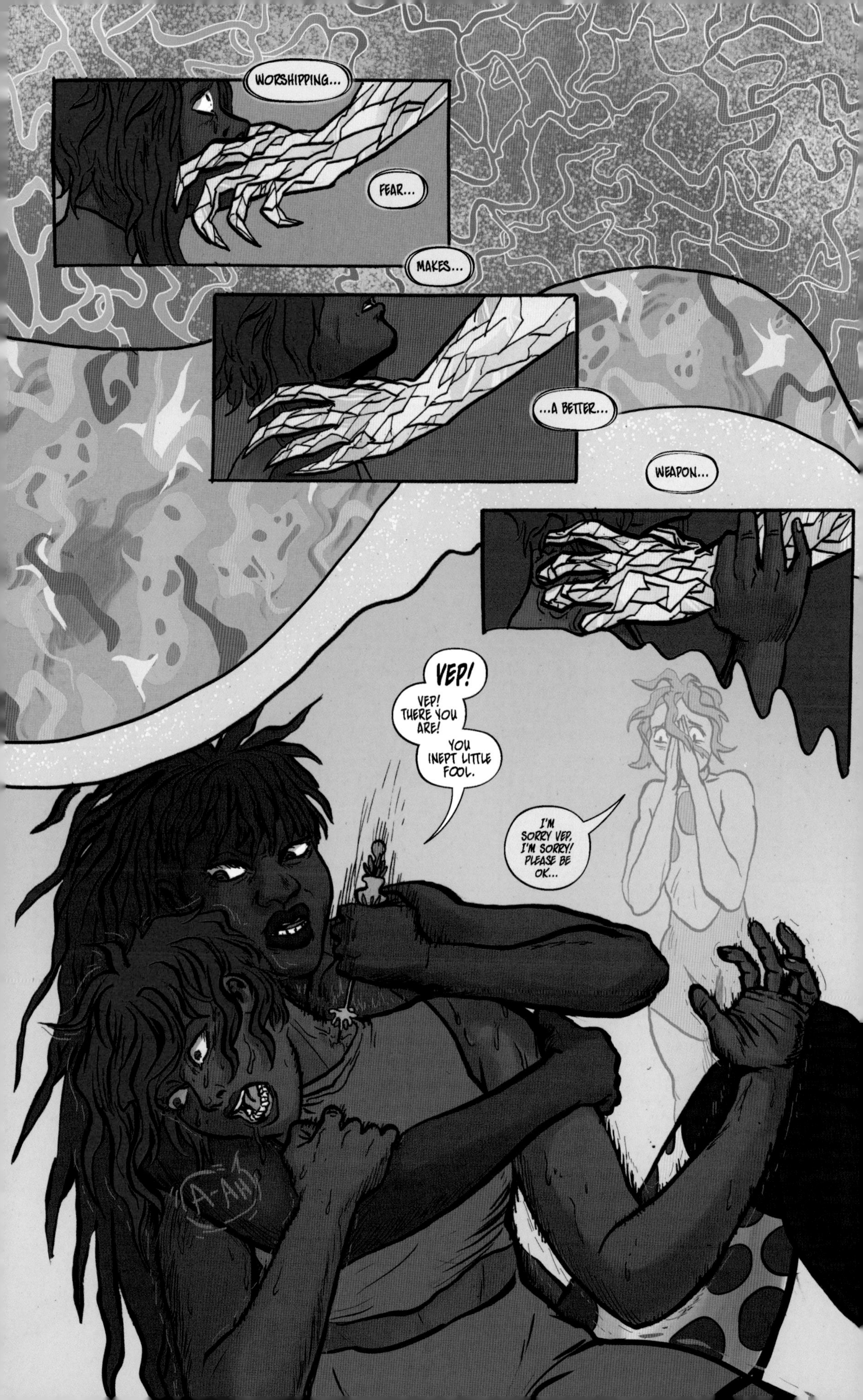
WORSHIPPING...
FEAR...
MAKES...
...A BETTER...
WEAPON...
VEP!
VEP! THERE YOU ARE!
YOU INEPT LITTLE FOOL.
I'M SORRY VEP, I'M SORRY! PLEASE BE OK...
A-AH

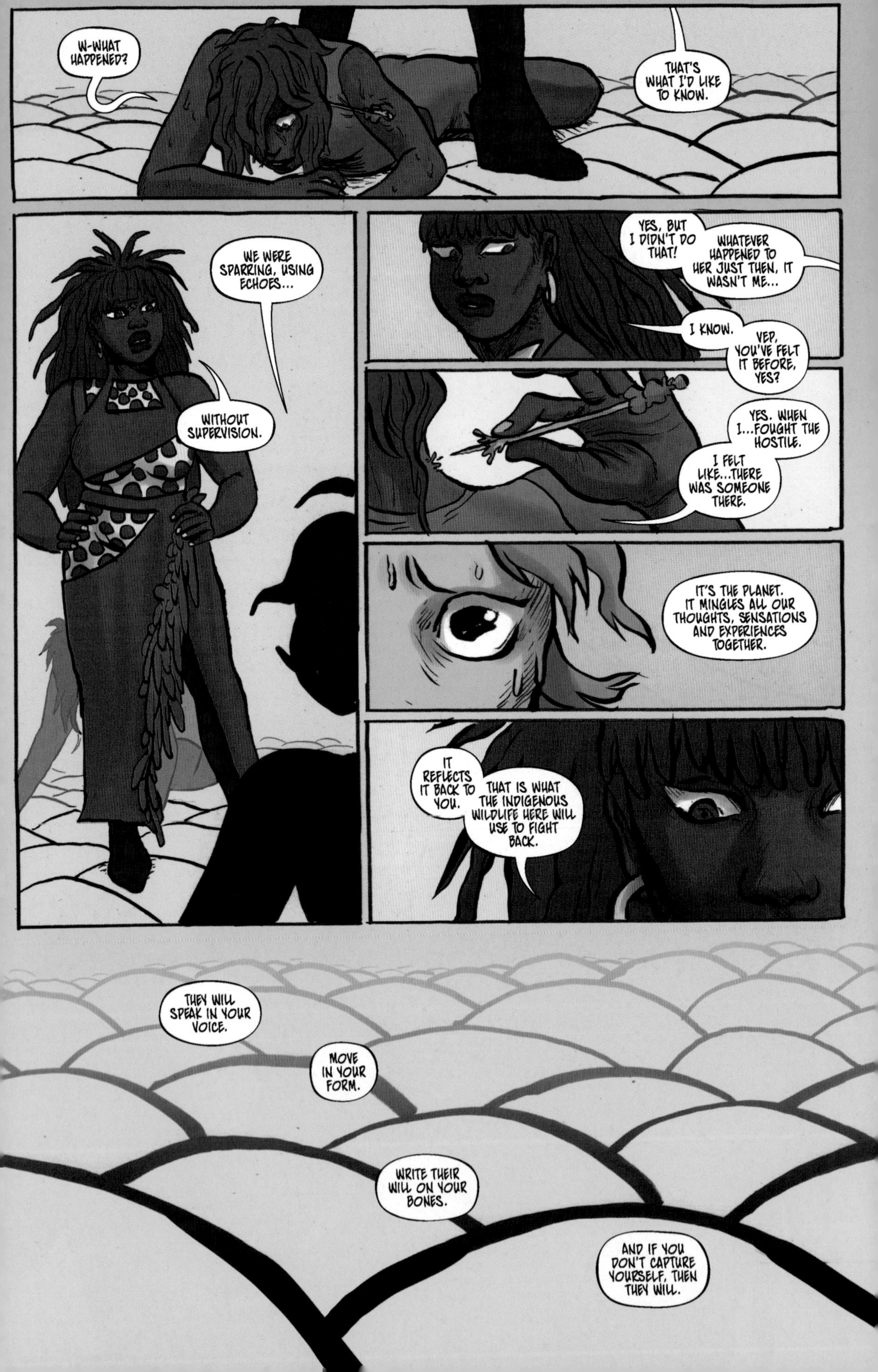
W-WHAT HAPPENED?
THAT'S WHAT I'D LIKE TO KNOW.
WE WERE SPARRING, USING ECHOES...
WITHOUT SUPERVISION.
YES, BUT I DIDN'T DO THAT!
WHATEVER HAPPENED TO HER JUST THEN, IT WASN'T ME...
I KNOW.
YEP, YOU'VE FELT IT BEFORE, YES?
YES. WHEN I...FOUGHT THE HOSTILE.
I FELT LIKE...THERE WAS SOMEONE THERE.
IT'S THE PLANET. IT MINGLES ALL OUR THOUGHTS, SENSATIONS AND EXPERIENCES TOGETHER.
IT REFLECTS IT BACK TO YOU.
THAT IS WHAT THE INDIGENOUS WILDLIFE HERE WILL USE TO FIGHT BACK.
THEY WILL SPEAK IN YOUR VOICE.
MOVE IN YOUR FORM.
WRITE THEIR WILL ON YOUR BONES.
AND IF YOU DON'T CAPTURE YOURSELF, THEN THEY WILL.

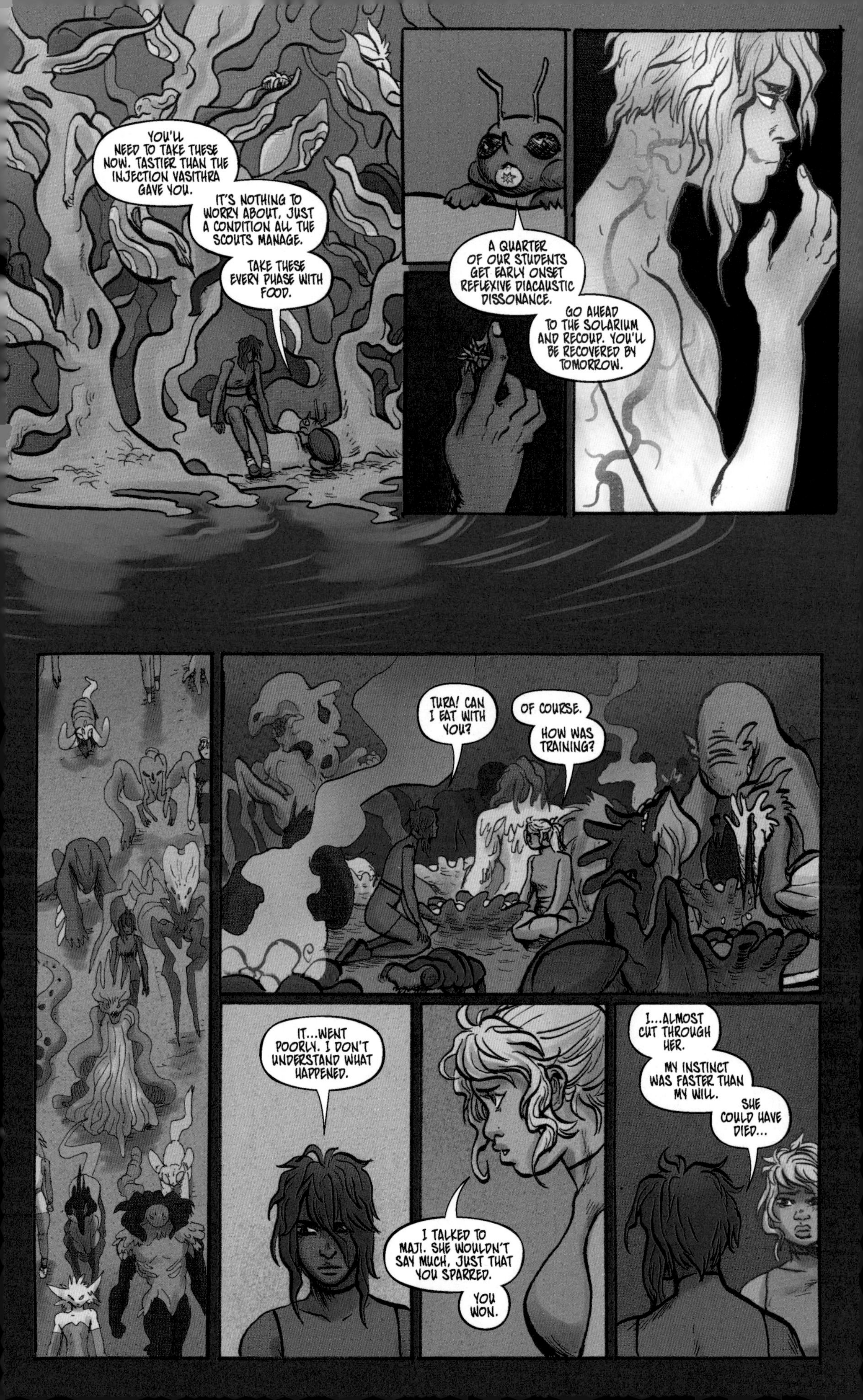
YOU'LL NEED TO TAKE THESE NOW. TASTIER THAN THE INJECTION VASITHRA GAVE YOU.
IT'S NOTHING TO WORRY ABOUT, JUST A CONDITION ALL THE SCOUTS MANAGE.
TAKE THESE EVERY PHASE WITH FOOD.
A QUARTER OF OUR STUDENTS GET EARLY ONSET REFLEXIVE DIACAUSTIC DISSONANCE.
GO AHEAD TO THE SOLARIUM AND RECOUP. YOU'LL BE RECOVERED BY TOMORROW.
TURA! CAN I EAT WITH YOU?
OF COURSE.
HOW WAS TRAINING?
IT...WENT POORLY. I DON'T UNDERSTAND WHAT HAPPENED.
I TALKED TO MAJI. SHE WOULDN'T SAY MUCH, JUST THAT YOU SPARRED.
YOU WON.
I...ALMOST CUT THROUGH HER.
MY INSTINCT WAS FASTER THAN MY WILL.
SHE COULD HAVE DIED...

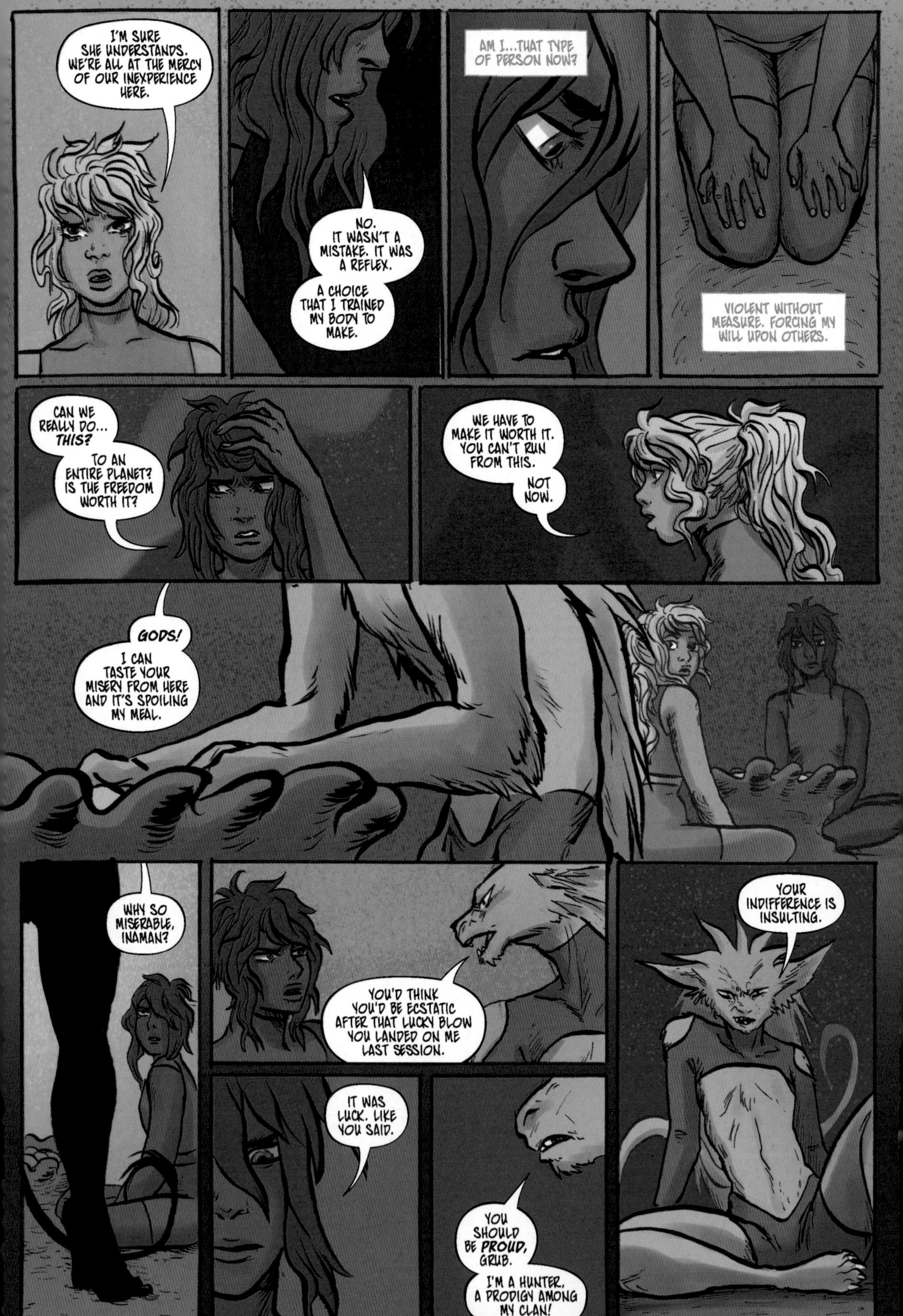
I'M SURE SHE UNDERSTANDS. WE'RE ALL AT THE MERCY OF OUR INEXPERIENCE HERE.
NO. IT WASN'T A MISTAKE. IT WAS A REFLEX.
A CHOICE THAT I TRAINED MY BODY TO MAKE.
AM I...THAT TYPE OF PERSON NOW?
VIOLENT WITHOUT MEASURE. FORCING MY WILL UPON OTHERS.
CAN WE REALLY DO... THIS?
TO AN ENTIRE PLANET? IS THE FREEDOM WORTH IT?
WE HAVE TO MAKE IT WORTH IT. YOU CAN'T RUN FROM THIS.
NOT NOW.
GODS!
I CAN TASTE YOUR MISERY FROM HERE AND IT'S SPOILING MY MEAL.
WHY SO MISERABLE, INAMAN?
YOU'D THINK YOU'D BE ECSTATIC AFTER THAT LUCKY BLOW YOU LANDED ON ME LAST SESSION.
YOUR INDIFFERENCE IS INSULTING.
IT WAS LUCK. LIKE YOU SAID.
YOU SHOULD BE PROUD, GRUB.
I'M A HUNTER, A PRODIGY AMONG MY CLAN!

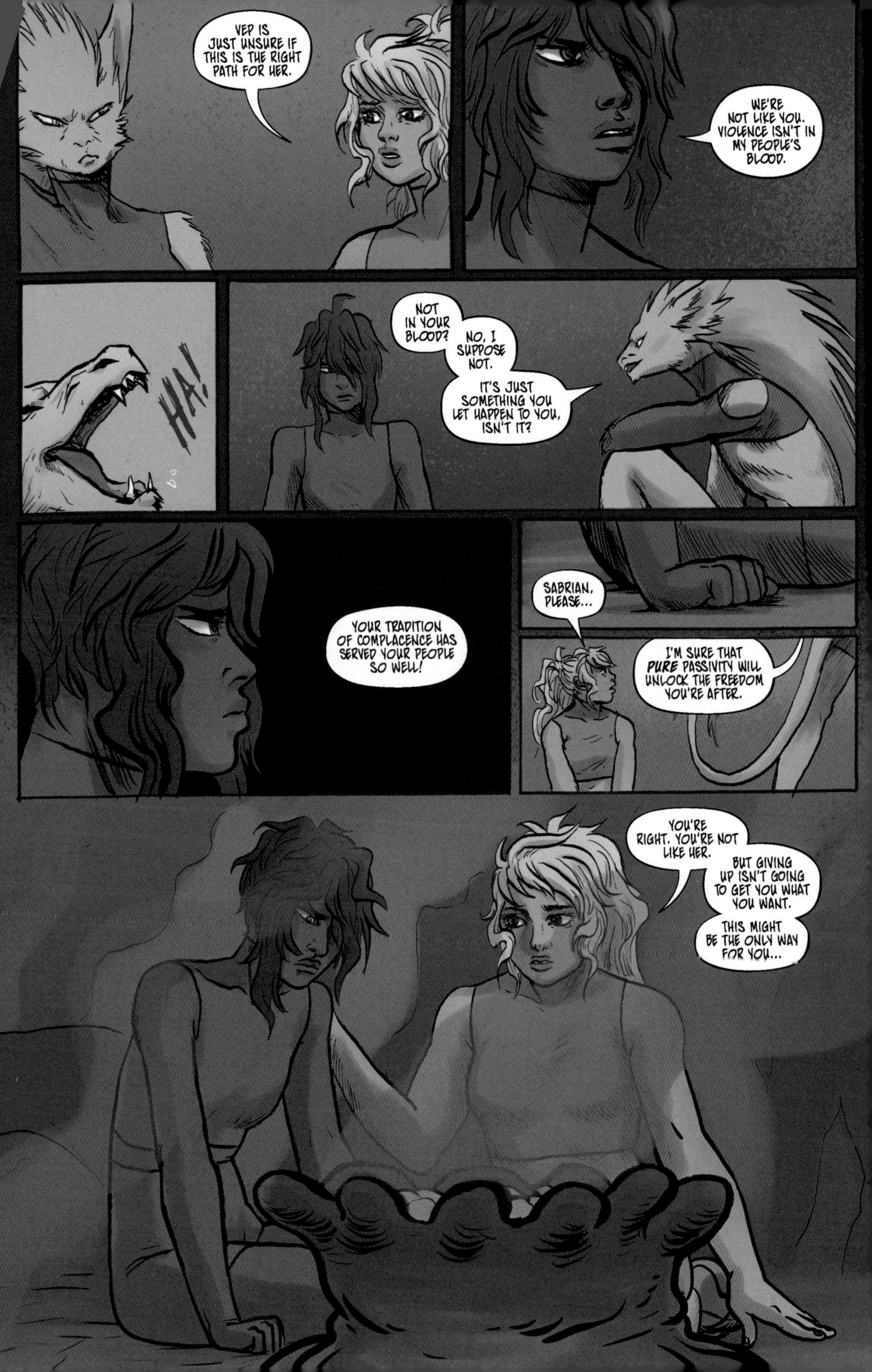
VEP IS JUST UNSURE IF THIS IS THE RIGHT PATH FOR HER.
WE'RE NOT LIKE YOU. VIOLENCE ISN'T IN MY PEOPLE'S BLOOD.
HA!
NOT IN YOUR BLOOD?
NO, I SUPPOSE NOT.
IT'S JUST SOMETHING YOU LET HAPPEN TO YOU, ISN'T IT?
YOUR TRADITION OF COMPLACENCE HAS SERVED YOUR PEOPLE SO WELL!
SABRIAN, PLEASE...
I'M SURE THAT PURE PASSIVITY WILL UNLOCK THE FREEDOM YOU'RE AFTER.
YOU'RE RIGHT. YOU'RE NOT LIKE HER.
BUT GIVING UP ISN'T GOING TO GET YOU WHAT YOU WANT.
THIS MIGHT BE THE ONLY WAY FOR YOU...

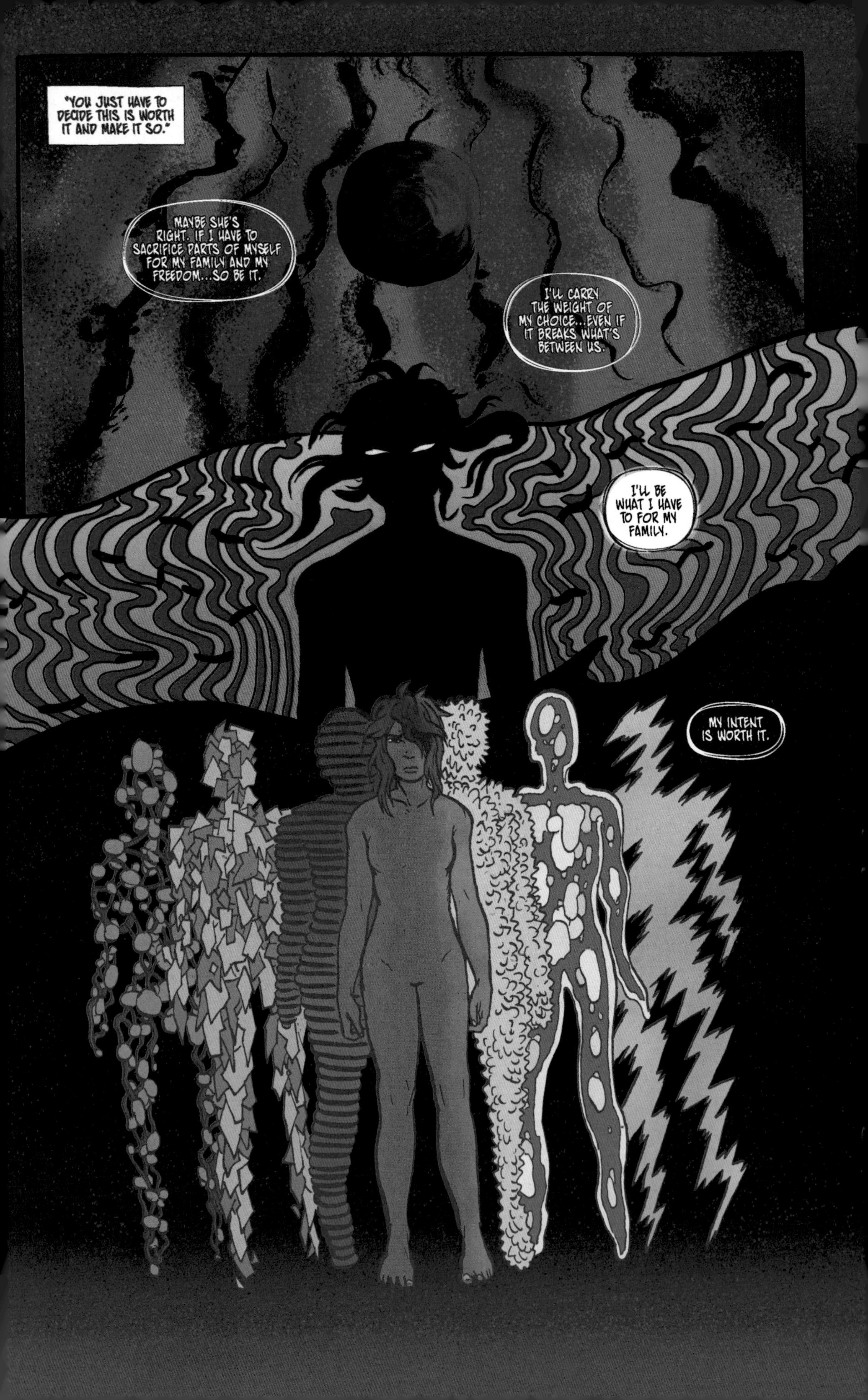
"YOU JUST HAVE TO DECIDE THIS IS WORTH IT AND MAKE IT SO."
MAYBE SHE'S RIGHT. IF I HAVE TO SACRIFICE PARTS OF MYSELF FOR MY FAMILY AND MY FREEDOM...SO BE IT.
I'LL CARRY THE WEIGHT OF MY CHOICE...EVEN IF IT BREAKS WHAT'S BETWEEN US.
I'LL BE WHAT I HAVE TO FOR MY FAMILY.
MY INTENT IS WORTH IT.

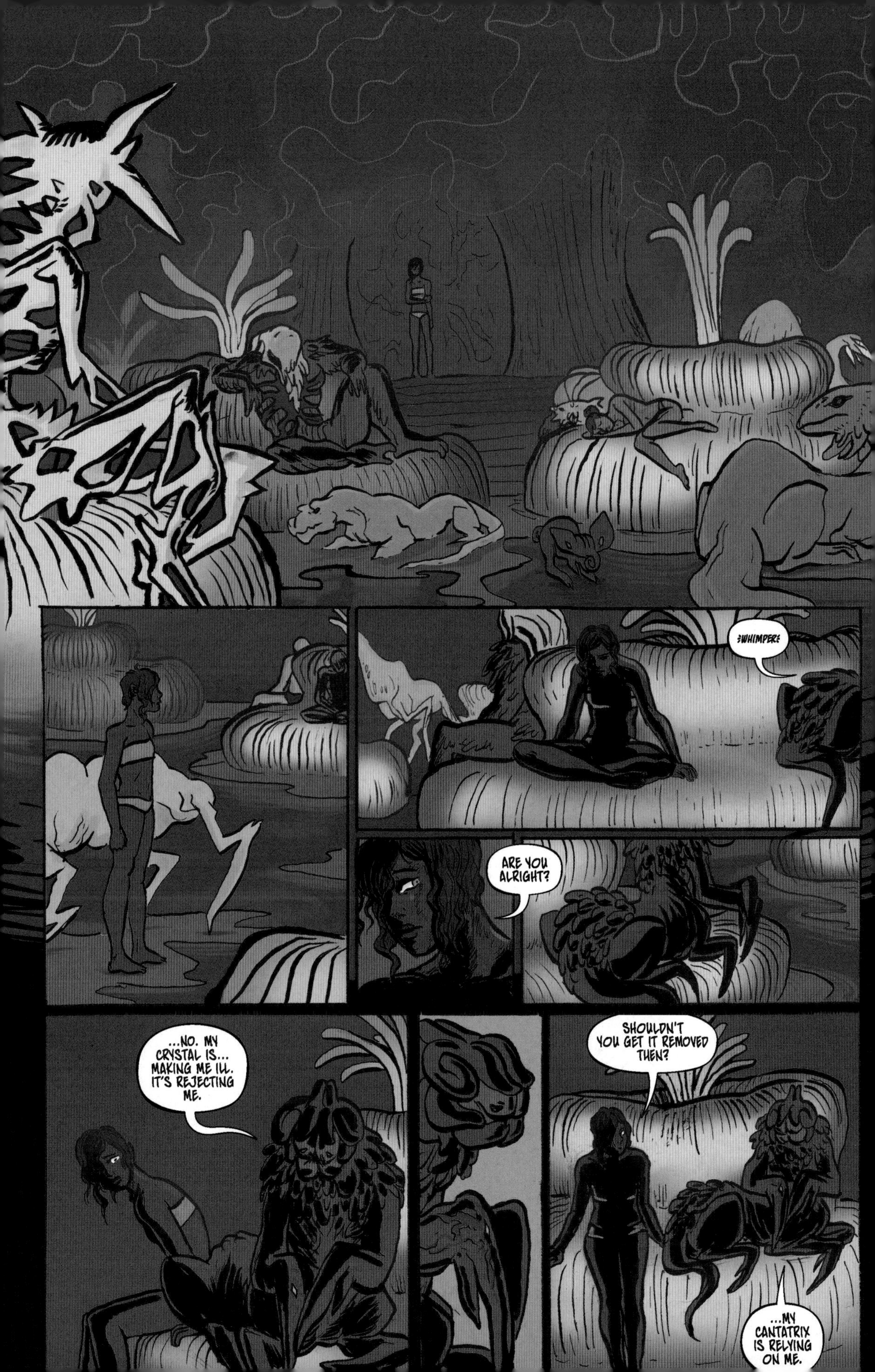

WHIMPER
ARE YOU ALRIGHT?
...NO. MY CRYSTAL IS... MAKING ME ILL. IT'S REJECTING ME.
SHOULDN'T YOU GET IT REMOVED THEN?
...MY CANTATRIX IS RELYING ON ME.

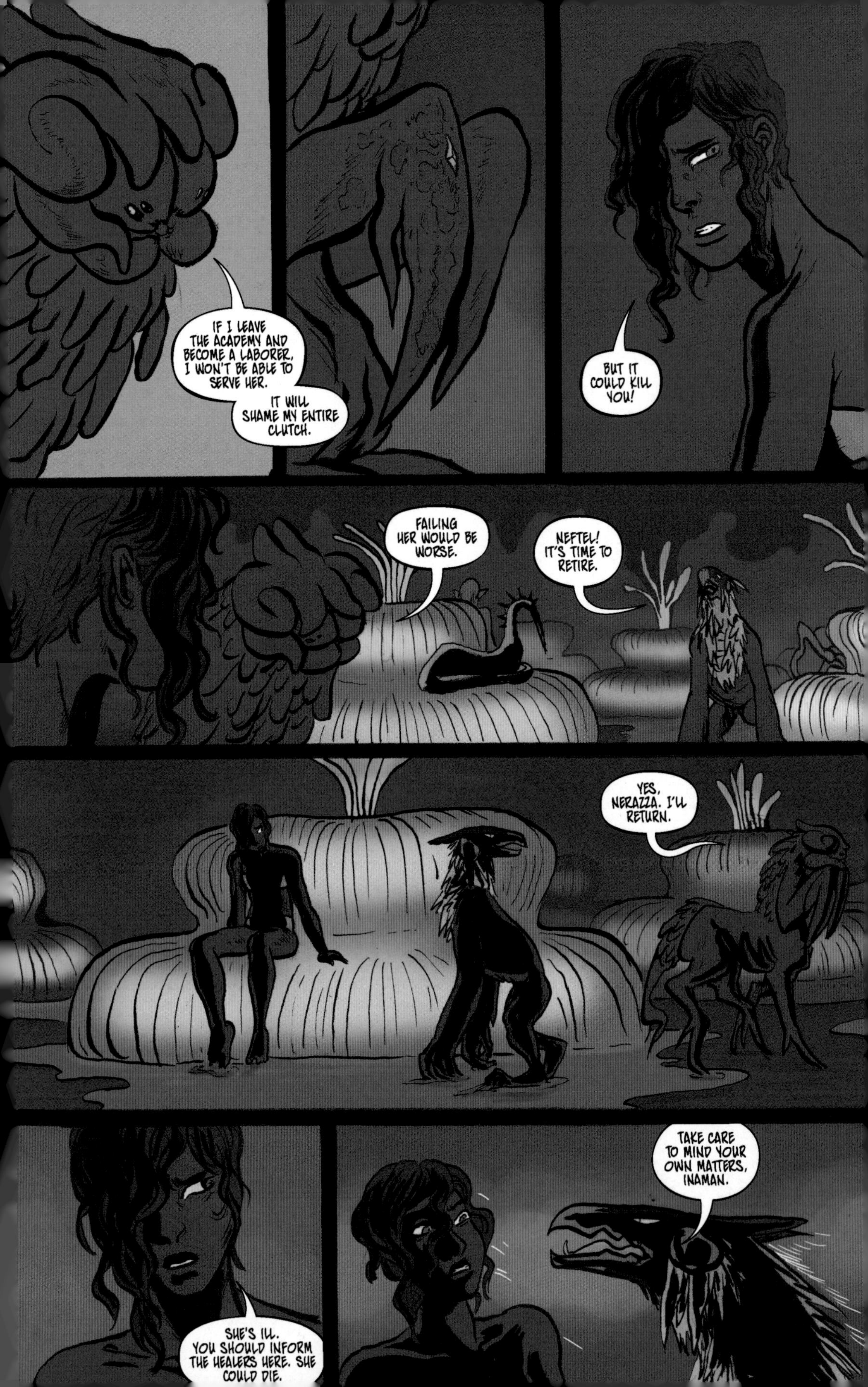
IF I LEAVE THE ACADEMY AND BECOME A LABORER, I WON'T BE ABLE TO SERVE HER.
IT WILL SHAME MY ENTIRE CLUTCH.
BUT IT COULD KILL YOU!
FAILING HER WOULD BE WORSE.
NEFTEL! IT'S TIME TO RETIRE.
YES, NERAZZA. I'LL RETURN.
SHE'S ILL. YOU SHOULD INFORM THE HEALERS HERE. SHE COULD DIE.
TAKE CARE TO MIND YOUR OWN MATTERS, INAMAN.

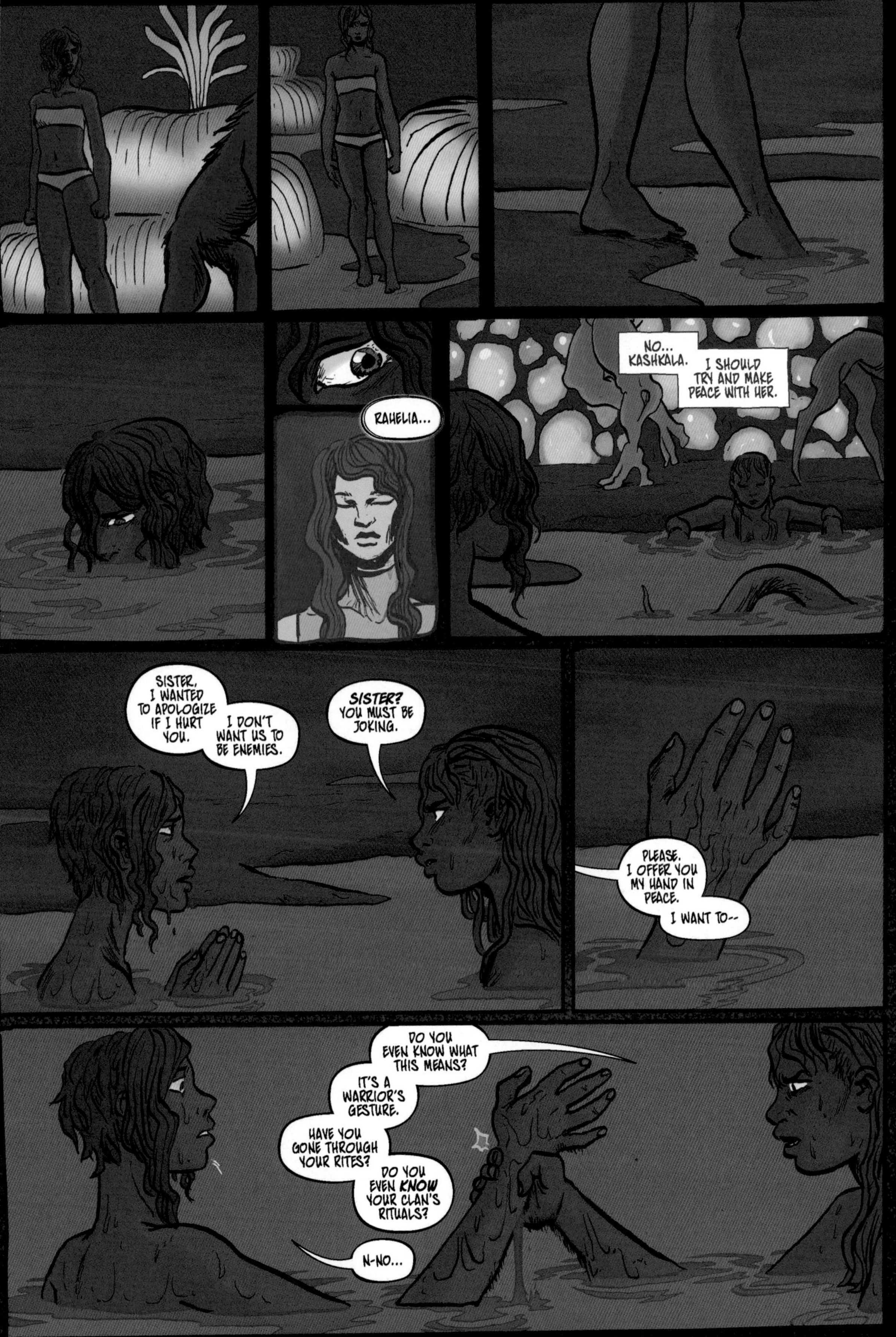
RAHELIA...
NO... KASHKALA.
I SHOULD TRY AND MAKE PEACE WITH HER.
SISTER, I WANTED TO APOLOGIZE IF I HURT YOU.
I DON'T WANT US TO BE ENEMIES.
SISTER? YOU MUST BE JOKING.
PLEASE. I OFFER YOU MY HAND IN PEACE.
I WANT TO--
DO YOU EVEN KNOW WHAT THIS MEANS?
IT'S A WARRIOR'S GESTURE.
HAVE YOU GONE THROUGH YOUR RITES?
DO YOU EVEN KNOW YOUR CLAN'S RITUALS?
N-NO...

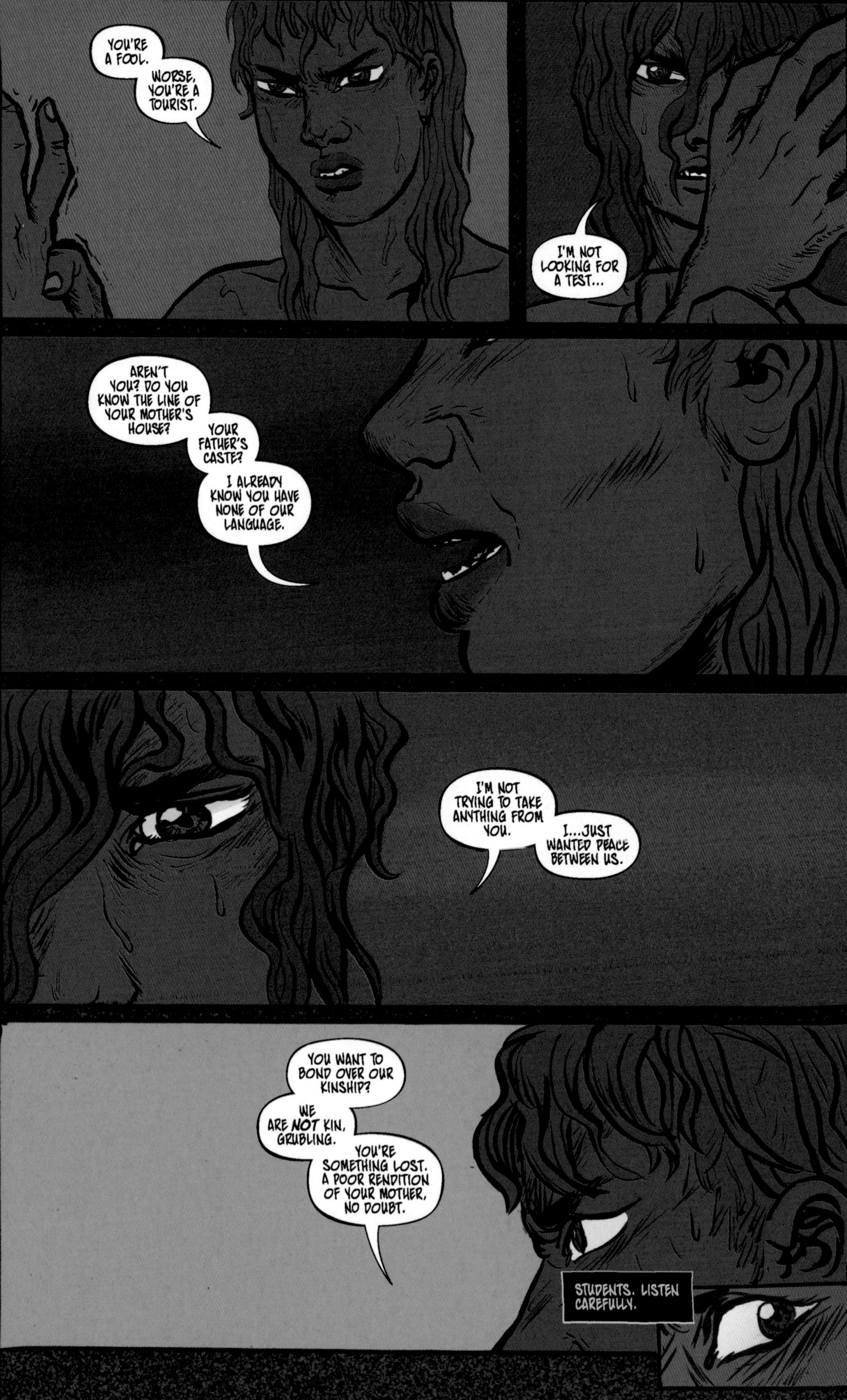
YOU'RE A FOOL.
WORSE, YOU'RE A TOURIST.
I'M NOT LOOKING FOR A TEST...
AREN'T YOU? DO YOU KNOW THE LINE OF YOUR MOTHER'S HOUSE?
YOUR FATHER'S CASTE?
I ALREADY KNOW YOU HAVE NONE OF OUR LANGUAGE.
I'M NOT TRYING TO TAKE ANYTHING FROM YOU.
I...JUST WANTED PEACE BETWEEN US.
YOU WANT TO BOND OVER OUR KINSHIP?
WE ARE **NOT** KIN, GRUBLING.
YOU'RE SOMETHING LOST. A POOR RENDITION OF YOUR MOTHER, NO DOUBT.
STUDENTS. LISTEN CAREFULLY.

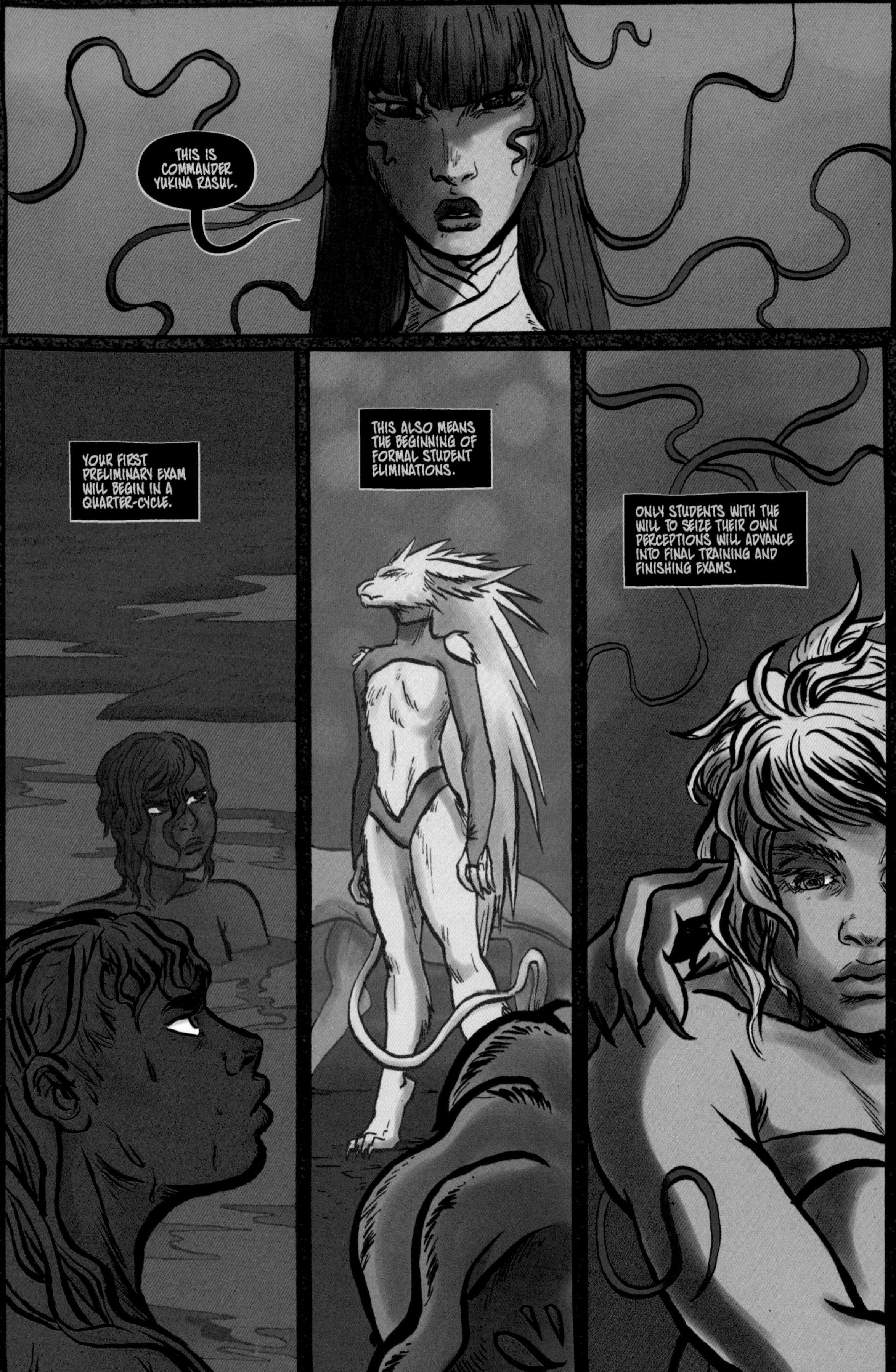
THIS IS COMMANDER YUKINA RASUL.
YOUR FIRST PRELIMINARY EXAM WILL BEGIN IN A QUARTER-CYCLE.
THIS ALSO MEANS THE BEGINNING OF FORMAL STUDENT ELIMINATIONS.
ONLY STUDENTS WITH THE WILL TO SEIZE THEIR OWN PERCEPTIONS WILL ADVANCE INTO FINAL TRAINING AND FINISHING EXAMS.

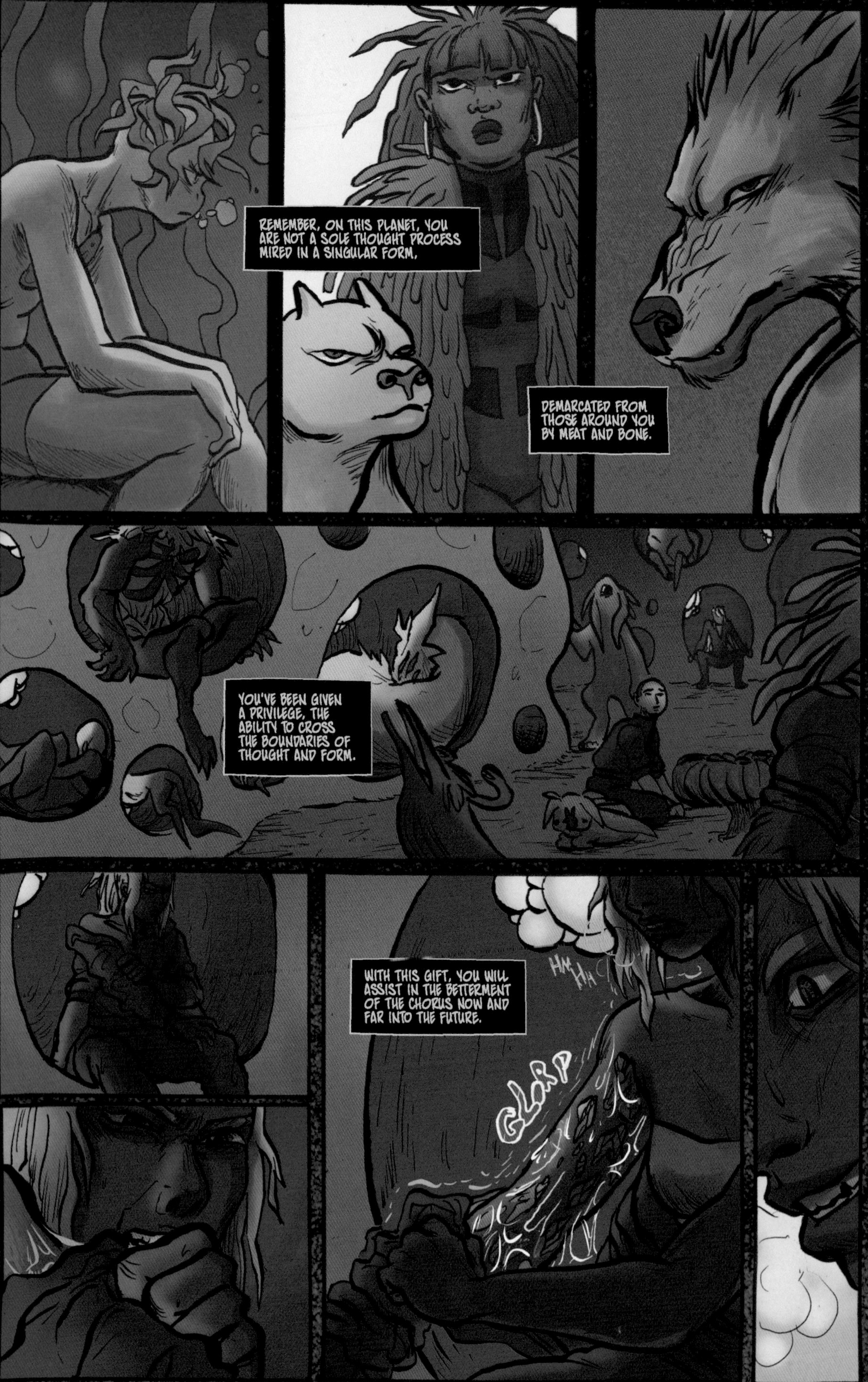
REMEMBER, ON THIS PLANET, YOU ARE NOT A SOLE THOUGHT PROCESS MIRED IN A SINGULAR FORM,
DEMARCATED FROM THOSE AROUND YOU BY MEAT AND BONE.
YOU'VE BEEN GIVEN A PRIVILEGE, THE ABILITY TO CROSS THE BOUNDARIES OF THOUGHT AND FORM.
WITH THIS GIFT, YOU WILL ASSIST IN THE BETTERMENT OF THE CHORUS NOW AND FAR INTO THE FUTURE.
HM HA
GLORP

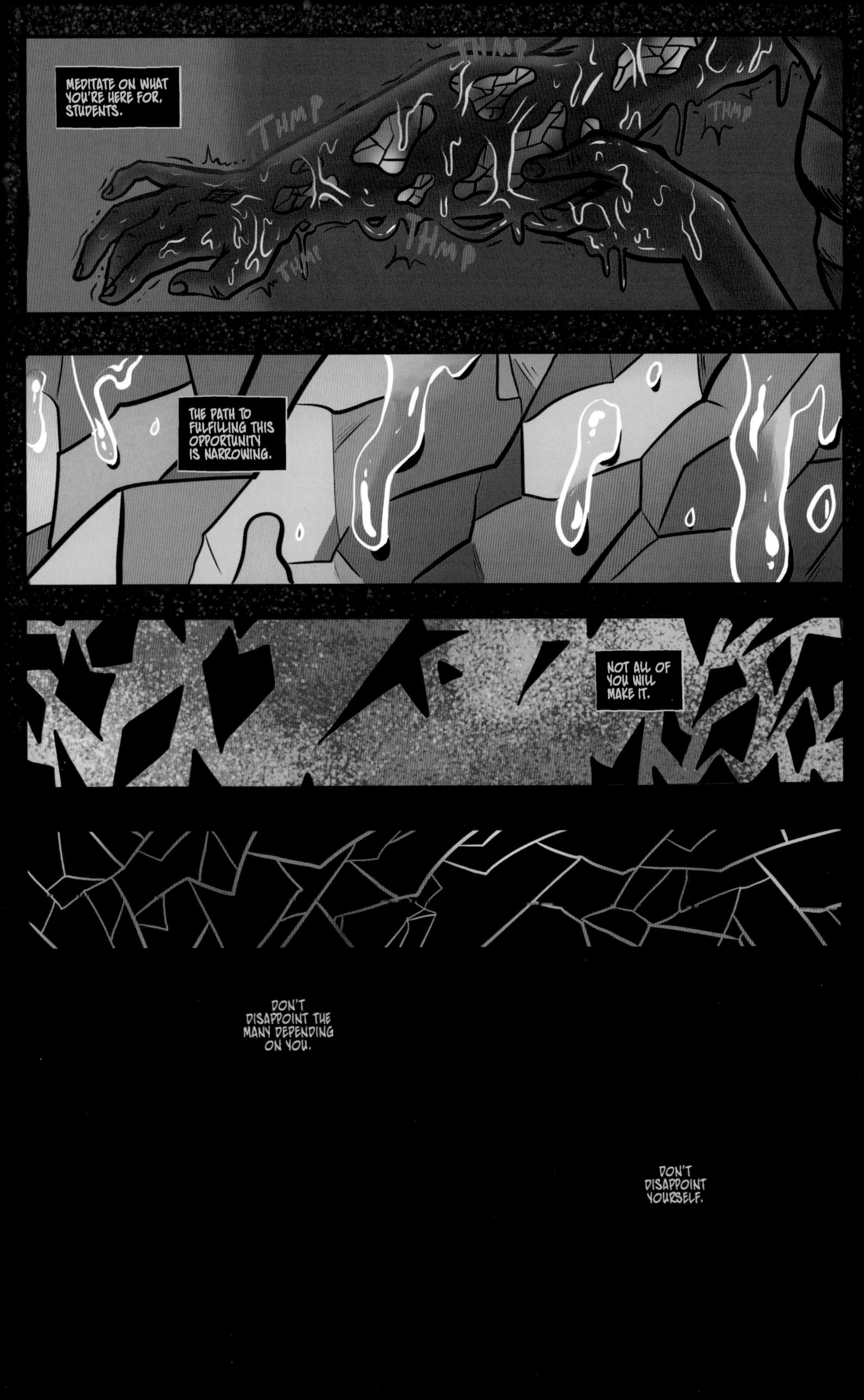
MEDITATE ON WHAT YOU'RE HERE FOR, STUDENTS.
THMP
THMP
THMP
THMP
THMP
THE PATH TO FULFILLING THIS OPPORTUNITY IS NARROWING.
NOT ALL OF YOU WILL MAKE IT.
DON'T DISAPPOINT THE MANY DEPENDING ON YOU.
DON'T DISAPPOINT YOURSELF.

AFTERWORD
BY AARON STEWART-AHN

"By degrees I made a discovery of still greater moment. I found that these people possessed a method of communicating their experience and feelings to one another by articulate sounds. I perceived that the words they spoke sometimes produced pleasure or pain, smiles or sadness, in the minds and countenances of the hearers. This was indeed a godlike science, and I ardently desired to become acquainted with it."

—Mary Wollstonecraft Shelley, *Frankenstein*

If I ask you what your first memory is, there is a mystery that neither you nor I can escape the gravity of, a black hole within every individual. No matter what that first image or thought is, we are all amnesiacs. Every human being's childhood is demarcated by a loss of conscious memories of the beginnings of our lives. As I write this, scientists posit that most of our earliest memories are likely inherited, often constructed by what we have been told by others who were present in those moments. It's astonishing, because it means that our earliest memories are stories we have been given, that part of our identity is stories we have been told.

Scientists also found something else in one of the few studies of this phenomenon[1] working in New Zealand, researchers found that of all the groups they tested, Maori children had the earliest recall of memories overall. It's far too complicated for me to parse here, and further studies continue to prove this and add to the complexity, so perhaps all this science is best described by a Maori proverb cited in the original study:

Kia whakatōmuri te haere whakamua.

I walk backwards into the future with my eyes fixed on my past.

Even in translation, one can recognize the faint traces of how language can reorder time. Further scientific studies would replicate and confirm these results. The very act of learning language appears to be inherently tied into memory. The structural underpinnings of how we form ourselves are as inherently related to the formation of language as the microstructures of cells within us. Organizing principles and power structures and the shape of thought are mirrored in syntax, conjugation, just as they are in the intertwining nature of double helixes and eukaryotic cells and mitochondria.

Language is so much like our own biology. It mutates over time as it's replicated, sometimes giving birth to entire new forms and species.

But for all this fancy-ass thought I'm digressing into, I keep thinking of that Maori whakataukī, or what we call a proverb, or others might know as a koan, 속담, 'Ōlelo No'eau, or just as something their mother might have said. And how through language and stories, one's perception can be altered to think of both the future and the past differently.

That's what Sloane Leong's PRISM STALKER does, and it's why I'm in awe of it. The other language she is drawing upon is visual, and so I think back to those first few pages, where I'm lost between image and words and becoming immersed in another consciousness outside of my own. It feels like the formation of memories. It feels like it's seeping into my own biology as images and words transmit themselves into my own eyes.

[1] Cross-cultural and gender differences in childhood amnesia
Shelly MacDonald, Kimberly Uesiliana, and Harlene Hayne · University of Otago, Dunedin, New Zealand 2000

It's an experience, one that is both complementarily (not paradoxically) foreign and familiar. PRISM STALKER is a little disorienting at first, but like the best sci-fi tends to be, that's because it's absorbing you into a totality of narrative in which everything you are shown and told has been created by another mind, and it's being shared with you.

And once it starts to resolve, as Vep's journey deepens and you go with her, you develop a fluency in her world, you are taken on a grand tradition of adventures stories. But...

In every single image and choice of word there is a deeper intent here, far more evocative than anything I could ever say to you. There is a dialogue going on between so many inherent tensions and power structures in our existence. Lurking in the adventure and the romantic sweep of PRISM STALKER and the images (that can provoke a physiological response from their sheer beauty, and yes I mean the transgressive, strangest ones most of all) is all the weight of what we know about how we have ordered time and the world.

And she could've taken the easy storytelling route, reduced things to their most simple, reductive symbols. But she's much more brilliant a storyteller than that. Like anyone who is displaced or colonized, Vep's own sense of self is struggling with history and genetics as much as she is about the identity she has formed for herself. She has no easy, clear, binary solutions. She is even burdened by how her knowledge of her own race is severed by memory and language while at the same time feeling the burden and responsibility of it. It's a staggeringly complicated idea to give to a heroine who is learning to fight psychic battles in a phantasmagorical academy.

And about that, yes, this is a story that has *psychic battles* with *rad creatures* that are both cute and / or vicious. But even there, Sloane takes the concept and mutates it into something even more compelling: a battle between form, word and thought. The catharsis of action in PRISM STALKER, which is badass and fun and terrifying, is rooted in making you conscious of how we perceive reality and what a struggle for survival it is to define and imagine and name things and purpose them with our will.

After all, language also becomes endangered. And even becomes extinct.

As I write this, there are seven known individuals alive who are the last speakers of their language, the majority of which are indigenous languages or ones that are perishing due to prior colonization.

Beyond the confines of human biology, we are living in an era of mass extinction. All over the world songbird populations are declining. Creatures with names like *wagtail*, *starling* and the *yellow breasted bunting* are in precipitous decline, which means that the biophony, the ever present ambient sound that emanates from our planet, is losing it's voices.

Although it's not very scientific of me to call it this, I ask for a poetic suggestion: that perhaps we are losing the language of songbirds from our collective stories. The names for those birds will be lost as much as their memories, when they are gone and our descendants don't know of them.

The struggle with human forces, social, political, economic, is clearly one of survival, then. It is not just science fiction where entire worlds are colonized. For that matter, the genre spent a few decades in the twentieth century putting stories about the glory of colonization at its forefront. Yet it's in our human history that people are enslaved or driven to reservations or exploited for labor that damages their lives and environment, and their collective memories are rendered traumatic and their languages are annihilated, and half of all species other than our own can vanish in a single human lifetime.

As I write this, I think of the Great Barrier Reef, a place I would have always like to have seen with my own eyes, but likely never will. Yes, it is dying, as the living symbiotes which compose its complex ecosystem cannot tolerate the heart of the oceans we have warmed. But something we hadn't counted on is possibly happening: the coral holobiont might be adapting, moving, changing. We hadn't accounted in our ability to think of the future for biology superseding our technology. That's the final thing I find so mysteriously compelling about Sloane's work, that hope may lie in the mysteries of biology. That biology, bodies and memories are just as parasitic, alive, gruesome and fleshy as our language. They might be the *same thing*.

About that research by those scientists working on earliest memories, years later, follow-up studies would find that another group of children had earliest recall of memories: children who lived through trauma at an early age. The emotive power becomes a fault line, a fissure by which the memory becomes stronger. That might mean that an imprint of emotion thus affects our biology, it inherently changes us on a physical level, even our neuroelectrical chemistry or the structure of our cells.

Which means that it's possible that receiving a story, having it imprinted into your memory, does the same. Stories are memories out of time, neither ahead, nor behind us. They reprise the memories of everyone who brought us here; they also whisper about things that have not yet happened.

I think of the effect of reading PRISM STALKER as one of learning a new language. It's one of those rarest, wildest works of the imagination, that becomes its own language, made up of the collective effect of its form, style, art and words. And we, its readers, are now its secret speakers.

We now live in a networked world where we have total hyperawareness but so little change. In learning PRISM STALKER's personal, private language, it leaves us open to change how we think of the relationship between time, memory, bodies, words and will. I believe this may be the most necessary, vital function of sci-fi, that we need more than ever. More of Sloane's story awaits us, more struggle for Vep and for us, and perhaps we will all find a way to some small crystalline, prismatic, foreign, shocking fragment of living hope and change within us. I cannot wait to see what more she tells us of it.

Aaron Stewart-Ahn
@somebadideas
NYC December 2018

Aaron Stewart-Ahn is a filmmaker and writer. He most recently co-wrote the movie MANDY, is finishing a documentary on police brutality, and published his first work in comics, *Work Nights*.

BONUS CONTENT

CREATION & PROCESS
AN INTERVIEW WITH SLOANE LEONG

BY TESSA STRAIN

PRISM STALKER is a really ambitious comic, and it's one you've said has been gestating for a long time. You make no secret of your influences, but at the same time it feels like a comic only you could make. What made this a story you wanted to tell and a world you wanted to create?

It was a story I hadn't heard told yet and I thought it was worth telling. The book is a reflection on my ancestral past and present, specifically a reflection on my Native Hawaiian and Native American ancestries, the social constructs imposed on those cultures and the oppression and evolution that followed. It's about how those past injustices and traumas to my people and the land they cared for reverberate through time and culture, twisting and warping, and rippled through the land itself. I've always felt a lot of conflict with the cultures I was raised in and bitterness over the indifference towards native peoples' rights to their homelands. I also felt a big disconnect to some of my cultures growing up because of displacement, the false notion of blood quantum and the general atmosphere of ubiquitous racism fragmented down to minute scales. Especially in Hawaii, where I grew up as a teen, those elements were always very present and tourism really drove home how other and lesser native peoples seemed to visitors. I've loved science fiction since I was a kid but have always felt left out of the genre, with native peoples being depicted as a primitive being or an alien. There was no native perspective in this genre, we were absent in others' imaginative gaze. PRISM STALKER is me filtering all these feelings and experiences into a loud, sci-fi kaleidoscope and carving out space in all those imagined futures for natives and other marginalized people who identify with Vep and her experience.

The look of PRISM STALKER is very texture-forward and biological (even in the depiction of deep space, which we so often see as something cold and inert)—what inspired that approach and how did you put your own stamp on it?

I've always been fascinated with nature and ecology, the human body and the diseases that pervade it. I wanted to attempt a world that was the polar opposite of what I had read and seen in popular SF media, of cold, angular architecture and rigid European-esque mono-cultures. Growing up in Maui, one of the world's most geographically diverse places concentrated into such a tiny area, I was surrounded by rich green jungles, black lava fields, sunset-colored coralscapes and flashing neon fish. I also drew a lot from Cronenberg and Octavia Butler and their takes on organic technology and hybridizing of humanity with alien species. Their architecture and technology are growing and alive, and the characters in their stories have actual impactful relationships with them. Those dynamics resonated with me, especially growing up in Hawaii, where the importance of and respect for nature was taught in schools and throughout the community. The world around us is alive and we are meant to be in a symbiotic kinship with it and I tried to translate that frame of mind in the environment of PRISM STALKER.

One theme throughout the comic is how colonialism makes its victims complicit in its horrors—as a reader there's a real tension between wanting Vep to succeed at the academy and be able to help her family and fellow refugees and the anxiety of knowing the moral cost that comes with that. How long can Vep walk that tightrope, and is there an inevitable breaking point for her?

Definitely. The toll the Academy is taking on her and fellow students is intensifying and she's becoming suspicious even as she's just barely scratching the surface of the Chorus's motivations. The Chorus has the potential to establish beneficial change for the majority but there's also a menacing and seductive veneer of altruism in the way the Academy presents itself and engages with the people living on the planet. The destruction it's reaping on the world will grow more and more apparent but so will the benefits of her participating in that violence and subjugation. Vep's life until this point has been unstable and traumatically alienating. When she gets the general shape of the Academy in this arc, she's unsure but also enchanted by how easy it is to assimilate and the allure of falling into a stable role. Those in power, the Academy and the Chorus, seem invulnerable to anything and so it's hard to question her role at first when the universe around her is falling in line.

There's this writer I like, Scott Alexander, that said: "The reason our current system isn't a utopia is that it wasn't designed by humans. Just as you can look at an arid terrain and determine what shape a river will one day take by assuming water will obey gravity, so you can look at a civilization and determine what shape its institutions will one day take by assuming people will obey incentives. But that means that just as the shapes of rivers are not designed for beauty or navigation, but rather an artifact of randomly determined terrain, so institutions will not be designed for prosperity or justice, but rather an artifact of randomly determined initial conditions."

Vep's story is about her realizing that these seats of power weren't made for justice or peace and that they're not infallible or indestructible. Vep is building up the confidence to forge her own path outside these compromised power structures but that isn't going to provide a clear and easy direction for her, especially when her actions have repercussions that will echo on a planetwide scale.

PRISM STALKER is rich in its visual metaphors—how do you integrate that into (and distinguish it) from a world that has so many fantasy elements? The Facture attacks Vep faces at the academy, for example, seem to be somewhere on the border between a fantastical reality and a metaphor for her experience of that reality.

It was difficult! And I don't know if I was actually successful in keeping the reality and the psychic expressions apart visually. But that confusion sits pretty well within the themes of the story so I don't hate it. Factures, which is a reference to my friend Zachary Braun's amazing comic *Nature of Nature's Art*, are personal expressions. They are heavily stylized and draw specifically on their umwelt—their perception of their physical world and how they create meaning from their point of view. Maji's facture draws on her fear of losing her egglings, a very literal fear but also a metaphor for losing out on potential futures. One of the creatures Vep kills has a facture that coerces her into following her primal instincts over her conscious mind. I tried to change up my own style for each facture in order to convey the different layers of reality but much of it bleeds together, especially in the beginning when most of the students are still honing their perspectives of themselves and the world.

Tell me about the music for PRISM STALKER. It adds so much to the experience of reading it and has a real harmony with your artwork on the page. How did you decide you wanted your comic to have a musical score, and what was the process of collaborating with Neotenomie like?

I had been following Riley [Neotenomie] and her frequent collaborator Porpentine, a writer and game designer, for a while and really connected with Riley's soundtracks for Porpentine's amazing games. Riley's music has this really reverberant underlying base to it and I knew she could capture the pulsating, echoing environments in PRISM STALKER while also conveying the inflections of subtle emotions that Vep experiences throughout the compositions. She created a series of lengthy, atmospheric vignettes that ended up being these perfect sonic snapshots of the world and of the story. I didn't have a lot to do with the creation of the music besides providing the comic for inspiration. I trusted in her skill and taste completely. The way I imagined a reader interfacing with the music and work was after the first read-through, the reader could go through the pages again to the beat of the music, letting it move them along at its own pace. It would let them experience a sort of tangible anticipation.

Language is a crucial motif throughout PRISM STALKER, and it's something the characters are deeply attuned to. Vep's captors treat her native language as a potential contaminant; meanwhile, her disconnection from her native language is used as a cudgel by other Inamans she meets at the academy. How does this figure into your characterization of Vep and her place in the world?

Language and the lack of access to it weighs heavy on Vep from the beginning of the story. Language is connective tissue to the past, a carrier of culture but also a tool of assimilation. It shapes our mental and physical realities. Most of the comic is spoken in a standard galactic common language, but when alien cultures can't communicate what they want in it, which happens often, their visual written language seeps through, usually indecipherable to the reader and to Vep. When Vep's elders talk to her in the first issue, we see her mother tongue in its native written form: she can't understand it, so neither can we. Language can be a brutal gatekeeper, an insurmountable wall. There is divide the other Inaman students at the Academy bring up in a social setting with Vep when they realize she can't speak their tongue, nor does she know many of her people's stories or customs. One of the most common ways to colonize a people is to destroy their language, "to induce a historical amnesia" and to reconfigure a culture's history so that it's seen with the colonizer's eyes—desolate, weak, defeated. Colonizers reframe the oppressed culture's history and make their [own] conquests romantic, seductive. If the language and therefore the culture is effectively obliterated, this leads to a cultural alienation and subsequently an identifying with the colonizer because to a colonial child, there is nothing else.

There's this example I always bring up from K. David Harrison from several years back, I'll quote it: "Tuvan [a Turkic language out of Siberia] has a word iy (pronounced like the letter 'e'), which indicates the short side of a hill. It turns out that hills are asymmetrical, never perfectly conical, and indeed one of their sides tends to be steeper and shorter than the others. If you are riding a horse, carrying firewood, or herding goats on foot, this is a highly salient concept: You never want to mount a hill from the iy side, as it takes more energy to ascend, and an iy descent is more treacherous as well. Once you know about the iy, you see it in every hill and identify it automatically, directing your horse, sheep, or footsteps accordingly." That's just a tiny example of how language is able to apprehend a feature that may go unnoticed in the world around someone. In PRISM STALKER, I'm extending this idea onto the entirety of this planet, where language is not going to just convey features of the immediate environment but foreign biological and cultural experiences, memories and inhuman sensations. This becomes one of the focal points of the story early on because translating previously unknown, indecipherable experience and knowledge is suddenly communicable and becomes a form of intimate psychic combat.

I love the visual diversity of the academy students and instructors. There is a scene in Issue 5 with a sick character that made my heart ache, and her face is basically a cluster of nodes—what was the process like of discovering ways to convey recognizable emotion and character through such a variety of faces and bodies?

I try and telegraph emotion in human ways like closed and open body postures, eyes, straining muscles, and creases but also animal ways like lowered ears, tucked or bristled tails, outstretched wings, and bared teeth. I feel like a lot of work is done by our own natural pareidolia and overlaying our own ideas of personhood on non-human beings. Still, there's some body language I tried to keep alien so there's not always a recognizable match to our own emotions. A grin isn't always a grin, it's a signal the alien is listening. An upraised pincer is a sign of offense. For each alien, I tried to think of their home culture and build their body language with that as a foundation.

The academy is such a fun setting, and it's part of a grand tradition of the action genre training camp (sports, too—I know you have an upcoming graphic novel about a girls basketball team), while also interrogating the concept as well. Do you have favorite examples of this that inspired you or that you wanted to subvert?

Takehiko Inoue's work comes immediately to mind when I think of stories focused around training the mind and body. *Vagabond* and *Real* were both influential on me, particularly in the way the characters are constantly grappling with their evolving philosophies as they develop their chosen skill. That obsession to achieve a certain end goal while also struggling with the ethics of the means to arrive there is an engrossing conflict I always find myself drawn to. On a more sentimental note, the training and tournaments arc in *Dragonball Z* and *Naruto* made a big imprint on me as a kid and I wanted to bring that excitement of potential lethality to the story. Training camps and tournaments are fun to watch in that they're intensely structured games with clear goals and rewards and gamifying elements of an institute or even a whole culture is an effective way to control people. The Academy carefully structures the experience the recruits have from the day they're taken from their homes. The benchmarks the students are pressured to meet, the atmosphere of competition in training and the upcoming Academy Tournaments (in Vol 2!) are arranged in such a way that thinking about the Academy's actual purposes will be buried beneath a mountain of distractions. Vep is slowly reaching a point where the game is failing to keep her attention.

Tessa Strain lives in New York and on Twitter (@tessastrain).
Her writing has appeared on *The Comics Journal* and *Bright Wall/Dark Room*.

THE SOUNDS OF PRISM STALKER

AN INTERVIEW WITH NEOTONOMIE

BY MARTY BROWN

One of the great pleasures of PRISM STALKER is its beguiling use of texture. Very early on, as Vep pushes herself through a viscous membrane that once seemed like concentrated mass, we learn that each substance has its own duality. Anything can be both solid and liquid. Thoughts themselves form pink ooze with the power to disassemble and reassemble a body. Color can be language; the verbal can be visual; and spoken words are tangible things that can be manipulated, even shattered.

Sound itself takes on a particular, er, resonance in this universe. Singing is used to for incubation, for nurturing; birth ritual. A subtle change in pitch can have life-threatening consequences. Communication is less about the word itself than the intoning of the message. Voices are things that can be consumed, gotten fat off of.

So it's no surprise that Neotonomie's PRISM STALKER soundtrack further expands the textural palate of Vep's universe without taking away any of its mystery. Voices swoop in and out of focus as snarling synths seem to pass through their own viscous membranes and become... what, pianos? Textures erupt and transform in the music with the same unnerving velocity as they do on the page.

Here, Neotonomie talks about her diverse discography, world building, and sculpting a physical environment out of sound.

So, the first thing I was drawn to from your non-PRISM STALKER discography was your version of "Goodbye Horses" on Superego Royal Jelly. Such a great song, and you really do it justice. Was there a particular inspiration behind that?

Thanks! When most people think of "Goodbye Horses" they think of Buffalo Bill, which I see as a sort of really unpleasant, retrograde caricature of a trans-feminine person. The song is so linked to that character that a lot of people treat the song itself as a joke. But it's such a beautiful song. You could call it synth-pop, I guess, but it's a lot more raw and driving than most of what's put in that category, but still very pretty and otherworldly. The "horses" are a reference to the five senses in Hindu literature, and to "fly over" them is to look beyond our limitations in the material world. And I read about the singer, Q Lazzarus, who was just a working-class woman trying to break into the music industry, which didn't seem to turn into much beyond this song. No one knows exactly what happened to her or even if she's still alive. It's a song about trying to see beyond what a mess life is, and the song itself has this accumulated history of misery and mystery around it. So I guess by covering it I wanted to lift it out of all of that context and show how beautiful it is to me. And a lot of the covers out there are really straightforward, so I tried to rearrange it like it was an original composition.

Totally. Good covers can illuminate both the original song and the artist performing it. Did I see that you did a soundtrack for a video game too? Do you often work with outside source material or is that just a coincidence? Do you enjoy working that way?

I did the soundtrack for a bunch of games by Porpentine Charity Heartscape, who makes both interactive fiction and graphics-oriented video games. The most popular one I worked on is probably *With Those We Love Alive*, which is a dark fantasy interactive fiction game about working as an artisan in the court of a monstrous empress. I'm also making most of the music for the game *Crypt Underworld*, which I Kickstarted with Lili

Zone and Zoe Sparks. It's a first-person exploration game about a netherworld that's a lot like our world, except even more horrifically saturated with consumer detritus. When I create music for its own sake I often find myself wanting to go in a million different directions at once, so having a project to tie the music to helps me focus. No matter what I'm working on it's really important to me that the music has a sense of place, like it's creating a physical environment around the listener. So having a visual artwork that I'm trying to complement takes care of some of that work for me.

How did you come to work on the PRISM STALKER soundtrack?

Well, Sloane knew Porpentine from the interactive fiction scene, and she's made artwork for a number of Porpentine's works such as *Love Is Zero* and *Psycho Nymph* Exile. She even worked Porp into the *Adventure Time* episode "Deep Purple" as the name of the evil soda that the episode revolves around – do check that out if you get the chance. But anyway, I guess we've been admiring each other's work for a few years now! Last year she contacted me about scoring her new project and I agreed to it without a moment's hesitation.

What's it like to make a score for a comic – to combine media in ways that don't immediately seem connected? What was your approach?

Well, I was turning the project over in my head, having read the first couple issues, and I was struck by how much territory each issue covered, emotionally, geographically, artistically. I wanted to do justice to all of that, so I decided to score each issue as if it was the score for an animated film, using the structure of each scene in the issue as the basis for each passage in the piece. I also had their idiosyncratic structures of the Oneohtrix Point Never's last couple albums in mind; I love when it feels like the entire piece is traveling or terraforming into a different physical space.

As you were working on these passages, did any of them surprise you? Were any particularly challenging to translate into sound?

The middle section of the music for issue 2 might have been the most technically challenging part so far… the story moves from Vep's vision of desperate hope inside a womb-like transfer pod to a scuffle among aliens in a passenger chamber. It's a pretty sudden tonal shift, so I kind of bent the baseline from the first part up into a sort of hideous wash to evoke Vep leaving the pod, and then cut to a call-and-response pattern of bells and chimes that represents the squabbling denizens of the passenger chamber. PRISM STALKER has been a great opportunity to play with sequencing as a transformation of raw waveforms, in ways that wouldn't necessarily make a lot of sense as sheet music.

Are there any parts of PRISM STALKER that particularly resonate with you?

Vep is living under this vast mega-culture that just casually instrumentalizes sentient life wherever it can. It reminds me of space opera in how it moves, but it's also full of this world that's deep into life under a messy but brutal kind of empire. Also I love how Sloane does so much by way of biology and mental communication, it's just a lot more interesting to think about and fun to look at than typical sci-fi world building to me. Like, you can only say so much about a computer at this point? I think? But this feels like it's really digging into how it feels to be a person, how we sustain those constructs over the mental and physical strain of survival. I hope that wasn't like spoilers or anything.

Ha, no, I think you're good. Alright, wrapping up, I want to talk about where PRISM STALKER is going—in a broad sense, not necessarily just plot-wise. How do you imagine the score evolving as Vep's world expands and the story unfolds? Are there any particular challenges in working on something sequentially over a long period of time? Anything you're looking forward to discovering or experimenting with.

I'm learning where the story is headed on an issue-by-issue basis at this point, so I wanted to touch on a lot of the different textures and moods that were possible right away to kind of establish to myself what the parameters of this sound-world were. A lot of the future direction depends on the content of the story, but I'd like to push to greater extremes in both the kind of lush emotive stuff and the hard dissonant rhythmic stuff seen in the first couple issues before the story's been told.

Cool. So, if people like the PRISM STALKER soundtrack, where can they find more of your music?

I have a SoundCloud (www.soundcloud.com/neotenomie) and an eponymous Bandcamp as well. But what I'm more into right now than my solo work is my electronic pop group with rooksfeather. You can download our debut album at Bandcamp (https://rookandnomie.bandcamp.com/), and also please check out rook's solo work (https://rooksfeather.bandcamp.com). She is the scariest critter and the sweetest girl you ever did meet.

Listen to the original soundtracks at PRISMSTALKER.COM.

Marty Brown is an actor and writer living in Brooklyn.

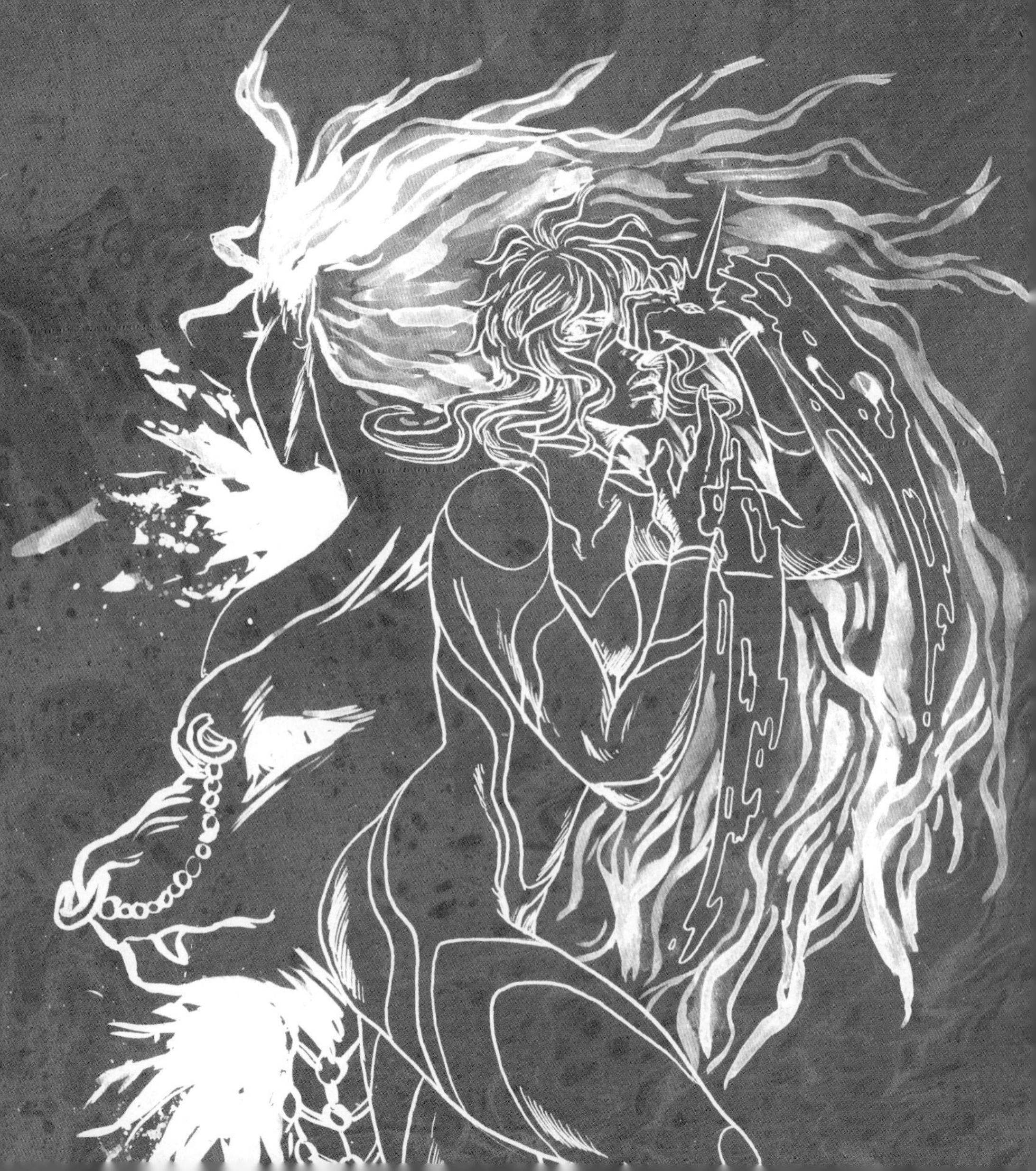

PIN-UP GALLERY

EMMA RIOS

JOANNA KRÓTKA

ARTYOM TRAKHANOV

MARIAN CHURCHLAND

TRADD & HEATHER MOORE

MARINA JULIA

KRISTINA COLLANTES

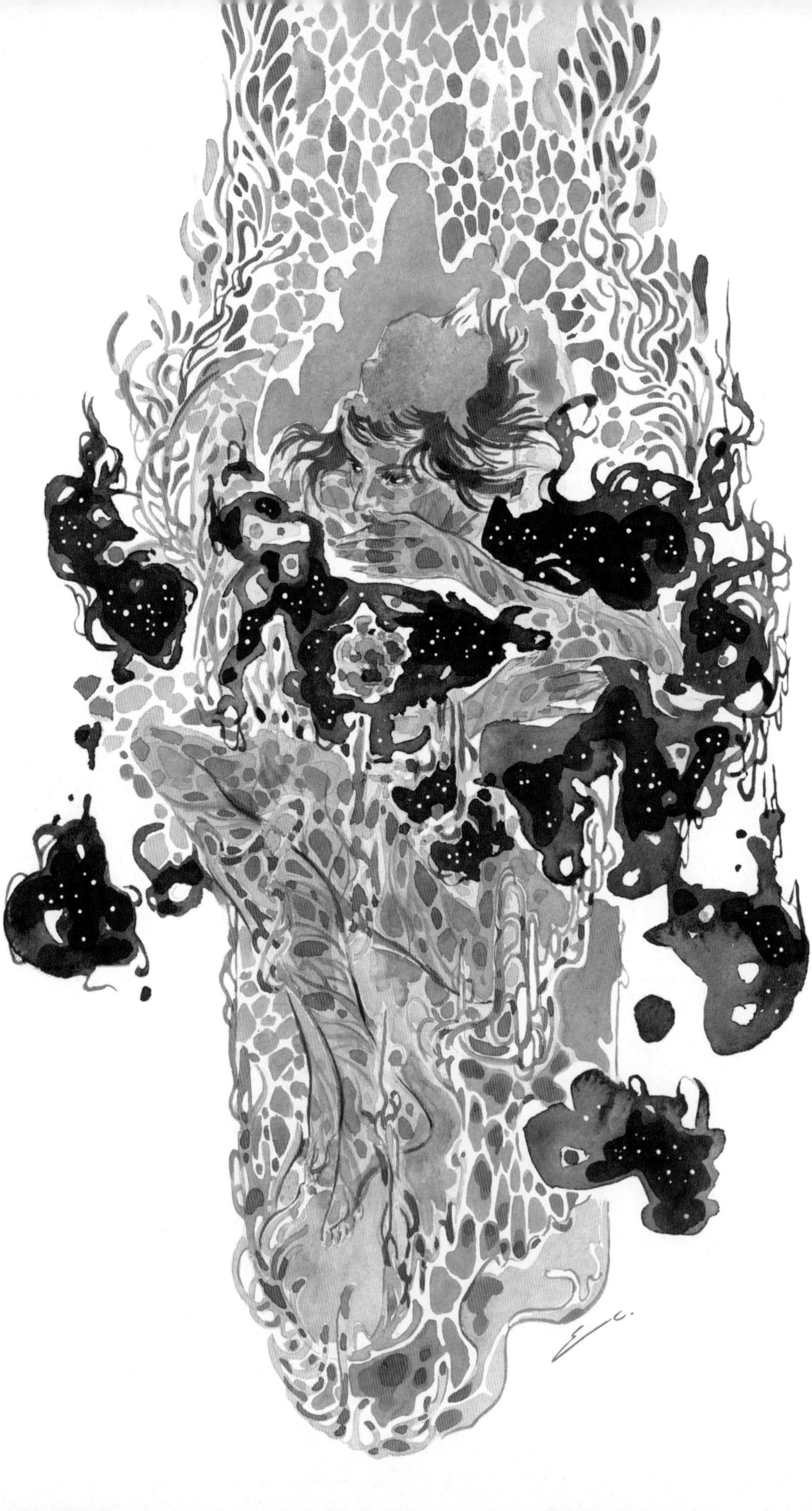

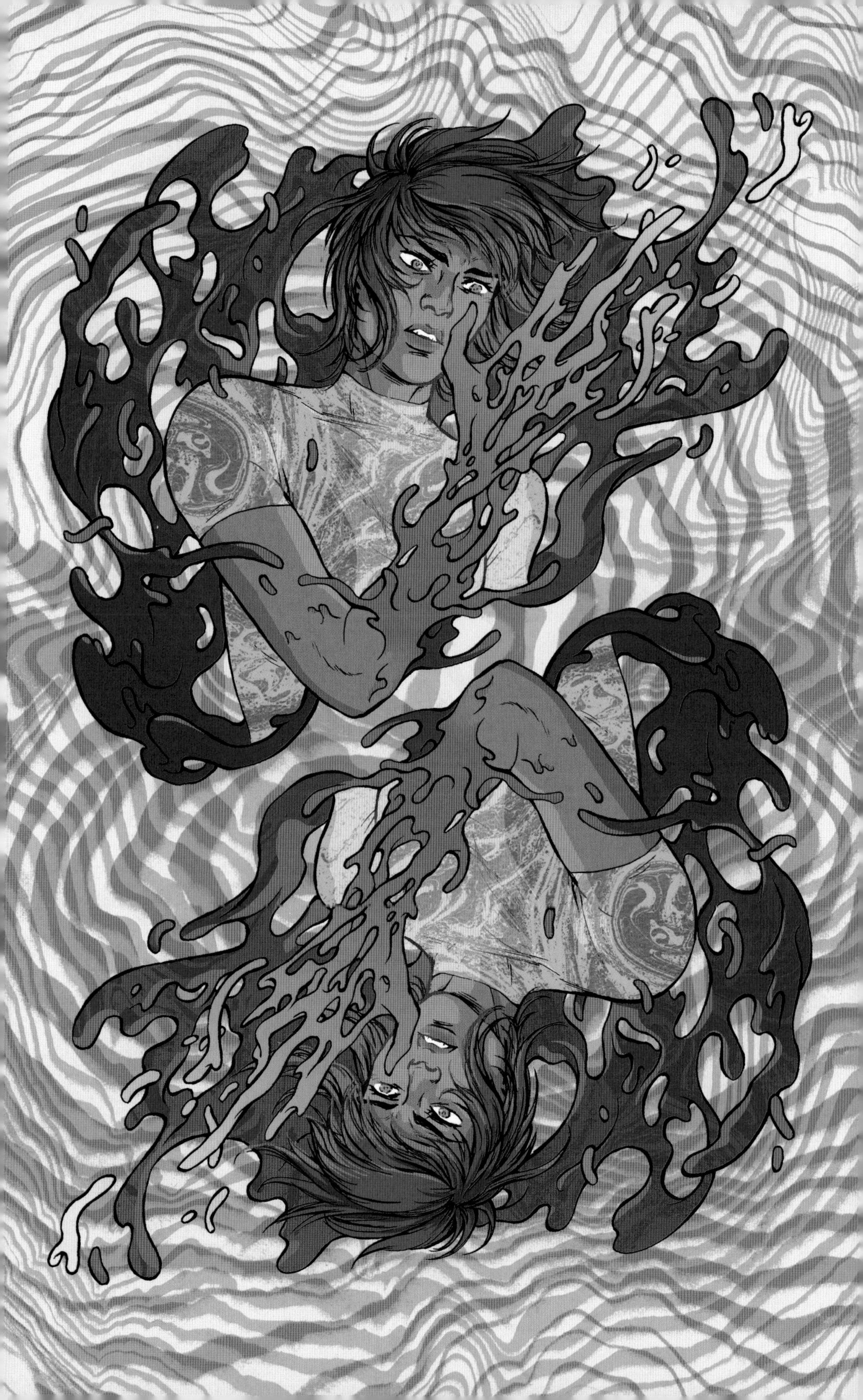

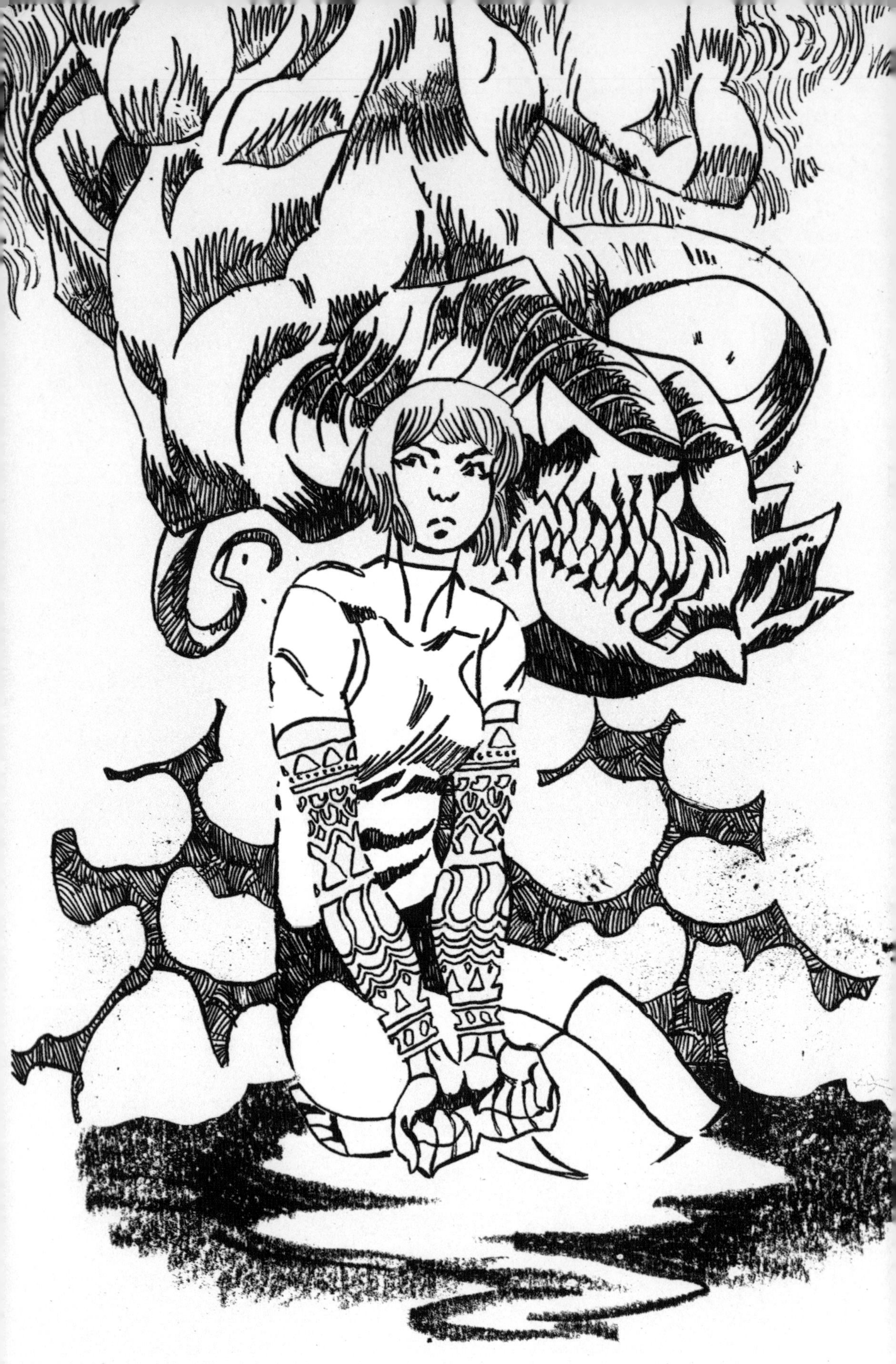

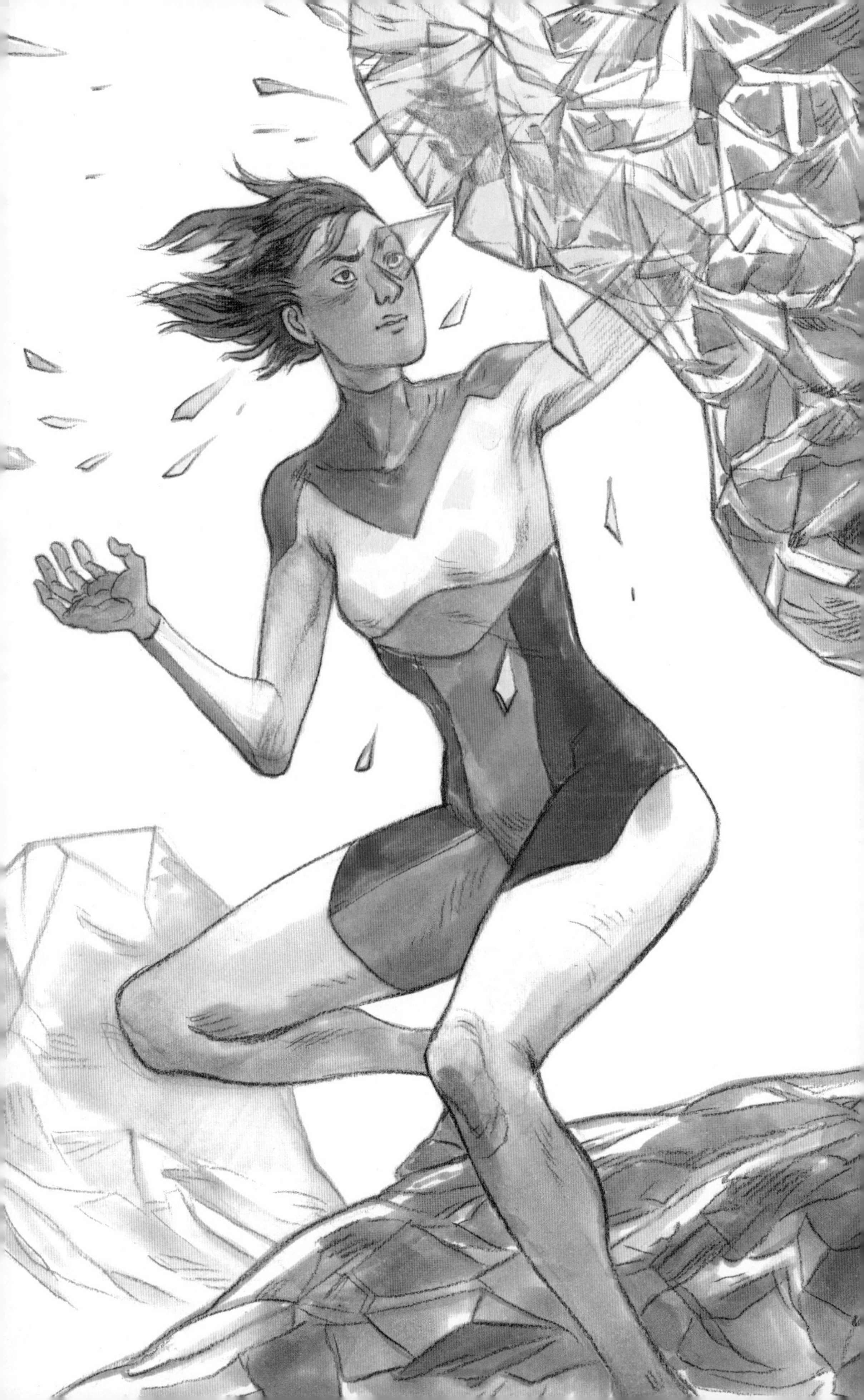

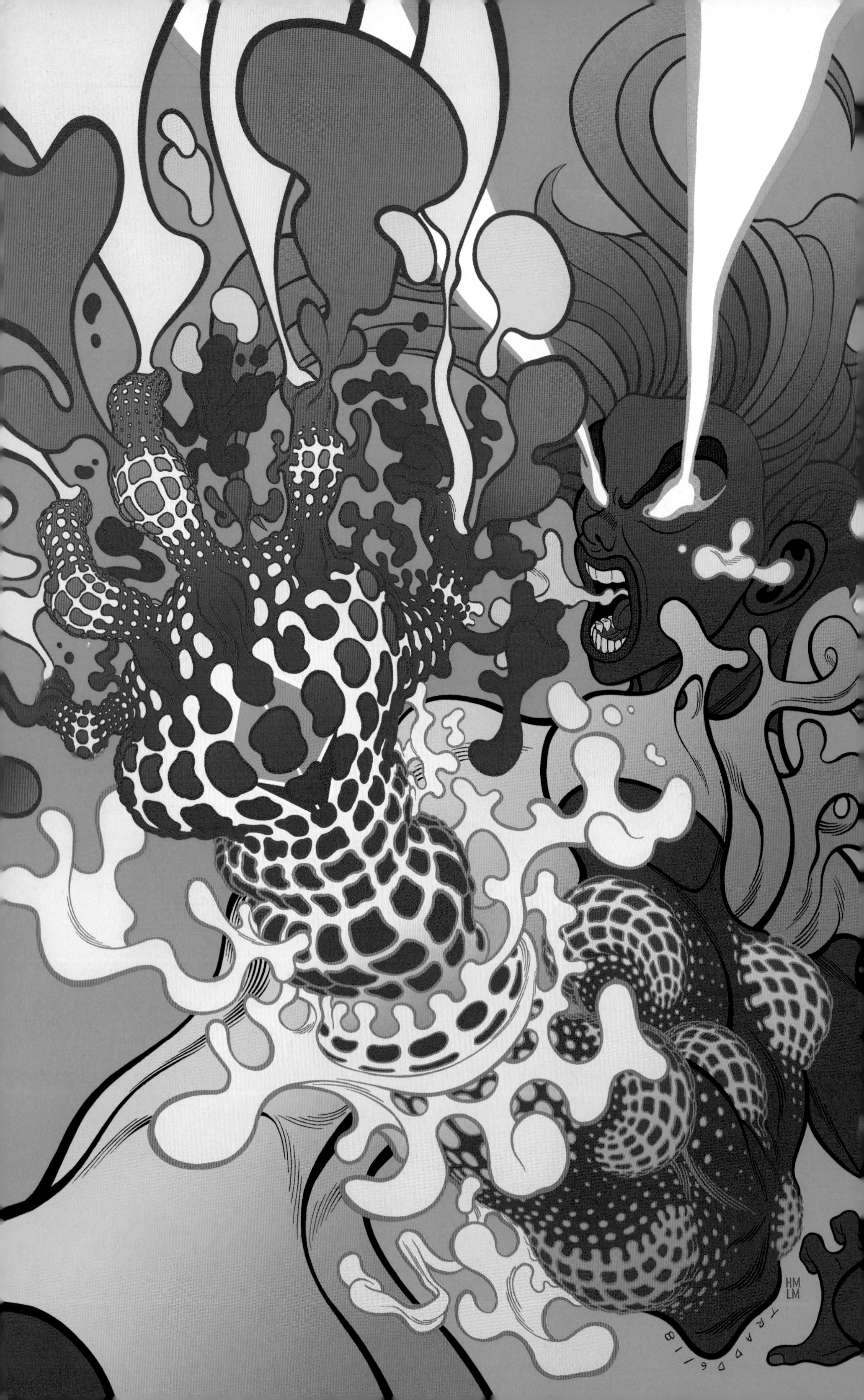
HM
LM
TRADD 6/18

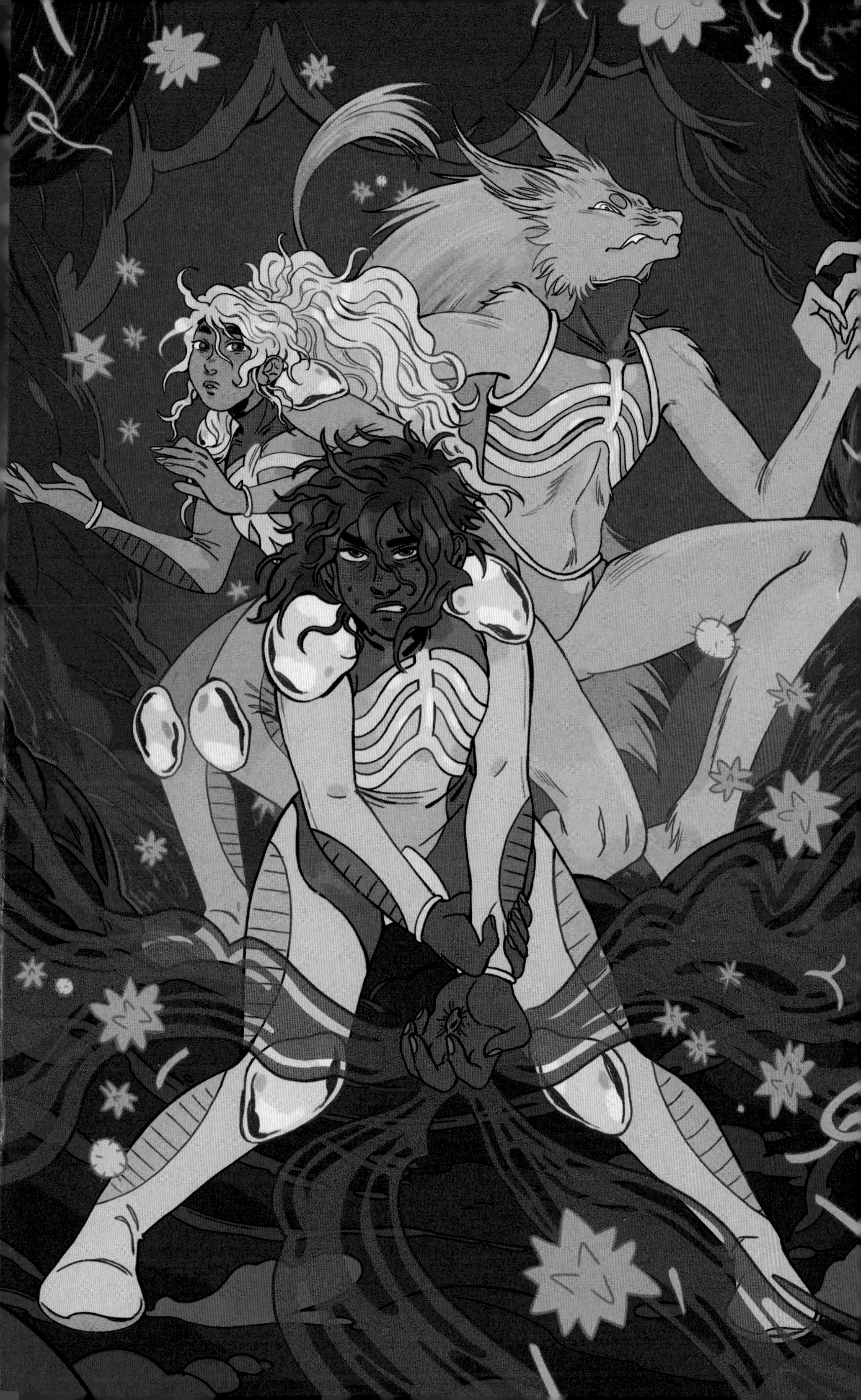

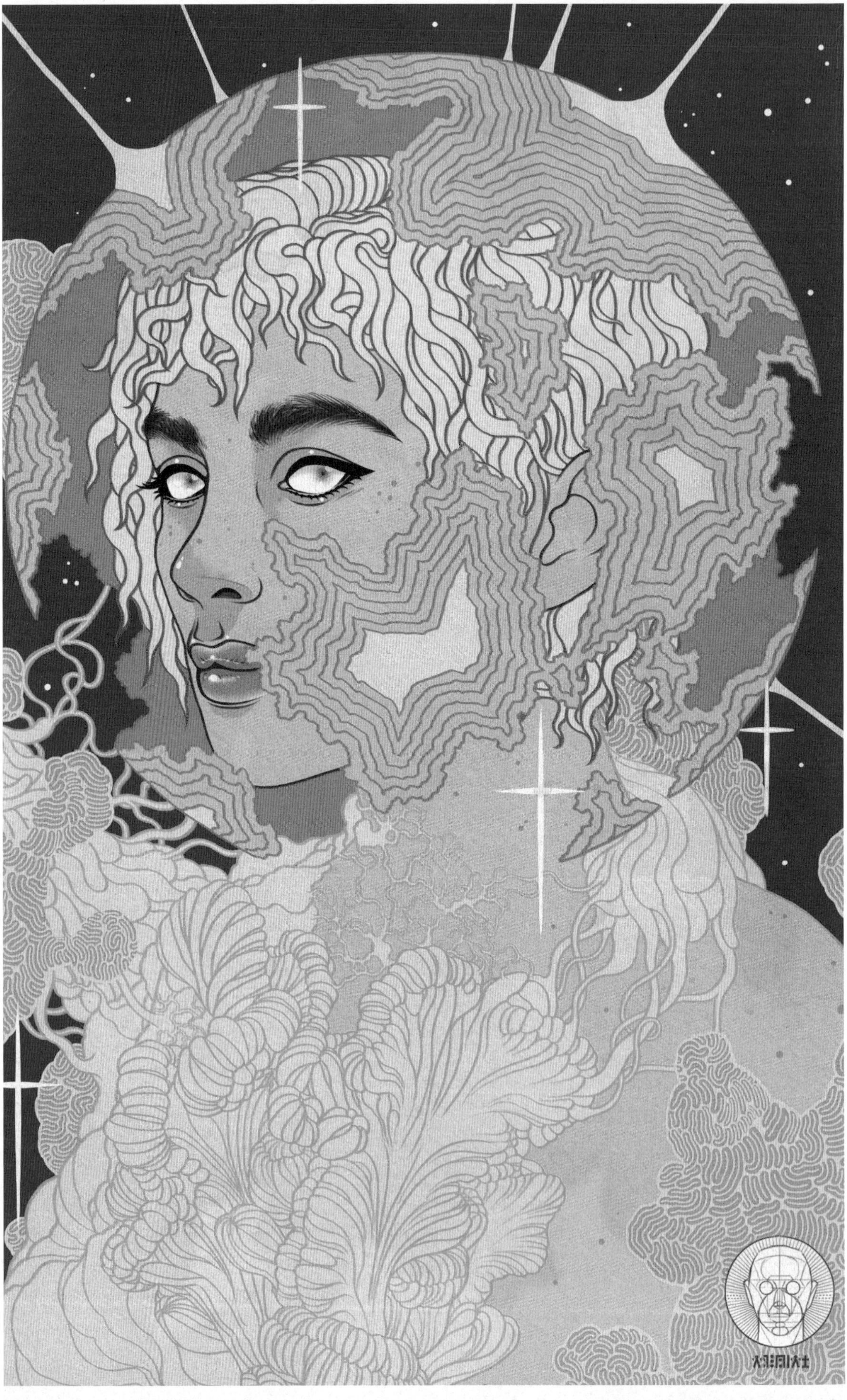